TIME
SHARDS

Also available from Titan Books and Dana Fredsti

The Spawn of Lilith

The Ashley Parker Novels:
Plague Town
Plague Nation
Plague World

A Man's Gotta Eat What a Man's Gotta Eat
(e-original novella)

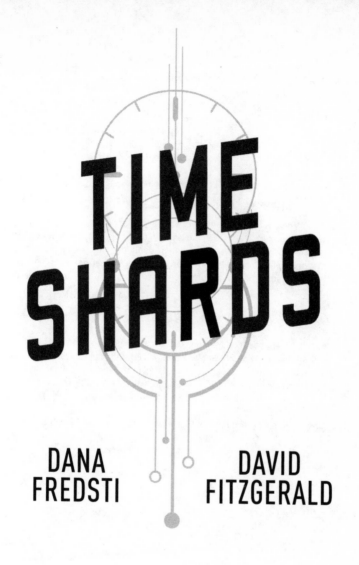

TIME SHARDS

DANA
FREDSTI

DAVID
FITZGERALD

TITAN BOOKS

TIME SHARDS
Print edition ISBN: 9781785654527
Electronic edition ISBN: 9781785654534

Published by Titan Books
A division of Titan Publishing Group Ltd
144 Southwark St, London SE1 0UP

First edition: January 2018
2 4 6 8 10 9 7 5 3 1

A CIP catalogue record for this title is available from the British Library.

Printed and bound in the United States

Did you enjoy this book?
We love to hear from our readers. Please email us at
readerfeedback@titanemail.com or write to us at
Reader Feedback at the above address.
TITAN BOOKS.COM

For Bill "Willy P." Galante & Lisa "Jei Jei" Brackmann

Imagine time seen as a continuum—an infinite line containing everything that was and everything that will be...

Time perhaps as a tangible object. One that can be touched, like a mural on a wall that stretches infinitely in both directions. Portraying everything that has happened, is happening, and will happen. In one direction is the future unfolding. In the other direction the past, much of it forgotten, back to the beginning of time itself.

Finally, imagine time as a stained-glass window. The story of everything laid out in a glittering mosaic of trillions upon trillions of moments, from the big bang to the fiery death of the universe.

Then the window shatters
Everywhere... and every when.

1

"Having fun?"

Amber nodded as Gavin smiled down at her from his standing position at the tiller, his irregular features drawn together by an engaging grin and a pair of killer hazel eyes. He propelled the little punt slowly down the river, using the pole with an enthusiasm that didn't match his expertise. She hoped he didn't fall in.

"It's really pretty here," she said, looking out past the grassy, tree-lined riverbank at the pastoral landscape beyond. Except for birdsong, it was blissfully quiet. Dipping one hand in the water, Amber dribbled some onto the back of her neck, stifling a small shriek when a cold rivulet ran unexpectedly down her spine.

Pulling down the hem of her skirt in yet another unsuccessful attempt to cover her knees, she discovered there was no real way to get comfortable in a punt, even with cushions tossed down between the seats. Certainly not while wearing a corset.

Why didn't I change out of my Codex costume? Even as she thought it, she knew the answers.

One, in Romford and the rest of Greater London, August was hot—much hotter than her hometown of San Diego. Two, she hadn't wanted to take the time to go back to her aunt's house for a different outfit, giving Gavin time to possibly change his mind. And three, she liked the look of admiration in her companion's eyes whenever his gaze wandered over her legs.

She just hadn't expected to show him quite so much, so quickly.

That morning, when Amber Richardson had walked into the dealers' room of ImagiAnimeCon—the largest science fiction and fantasy convention event Romford had ever hosted—she'd instantly noticed the dashing, if somewhat skinny, retro Han Solo. They'd locked gazes over a table covered with action figures and other toys. He'd grinned, and Amber had turned to look behind her, certain he was smiling at someone else. Like maybe the petite blonde showing improbable mega-cleavage in her Sue Storm costume.

As it turned out, Gavin preferred *The Guild* to *Fantastic*

Four, and redheads to blondes. He was charming, intelligent, and had an accent as sexy as any of the current crop of Doctor Whos. So when he'd suggested a picnic on the nearby river, Amber had given an immediate yes, even though it meant missing the *Firefly* panel and the actor who played Wash.

Priorities.

Now here they were, floating lazily past picturesque landscapes straight out of a Merchant Ivory film. Gavin had even brought a picnic basket, one of the old-fashioned ones made of wicker, with flaps that opened upward on either side. It was nestled against Amber's legs, next to her ever-present burgundy backpack. Her Codex staff was tucked through the sturdy top loop so that it stood nearly upright like a flagpole.

"So how do you like the con?" Gavin said, dipping the pole into the river to propel them a few more feet downstream.

"It's nice," Amber replied. "Especially after how nutso Comic-Con has gotten the last couple of years."

Gavin nearly dropped the pole. "You've been to Comic-Con?" His tone oozed pure envy.

Amber hid a grin, pleased to have impressed her date. "Yup. Twenty-four years—every year since I was born. My dad is a raging geek. The first year I went, he dressed up as Kuato from *Total Recall*."

Gavin looked blank.

"You know, the guy with the parasitic baby growing out of his stomach?" she said. "I was the baby."

"Okay, yeah." Gavin gave a nod of recognition. "Wicked! I wish my dad was even half as cool."

Amber thought of all the times her dad had picked her up from school in his ancient VW bus covered in *Star Trek* bumper stickers. I FIND YOUR LACK OF LOGIC DISTURBING, CAPTAIN PICARD FOR PRESIDENT, and more recently, KIRK/SPOCK 2016. The cool kids hadn't been impressed, and her Star Fleet Academy computer bag hadn't helped. She gave a rueful smile and shook her head.

"No, you really don't."

He nodded and fell silent for a bit, his attention devoted to navigating the punt around a bend in the river. Amber didn't know if she was relieved or disappointed that he didn't ask her to elaborate. On one hand, she was happy not to talk about life as an excruciatingly shy middle child in the midst of a loud and chaotic family, with a bubbly older sister and an up-and-coming jock for a younger brother.

On the other hand, guys as a general rule weren't interested in anything personal unless it was about *them.*

Maybe it's just because you're boring, she told herself, giving her skirt another self-conscious tug. She looked up in time to see Gavin's gaze directed toward her bare thighs, flickering away when he saw that she'd noticed.

She lowered her head, hiding a smile.

Okay, maybe not so boring.

The punt hit something in the water, sending Gavin tumbling forward. The pole dropped into the river as he sprawled across the seats, face down, his head on the bench next to Amber.

"Omigod, are you okay?" Amber stared down at the back of Gavin's head as he groaned and pushed himself slowly to a sitting position on the seat in front of hers, legs straddling the cushioned bench. A small but steady trickle of blood ran from a gash on his forehead.

"Ouch," he said simply.

"Hold still." Searching in the picnic hamper, she extracted a white linen napkin and gently pressed it against the injury to staunch the bleeding. Gavin groaned, and she looked at him in concern.

"Is that too hard?"

He shook his head, wincing as he did so. "No, it's just my sister is going to kill me for mucking up one of her good napkins."

"Oh jeez, I'm sorry!" Amber started to snatch the napkin away, but Gavin quickly grabbed her hand, holding it and the cloth against his forehead.

"It's too late for that now," he said sadly. "I'm done for, so I might as well enjoy the moment, don't you think? My last sight on earth shall be that of the beautiful Codex, tending my wounds."

Amber laughed, the sound soft and low. Her dad called it "stealth laughter."

Gavin's hazel eyes darkened as he reached out with his free hand and touched Amber lightly on one cheek. She held her breath as he traced a line along the side of her face, his touch sending a pleasant shiver down her spine. Most of the kisses she'd experienced in the past had been planted on her forehead by her parents, and a memorable-in-all-the-wrong-ways make-out session with Danny "Lizard Tongue" Metcalf at his senior prom.

That had ended badly. Since then she'd pretty much ignored dating and immersed herself in the three C's—college, career, and cosplay. Now she thought she might be ready to expand her horizons.

Gavin leaned toward her then, still holding her hand and the napkin against his forehead. She didn't know how to react, and was afraid if she tried to say anything, it would come out as an inappropriate giggle.

So she held perfectly still and waited to see what would happen next.

2

The western border of the Trinovantian kingdom, Southeast Britain
AD 9

Two Celts hid under a veil of dangling willow branches, peering out across the river they called the Leagean. Dawn had broken, but the sun would not cut through the gloom until midday, leaving the world below in a dim half-light. On the opposite bank, strands of mist wove through the reed beds and the woods beyond, cloaking the alders and black poplars with a gray mantle. The only sign of movement was a pair of ravens hunting along the water's edge. The two young men kept their watch all the same.

"I thought I heard it again," the younger of the two whispered. He was Camtargarus, son of Cattus. His black hair was short but shaggy, his brow heavy and his eyes serious.

"Are you sure? I don't hear anything."

Cam glanced at Kentantorix, son of Exkamulot. A year older, slightly taller, in Cam's eyes he could do no wrong. By long and ancient tradition, the Celts did not raise their sons in their own households. Instead, the two had been brought up together for seven years across the sea, in Gaul. The bond of the two foster brothers was closer than that of blood kin. Either might be a king some day.

They fell silent, listening intently.

"There," Cam hissed.

Odd snatches of sound came just over the rushing of the water. The clink of harnesses. Creaking of wooden chariot wheels. Barked orders.

No one needed to tell them who moved unseen through the forest. The choices were few.

To the east lay the Mór-Maru, the Dead Sea. To the north, a long line of earthen ramparts and ditches marked their border with the mighty Iceni tribe. The great estuary of Tamesas, the Dark River, separated them from the Cantiaci to the south. But to the west, they had only the Leagean, the Bright River, to keep their uneasy border with their hungry enemies, the Catuvellauni.

War is coming. A chill reached in and grabbed Cam, colder than the damp in the air. He turned to Kentan. "We need our swords."

"We need a hunting horn," Kentan countered. "One that can be heard all the way to the sea. Come, let's get back to the horses and ride as fast as we can to sound the alarm." The pair turned and rose to their feet to climb back up the riverbank. Kentan stopped short to put his hands on Cam's shoulders, leaning in until their foreheads were touching.

"Listen," he told him softly. "Don't be afraid, but if anything happens—"

A soft cracking noise from above cut Kentan off before he could finish. Both looked up to see a trio of Catuvellauni scouts staring down at them from the top of the rise. They were bearded and bare-chested under their thick wool cloaks, except for sharp triangles of red and black war paint. Their swords were drawn and their grins unpleasant.

"Riddle me ye…" their leader called down softly.

"Tell me three…" the warrior to his left responded.

"Three things that are—" the one on the right said.

"—easy to take hold of." The leader's stare locked on the two of them. He took a step forward as he answered.

"Eggs from a nest…" The one on the left took another step.

"A mouse in a serpent's hole…" chanted the one on the right, taking a step closer as well, flanking them.

"A pair of hapless young maidens lost in the woods without their mother." The leader's eyes, teeth, and blade all gleamed. His warriors laughed—an ugly sound.

"We are Trinovantes!" Kentan stood his ground, facing them. If he was afraid, he didn't show it. "Go back across the river, or by the treaty your chieftain Cunobelin signed with Caesar, your lives will be forfeit."

"Haven't you heard?" The lead scout snorted with contempt as his scouts edged forward. "Little Trinovant whelps. Your friend Augustus Caesar is far away, and has troubles of his own. The tribes of Germania have banded together and killed three full legions of his soldiers, along with all their horsemen and cohorts. They've crossed the Rhine and swept away all his forts and cities.

"The tribes have sent the Romani packing," he continued. "Caesar won't be coming to save you. Cunobelin is chief of the Catuvellauni tonight, but he will be king of the Britons tomorrow."

They were dangerously close now. Cam took a step nearer to Kentan, to stand by his side, but his foster brother pushed him back. Kentan's other hand rested on the hilt of the knife at his belt, and he whipped out the blade, holding it out in line with the leader's eyes.

"Take another step and you'll never see his coronation," he said grimly.

The Catuvellauni only chuckled. "Your head will sit nicely in the lintel of my house."

Kentan risked a glance back at Cam.

"*You have to warn them,*" he hissed. "*Go!*"

Cam shook his head. "No! We'll fight them!"

Kentan turned on him, his eyes furious.

"Run!" he shouted. "*Now!*"

The lead Catuvellauni saw his chance and rushed Kentan, stabbing out with his short sword. The blade pierced Kentan's side and he screamed in pain. The scout to his left leapt forward with his sword raised. Reeling, Kentan grabbed his first attacker for support and plunged his knife up into the man's neck. It sunk to the hilt—then the second man's blade dropped down on him, sending Kentan and his stricken opponent to the ground.

"Kentan!" Cam screamed, momentarily frozen. The third scout was on him in an instant, his sword slashing in a wide arc. Cam twisted away just enough to avoid decapitation, though as it passed his face the tip of the blade cut a harsh red line across his cheekbone. His assailant's momentum carried him forward and both went sprawling on the treacherous ground. The scout crashed over him and fell into the mud and reeds of the river, cursing. Cam kicked off him, regaining his feet, and ran along the riverbank as far as he could, but all too soon the gnarled roots and trunk of a great old oak at the water's edge blocked his path.

He hazarded a glance behind, only to discover that his pursuers were hot on his heels. A dagger spun through the air toward him. He ducked and the blade sunk into the oak trunk instead of his head. Cam scrambled up the steep bank, only just avoiding the grasping hands below. Then he was tearing through the undergrowth and between the trees.

The men hunting him bayed like hounds, pounding the earth after their prey. Cam's woolen cloak trailed behind him, flapping wildly in the air and threatening to choke him. He clawed at the clasp to release it. A stray branch caught it and tore both cloak and jeweled brooch away, nearly yanking him to the ground in the bargain.

Kych-an-broc! he swore silently. His mind was a torrent of confusion, pain, and fear. *Where are the horses? How close are the scouts? How long can I outrun them? Nev Kawgh!* Shame burned on his cheeks, in his chest. Tears blinded him and he tried to swipe them away, raging at himself. *I can't cry. I'm a man, not a boy. I* can't *cry.*

They'll kill me if I cry. Any thoughts of valor, honor, and glory had gone. All hope of seeing his brother again had fled, along with any hope of vengeance. He had never felt further from being a man. Now there was only survival. He had to get word to his people, to save his tribe… if he could.

I couldn't save my brother. Can I save the tribe? Can I even save myself? He ran on through the gauntlet of the forest, desperate to shake his pursuers while he still had hope to fuel him. The sounds of pursuit began to fade.

Abruptly, he startled a bevy of grouse—the flock burst into noisy flight all around him, followed by coarse laughter and more baying from behind him. His legs and lungs burned as he strained to push his body to its limit, ducking low-hanging branches and crashing through thistles and brambles that cruelly bit the flesh of his hands and legs. His breath came ragged and sharp, as if a knife were working its way into his chest. His greatest pride, the silver torc given to him when he became a man, now clamped down on the corded muscles of his neck.

Even in his desperation, he fought to think.

I can't outrun them. I have to try and outwit them. He took a sharp turn to the left, then to the right, seeking to throw them off his trail. He repeated the pattern, then again, and in one particularly dense thicket of alders he jerked to a stop and ducked behind a trunk, fighting to stay still.

I can't make a sound.

I can't make a sound.

I can't make a sound.

Long agonizing moments passed while he waited and listened for his pursuers, hoping they would race past him. His aching legs and arms trembled, his heart thumped loud and rapid as a bodhrán drum, and his chest rose and fell as he struggled to breathe and stay hidden.

Where are they?

Had he finally shaken them?

Suddenly they appeared, barely two paces away, grinning like skulls and howling in triumph. His failed ruse had only allowed them to close the distance. Cam pushed off the tree and tore away again at a new angle, yet both hunters and prey knew the game was coming to an end.

He was becoming dizzy from the chase, his steps growing more unsteady, and more than once he tripped over a stone or unseen root and stumbled toward the ground, only to force himself up to his feet again. The Catuvellauni never slackened their pace for a moment, and he became certain they were toying with him.

Cam prayed to the spirits of the trees and stones. *Forgive my trespass. Please give me your aid.* As the fire in his lungs turned white-hot, a strange light appeared somewhere up ahead, catching his eye. Without knowing in what direction he was going, he turned and ran toward it, hoping against hope that he had reached his kinsmen. As he ran into the light, however, a flash of a warning struck him.

What if it is the enemy?

It wasn't. It was nothing more than a small break in the trees, a tiny green meadow lit by the few stray shafts of sunlight that could breach the leaden sky. Bursting out, Cam came to a ragged stop, trying to catch his breath. With a shock, he realized he had trespassed into the center of a fairy ring of mushrooms—very bad luck indeed.

And then it was too late.

The Event radiates out from a single point on the timeline, a cataclysmic energy surge that reaches a critical threshold.

The result is a shockwave that shatters six hundred million years of space-time into an untold number of fragments. The overwhelming majority of them are instantaneously converted to energy or blasted into subatomic particles. Only a tiny fraction of a single percent of the timeline remains, to coalesce back into a semblance of the original order.

It is both the end of the world...

...and the beginning.

3

Gavin's lips had barely touched Amber's when the boat started shaking.

Her eyes flew open to see the formerly quiet river now bucking and heaving beneath the punt, water bubbling and frothing like a pot of soup left too long on a burner. A high keening noise replaced the sounds of the birds. The smell of ozone, charred wood, and cooked seafood filled the air.

"What's happening?" Amber looked about wildly as fish floated to the top of the now boiling water. Gavin shook his head, confusion stamped on his face.

"I don't know!"

A deep, unnatural thrumming began, like an

industrial-sized dynamo firing up just below the boat. It resonated through Amber's body, in her very bones, prickling along the skin of her arms and setting her teeth on edge. Droplets of water and tiny will-o'-wisps began to slowly jitter and float up into the air in an impossible, chaotic swirling dance, as if the laws of physics were fraying at the edges.

Her hair whipped around her face, crackling with static electricity, and she clutched Gavin's hands. Then the air erupted all around them. Amber screamed, but the sound was lost in the roar as a streaming wall of brilliantly colored light, both beautiful and terrifying, rose up through the center of the boat, stretching up into the sky.

It flowed like a gravity-flipped Niagara Falls of raw power and light, just a foot from their faces, roaring with fury. The heat coming off the wall was close and searing. Only it wasn't just a wall—it surrounded them until they were in the center of a tube of fiery brilliance.

The keening noise spiraled into a wailing cry that threatened to burst her eardrums, the sound driving a spike of pain into her head. Just when Amber thought her skull would break open, the towering walls of light were gone again, and the deafening sound cut off as abruptly as it had started. Her hair settled back against her head, although her heart still pounded wildly.

The boat seemed oddly frozen in place.

An instant later it lurched to life again, but it was moving *down*. It fell a yard or so until they hit bottom with a bone-jarring, squishy thump. Amber threw herself backward, still clutching Gavin's hands as water rushed toward them, filling the inside of the boat.

There was an odd whooshing noise, almost like water running out a drain, as the boat gave one last dizzying lurch, pitched forward at a crazy angle, and then slid further until it came to a sudden, ungainly halt. The water drained back away from them until only a trickle remained.

What was *that?*

Adrenaline coursed through her body as she peered cautiously over the side of the punt. They rested on top of mud, dead fish and frogs littering the muck that until recently had been covered by the river.

"Omigod," she breathed. "That was the freakiest thing I've ever seen!" The quaver in her voice came as a shock. "Gavin, what's happening?"

He didn't reply.

Suddenly she noticed how limp his hands were in hers, and wondered if he'd been knocked unconscious. She looked down at his face, noting the expression of surprise on his handsome features, his head lolling to one side.

Amber let out a throat-wrenching shriek as she frantically let go of Gavin's hands. Deprived of that last support, he slumped down to the bottom of the boat, resting face down against her feet so she had a clear look at him.

He'd still been straddling the middle seat when he'd leaned in to kiss her, twisting his body a bit awkwardly forward, so most of his torso, right hip and leg, and both arms now lay at an odd angle.

Everything that had been on the other side of the wall of light—including the other half of Gavin—was gone.

4

The western border of the Trinovantian kingdom, Southeast Britain, AD 9

The pair of Catuvellauni scouts burst out of the dark of the trees into the bright clearing. They smiled in triumph, swords ready for the kill.

Cam raised his eyes to the sky.

Gods of my father, hear me. Andraste, Goddess of Victory, grant me the chance to warn my people. Camulos, Lord of War and Sky, grant me strength.

A ghostly calm emptiness filled him, his heart crushed down to a jagged mass of broken hopes in the pit of his stomach. Nothing remained but to fight and win, or die well. He reached for the knife at his belt. It was gone. He looked around for a weapon—a branch, a rock—then settled for two fists. His killers laughed, flanking him as they slowly closed in. Wind began to whistle through the pines and oaks, keening as if the wood spirits were already howling to avenge his death.

Then the trees themselves came alive, trembling and shaking their rage. The scouts stopped in their tracks, for the first time seeming uncertain and frightened. The eerie sound rose until it filled the air, and then with a mighty roar, a sorcerous wall of shining green and violet eldritch lightning-fire came to vivid life behind him. As he turned its light split the clearing in half and stretched off into the woods on both sides. The towering wall reached up and grew toward the clouds, casting a strange glow on the overcast sky.

Cam threw himself to the ground, and the Catuvellauni scouts followed suit. The thunderous thrumming of sheer power that came off the shimmering wall of light echoed in his breastbone and made his head spin. An endless storm of banshees continued to rush out of the very earth, wailing into the heavens above. Then without warning, the wall was gone again.

A new and very different forest lay beyond it.

Denver, Colorado, AD 1924

When the house started shaking, Maddie's first thought was for her bread dough, rising in the oven. It would fall and give Jared another reason to find fault with her, although lord knew, she couldn't control nature if it decided to throw an earthquake into the mix.

Her second thought was that the shaking was oddly rhythmic for an earthquake, punctuated by loud, evenly spaced thuds that grew closer and more violent with each impact. Tea sloshed over the rim of her cup and the couch bucked, the legs almost coming off the ground. Her wedding china clattered in the rosewood hutch, saved from shattering to the ground by the thin railings around each shelf.

A terrified yell brought Maddie to her feet, her bread dough forgotten as she made her way to the back door, throwing it open. She stopped in her tracks as she saw Jack, their cheerful mailman, staring up in terror at what looked like a giant feathered lizard with an oversized head.

As Maddie watched, the creature dipped that big head, seizing the mailman between razor-edged teeth. His scream was cut off as the creature bit down, swallowing the top half as Jack's legs fell to one side, hitting the ground with a dull thud. The thing scooped up the remains, chewing as it stomped further down the street, into unfamiliar swampy land that lay beyond. That swamp replaced the cheerfully painted houses and white picket-fences that had been there that morning.

Maddie shut the door quietly, backing up until

she'd reached the couch, where she promptly curled up under her grandma's quilt. She thought she'd stay there for a while.

Island of Oahu, AD 864

The strange storm faded in the span of a few heartbeats, swifter than the conch shell blasts the holy men had blown to warn the islanders that the gods had descended. Waves of divine lightning had scarred the sky above the seas, leaping forth like a waterspout from the deep. From atop the promontory their people called Lē'ahi, the two young sisters who spent their mornings tending to the sacred fires had been graced with a magnificent view.

They witnessed the gods of storms and seas at play.

In respect and fear, the sisters bowed and averted their eyes until the sun returned and smiled upon them. Only then did the teary-eyed girls dare to look up and hug one another, shaken and yet elated. They had witnessed a miracle.

Holding hands, they turned from the clifftop to return to their village below—only to catch sight of a second miracle. Below them lay Waikiki, which, until a few moments before, had been a swampy place of rivers and streams that fed the turquoise sea.

Now a gigantic structure stood there. More like a

mountain than a hut, far too immense to have been built by mortal hands. It was wide enough to cover a village, perfectly square like a *konane* board with edges straight as fishing spears. It towered into the sky as high as the hills, shining like the sun.

High up in the towering structure, a man slid open an invisible door and stepped out onto a shelf that projected there. He whistled and called out,

"Baby, you would not *believe* the view from up here!"

Mount Vernon, Virginia, AD 1789

"Mr. President!"

Excited steps clattered down the hall, then George Washington's secretary burst into the study. The president looked up from his writing desk in surprise. As he did, he noticed a keening wail coming from somewhere in the distance, impossible to localize.

"Tobias, is the coach here already?"

"No, sir. It's not that. It's outside—come quick, please!"

Washington furrowed his brow, but arose to follow Tobias Lear out back to the mansion's piazza. Tobias shielded his brow with one hand and pointed to the sky.

"Look, sir!" he said. "Can it be some manner of lightning storm? Or the Aurora Borealis?"

A cyclopean curtain of brilliant light obscured their view of the Potomac. The mysterious phenomenon appeared to have completely encircled the mountain on which the estate stood. Its rays reached up high overhead. Soon the shimmering walls blocked out the sky entirely, and the two men stood staring up as from the bottom of a fiery well.

"It's like nothing I've ever seen before in my life," Washington murmured in awe.

Tobias nodded. "It beggars belief."

As the two men continued to stare in wonderment the sound grew louder, more piercing, and then... the spectacular show of light simply vanished.

Along with it went the river valley below. With a boom of thunder, a chilling blast of frigid air blew past the two men, startling them—but not as much as the new vista that lay before them. Mount Vernon had become an isle of green in a sea of pale frozen tundra. Where the Potomac had flowed was now a river of another kind—a moving carpet of huge tusked beasts with shaggy fur.

"Great God in Heaven!" Tobias stammered in disbelief. "It looks like a migration of... elephants."

"Not elephants, Tobias," Washington corrected, even as he struggled to comprehend the sight below. "Mastodons."

Upper Makefield Township, Pennsylvania, AD 1776

A fine Christmas night, General Washington thought, huddled in the Durham boat with his men, cold and wet.

A damp cloak of uncongenial drizzle had been cast off in favor of the mantle of winter in full force. Biting rain, then sleet, then snow. Save for the ice floes clogging the way and crunching against the sides of the boats, the Delaware was an inky black void of freezing water, choppy and treacherous. Few of his troops could swim.

We need a victory.

He considered the fourteen hundred Hessian mercenaries quartered in Trenton. Summer and fall had yielded nothing but one painful defeat after another. The morale of the Continental Army was spent, and their enlistments would expire soon. Tonight's sneak attack was his last chance, and its outcome would make or break the entire revolution.

"Well, I'll be a lobsterback's daughter," one of the oarsmen muttered in disbelief. "Look at that now. The damn river's boiling!"

It was true. Despite the dark and the damp, great curls of steam were billowing from the black water. The inky river, so heartless and cold before, now roiled and churned with an angry new passion, and far down in its depths a growing light burned below them.

Washington half stood to marvel at this odd turn, but

before he could decipher its meaning, an eerie sound filled the air. A rising drone that tingled in their teeth and breastbones. Enormous walls of light burst into life, ringing the far horizon on all sides of the soldiers with a shining flame that banished the icy winter night.

The vision lit up the river and the tiny men in their cramped boats, bathing them in the brightness of noonday, walls of angelic light towering above and encircling them in a shuddery, thundering brilliance that continued to rise into the heavens as far as they could see, reaching up to the stars.

Then the waters and ice floes of the river—all the boats, with all the men and horses and cannons—were thrown into the sky and consumed in a final destroying blast of raw energy as everything in sight tumbled up and away into the void.

On the road to the Theater of Pompey, Rome, March 15, 44 BC

Beware the Ides of March.

Above the thronging crowd along the Via Lata, borne by eight red-headed Thracian slaves in his sedan chair, Caesar kept his face proud and unreadable, but his thoughts were dark as the hateful phrase returned yet again, unbidden.

Beware the Ides of March.

He dismissed it. There was too much to be done. In three days he would lead the army against the Parthian Empire, far to the east. A chance to regain Rome's honor following their most recent defeat at Carrhae. With that victory under his belt, the last resistance of the senate would be gone. But this morning one last senate meeting remained, before he could get on to the greater task before him.

And yet, always obstacles.

Rumors of ill omens ran wild through the city. To have well-drawn plans and the careful work of years continuously undone by rank superstition and fear... that was vexing.

Men worry more about what they can't see than about what they can.

At yesterday's supper, the question had arisen as to what sort of death was the best. He had quipped, "An unexpected one." Everyone laughed. Then last night he dreamt of flying above Rome, above the clouds, clasping the hand of Jupiter himself.

But his bold and intelligent wife, no superstitious fishmonger's doxy, had been beset by nightmares about his safety. In the morning, her eyes red and slick with tears, she pleaded with him not to go out, begged him to postpone the senate meeting instead. He had never seen her so disturbed.

Beware the Ides of March.

March 15, the day of the Ides—today.

The slaves were hard-pressed to navigate the sedan chair through the throng. A familiar figure jostled through the crowd, waving a scroll frantically and shouting to gain his attention. It was Artemidorus, the rhetorician. The little man leaned as close as he dared and stretched out a lanky arm, and Caesar deigned to take his scroll. He handed it in turn down to a servant, who would hold it for later. This alarmed the Greek.

"Sire!" he protested. "The letter is of the utmost importance to you—I pray you, read it at once. I pray you!" But Artemidorus was left behind, mired in the crowd as Caesar's retinue continued on its way. His desperate pleas were drowned out by the clamor.

When they came at last to their destination, and Caesar stepped from his litter, he spotted a less welcome figure haunting the entrance to the Curia. Spurrina, the cadaverous haruspex who had started all this talk of bad luck with his damned prophetic mutterings. Caesar vowed to himself that on his return from Parthia, he would remember to have the miserable old storm crow quietly eliminated. For now, however, he would content himself with a public rebuke.

"The Ides of March have come, old man," he said pointedly.

The old seer bowed his head and answered softly. "Aye, they have come."

Caesar allowed himself a small smirk of triumph before Spurrina murmured further.

"But they are not gone."

A chill came over Caesar as he left his servants and entourage behind to enter the marble hall. The senate rose to greet him and he strode through their midst to take his seat at the base of Pompey's statue. This was a snake pit, but he knew his friends here. Many of the senators here now were his men. Appointing his own partisans had weakened the old aristocracy's hold, making the senate increasingly subservient to him. They knew it. And they hated him for it.

Let them.

Scarcely had he taken his seat before senators were jostling to reach him, petitions in hand. He allowed a group of his most trusted appointees to approach first, including pale, hungry-eyed Cassius. He was followed by Gaius and Servilius, the loyal Casca brothers, and then his heirs, Decimus and Brutus—both distant cousins, but more like sons to him. Another of their fellow supporters, loud, bold Lucius Tillius Cimber stepped up, and the others crowded closer to offer their hot-headed friend their support, wordlessly fanning out around Caesar.

"Noble Caesar," Cimber's voice ached with quiet desperation, "I implore you for the sake of—"

"No, this needs to wait, Lucius." Caesar would not need to read his petition to know what the man wanted—to have his brother recalled from exile. But damn the man, the legions would march on the Parthians in just three days. Besides, the ruler liked Cimber's brother exactly where he was. "There are more pressing matters for today." He rose to address the senate and waved him away.

Cimber did not leave, but only fixed him with a hard, unreadable glare for a fleeting but uncomfortable moment. Then, without warning, he dropped his petition scroll and violently seized Caesar's tunic with both hands, jerking it down.

Thunderstruck, Caesar bellowed, "What is this violence?"

As if in answer, a low rumble, then a howling, keening shriek suddenly filled the chamber. It echoed off the spotless marble floors, growing to a piercing storm of screams, as if the furies themselves had come into the hall, wailing in outrage.

Caesar felt himself trapped as if in a dream, his limbs moving at a snail's pace as he fought to rise and free himself from the man's grasp. The others around him were reaching for him, but they were caught in the same heavy grip, like divers struggling to swim to the surface of the sea before they drowned.

The hall filled with brightness as brilliant lightning-fire roared up like a living curtain from the floor, barely two paces away from him, and shot skyward through the high-arched ceilings. The eerie, roaring wall of lightning ran in a crooked line from wall to wall. It cut through the line of men in front of him and they died screaming. Cimber released him in shock, and stumbled against the fiery barrier. It devoured him entirely, as if he had backed into an open furnace.

Overhead, large portions of the majestic ceiling arches, now unsupported, came tumbling down. Some blocks fell into the blazing wall and vanished before they could touch the floor, others fell on the senators below.

And then, as swiftly as it had come, the ear-bursting wall of Tartarus-fire was gone again. The marble-clad floors, columned walls, and arched ceilings were still pristine… except where the terrible veil had stretched across. Like a knife cutting a wedge of goat's cheese, it had split the building apart, leaving nothing on the other side. No senate hall, no senators—nothing beyond but a dismal new landscape. There stood tall, ruined buildings of a curious design. The bright morning sky was replaced by another, smudged black by fires, the smells of spring mixed with that of ash and gloom.

A pair of dark figures stalked the streets, wearing somber robes, slowly swinging braziers of burning incense. Their faces were obscured by ominous blackened leather hoods in the shape of bird heads, each with a long beak and large round glass baubles for eyes. Behind them trailed a slave, the lower part of his face hooded with filthy rags, leading a cart pulled by a starving donkey.

Blotched gray corpses filled the rickety wagon.

Caesar turned from the nightmare outside and looked down at the bodies of his dead friends. Of those taken by the veil, nothing was left but stray scraps of silk and flesh. At his feet lay Cassius, Gaius, Servilius, and Decimus. All dead, all broken by fallen masonry.

Were there no survivors?

He looked about for anyone else alive. Turning, he saw his beloved Brutus lying beside him, a puddle of blood expanding beneath him. His body had been crushed by a sharp-edged block of marble. Caesar knelt down and cupped his head. The younger man's eyes fluttered, and he tried to speak, but no words could escape. He looked up into Caesar's eyes, and then his gaze faded away. The closest thing to Caesar's son was gone.

"You too, Brutus?" His voice cracked. The portents were clear. The gods themselves had rained down punishment, in payment for his hubris, and Rome itself had paid the price with him.

A gleam caught his eye. A dagger lay in Brutus's hand. Had the gods placed it there to give to him? He gently pried it from his heir's fingers and rose. Like a gladiator, he raised it to heaven and saluted the gods.

"Then fall, Caesar!"

He fell upon his blade.

Upminster, United Kingdom, AD 1955

He smiled down at his guest, enjoying the raw fear in her eyes, visible above the swatch of duct tape that covered her mouth. Tears dripped down her cheeks and she struggled to breathe through mucus-filled nostrils. He'd take the gag off… eventually. His basement was soundproof, but he'd wait until she was close to suffocation, terrified that she'd asphyxiate on her own snot. She'd be so grateful for air, so relieved to take those first few breaths… until she saw the toys.

By the time he'd finished with her—and oh, he planned on stretching things out as long as possible— she'd be praying for an easy death like suffocation.

He'd watched her for several months, getting to know her routines, any variations and how often they'd occur. Not often—a point in her favor. Grocery shopping on Sunday, nine-to-five receptionist at a local dentist's, dinner with her mum on Wednesdays, pub with her girlfriends on Fridays and the occasional Saturday, and the bi-monthly visits to the cinema on Saturday afternoons.

After careful consideration, he'd chosen Saturday night to take her. Her friends would be pissed up when they left the pub, and down with raging hangovers most of Sunday. No one would notice her absence until Monday morning when she didn't show up for work.

All he'd had to do was wait until she parted ways with her friends and started on wobbly feet down the little alleyway that led to her basement flat. There he'd quickly overpowered her, tossing her unconscious body into the boot of his car.

Now he picked up a black canvas bundle, slowly pulled on the ties that held it shut, and allowed the heavily weighted length to unfold, displaying a glittering array of knives in a variety of shapes and sizes, taking care to make certain his guest got a good look at them.

"You like these? Sheffield steel. Nothing but the best for my company."

Her eyes widened and she whimpered, the sound frantic under the tape.

He smiled, full of good cheer at the thought of the hospitality he was about to inflict on her.

Life was good.

She whimpered again, sounding like a whipped puppy. That made him frown. He liked puppies. He'd never found pleasure in hurting animals. Just people.

An empty space on the carefully organized display caught his eye. One of his favorite knives, a filleting blade, wasn't in its spot. He cast his mind back to the last time he'd used it. His previous guest had visited more than a month ago. Had he used it since then? He chuckled to himself. Yes, he'd deboned a whole salmon for dinner the week prior. Must have left it in the dish drainer. Careless.

"Damn," he murmured. "If you'll excuse me, I must retrieve something. Can't get close to the bone without it." He grinned as she started thrashing again. Anticipation made this *so* much fun. "Be back in just a tick."

He stepped out into the main portion of the basement, closing the heavy iron door behind him and twisting the lock shut. Not that she could get out of the shackles, but one couldn't be too careful. Taking the basement stairs two at a time, he whistled a jaunty little tune.

Sure enough, the filleting knife rested in the bottom of the dish drainer, waiting for him. The sharp metal glinted under the kitchen lighting, almost as if it were winking at him. He grinned to himself, liking the fanciful thought of his knives having their own personality, even if he knew it was utter rubbish. He didn't have voices in his head, or some big man in the sky telling him to kill people.

He did it because it was fun. And wasn't that the best reason to do anything?

The floor shifted under his feet with a suddenness that nearly threw him to his knees. He grabbed the edge of the worktop, holding on as the house shuddered around him, groaning and creaking like an arthritic octogenarian. There was a loud ululation, rising to a painful shriek. Dishes danced on the cheerful yellow-tiled counter, a plate leaping off the edge to shatter on the floor.

The shaking stopped as abruptly as it started. The

house settled with one last creak. Something upstairs fell with a heavy thud. And then, nothing.

A superstitious man might question whether this was a sign from God Almighty, he mused, telling him that his hobby somehow was wrong. A small smile played across his face. He had no such internal struggles, theological or otherwise.

His guest would be beside herself. What if something had fallen on her? She might be seriously injured, or worse, dead.

Then what fun would she be?

The mess in the kitchen, and no doubt elsewhere in the house, could wait. He needed to check on her right away, and hurried back down to the basement. Turning the lock, he threw the door open.

A gust of frigid air greeted him.

His playroom—along with his new toy—was gone. The room, the walls, the council house that butted up against his directly across from the door.

All gone.

Cautiously, slowly, he peered around the door, first to his right and then to his left. The street he'd grown up on still remained.

In front of him, however, lay an expanse of grass as far as he could see, the sky above a cold slate gray. The word "tundra" came to mind, one of those stupid bits of information that had stuck from school. He couldn't quite remember what it meant, but it seemed to fit the scenery in front of him.

Crazy.

Someone screamed off in the distance. Closer to home, he thought he heard the mutterings of incoherent prayers.

He grinned.

This could be fun.

He decided to dress for any occasions that might lie ahead.

Sea of Tranquility, the Moon, AD 1969

The radio beeped again. Mission Control's voice crackled in his ear.

"Okay. Neil, we can see you coming down the ladder now."

Commander Neil Armstrong carefully backed through the *Eagle*'s forward EVA hatch. Even in one-sixth Earth gravity, his cumbersome space suit made him feel like Frankenstein's monster as he stepped off the egress platform and carefully, slowly, lumbered his way downward.

The landing had been so soft that the *Eagle*'s shock absorbers hadn't compressed. He had to hop down from the last rung to the footpad of the module. He paused a moment to make sure they would be able to climb back aboard, and then dutifully reported the situation.

"Okay. I just checked getting back up to that first step, Buzz. It's... the strut isn't collapsed too far, but it's adequate to get back up." The radio let out another piercing high-pitched peep.

"*Roger*," Houston responded. "*We copy.*"

"Takes a pretty good little jump," Armstrong said. "Okay. I'm at the foot of the ladder. The LM footpads are only depressed in the surface about one or two inches, although the surface appears to be very, very fine-grained, as you get close to it. It's almost like a powder. Ground mass is very fine."

He paused for a moment on the metal footpad, his last touchstone with Earth. Up to now in the mission, the constant stream of tasks at hand had taken the lion's share of his attention. Now, here at the brink, unbridled and oddly poetic new thoughts unexpectedly presented themselves.

He adjusted his sun visor. The sky was an unrelenting midnight black, but it still felt like daytime. The pure, unhindered sunlight burnished the lander to gold and silver and tinted the brilliant lunar surface a welcoming grayish cocoa. The horizon wasn't quite right—it was too close, its curvature so much more pronounced. The absolute lifelessness of the vista fascinated him.

Nothing has changed here for hundreds of thousands of years, he thought. *Generations of humanity emerged from the trees… and in all that time, all of this has looked the same.* A new realization began to eclipse the rest of his thoughts. Over half a billion people were watching him at this utterly unprecedented moment. He swallowed. He blinked.

The radio beeped again in his ear.

He pulled himself together.

"Okay. I'm going to step off the LM now."

With both hands secure on the ladder, he cautiously stretched out his left foot, leaving the other on the safety of the lander's footpad. His boot sank a fraction of an inch into soft, fine lunar dust, sending grains of it leaping away in an unearthly—*literally unearthly*, he thought—fashion. The regolith clung to the sides of his boot in fine layers, like powdered charcoal.

That bootprint could remain there for eternity, he realized. Armstrong cleared his throat, thinking of the right words to say.

"That's one small step for man…" He glanced up at the minuscule thumbnail of the Earth, floating so serene in the blackness. *How fragile it is… so small, so very colorful. I could blot it out with my thumb…*

As he watched, the tiny blue planet splintered. A thousand brilliant cracks appeared, as if the Earth had been hiding a sun inside—one that had finally grown strong enough to burst through its ancient cocoon. The slender rivulets of fire ran from pole to pole and across the globe, its cloudy blue-green ball spider-webbed by a million blazing electric filaments.

Armstrong stared in speechless horror as the light from the fractures speared out into space. He lifted his hand to shield his face from the blinding light that had been the Earth.

Just as suddenly, the exploding glare was gone.

So was the Earth.

Armstrong collapsed to the dusty ground, his limbs gone to jelly, his eyes wide and raw and wet, still staring—unbelieving, uncomprehending—at the empty sky. He sat there, utterly alone, quivering within his pressure suit in stunned silence.

And then…

The Earth was back.

5

Once the sound and fury had passed, Cam was the first to rise back to his feet. When he did, he stared in wonder.

Gods of my father…

Beyond where the colossal wall of druid-fire had arisen, a strange new vista now lay before him. The trees were like none he had ever seen. No oaks, birch, poplars, ash, or alders remained. There were reeds and ferns, clubmosses and bracken in abundance—indeed, it seemed as if even the trees themselves were ferns of enormous size.

Lizards skittered up every scaly trunk, pursuing huge beetles. The dense warm air buzzed with brilliant gleaming streaks of armored dragonflies as they dove and circled, hunting smaller winged insects. Each one was at least as long as a tall man's arm, in jeweled hues of emerald, azure, or reddish-gold amber. Off in the distance, strange bellowing sounds echoed, like those of a great elk, but deeper and louder than any he had ever heard.

This was no land of mortal men. It could only be a realm of the Sídhe, the folk of the enchanted world. Cam knew his own lands and people lay beyond this fey realm. He stared into its strange depths, took a quick breath and nodded to himself.

No choice now but to cross it. Without hesitation, he bolted for the line of division and crossed over into the Otherworld.

His deerskin boots were quickly soaked. It was warmer and wetter here, and the ground was marshy at best, much of it no more than stagnant pools and dank fenlands. Yet he had a second wind now, and this time he swore he wouldn't give his pursuers another chance to close the gap—if they dared to follow him through this maze of lush ferns and uncoiling horsehead plants.

No jeers or war-howls rose behind him, but he raced on ahead all the same, for as long as his tortured legs and lungs continued to pump. When at last he reached his limit and staggered to a clumsy stop, he dove into the undergrowth and lay there hiding, listening for any sign of pursuit. His chest rose and fell while his runaway heartbeat slowed and fern fronds tickled his face. Still no human sounds came to his ear.

Once he caught his breath again, he peered around

and risked standing. There he watched, waited, and listened, perfectly unmoving. His cheek stung, so he reached up to touch it. A veil of blood had crusted on his face from the fresh scar below his right eye.

Ignoring the burning cut, he cautiously began to move and made his way silently through the curious landscape. A chorus of insects announced his every step. As he passed the deeper pools, fish darted away, and the biggest newts he had ever seen scattered from the muddy water's edge.

Strange that there are no birds. Cam wondered if this was an ill omen.

Here and there, misshapen frog-things the size of wild hogs sat and regarded him implacably, tracking him with their fat-lidded eyes, as if deciding whether he was an unusual new bug worth snapping up for a meal.

Circling carefully around pools, fallen logs, and tree trunks, Cam lost all sense of direction and time. He might have been wandering for one hour or many, for all he knew. The strange fern-trees loomed over him, casting sinister shadows and blocking the sun more with every step he took into their canopy. The constant drone of chirping insects, the calls of the frogs and of less familiar creatures, and the thick, rich air all wove a spell over him. Increasingly he felt as if he had entered an enchanted labyrinth.

Gods and spirits lived in all the pools and trees of

home, but he did not know the names of the forest gods that dwelt in the sacred places of this realm. He touched the tree trunks with humble reverence and offered their spirits quiet words of honor and supplication. If they accepted his offerings, they gave no sign.

He forged on.

Cam recalled the old stories of those who had entered the fey world, and returned to the mortal realm to find that years had passed, though it seemed like days to the traveler. If he came across a damsel or lord of the Sídhe, he would have to remember to be courteous, but to steadfastly decline to eat or drink anything they offered. Otherwise, when he returned, he might find he had been away for a hundred years. Or perhaps he would never be allowed to return at all. The ways of the fair folk were strange and unpredictable.

A sharp pang struck him as he realized it had been Kentan who had told him so many of those stories. He caught his breath, fighting back tears that threatened to burst out. The sorrow was so strong it made his chest and limbs ache.

He was utterly alone now.

A blood-chilling war cry split the air. The Catuvellauni had followed him. Without thought, Cam instantly cut hard to the left, splashing across the shallows of the closest pond. His pursuers yelled and howled like wolves after a wounded stag. He leapt over mossy stones and decaying tree-fern trunks. The warriors kept pace, clearing each hurdle with the same ease. He did not dare look back, but from their howls he knew they were closing in.

In the gloomy depths of these otherworldly woods, Cam could barely see the obstacles in his path as he plunged ahead in desperation. He slipped around a brace of ferns—and ran into a dead end of deep water.

"*Nev Kawgh!*" he hissed in surprise.

He spun around and looked for a way past his pursuers. There was no escape.

With a desperate war cry of his own, the unarmed youth charged toward them, but the lead scout hurled his short sword at Cam's feet. The whirling iron blade struck him heavily in the shins, pommel first. Cam tripped over the blade and tumbled down to the damp earth. He looked up to see the man draw his dagger and raise it high as he made a mighty leap for Cam, howling in triumph.

His victory cry was cut short as a massive shape thundered out of the dark. Mighty jaws snatched the man out of the air like a lark catching a kicking grasshopper on the fly.

Cam stared in disbelief. The thing was taller than a grown man by twice over, and its hulking body wider than a war chariot, carried by four legs thick as ancient tree trunks. Hungry eyes like slick wet river stones gleamed in a great green scaly head larger even than a cave bear's—more like a boulder—with a mouth full of teeth like spearheads. Its backbone was a ridge of pikestaffs connected by a thick web of skin, almost like a sail.

A dragon! Kych-an-broc!

The gigantic beast's growl almost drowned out the screams of the warrior being chewed apart by those horrible jagged teeth. In a few shakes of the beast's head, what little was left of the man fell to the ground in ragged red chunks.

The hungry monster turned its head to the other warrior and roared again. Cornered, the Catuvellauni backed up until he was hard against a thick tree trunk, fear-frozen. Again and again he slashed out with his blade, striking against the thing's thick bony skull as it closed in on him.

Still sprawled out on the marshy ground, Cam saw his chance to escape while the dragon was fixed on its new prey. He rose to a crouch, preparing to take to his heels and be gone before the monster even realized he was there. Yet he could not move, transfixed as he was by the sight of the other man struggling for his life. In that moment, he knew he could not leave him to fight alone.

No, he thought. *Not even an enemy. Not even my brother's killer.* He would take his vengeance, but the beast would not take it for him. Taking up the sword that downed him, he rose to his feet.

This is it.

With a harsh battle cry, he charged the dragon. The monster made no indication that it heard him, but remained fixated on its prey, like a cat with a cornered mouse. The Catuvellauni was still desperately on the attack, but the creature kept snapping at him hungrily.

Running up to the great beast, Cam reversed the grip on the weapon and took it in both hands. Raising it overhead, he plunged it down with all his strength into a spot on the beast's skull. The sword bit deep, and he put his back into forcing the iron blade down even further, hoping for a death blow.

No such luck.

The monster roared in pain and reared up, twisting its massive head. Still grasping the hilt with both hands, Cam was first lifted and then shaken off, thrown far through the air to crash with a painful thud that pounded the breath out of him. The dragon continued to stamp and twist, with every step hammering the ground like a mountain giant's fist. One gargantuan taloned foot came down on the Catuvellauni, crushing the man's leg with a sickening crunch and pinning him to the ground. Noticing its prey again, the dragon ceased its thrashings and proceeded to eat the screaming man in huge, leisurely bites.

Cam caught his wind once more, but tiny bright blue fairies swam before his eyes and played dreadful piping music in his ears. He staggered to his feet, but no sooner had he regained his footing than the dragon's tail swept the ground and slapped him like a fly.

Merciful blackness took him before he hit the ground.

What was left of Gavin reminded Amber of the colored cross-sections in her anatomy textbook. Organs, muscles, bones, sinews all in place and oddly bloodless, as if he'd been cut by a giant razor blade that had cauterized everything as it sliced through his body.

The smell of charred flesh wafted up, reminding her perversely of summer picnics and barbecued steak.

"Oh god."

Before she could stop it, her breakfast came back up in a violent surge. She managed to grab the side of the punt, hanging over the rim just in time to prevent her vomit from splashing onto Gavin's remains. Even after there was nothing left inside to throw up, Amber dry-heaved for several minutes, then let her body slowly slide back into the boat. She rested her forehead against the wooden seat, waiting for the dizziness and nausea to subside.

She had no idea how long she remained in that position. Maybe if she stayed there long enough, she thought, she'd wake up and the smell of charred meat would be gone.

Because this has to be a nightmare, right?

It had to be. There was no other explanation.

She waited for the odor of human barbecue to go away and for the hard wood under her forehead to morph into soft pillows. Neither of these things occurred, however, and Amber became gradually aware that the former heat of the day had been replaced by noticeably cooler weather. A chill breeze raised goose bumps on her bare arms and legs and she shivered.

I should get inside, get more clothes on.

That thought, combined with an even colder gust of air upgraded from breeze to wind, finally convinced Amber to take stock of her surroundings. Her next thought was to call someone for help.

Reaching out one arm, she pulled her backpack toward her and fumbled in one of the outer pockets for her iPhone. With shaking fingers she hit the home button, punching in her passcode. The screen lit up and she used the touchscreen to pull up the phone app.

Do they use 9-1-1 in the UK? She stared at the screen for a minute, then remembered, *No. They use 9-9-9.*

She hit the numbers and held the phone up to one ear. Nothing.

No ring tone, no mechanical voice telling her there was no signal. Just silence. She looked at the screen. Her battery charge was at ninety-seven percent. The words *No Signal* sat in the upper left-hand corner where bars should be.

Still, there should at least be a ring tone, right?

She set the phone on low power mode before putting it away, and pushed herself up to a sitting position, taking care to move slowly just in case the dizziness hit her again. She tried not to look at Gavin's remains or to breathe too deeply, instead focusing on her immediate surroundings, trying to center herself.

Her heart clenched, her stomach tightened, and she nearly curled up into a fetal ball.

Gone was the peaceful Thomas Gainsborough landscape of willow and oak trees, the gentle river with sloping banks, and the songbirds. In its place were what seemed like endless miles of stark grasslands, the pale yellow grass tipped with frost. Overhead the atmosphere roiled and twisted in a meteorological dogfight. The blue sky was swiftly changing now to a slate gray, clouds heavy with the threat of rainfall. The only sound was that of the wind rustling through the tall vegetation.

For the first time, she noticed that the punt had also been sliced in two, the edges shaved off with a supernatural perfection. The other half of the little boat was just… gone.

Amber shook her head. Maybe if she shook it hard enough, things would snap back to reality as she knew it. All the motion did, however, was make her want to throw up again. She sat still, her brain constantly trying to make sense of what she saw.

The only trace of her former surroundings lay directly

next to and behind her. Remnants of the riverbank bracketed what was left of the punt. Several willows still stood, though one was only half a tree, bisected directly through its trunk from top to bottom in a perfect split. The other half had just vanished, much like Gavin and the punt. The banks ran about twenty feet behind her, then ended sharply, as if the river had been punched out with a Godzilla-sized cookie cutter. Muddy ground and a few puddles were all that remained of the river itself.

In front of her, it was as if the river had never existed.

A mournful howl off in the distance broke the silence. Amber sat bolt upright.

Wolves? Are there wolves in England?

The howl was answered by another sound, deep and guttural. More like a roar.

Primordial, maybe. Amber didn't know where that thought came from, and she didn't want to think about it. She needed to find her way back to Romford and normality.

Another gust of wind blew across the grass, the cold cutting through the thin fabric of her dress. She looked around and spied the picnic hamper next to her feet. Maybe there was a blanket inside, something she could drape around her shoulders until she reached the hotel and the convention. Sure enough, a cheerful blue and white checked flannel cloth was tucked into one side, cushioning two cut-crystal champagne flutes, a bottle of Prosecco, and a bottle of sparkling apple juice, as well.

Gavin had covered all the bases.

As she reached for the cloth, she noticed Gavin's Han Solo jacket on the floor where it had fallen off the picnic hamper. The sight of it hit her like an electric shock, and she stood there momentarily paralyzed, unable to move or look away as the reality of his death hit her. She caught her breath with a ragged gasp, sorrow and fear bubbling up inside her, eyes welling with unshed tears.

With grim determination, she forced both her tears and emotions back down, then slowly, deliberately, she stooped to pick up the jacket, donning it over her bare arms and shoulders. The little epaulets of her costume made the jacket stick up a bit at the shoulders, but now wasn't the time to worry about how she looked.

I should take the food with me. The thought came out of nowhere. Her more conscious reaction was, *That's just silly. I'll be back at the hotel soon. Why would I need it?*

Then she looked in the direction of where she thought Romford should be, back the way she and Gavin had traveled on the river, at the expanse of grass and nothing else. Without questioning her reasons, she rummaged in the hamper and pulled out everything edible, including two carefully wrapped sandwiches, cheese, apples, packets of chips—

They call them crisps here, she thought vaguely.

—and two eight-ounce plastic bottles of water. There was even a large Cadbury Fruit and Nut bar.

All of this went into her backpack, along with the Prosecco, a couple of forks, a sharp knife, and another linen napkin.

Again a howl rose above the wind, this time joined by several others in a lusty chorus that sent chills up Amber's spine. She knew wolves got a bad rap, and didn't usually eat people... but what if they were hungry? Also, she didn't think wolves were the only wildlife lurking out there.

She hurriedly zipped shut the main compartment of her backpack, then opened it again, grabbing the knife. Just in case. Then she looked at her Codex staff where she'd leaned it against the seat. The body of the staff was painted wood—not the sturdiest weapon she could ask for—but it was four feet long and the axe-shaped blades around the orb were aluminum. Four feet between her and whatever might be out there seemed like better odds than a close encounter with only a cheese knife for protection.

The knife went back in the backpack, which she zipped shut and slid onto her shoulders. She picked up the picnic blanket, thinking to wrap it around her for extra protection against the cold. She held it against her cheek. It felt very warm and comforting.

She turned to look at Gavin. His face was still frozen in that look of surprise, his hands open and empty. It hurt her heart to look at him, so she quickly and gently draped the blanket over his partial corpse. It was the least she could do.

Then she stood, swaying unsteadily for a minute as she steeled herself to leave the scant shelter of the punt and step out into a landscape that shouldn't be there.

You can do this, she told herself. *You* have *to do this.*

Amber decided to climb over the side of the punt, unable to bring herself to step over Gavin's remains even though it would have been an easier exit. She scraped a knee on the wooden rim as she clambered over, but managed to keep her balance as she dropped the few feet to the ground.

Her low-heeled sandals immediately sunk into mud, the ground squelching beneath her feet as water seeped up between her toes. Thankfully she'd missed stepping on one of the boiled fish littering the riverbed, but still...

Ugh.

She carefully picked her way out of the mud and climbed onto the firmer ground of the grasslands that started where the punt had been halved. If she stared hard enough in that direction, she thought she could see splashes of green and brown on the horizon, maybe trees and buildings.

The chorus of howls started up again, followed by another one of those deep guttural roars.

Definitely closer than before.

Amber started walking toward the green and brown shapes in the distance. Maybe when she reached them, things would be back to normal.

6

Cam groaned. His eyelids fluttered, once, twice, and cracked open. There was nothing to see but green-tinged haze.

How long have I been here?

He thought about wiggling his fingers, then realized one arm was stretched out and the other twisted at an awkward angle beneath him. He untangled himself and tried to rise up on his elbows.

That was a mistake. The dragon's foot had come down and crushed Cam's skull like an eggshell, smearing its contents in a messy streak along the ground. Surely that was the only explanation he could conceive for the pain he now felt.

Kych-an-broc...

He clutched his head and groaned again. To his surprise, his skull was perfectly intact, yet somehow unseen chariot wheels were rolling back and forth over it, and he could see the fairies again. Jangled memories flittered off like moon-moths, and he couldn't think straight. He had to stack his thoughts one painful word at a time, like piling stones on a cairn.

Where am I?

What happened?

The woods…

He had been in the woods—a strange sort of woods—and someone had been chasing him… Slowly his vision cleared, and he saw he was splayed out in a patch of fern. *Huge* fern. But why? A loud bellowing echoed from nearby, and the sound quickly shepherded back all his meandering thoughts in vivid flashes of memory.

The Leagean.

Kentan.

The Catuvellauni.

The dragon!

The punch-drunk spell instantly sobered, and he swiftly ducked his head back down into the undergrowth, then peered out to spy where the beast was now. He rose to a crouch and cautiously parted the ferns to take a look. Nothing was moving but the scurrying lizards and flying insects. The dragon's thrashing had stamped out a new clearing at the water's edge. The rich red ground was pockmarked with its clawed footprints, all filled with dark pools of the scouts' blood. Tattered bits of their gory remains lay scattered about.

Cam stood, silent and watching, poised to sprint or fight. The tracks led off into the deep pool that had blocked his escape. It still rippled from the beast's passage. He remained still, listening carefully as, somewhere in the distance, a bellowing roar sounded the dragon's departure.

Only then did he move on.

Directions were capricious and treacherous things here in this strange and murky realm of the Sídhe folk. Cam swatted away another unduly large insect that buzzed around his head as he slogged further through the swampy Otherworld.

He had been sure he would have come upon some fabulous palace or ring-fortress before now. His plan was simple. He would stand before the fey lords and ladies, behaving most courteously, and get their help. He bit his lip in determination, trying to think of the right words to say.

"My lords and ladies of the fair folk," he practiced aloud, "I beg your forgiveness and grace, and do come before you in all humility and in great and desperate need. I… I would not dare…"

What was it the nobles would say? The words came to him.

"I would not dare trespass against your custom or your realm, nor intrude upon the peace of your court. Yet so urgent is my mission and dire our circumstance, I but ask your aid to bring me swiftly back home." He paused and mulled over his words, then continued. "Even now, our enemies, the Catuvellauni, have broken the peace and cross the Bright River to make war upon us. I must warn my people, my lords and ladies. Will you help me?"

Surely for a cause so noble they would grant him that small a favor. If the Sídhe could read the hearts of men, they would see that his was pure. Perhaps his plight would touch them, and they would grant him a magical horse whose enchanted hooves could cross many leagues with every step.

Or maybe they would see the muddy wool cape and the battered old short sword he had taken from the dead scouts, take pity on him, and replace them with a Sídhe-forged blade of steel and a shirt of glittering gold ring-mail.

His eyes lit up, picturing the sight of his return.

But… what if they refuse me and I'm trapped here forever?

The sudden thought terrified him. His brow furrowed as he came to a hard decision.

Whatever they demand of me, he thought, *whatever they ask, I will do it. Even if it means I have to return after the battle and serve them for a hundred years. Even if it means remaining here forever.*

He frowned as his bleak thoughts lost ground to a still darker one.

What if I never find the Sídhe at all?

What if their castles were hidden from mortal eyes by magic? The further he went, the more the twists and turns of the swampy woods gave him scant hope. Cam prayed he wasn't just wandering in circles. Would he ever get out of this maze? Lost in thought, he didn't notice what was in front of him until it struck him in the eyes.

The sun.

With a single step, Cam emerged from the dank fen into the light of day. Soft meadowlands stretched out before him, green and inviting, rich with wildflowers in yellows and violets. Even the leaden sky looked fair and warm. A flock of starlings twisted and dove overhead and flew away again.

He blinked at the sight for a few moments, before surprising himself with a single quick, unexpected laugh of sheer relief.

Have I returned home, just like that?

It looked like his own land, and yet…

He turned back to the dark forest behind him. Something was wrong. It was the way the otherworldly forest ended and the meadow began. At first he couldn't sort it out. Then he realized there was no gradual tapering off of the trees—no meadow grasses growing between the trunks of tree ferns. Instead, there was a jagged line of division from one terrain to the next, like two scraps of cloth sewn together. Even the soil was a different shade on either side of the line.

The trees of the strange forest didn't simply stop at the line. The division sliced *through* them, branches and trunks alike, as if a giant scythe had followed the cut of the line with perfect precision. It was unnatural and disquieting, but perhaps it was to be expected with the Sídhe.

Shrugging, he set off at a brisk pace, heading due east toward the interior of the Trinovantes' lands. At the first fort or homestead he came to he would beg a horse, and ride like the wind to raise the alarm.

7

Amber walked with no real idea of how much time actually passed. It might have been minutes or hours. The horizon didn't change. The same grasslands stretched out on all sides, no matter how far she went or how much her feet throbbed, skin chafing where the straps rubbed against the flesh.

Funny, she'd chosen the sandals for comfort. They were supposed to have heels, but since this was just a hall costume she hadn't worried about accuracy. That had been with the expectation of a day on her feet at a convention. Not hiking miles across half-frozen ground.

She'd started out at a brisk pace, anxious to get back to the normality of Romford, have a "cuppa" with her aunt, take a hot shower, and change into pajamas. But no matter how fast or far she walked, the smudges of green and brown in the distance didn't seem to come any closer. They were a mirage. A perverse trick of the imagination.

After a while her quick steps slowed to a steady walk, and then to a weary trudge, until each step was an effort of will, even aided by her Codex staff. She shivered as another cold gust of wind cut through her clothes, the tall grass bending sideways under its passage.

Each step hurt.

She was pretty sure blisters had risen, burst, and were now bleeding, but she didn't look. If she didn't look, it wasn't real. If she looked and saw blood trickling down, pooling between the soles of her feet and those sandals, then she couldn't pretend anymore.

I'm like the Little Mermaid, she thought. Every step like knives in the feet, all for the sake of a handsome prince. Only her prince was dead, cut in half with no warning or explanation. It wasn't real. It *couldn't* be real.

This has to be a dream, right?

Her right foot slid inside its sandal, slick with wetness.

A sob bubbled up in Amber's throat but she choked it back. If she let herself start to cry, she wouldn't be able to stop. She'd crumple to the ground and cry until she froze to death, or died of starvation.

Another of those guttural sounds echoed across the tundra, summoning up visions of monsters. Every stupid giant crocodile movie she'd ever seen sprung to mind, only they didn't seem so funny now. Amber shuddered.

She didn't know what was behind the freaky noise, and she didn't want to find out. The intermittent howling was bad enough, but at least wolves were something within the framework of her reality.

As long as she kept her eyes to the ground, she could tell herself the next time she looked up, things would be back to normal. If she kept staring at the seemingly endless vista of grass, she would lose it.

Put one foot in front of the other... and soon I'll be walking out the do-o-or...

Maybe she *was* crazy.

It didn't matter. What mattered was getting back to civilization, and then hopping on the first plane available back to San Diego and her family.

Put one foot in front of the other...

Each step through the knee-high grass, each rub of leather against chafed skin brought her that much closer to her goal.

After a while, she didn't see anything other than a grayish-green blur beneath her feet. So when she stubbed her foot on something rock solid, it came as a complete surprise.

Yelping, she bent over as the big toe on her right foot expanded into a ball of outraged nerve endings with the kind of abrupt and excruciating pain that caused people to punch walls or break inanimate objects. She waited until it subsided, giving an exploratory wiggle to make sure nothing was broken.

Only then did she look down to see what she'd hit.

It was a strip of concrete about six inches high and twice that in length, rising into another one, and then another, like—

Stairs.

Stairs!

Amber raised her head and caught her breath. A flight of stairs, set into a gentle slope of well-tended lawn a few hundred feet across. It butted up against an asphalt drive that curved under an overhang, marked by the letters of a sign.

ROMFORD
ARMS HOTEL

She'd made it back! She could use a phone inside and call her aunt. Or even better, call her family in California! Amber ran up the stairs, nearly slipping on a patch of melting snow on the top step and—

Patch of snow?

Slowly she walked across the drive to the hotel entrance, noticing more puddles of slush and patches of dingy gray ice pushed up against the curb.

The marquee listed upcoming special events.

✦ BAYLOR-HODGESON WEDDING ✦
✦ ROMFORD MODEL RAILWAY SOCIETY MTG ✦
✦ CONGRATULATIONS CLASS OF 1993 ✦

Amber took a second look at the building's façade. The semi-enclosed parking garage—"car park," Gavin had called it—was there on the right, but it looked as though someone had chopped it in half with a giant guillotine. All three stories. More grasslands lay beyond the part that remained, but in between the grass and the concrete stretched a sliver of cobblestones. Splashes of dark, red-stained grass, cobblestones, and concrete.

Amber hurried to the hotel's glass double doors, shoved them open, and ran inside. All she wanted right now was to get out of the frigid wind and safe from whatever—

The smell hit her first. A thick, nauseating blend of the coppery scent of blood mixed with fecal matter, spilled guts, and the contents of shredded intestines. Not even the harsh, cold wind blowing past the check-in desk could mask the odor of death.

Then, as if someone had superimposed the images after the fact, Amber saw the bodies scattered around what was left of the darkened lobby. Pieces, parts, shredded and pulped. Hands, arms, chunks of meat barely identifiable as human littered the gore-smeared parquet flooring. Blood spattered the furniture and walls. Part of a woman was draped over the concierge's desk, mouth open in shock. Amber noticed almost absently that the dead woman's hair was retro-styled in what her mom referred to as "secretary hair," the bangs poofed up and heavily lacquered in place.

Her staff dropped with a clatter, landing by her feet. She let the doors fall shut behind her, and stared at the carnage spread across the hotel lobby—or what was left of it. It wasn't quite as hollow as a movie set—maybe a few hundred feet with lobby furniture, fountain, and the check-in desk.

Most of the check-in desk, anyway.

The wall behind it was gone.

Amber would have said "missing," but as with the punt and Gavin, it was as if the wall had never existed. The ever-present grasslands pressed up in a straight line where the parquet floor ended.

Lovecraft had it all wrong, Amber thought. All that stuff about non-Euclidian geometry, things like triangles with five sides driving men mad… that was nothing. Her world had been cut into slices with the precision of an X-Acto knife drawn against a ruler. Now *that* won the "insane" prize, hands down.

Somewhere, not nearly far enough in the distance, fierce howls rose in the darkening sky.

Oh, god…

They sounded hungry. How could whatever made those noises still be hungry when they'd already eaten—?

Amber blocked the rest of the thought. She was close enough to the edge as it was.

More howls, closer.

The shadows lengthened.

Then that guttural roar, like something had crawled from the primordial ooze. This time, however, it was accompanied by the sound of footfalls. What was left of the walls shook with the force.

Amber fell to her hands and knees and scuttled along the lobby floor toward the relative safety of an unlit corner. She slid behind an overstuffed couch half-hidden in a patch of twilight. She bumped into something in the shadows and stifled a scream, finding herself face-to-face with an open-mouthed rictus of fear and pain, on a girl maybe half her age. A bare sliver of light revealed the girl's body, shredded from the waist down, reminding Amber of bloody pulled pork. The thought nearly made her puke again, even though she was pretty sure she had nothing left to vomit.

"Help me…"

Amber jerked in surprise, nearly falling into the pool of gore puddled in front of her.

Still alive.

The girl was somehow still alive.

"P… please?" Small fingers wrapped around Amber's wrist.

"I… I don't…" Amber swallowed hard, fighting the

urge to pull away. Instead she reached out with her other hand and smoothed some blood-matted blonde hair away from the girl's forehead. "It's okay," she said, knowing she was lying. "You're going to be okay."

"Mummy?"

"Yes," Amber murmured. "Yes, it's me."

"It hurts, Mummy…"

Amber blinked back tears. "I know it does. Here, I'll kiss it and you'll feel better."

Her words brought a flicker of a smile to the child's face. Amber leaned down to plant a kiss on the girl's forehead.

Her lips had barely grazed the skin when something unseen jerked the girl's torso, and dragged her off into the darkness. A brief scream, filled with inescapable pain and terror, then came the sounds of flesh being ripped from the bone.

Ohgodohgodohgod…

Somewhere deep in her mind Amber realized she had two choices—either freeze in place and wait for whatever took the little girl to come back for her…

Or find a place to hide.

Her fight-or-flight instincts kicked into overdrive. She glanced frantically around the lobby, looking for a safe place to hide before finally lighting on a closed door, catty-corner to the front desk.

More howls sent Amber scrambling on hands and knees across the slippery gore-spattered floor, moving so rapidly that she reached the door before realizing it, smacking her head against the hard wood paneling with a painful thud. Reaching up blindly, she clutched the doorknob and twisted, pushing the door open and falling into a small room stacked with suitcases and boxes.

Amber slammed the door shut behind her and dragged several large suitcases in front of it, stacking them one on top of the other with clumsy effort. When she swung the last one up, it fell short, swinging back to smack her in the chest. She stifled her yelp of pain and heaved the suitcase up again, this time managing the extra inch needed to slide it on top of the stack.

Then she shoved as many additional bags and boxes as she could up against the suitcases, creating a barricade that would hopefully keep whatever was out there at bay. Finally, she huddled as far away from the door as she could get, trying to calm her breathing and remain as silent as she could.

There was a muffled padding of feet, followed by a crash as something—maybe one of the little Tiffany lamps—fell over and shattered. Sounds of snuffling and, more horribly, chewing. All of this punctuated by snarling and snapping as whatever they were fought over their meal. There was a thump as something softer hit the ground. More ferocious growls, and then the sound of something heavy being dragged across the floor.

It stopped right in front of the door.

Amber pressed both hands to her mouth, holding back a scream as she listened to more of those horrible, wet rending noises, accompanied by heavy breathing like a dog panting in the heat.

She prayed it wouldn't even notice she was there. It couldn't see through walls, right? And with all the blood and stuff, it shouldn't be able to smell her, even if it—they—*were* wolves, and had noses like bloodhounds.

It's not like they'd have my scent.

Unless they followed the trail of blood, dripping from her feet and ankles.

The thing outside gave a low, wet growl and started clawing at the luggage room door.

8

Cam was lost.

He had crossed through a supernatural realm and come out the other side again, but where had he emerged? The land resembled the fields of home, all grass and flowers. The breeze carried the same familiar chill, the heather and wildflower scents... but where were the farmsteads and roundhouses? Where were the defensive walls and border forts, the cattle and crops?

Where were the people?

Surely I'm within the kingdom of the Trinovantes, he thought, but after running for miles, he was no longer so sure that was true. Slowing his pace to a walk, he scanned the horizon. There were no signs of habitation anywhere.

"Where am I?"

He looked to the sky, then hung his head with a deep sigh, rubbing his temples. The sword-cut on his cheekbone burned from the salt of his sweat. He thought of his village, his family, everyone he knew. He thought of the Catuvellauni war chariots coming for them.

How can I warn anyone, if I can't find them?

Helplessness warred with rage within him.

"Where *are* you?" he shouted to the sky.

No one answered.

Where should I go now?

Every direction looked the same. Casting his gaze about, Cam spotted a break in the meadow off to his right, and walked over for a closer look. At first glance it appeared to be a pond, but as he drew near he saw a large patch of rocky earth, about the size and roughly the shape of a sailing ship. Wide in the middle and narrowing toward the ends, with ragged edges here and there, almost flame-shaped.

Reaching the patch, he walked across its surface. The ground was completely free of any sort of grass or plant. In fact, it wasn't ground at all, but blocks of square gray stones. Hundreds of them, all carefully laid out in tight formation and anchored with mortar.

Just like the trees in the fey woods, the bricks along the edges had been sliced as if by a knife. The meadow surrounding the curious stonework fit exactly, as if turf and bricks had been perfectly cut to match one another. Yet who would build a Roman-style plaza in the middle of a wilderness, and in such an ungainly shape? It made no sense.

He stared for a bit, and then shook his head impatiently, leaving the mystery behind as he continued on. Judging by the sun, he traveled toward the east—the direction that gave him the best chance of reaching his tribe. Or so he had thought when he first emerged from the forest.

Cam was no longer sure of anything.

More oddities appeared in his path. First, what he took to be a tower off in the distance, turned out instead to be a tight stand of pines rising a hundred paces high. The grove was a dense forest, thick with undergrowth and fallen logs, and yet the whole affair was enclosed in a crude circle barely three paces across. Even the tree branches had been sheared off from bottom to top all along the rim of the tiny woods, separated from the surrounding meadow in the same precise way as the plaza had been.

An hour or so later he came upon another peculiar island in the sea of grass and wildflowers. This one was bigger than those he had passed before. It formed a great uneven swirl about three hundred paces long, curling out from a tapered point into a wide, rounded droplet shape as white as snow. His eyes went wide when he realized it was just that—an enormous, pristine snowbank, surrounded by summer on all sides.

Offering a quick prayer to the snow spirits, he scooped cold handfuls into his mouth. It was agony to his teeth and throat, but it slaked his thirst until a sharp icy pain in his head made him slow down. He breathed deeply for a moment, then rubbed a little snow on his cheek to ease the sting of the cut before moving on.

Soon thereafter the meadowlands ceased to dominate the landscape. Cam passed through other odd patches of terrain, some no bigger than a pace or two across, others stretching as far as the eye could see. Dry dead grass. Forests of birch, pine, hazel, oak, or elm. Unnatural tarns of brackish green water. Orphaned segments of rivers and streams.

There were signs of men, as well. Tilled soil without fence or a farmer. Strands of cobblestone. He saw blasted, scorched regions of choking ash and tortured blackened stumps. It was as if the spirits of a dozen different seasons had all set down on a different scrap of land and claimed it for their own.

The sun was nearing dusk when, at the top of a low ridge, a standing structure caught his eye, off in the distance. A post. It looked like a marker. Which meant—

"People!"

He ran the entire way to the top of the rise, and found a square sheet of tin mounted on a pole of metal. The workmanship was very fine, the panel's edges perfectly straight and even. He walked around to the front of the marker. It bore a message, painted in a bright blue, with thick white letters painstakingly and perfectly written in the script of the Romani.

DUAL CARRIAGEWAY
2 MILES AHEAD

Cam spoke and read Latin passably well, but these words puzzled him. He recognized the second-to-last one—a *miles* was a foot soldier. He knew "duo" meant two, and "ala" meant armpit, but what did "dual" mean? "Carri" was a wagon—was "age" short for *agellus*, a little plot of land?

Whoever wrote this is a terrible scribe, he thought, *or his Latin is even worse than mine.* The rest of it baffled him as well. Some of the marks looked like Greek letters or runes of the Northmen. What about the fourth word, "ahead"? "Ahenea" meant bronze, didn't it? And "ad" meant "toward."

Cam chewed his knuckle and tried to put it all together:

"Two armpits? Wagon-field—or field-wagon? Wagon-*something...* Bronze to the foot soldier?"

If he had to guess, it seemed to be announcing that someone had awarded a foot soldier a double-armpit-wide bronze field-wagon, whatever that was. The more he thought about it, the less sense it made... and what was this bizarre message doing here? He scratched his head and looked around for clues.

There. A strange road lay below him, on the other side

of the little rise. One end stretched away to his left, and the other disappeared around a bend to his right.

Cam trotted down the rise to investigate more closely. It wasn't a Roman road, made of stone slabs and cement. This had a smooth black surface, with long white lines painted along either side, and a broken white line going right down the middle. He had never seen anything like it.

Taking the left-hand route, he followed it straight for a few hundred paces before it ended in yet more grassy meadow, again sliced off with the same eerie precision he'd been seeing all day since emerging from the Otherworld. Crouching down, he could make out the split between the meadow grass and the grass growing alongside the black road.

Cam rose and turned the other way. Walking back, he saw that the sign had been placed so that it could be read by passers-by traveling in this direction. Maybe that meant he was headed the right way to find some answers.

His soft deerskin boots barely made a sound as he strode down the strange black road. Rounding the bend, he caught sight of a boxy obstruction up ahead. It looked more than anything like a large armored wagon, halted upon the road and painted as bright yellow as a wagtail's feathers. He approached it cautiously, noting that the body and roof were made of metal instead of wood.

All four sides of the strange wagon had square openings, clad with sheets of some material much like polished horn, but perfectly transparent, clear as spring water. The wagon's wheels were short, fat black things surrounding a core of metal. He didn't know what they were made from, but it wasn't any material he recognized.

Cam looked through the windows and had a shock of surprise. Two figures were inside, their backs to him.

"Hey!" he called out, raising an arm. "Hello in there!"

They gave no response.

Cam called out a few more times, in both Briton and Latin, to no avail. Realizing he had his hand on his sword, he lifted it and kept both hands up as he came closer.

The wagon was adorned with all kinds of curious little metal trimmings and panels of crimson and amber. He approached the side of the cart, walking slowly and trying to give no show of hostile intent. There were lines of green Roman lettering painted on the side, the largest of them reading TELECOM. Another word that made no sense.

"Can you hear me in there?" Cam kept his tone gentle while he rounded what had to be the front of the cart. "I'm no bandit. I'm only a traveler like…"

His words trailed off mid-sentence as he came face to face with the corpses of two men. Both stared at him unseeing, faces frozen in wide-eyed rictuses of horror.

Something massive had smashed head-on into the wagon. The impact had shattered the clear substance in the front window, and crumpled the metal body so badly that there was no sign left of the shaft or the harness for the horses.

Both men wore odd tunics of a style Cam didn't recognize. One had a tight curly mane and skin as dark as Cam's own hair. When he was in Gaul, he had heard stories of Nubians and their faraway country, but never thought he would ever see one in the flesh. The other was red-haired and pale, either a Celt or a Northman from Skandia, beyond the Dead Sea. Whatever impact destroyed the wagon had also left the men with horrendous chest wounds, as though each had been impaled by a stake carved from a good-sized tree.

"*Kych-an-broc,*" he murmured softly, both awestruck and horrified by the wreckage and human remains. The thought of the strength and size needed to cause such destruction made the hairs rise on the nape of his neck. Vivid memories sprang to mind—the terrible thrashing tail, the chomping mouth full of dagger-teeth, and the blood-roar of the dragon…

Suddenly he wished he was anywhere but this place.

I should try to find the horses that pulled this wagon, he thought. If he could coax one into letting him ride, he'd make better time cross-country. He turned and raised a hand to his brow to scan the landscape.

Up ahead the strange road continued straight into a stray bank of mist, and Cam spied shapes moving around in the gray gloom. But they were too large to be horses.

Oxen, perhaps. One of the big draft animals wandered a few steps closer out of the fog and looked over at him.

Not an ox.

Not oxen at all.

These were much larger animals. If an ox could stand on another's shoulders, they would still not be as tall, nor would two oxen standing side by side be as wide as one of these beasts, these cattle for the giants.

More appeared out of the fog, at least a dozen or so, and each one's skull sported a massive bony frill with two long fearsome horns, protruding from the forehead. The horns were as long as two-handed great-swords, and a thick, shorter one jutted out just above the birdlike, beaked mouth. Their rust-colored skin was thick and pebbly, their huge limbs and flanks like boulders come to life.

The closest turned to face Cam, staring at him intently. The great beast snorted, and stamped its foot, shaking its head at him.

The horns were stained a dark brown.

Cam's legs, until now frozen in place, took a step back without his permission, smacking into the hard embrace of the wagon's crushed remains. More of the gigantic beasts emerged, until all of them faced him, the bigger ones forming a wall around a smaller one. The bull raised up and bellowed a warning challenge.

Then it charged.

"*Kawgh!*" he cried.

The horned monster rushed forward with unexpected speed, pounding down the road straight toward Cam. His legs failed—fear rooted him in place. He reached out his arms and realized he was hemmed in on either side, caught in the depression of mashed metal.

The ground shook like an earthquake as the creature barreled directly at him. Cam half-twisted at the last moment and tried to scale the front of the armored wagon, but only caught shards of the clear stuff. It came loose and he crashed down hard onto the black road—

just as the roaring beast slammed the wagon.

The battered metal screeched and the whole wheeled contraption buckled from the impact of the creature's stony skull. Cam squirmed beneath the thing's enormous chin as it shook its horns loose from the impaled wreckage, sending bits of debris raining down on him. As it pulled free, he scrambled on his belly deeper beneath the security of the wagon.

The undercarriage stunk of something like naphtha oil or pitch.

The beast twisted its neck, fishing around for him with one long horn, so close Cam could feel its enraged snorts of breath. He kept scuttling backward in the cramped space to keep his head away from the sharp point as it jagged back and forth in front of his eyes, scraping metal and carving grooves when it caught on the road.

The other horn snagged on the undercarriage, hindering the monster's efforts to kill him. It roared its frustration, the sound deafening at such close quarters. Then the three-horned beast jerked its head up, lifting the front of the wagon and dropping it just as suddenly. Cam ducked his head, and only the thick wheels kept him from being crushed. He lay as flat as he could with his eyes shut, cheek pressed to the road, flinching and gritting his teeth with each bone-rattling impact as the beast slammed the wagon again, and then once more.

He braced himself for a fourth, perhaps final crash, but none came.

After a few moments there was silence, and he dared open his eyes. Abruptly the road beneath him rumbled as the beast came rushing up from another angle. It struck the corner of the wagon this time. The black wheel burst apart with a loud noise, leaving strange, almost ropey chunks and the smaller metal wheel at its core. The front end of the wagon collapsed, nearly pinning Cam's head under it. He tried to push his body backward, but the increasingly narrow space made it hard to move, and he only managed to wedge himself in.

Between the rough road and the sooty metal, his palms and knuckles were being scraped raw.

The beast stomped off again, and Cam realized he needed to go forward in order to go backward. He pulled himself up with his elbows and shifted toward the other front corner in an effort to better center himself. His head nearly touched the remaining front wheel when the bull-beast smashed into that corner of the wagon, striking so hard that the wheel bent in at an angle.

Cam twisted away and wormed his way straight back. The beast slammed the same corner again, and this time the wheel burst, bringing the entire front end of the wagon crashing down where Cam had been just a few heartbeats earlier.

Continuing to inch back, he finally slipped out from under the wagon, clambering to his feet. There was a ladder of silver metal fastened to the back of the strange yellow conveyance. He quickly swung himself up it and took to the roof.

Flattening himself there, he tried to keep out of sight of his rampaging attacker, which suspiciously sniffed the air. After a minute or so, the hulking creature seemed satisfied that it had crushed him. It turned and ambled back to its herd. They spread out in the grass and surrounded Cam on all sides, grazing on the lush meadow greenery.

Exhausted, he rolled himself in the wool cloak and waited for them to get their fill and move on.

9

The exploratory snuffling and scratching became an insistent scrabbling, with claws that sounded as if they were made of steel. Amber shoved her hands to her mouth, trying to keep her presence undetected. With a sickening realization, however, she knew the smell of her blood was enough to set them on her trail—whatever these things were.

How long would it take them to get through the door? The suitcases she'd piled up seemed as flimsy as cardboard in the face of an animal that was even now penetrating the heavy wood.

Pleasepleasepleaseplease.

The silent mantra ran through her head.

Please let those creatures lose interest and go away. Please let some miracle occur to get her out of this alive. Please let her wake up and find herself back home in San Diego.

If this *was* a dream, and she died while dreaming,

would she die in real life? Would the shock be enough to stop her heart?

She thought it might.

The snuffling turned into a deep liquid growl. The sound dripped with saliva and hunger.

Amber burrowed deeper into the coats. She wanted to close her eyes, to pretend this wasn't happening, but they remained stubbornly open, fixed on the door. It splintered about two feet from the floor, and two claws appeared. Claws that looked as sharp and sturdy as steel nails, tipped with blood.

Her heart pounded so hard she thought it would burst out of her chest before whatever was out there ripped it open. The rapid drumming filled her ears, almost drowning out the sound of the razor-sharp talons breaking through the barrier.

An oversized muzzle pushed its way through the small gap. Gore-stained teeth chewed at the splintered wood around the edges. The hole widened, allowing Amber to see even more of the head. It looked like some sort of wolf, but huge. Twice, maybe three times the size of anything she had ever seen at the zoo.

It stared at her with eyes golden and malicious. Amber locked gazes with the creature, and in those eyes she saw her death.

A cracking sound cut through the sound of her heartbeat.

A gunshot?

The beast at the door yelped in pain, suddenly sounding like a dog. Deceptively normal. Another sharp report, followed by two more. The blood-stained muzzle retreated, and something big collapsed against the wood with a meaty thud, the impact sending splinters showering down into the closet. Then...

Silence.

Amber stared at the door, hands still pressed against her mouth. She heard the sound of something being dragged away, along with an expulsive grunting, like someone lifting heavy weights. Then she heard footsteps.

"Hello? Is anyone in there?"

A male voice, deep and definitely British. What her aunt would call a BBC accent. He rapped decisively on the door. Three in a row.

Was he friendly? Would it be safe? Or had she traded one danger for another?

Amber didn't know. Some of her friends insisted that every man was a potential rapist and given the chance any one of them would take advantage of a woman. For all of her shyness, however, Amber had never been one to live her life afraid of the opposite sex. Her dad was too good a role model for that.

This was different. She was alone in a world gone mad, and this guy had a gun. In her family, that by itself was a big fat no-no. But without it, he wouldn't have been able to kill the monster trying to eat her.

"Hello," he said again. "Look, I'm not going to hurt you. I'm here to help."

She'd have to risk it.

"I'm—" Amber's voice cracked. "I'm here."

The man turned the knob and pushed, but damaged as it was, the door stopped against her suitcase barricade.

"Hang on," she said, and she began pulling the boxes and suitcases out of the way. The top ones tumbled to the floor, blocking the path even as she tried to clear it. Like digging a hole in the sand and having it fill back in before any headway could be made.

Finally she succeeded in clearing the way. She reached for the knob just as the man on the other side turned it and pushed the door open.

He was older, in his late thirties or early forties. Tall, dark hair cut short under a dark green beret, the wool pilling in places. Strong features set in harsh lines. He wore olive drab trousers tucked into khaki gaiters, combat boots, and a long-sleeved cable-knit sweater in the same olive as the trousers. The sweater was liberally splattered in dirt and what had to be blood. There was a splotch of dark red in the shape of Florida on the front of his sweater.

It's a red state, she thought, and the idea made her giggle. The sound morphed into a gasping sob before she realized it was going to happen. She jammed her fists back up to her mouth, trying to hold onto some control.

The man's grim expression softened.

"I'm Blake," he said, holding out a hand. For one crazy minute Amber was sure he was going to say, *"Come with me if you want to live."*

He didn't.

"Are you hurt?"

Amber stared at him. Was she hurt? A better question would be "Are you crazy?"

"Are you hurt?" he asked again, impatience edging his tone.

"N… no. Not really," she managed, looking down. "Just blisters."

"We have to move. Can you walk?"

Amber nodded. She'd already made her choice. Man with a gun, or big scary animals? It wasn't really a choice at all.

Taking his hand, she let him help her to her feet. He was tall—her head only came to his shoulders. She took a step and nearly collapsed as pins and needles shot through her legs and feet. The man—Blake—steadied her with a strong arm around her waist, glancing down at the blood pooling in her sandals.

"We'll have to take care of that," he said. "No time now, though." More howls sounded in the distance. His face tightened. "We need to leave."

Somehow Amber managed to stay on her feet as he

propelled her through the lobby-turned-charnel house, pausing briefly to snatch up her staff before they exited into the cold unforgiving landscape where the back of the hotel used to be. The howls grew closer. Amber's new companion glanced sharply around as if gauging the distance. He led her out toward the car park.

"We need to find a place to hide, where they won't see or smell us. Once they pick up the smell of prey, it's hard to shake them off. But if we can throw them off the scent... they may go away."

They both looked at the bloody footprints Amber was leaving behind with each step.

"Quick, take that off." He nodded at her backpack.

"I'm not leaving it behind," she said.

"I'm not asking you to leave it," he replied impatiently, "but I can't carry you with that rucksack on your back."

Amber knew her blood left a trail that might as well have been a formal dinner invitation to the carnivores. So she shrugged off the backpack as quickly as possible, then clutched it in her arms as, without another word, he scooped her up. Striding rapidly and with purpose to the stairwell, he ignored the elevator.

The stairwell door was open, a metal doorstop holding it ajar. The man stepped inside the stairwell and took a quick look at the lock, making sure it wasn't engaged before kicking the doorstop up and letting the heavy metal door slam shut.

"We don't want to be trapped inside," he said. "Starvation and dehydration might not kill us as quickly as those things, but it would still do for us in the long run."

He carried her easily up three flights of stairs, making sure the doors on each level were also closed. Once they reached the top, he scanned what was left of the deserted third level, staring at the various cars with a perplexed expression.

"When the hell did *these* come out?"

Amber looked at them. "I think they're all from the nineties."

"Don't be ridiculous," he scoffed. "They didn't have cars back then."

Confused, Amber kept silent as Blake marched over to a shiny sky-blue vehicle that looked like a short station wagon, and set her down carefully on the hood.

"Try not to let your feet touch anything," he cautioned. "We don't know how good their sense of smell is, but best not to take any chances."

The windows of the car were partially rolled down. Blake reached in and unlocked the front right-hand door.

"Not very smart on the part of the owner, but good for us."

He rummaged around inside, leaving Amber to stare at an abrupt drop-off about twenty feet away. The wall on that end of the car park was gone. The entire row of cars parked there were cleanly sliced through the hoods, a visceral reminder of what had happened to Gavin. She shuddered uncontrollably, both from the memory and a gust of freezing wind blowing in off the grasslands.

Blake emerged from the car, holding several cans of soda, some bottled water, and a plaid blanket much like the one Amber had used to cover Gavin's body. He took his finds over to the stairwell, then came back to Amber and handed her one of the sodas, a Coke.

"Didn't know this came in cans, but at least I recognize the brand. Should pep you up a bit. I'm going to search the rest of the cars on this level and see what I can scavenge before we lose all the light. Then we'll look after your feet. In the meantime, keep your eyes and ears open."

Amber nodded, too tired and stunned by the day's events to object to his brusque take-charge manner, or question why he was unfamiliar with canned soda. She popped the tab and took a sip of the ice-cold Coke, savoring the bubbles and the caffeinated sweetness.

She hadn't realized how low her blood sugar had gotten until her brain and body perked up. Then she wished it hadn't, because now her mind insisted on thinking about the horror and impossibility of everything that had happened since the world went mad.

I won't think about it right now, she thought. Instead, she decided to focus on whatever she needed to do to survive.

So she kept careful watch while Blake systematically checked the doors of all the remaining vehicles, searching the interiors of those that weren't locked, depositing anything of interest in the stairwell. The last of the daylight was fading, so he produced a flashlight, which he used to help his search. Amber was intrigued by the light—an old-school military style, meant to be held upright, with an angled head that made it look a bit like a little periscope. He made his rounds, looking in the cars that had been bisected as well, taking care to keep his weight away from the drop-off.

Smart, Amber thought.

She was watching him poke through part of a Mini Cooper when something roared, off in the distance. She gasped at the loud reverberating thuds of its footfalls. They seemed to be coming closer, increasing in volume and force, shaking what was left of the car park. All-too-familiar howls started up, as well. Amber thought she heard the clicking of toenails on the cement below.

Blake immediately abandoned his search and strode back over to Amber, scooping her up without a word. He carried her back to the stairwell.

"We'll have some protection against the cold in here," he said as he set her down gently on the blanket, which he'd spread out on the cold cement.

"Not to mention opportunistic predators."

He glanced at her in surprised approval, as if she were

a Barbie doll who'd suddenly offered up an intelligent opinion. In another lifetime Amber would have been offended. Now she couldn't summon the energy.

"Yes," he agreed. "That as well."

He set the flashlight down next to her before shutting the door.

His findings sat in the circle of light. Bottles, cans, bags of crisps, bars of chocolate, a couple of slightly brown apples, a first aid kit. Various items of clothing, a pair of bright pink Converse high-tops, several more blankets, and a sleeping bag were stacked against one wall, along with two more flashlights. He switched one on and handed it to Amber, sitting down next to her. She tried not to flinch as claustrophobia and paranoia wrestled for control of her tautly stretched nerves.

"We'd best take care of your feet." He snagged the first aid kit, a small one with a few antiseptic wipes, antibacterial ointment, and bandages, then scooted back against the door and spread a denim jacket on his thighs.

"Put your feet here and keep the light on them."

Amber reluctantly did as he said, stretching out her legs and resting her feet on the faded denim. She winced, giving an indrawn hiss of pain as Blake undid the straps wrapped around her calves and pulled them away from the skin. When he unwound the straps from her ankles, however, she had to suppress a scream as the leather stuck to the bloody welts they'd rubbed in her flesh.

When he finally removed her sandals, Amber could barely look at the bloodied hamburgers that were her feet, even in the dim glow of the flashlight. There were blisters—some whole, some burst—on the soles, insteps, sides, and ankles. Blood congealed in places, fresh and still dripping in others.

"Here." Blake fished out two packets of paracetamol from the first aid kit, along with a bottled water. He eyed the plastic bottle with a quizzical raise of one eyebrow, thumping it with one finger before handing it and the pain meds to Amber.

"Thanks." She downed all four painkillers with a hefty swallow of water. She took another few sips, then held the bottle up to her rescuer.

He nodded his thanks and drained the rest of the contents before getting back to work on her feet and calves. Another bottle of water was sacrificed to clean most of the blood off her skin and rinse the abrasions. Then he went after them with antiseptic wipes, the resulting sting causing Amber to stuff her hands into her mouth to prevent her from screaming. He might as well have used acid.

"This should help." He smoothed on some sort of ointment, then pulled Band-Aids from the first aid kit. "Hold still, let me just put on some sticking plasters."

Though uncomfortable having this stranger handle her feet and calves in such a familiar fashion, Amber tried to stay still as he finished his ministrations.

"I don't know if these will fit you or not," he said, holding up the high-tops. "And the color is far too bright. We'll want to muck them up a bit, but they're better than your sandals. What on earth possessed you to wear those?"

"They weren't meant for walking long-distance," she replied defensively. "They go with the rest of the costume. I didn't expect to be hiking." She thought he'd ask her about her costume, but he didn't. Evidently her explanation satisfied him.

"We should eat something," Blake said, "and then try to get some sleep. Hopefully those things will have cleared out by the time the sun comes up."

"I've got some food." Amber carefully shifted to get her backpack, but before she could reach it, Blake had snagged it.

"In here?" He started to open the flap.

"Please don't." Amber's tone was sharper than she'd intended. He looked at her in surprise.

"You do realize that if we're going to survive, we need to share."

"I don't mind sharing," Amber said. "I'll share whatever I have with you. But the backpack… I mean, I wouldn't go into your pockets without your permission. It's just not polite."

What she couldn't quite articulate was that for all she

knew, the backpack held all of her belongings left in the world. Maybe she'd eventually find her way back to San Diego. Maybe her childhood still existed at her parents' house, all of her art projects, costumes and photos… everything. Her history.

But right now?

The contents of that wine-colored backpack— expensive and built to last—were the only connection she had left with her life as she'd known it. The backpack itself had been a birthday present from her dad. Having some stranger pawing through it—even one who'd saved her life—seemed somehow unbearable.

Blake tilted his head to one side, then handed the backpack over to Amber without another word. She opened it and dug out the remnants of her aborted picnic with Gavin—the sandwiches, cheese, apples, chips— and divvied it up with Blake.

"These will last a few days," he said, holding up the apples and chips. "So we should save them for now." Amber nodded her agreement, trying not to let his take-charge attitude overwhelm her. Bottom line, he was right.

They ate the sandwiches and chunks of cheddar cheese, washing the meal down with Coke. A flashlight propped up against the wall provided some light. Even with the sugar and caffeine boost from the soda, Amber felt her eyelids droop, as if her eyelashes had turned to lead.

"What's your name?" Blake asked, almost as an afterthought, as he took a swig from his soda.

"Amber," she said, the word followed by a jaw-cracking yawn.

"Well, Amber, we'd best get some sleep."

He spread the sleeping bag on the landing, handing Amber two of the blankets he'd scavenged, keeping only one for himself. He rolled up the denim jacket. "You can use this as a pillow."

"What about you?"

"I'll be fine. Now get some sleep."

He turned and lay on his side, his back to Amber, his feet sticking out from the blanket. She slowly followed suit, facing the opposite direction. She could feel the cold from the cement trying to creep through the down-filled layer of the sleeping bag, but the blankets and her utter exhaustion helped her overcome the chill.

The guttural roar sounded again, closer this time, the echo reverberating through the stairwell.

Amber drifted off to sleep.

Blake leaned up against the cement wall, head falling back to rest against the unyielding surface. He allowed himself to relax ever so slightly for the first time since he'd found the girl. Amber. She slept now, tucked underneath the blankets. He couldn't see her in the darkness of the stairwell, but he could hear the sound of her soft and rhythmic breathing.

It soothed him.

It would be a while before he could sleep. He pulled out his Fairbairn-Sykes knife, along with a whetstone, and commenced sharpening both edges of the blade, slowly, rhythmically.

His companion gave a small cry in her sleep. He put the blade down, replacing it with one of the electric torches. Switching it on, he shone the light slightly above her, not wanting to wake her up. Her face was mostly buried in the blankets, only a partial profile and a swatch of fire-bright hair visible. What little he could see made her look so very young and vulnerable.

He didn't have a good read on Amber, not yet. She seemed soft, easily broken, and yet she'd been through a nightmare experience in the hotel and still appeared to have her sanity. She could be a fighter.

He hoped so.

It would make their time together infinitely more rewarding if she was.

10

When Cam awoke, hungry and cold, the sky had gone from blue to black, with little more than a pale moon, filtered by clouds, to cast light on the herd of three-horned beasts that still surrounded him.

He sighed and lay back down again. If they weren't going to leave, perhaps they would at least sleep soon and he would have his chance to slip away. He closed his eyes, and tried to ignore the hunger in his belly. The giant horned cattle-things continued lowing to one another.

It was going to be a long night.

A moment later, the underbellies of the leaden clouds overhead lit up like a lantern and a great chorus of booming thunder split apart the gentle pastoral silence. The anxious beasts lifted their great heads and bellowed in alarm. Cam sat up, too. The flashes of brightness lasted for no more than a heartbeat before fading away, only to return again with another resounding drumroll of thunder.

There was neither rain nor bolts of lightning in the night sky, but the thunder and the strange light that accompanied it continued. Both the lights and the dull roar seemed to be coming from further to the east.

One of the nervous tri-horns broke ranks and ran, and then the entire herd bolted as one, following at full speed. Cam grasped the wagon's thin metal rails as they rumbled past, shaking his precarious little metal island as they fled in terror. The jostling stampede of ponderously heavy bodies retreated past the black road and up and over the low rise, like an army of spiked boulders.

When the last of them had disappeared over the rise, and he could no longer hear their panicked bellowing over the sound of the distant booming din, he fastened the clasp on his stolen wool cloak and swiftly climbed down the ladder. He set off east again, away from the giant beasts and toward the lights flashing above from the valley of thunder. For that way lay home.

The smooth black road soon came to an end, cut off as abruptly as it had been at its other end. It gave way to more flat grasslands, turned silver now by the moon. Cam kept his eye on the play of light on the clouds. He had walked many, many miles since rising that morning.

Just a few more miles lay ahead of him before he might discover the source of the fire in the sky.

By the time Cam surmounted the last gentle rise, the dull booming had grown into a painful furor that jangled his bones with every new burst. Other sounds joined the tumult—drums and war cries. Shrieks and strange whistlings. Horrendous sounds of terrible impacts and of wood and stone blasted into splinters.

Screams of horses.

Screams of men.

The ring of steel upon steel.

With trepidation he looked out over the rise, though the fickle moonlight only allowed mischievous hints of the movement below. Men fighting on foot and on horseback, gleaming points of cold moonlight off helmets and armor, and bristling forests of pikes and banners. The battlefield seethed with over a thousand combatants fighting for their lives in the night. With every booming blast came another source of light—fire and smoke spitting out of the dark from strange half-seen shapes, cutting through the air. The smoke they belched hung on the ground like tendrils of fog.

There were large, great dark pipes mounted on wagon wheels. Crews of men tended to each of them, moving swiftly to stoke them with long rods and load them with round iron balls. At each barked order, shouted out in some barbarian language he did not recognize, a blast would follow.

Others carried fire-weapons that were only the size of a druid's staff. Ranks of fighters, lined up like archers, each held a single weapon, resting one end on their shoulders and using both hands to point them lengthwise, launching their own fire at their foes.

Cam could make no sense of who these unknown warriors might be. Neither side were Romani or Celts or Picts, nor Northmen or Germani. The clothing they wore was neither Briton nor Roman style. They wore trousers like Celts, but theirs were baggy, and without plaid designs. Some wore breastplates of armor, something like those of the Roman soldiers. They wore helmets of steel, or floppy cloth hats.

Something whizzed past Cam's face. He turned to his left to see a handful of warriors advancing on him. One had a smoking hand-weapon pointed at him—it had just missed him by less than a hand's breadth. Another brought up his staff and aimed it at Cam's heart.

Kawgh!

He turned and ran as the thing roared with a blast of flame. An object traveling too fast to see flew past his ear, a thumb's breadth away. The warriors charged after him. Another shot tore past his face.

This one from up ahead.

Kych-an-broc!

Horsemen were charging toward him at full gallop.

The leader had his curved sword raised and, as he thundered up, swung it downward. Cam pitched himself to the ground and rolled, narrowly avoiding both the slash of the blade and being trampled by the riders who were following behind.

Splayed out on the ground, he raised his head and looked back at the galloping horses. The two groups were locked in battle, fighting with swords and the booming fire-weapons. He scrambled to his feet and ran, putting the battlefield and its bizarre warriors behind him.

11

When Amber woke up, she felt oddly rested. She'd slept deeply and dreamlessly, exhaustion overcoming fear to give her at least a few hours of much-needed rest. Godzilla could have stomped through the car park, smashing the remaining vehicles into smithereens, and it probably wouldn't have roused her.

For an all-too-brief moment she could almost pretend the events of yesterday hadn't happened. Then she opened her eyes and saw the dingy concrete ceiling of the stairwell above her, and the descending stairwell on her far right, below her feet.

"Awake then, are we?"

Amber jumped. Blake sat leaning against the wall across from her, sorting through the stuff he'd scavenged from the cars, dividing it into piles. The sight of her rescuer's unsmiling face was the next step in the morning's unwelcome reality check.

Her attempt to sit up was the third.

As soon as she moved, her muscles screamed in protest along with a chorus of shrieks from all the abrasions on her feet and ankles. That was bad enough, but then her calves knotted up, doing their best to put a double charley horse whammy on her. Immediately she reached down under the blankets and began frantically massaging both lower legs, trying to unknot the muscles before they clenched up past the point of no return.

"Muscle cramps?"

Amber nodded, unable to get the words out. If she opened her mouth, she knew all that would come out would be a pained squeak.

"Grab your toes and pull them towards your knees," he said. "And breathe."

She did as he'd advised, finding almost instant relief from the relentless bunching of the calf muscles. She also gave silent thanks that he hadn't tried to rub the cramps out himself. She felt like an ungrateful shit for the thought, but something about Blake…

Well, he didn't exactly give her the creeps, but there was something *off* about him. Then again, who knew what he'd been through before he'd stumbled upon her and rescued her from being devoured by giant wolves, or whatever the hell those things had been. As the cramps abated, Amber resolved to try and back off the mistrust, since he'd given her absolutely zero reasons to doubt his intentions.

"Better?"

"I think so."

She cautiously released her toes and flexed both feet a couple of times. The muscles were still tight, but the agonizing cramps had eased.

As she managed to get to her feet, Amber was suddenly aware of the need to pee. The chill in the morning air cut through her flimsy dress and the jacket she'd taken from the punt, so she grabbed one of the blankets from her pile of bedding and wrapped it around her shoulders. She thought about putting on the high-tops, but couldn't quite bear the thought of any pressure on her feet quite yet.

The icy cold concrete against her bare soles nearly made her change her mind.

"Is there any toilet paper or Kleenex?" she asked.

"There's some tissues here somewhere." He rummaged in the pile and pulled out a square box of Kleenex, the cardboard a cheerful pink. "I used the half landing below," he said. "I suggest you do the same. We don't want to take a chance of being caught in the open with our pants down."

Amber waited for him to add "so to speak," and then realized he was being quite literal. Nodding her thanks, she took the box of tissues and carefully made her way down the stairs, making sure to be well out of sight of the landing above before relieving herself.

She couldn't do it fast enough to suit her, both because of the feeling of vulnerability and the ever-increasing chill penetrating the bottoms of her feet. It felt like they were on fire. As soon as she was finished, she ran up the stairs as quickly as her aching muscles would allow her. Her teeth chattered uncontrollably, and she hurried over to the sleeping bag and blankets, pulling them over her feet.

Blake sorted through the items against the wall. He held up an old canvas duffle bag, sturdily built with a thick shoulder strap.

"Found this in one of the motor cars I didn't have time to search last night. It should come in handy."

Amber nodded, noticing more cans of soda and some Cadbury Dairy Milk bars added to the stash, along with a faux fur-lined leather car coat. Under normal circumstances the dichotomy would have made her laugh. She sincerely hoped he'd grabbed it for her.

"We should change the dressings on your feet," he said. "Then we should pack up and leave this place."

A… are th…" She waited for her teeth to stop chattering before continuing. "Are those things gone?"

Blake shrugged. "No sign of them when I was outside. They may have eaten everything there was to eat in the hotel, and headed elsewhere."

"Everything" being people. Amber suppressed a shudder.

"What if they didn't?" she said. "What if they're still around?"

Blake shrugged again. "Either way, we can't stay here. We'll either die of starvation or exposure. I'm not sure I wouldn't prefer to be eaten. At least it would be quick."

This time she couldn't hold the shudder back. None of the options appealed.

"Where will we go?"

"Whitehall," he said decisively. "Whatever's happened, they'll know what to do."

"Who?"

"The Ministry of Defence and Her Majesty's government. It's their job to know what to do in situations like—" He paused briefly as if considering his words. "In emergencies."

Whether this was true or not, the idea of someone in charge, someone to make decisions and figure out how to restore the rightful order of things, appealed to Amber. It was, after all, what governments were supposed to do, right?

Besides, she didn't have any better ideas. This wasn't even her country. She needed to trust someone else to know the right thing to do. In this case the "someone else" was Blake, and at least he had a weapon to protect them.

Reluctantly she pulled her feet out from under the

blankets. He changed the Band-Aids and gauze bandages, using the antiseptic wipes and antibiotic ointment again. It hurt when he removed the old bandages, but not nearly as badly as it had when the sandals had come off. Without so much pain, however, she found herself more conscious of her short skirt. She needn't have bothered, though—he didn't even seem to notice.

When he was finished, he handed her a pair of white socks.

"These should help keep you comfortable."

Carefully Amber pulled on the socks, making sure not to dislodge any of the bandages or Band-Aids. *Plasters*, he'd called them last night. Yet another weird Britishism to add to the list. Then the shoes, which were about a half-size too big. Probably better than if they'd been too tight. Still, her feet weren't happy.

She didn't have a choice, though. It was either wear shoes more suited to a Japanese schoolgirl, or go barefoot. Not really an option in this weather.

She took four more of the paracetamol, wishing for something stronger. Maybe a couple of Valium, as well. She'd never actually taken Valium, but right now she'd welcome anything to reduce the anxiety that was bubbling in her stomach and knotting up her chest at the thought of leaving the safety of the stairwell.

They packed everything, dividing up the food. "If we're separated," he explained, "you'll still have the basics you'll need to survive." Once the supplies were stowed, Amber carefully wrapped the bloody laces around her sandals, and then stuffed them into her backpack.

"Why on earth are you taking those?"

Amber looked up. Blake was frowning at her.

"We'll want the room for things we can use," he added in his take-no-prisoners way.

"I just—" Abruptly Amber stopped, again struggling for words that would explain her feelings. She had a feeling Blake would think any kind of sentiment to be a waste of time.

"They don't take that much space," she finally replied, trying to keep the defensiveness she felt out of her voice. "Besides, the leather might come in handy later."

Blake just looked at her, and didn't say anything else about it, but Amber was conscious of his disapproval. She told herself she didn't care. That it was none of his business. She wasn't asking him to carry them. Besides, she was used to having people—including most of her family and friends—dismiss her ideas.

She compensated for her vague feelings of guilt and inadequacy by stuffing her backpack almost to bursting. Blake used the old duffle bag, into which he stuffed the blankets, the sleeping bag, and the heavier items such as sodas. He handed Amber a crowbar.

"You'll want something to protect yourself with, if anything happens to me," he said simply. She took the tool without argument, threading it through an elastic loop on one side of the backpack. That left her hands free for her staff, which would double as a walking stick.

Between the two of them they managed to gather up all of the items. They each breakfasted on an apple and remnants of cheese from the picnic. Amber would have happily killed for a cup of coffee. She had some packets of instant from Starbucks, but no hot water.

"We'll want to forage for more food and drink where we can," Blake said unnecessarily—at least from Amber's point of view. She felt like an audience to a one-man show. At least it seemed to be a one-man survival show.

"What about what's left of the hotel?" she suggested. "They must have vending machines, if nothing else."

Blake paused, thinking about it briefly before finally shaking his head.

"If those creatures are going to be anywhere, it's bound to be in there with all of those dead bodies. Not worth the risk. If they *are* still there, we sure as hell don't want to attract their attention."

Secretly she was relieved. As much as she wanted to find more food, she didn't want to go back inside the abattoir that used to be the Romford Arms. Besides, there were sure to be food and other supplies when they reached Whitehall. At least she hoped so.

They walked slowly and cautiously back down the

flights of stairs, past the smell of urine on the second landing. Blake ignored it, so she tried to do the same.

She wore the car coat for warmth. It was made for a woman a few sizes larger and several inches taller than she was, the hemline ending just above her knees instead of right below her hips. She felt a bit like one of the Pevensie kids entering Narnia, wearing coats borrowed from the magic wardrobe.

When they reached the bottom landing, Blake held a finger up to his mouth. He opened the door an inch at a time, pausing to listen and then look out through the widening gap. Other than the eerie whistling howl of wind, it appeared quiet.

Finally, he pushed the door open all the way, taking a cautious step outside and scanning in all directions. After a moment he gestured for Amber to follow him. She clutched her staff tightly in both hands.

No giant wolves, no people. Just the same seemingly endless grasslands circling bizarrely truncated chunks of buildings, the neatly kept hotel grounds and—

"What about in there?"

Amber pointed to Lottie's, a small tearoom catty-corner to what was left of the hotel. The door was shut, windows still intact. It looked as though the little one-story shop had survived whatever had chopped through the other buildings. Blake followed the direction of her finger, and nodded.

"It's far enough away from the hotel to make it worth a go. Well spotted."

She tried not to feel pleased at the praise, but couldn't quite help herself.

"We'll do a quick check," he continued quietly, "and then head southwest towards London proper and Whitehall."

"How far is it from here?"

"Twenty-six kilometers, give or take," Blake said, giving her an amused side glance. "That's sixteen miles in the Colonies."

Ha ha, Amber thought. "Do you think it's going to take us very long to get there?" she said aloud.

"Under normal circumstances I would've said no. Even walking at an easy clip, probably six hours, tops. But—" He shook his head, his expression baffled and angry, as if he faced a problem he couldn't solve. "Most of the signage and the roads are gone. The terrain itself has changed, and while I have a compass, we don't know what we might run into along the way."

"What do you think happened?"

There. She'd finally voiced the question out loud.

"I don't know." There was no hesitation in his reply. "I've seen places that have been scorched by bombs and missiles, but at least there was rubble left behind. You knew there'd been buildings there before they'd been destroyed. This—" He gestured to the vast open spaces around them. "I've never seen anything like it. We might be in a different part of the country altogether."

"Or on a different planet," Amber said softly. He ignored that.

"All I know is that in order to survive, we need to stay on our toes, and make our way somewhere secure."

She nodded, having nothing to add.

They walked quickly over to Lottie's Tea Shoppe, Blake keeping a close watch on their surroundings. He moved like someone used to being shot at. When they reached the corner of the building, he once again motioned for Amber to stay where she was. She did her best not to let it bug her. Obviously the guy had experience in life-threatening scenarios, whereas the most hostile situation she'd faced was Cammie Baxter and her pack of bullies in seventh-grade gym class. She had to ignore the fact that Blake came across like a real old-fashioned sexist. Her ego had to take a backseat to her survival.

He looked in through one of the side windows, frowning slightly.

"It looks safe enough."

He tried the front door.

"Locked."

"That means there could be somebody alive in there," Amber offered.

"We haven't time for politely knocking on the door and waiting for an answer," Blake snapped, as if she'd said something remarkably stupid instead of making a logical observation. Mortified, Amber felt her cheeks heat up, and ducked her head to hide the telltale flush. Not that he would have noticed. He was preoccupied with the doorknob, gripping it tightly with one hand and giving the door a solid shove with his shoulder.

It popped right open.

Blake nodded in grim satisfaction before going inside. He poked his head out and gestured for Amber to follow him.

She'd been in Lottie's Tea Shoppe once before, the day before the convention had started. "Lottie" was actually James Lott, a big man in his late forties with a fringe of still-flaming red hair that refused to give up the good fight against male pattern baldness. He ran the shop with his son Jimmy, a thinner version of his dad with a full head of equally red hair. Both men had teased Amber about being a member of the "Ginger Club."

"If you were to marry her," Lott Senior had said, elbowing his son in the ribs, *"I'd be sure to have a lovely little ginger grandson."*

The shop itself had been as welcoming as its owners. Cozy décor with butter-yellow curtains, matching tablecloths on the half-dozen or so tables. A glass-front cabinet showcasing the baked goods for sale, either to go or for eating in house. Their currant scones and clotted cream were to die for. She'd eaten two of them, washed down with a pot of Red Rose tea.

Was that really only two days ago?

The glass-front cabinet looked much the same, still stocked with scones, eclairs, cookies and other tea cakes, but the curtains and tablecloths were now cream colored, with a thick edging of crocheted lace. Amber frowned, but *supposed* it was possible that Lott had changed décor. Somehow, it didn't seem likely.

These curtains looked as if they'd been hanging in the windows substantially longer than two days. A light layer of dust nestled in the creases of the fabric as though someone had forgotten them on laundry day. Dim light filtered through them, the diffused gray light of winter. It looked almost as if the tea shop was under water.

There was a red splotch on the beige tablecloth of the closest table. Her stomach clenched until she realized it was preserves—not blood—staining the fabric. Still, underneath the faint pleasant fragrance of baked goods, something smelled off. Blake noticed it too, sniffing the air as suspiciously as a drug-sniffing K-9, head cocked to one side as he listened for any possible dangers.

Finally, he shook his head and pointed to the counter.

"Take as many of those as you can carry. The scones and crumpets and such. Nothing with cream, or anything that will spoil. I'll check the kitchen for anything useful." With that, he vanished into the back of the shop.

Amber grabbed a plastic bag from behind the counter. She proceeded to fill it according to Blake's instructions, stuffing a cream-filled mini éclair into her mouth while doing so. She nearly spat it out after the cream hit her taste buds. It had started to curdle. That probably accounted for the unpleasant odor underneath the hints of sugar, butter, and chocolate.

As she rummaged through a drawer below the cash register, a stack of newspapers next to the register caught her attention—the *Romford Bee*. She picked the top one off the stack and scanned the headlines, hoping against hope for something that hinted at the cause of whatever had happened. A quick skim of the headlines drew a blank. She flipped open the paper, taking a closer look at the articles, noting an upcoming David Bowie concert this Saturday at—

No, that had to be a mistake.

Bowie had died a few months ago.

Then the date caught her eye.

October 15, 1993.

Is this some kind of a joke?

She started to call Blake's name, but then her mouth snapped shut as she glanced over at a table in the far corner of the shop. A shelf stocked with teapots, mugs, and other merchandise stuck out into the room, creating a small alcove. It gave the occupants a semblance of cozy privacy.

A pair of legs protruded from behind the shelving unit.

Newspaper still in hand, Amber walked slowly over.

The table was the only one in the shop with cutlery and plates. It looked as though an entire tea service had been in progress. There was a three-tiered pastry platter, with a few pastries still remaining. A teapot sat next to it, with a half-filled cup on a china plate. As she moved closer, Amber saw the remains of another cup shattered on the floor, a small puddle of tea spreading out from the shards.

Then she got a better look at the body. A man, bright red hair just starting to thin near the crown. *Lottie's son,* she thought. He held a toddler in his arms, a little boy with the same ginger hair. In death their faces were relatively peaceful. A pill bottle lay tipped over on the table, empty.

Her stomach turned in a slow, lazy circle. She pressed a hand to her mouth, trying not to throw up her breakfast for the second time in as many days. A hand fell on her shoulder and she gave a yelp, which pierced the silence, then felt like an idiot for doing so. It was Blake. The man moved like a ninja.

He looked dispassionately at the corpses.

"That explains the smell." Then he noticed Amber's expression. "If it's any consolation, they don't seem to have suffered at all."

Amber nodded, unable to speak as tears welled up in her eyes. She knew he was right. At least the toddler hadn't died in pain and terror, ripped to pieces by monsters. Instead, one last tea time before the end. Still, the sight of the little boy's hand, tucked inside his father's, broke something in her heart.

"We should leave," Blake said. He gave her shoulder a reassuring squeeze and walked over to the door where he'd left the duffle bag. Amber started to follow, then stopped, remembering what Lott Sr. had said to his son about getting married and giving him a grandson. Why would he have said that if—

"Blake, look at this." She held up the newspaper, hurrying over to him.

He looked over and frowned.

"What is it?"

Amber pointed to the date. He glanced at it.

"It must be a typographical error."

She shook her head. "I don't think so."

"Then someone's idea of a joke."

"Look," Amber said, desperate for him to believe her, "when I was in here two days ago, I met the owner and his son. The dead man looks kind of like the son, but older. And he hadn't had any kids of his own yet."

"What's your point?" Blake stared at her with barely leashed impatience.

"I think the dead man is James Lott, and the little boy is his son. Except when I met them, they were both twenty-three years older. Which is why the paper's out of date by twenty-three years."

Blake gave a short, derisive laugh.

"You sound stark raving mad. What you're saying is utterly impossible."

"Fine," Amber snapped, both frightened and angry enough to stand up to him. "You tell me what year it is, then."

"Oh, good lord," he muttered with a shake of his head. Then he looked at her, both pity and condescension clear in his expression.

"It's 1953, of course."

12

Sally was lost. Not lost as in "got pissed and wandered down the wrong street." She'd done that before, and while it had been scary, she'd eventually found her way home no worse for the experience other than for the blisters on her feet.

This was so much worse.

She'd been out with her friends at the pub, enjoying a few pints. Sally wanted to go to the new wine bar a few streets over, but had been overruled. Budget over trendiness. She hadn't minded so much. Not like there wouldn't be another chance some other evening, even if she went on her own.

Sally had gone to the loo three pints into the evening, anxious to escape from a loud-mouthed wanker who wouldn't take "no" for an answer. She'd felt a bit of a shake while in there, but hadn't thought much about it. Earthquakes were rare, but not entirely unheard of. Nothing to worry about, especially when the walls and floor were already starting to spin. She'd slow it down, drink some water. She'd be fine.

Then the sound started—building to a wail so loud that she would have pissed herself if she hadn't already been sitting on the toilet. When it stopped she'd gathered herself and bolted for the door.

When she came out, however, there wasn't much left of the pub—just a foot or so of the hallway leading to the bathrooms—and there'd been nothing at all left of her friends, or anyone else who'd been at the Lucky Duck that night. Sally had been left with nothing but the clothes on her back and her handbag.

"Huh."

She took in her new surroundings.

Outside, instead of the streets of Ilford with the chill crisp of winter, she found herself staring at damp swampland, the air so thick and humid it seemed she could slice it with a knife.

Sally stepped back into the loo and shut the door.

Maybe the wanker had slipped something in one of her drinks. Her last pint, hadn't it tasted a little off?

Yes. Yes, it had.

This had to be a dream, or some sort of hallucination from a failed roofie attempt. The more she tried to sort it out, the more her head hurt. So she curled up on the tiled floor and went to sleep for an hour or so, figuring when she woke up things would be back to normal.

They weren't.

The buildings were still gone, the air still warm and oppressive. Sweat beaded up under Sally's bra and sweater as she stood at the bathroom door, staring out into a world that made no sense.

She hadn't napped long enough, however, to sleep off the alcohol still buzzing through her system, so the thought of trying to find her way home through the unfamiliar landscape seemed like a good idea. She stepped down onto the ground, unsteady in her stiff new ankle boots. She'd got them cheap. Faux leather with fringe hanging off the sides. The chunky three-inch heels immediately sank into soggy ground.

"Shit," she muttered.

Steeling herself, she set out in the direction of her flat, a good two miles down the road. Except there was no road. Just sticky mud and plants that looked like they belonged in the Amazon, not East London.

Strange noises rustled in the foliage around her, and others sounded off in the distance. If she hadn't been so drunk, Sally thought, she would have been a lot more frightened. As it was, she figured she only had to find her way home and into bed, and things would be back to normal when she woke up in the morning.

Plants gave way to trees.

Something growled off to her left, the sound menacing enough to cut through the alcohol haze.

"What the bloody hell," she muttered, picking up her pace as best she could and hurrying away from the growling. The ground became even softer. A sucking sound accompanied each step as she pulled her boots out of the hungry mud. She wished she could see, but the only illumination came from the moon and the stars, which had become increasingly obscured by large trees, the branches above blocking out the light.

Suddenly her right foot and leg sunk into water up to her knees.

"Shit!"

Bracing herself to keep from falling, she continued onward, tripping at one point on something under the water and dropping to her knees. She picked herself up, cursing softly as she pulled her handbag out of the bog and kept going. Soon she was submerged up to her waist.

"Bugger this!"

Something growled again, the sound liquid and dangerous.

Sally gave a frightened sob and kept slogging through the fen. She finally found her way back into shallows, the water only coming up over her knees again.

"Come on, Sally," she muttered, more for the sound of a human voice than anything else. "You can find your way out of here." She wished she hadn't spoken. Her voice sounded hollow and muffled, not comforting at all.

She had to pee again already. Beer always had that effect on her, but she'd be damned before she stopped to do her business in this nightmare landscape. Something hit the water behind her with a loud splash.

Freezing in place, she listened for a good minute or so.

Nothing. Even the rustling stopped.

Sally heaved a sigh of relief.

Then something with horribly sharp teeth latched onto one calf, yanking hard and pulling her under the water.

13

"I don't get it," Amber said, trailing behind Blake by several feet. "The world has gone totally insane. Big chunks of it are gone, giant wolves are eating people, and it looks like we're in the middle of Siberia instead of England. Why is it so hard for you to believe that it's not 1953 anymore?"

Blake didn't answer.

Ever since they'd left the remnants of Romford behind, he'd set a pace just short of grueling, always managing to stay a few feet ahead of Amber but close enough to protect her if necessary. It was like traveling with a living, breathing G.I. Joe, only British. It was also the most macho example of passive-aggressive behavior she'd ever encountered. In other circumstances—normal ones—she'd have found it funny. Now, however, it was both infuriating and exhausting.

Every time she tried to bring up the date on the *Romford Bee* and what it meant, Blake would lengthen his stride just enough to make it impossible for Amber to carry on a conversation without yelling at his back. No telling what predators that would attract, and she wasn't willing to risk their safety for the sake of an answer. So she would fall into a frustrated silence and follow in her companion's determined wake.

Her feet and ankles throbbed continuously. The bandages and socks helped, but the damage had already been done and it would take time for the skin to heal. At least the pain was bearable, thanks to Blake's ministrations. The coat he'd found kept her warm, too, even with the cold wind constantly blowing over and through the grasslands.

She tried to temper her irritation with the certain knowledge that he was the reason she'd survived the night. Even if she hadn't died in the hotel, without his help she couldn't honestly say that she would've thought to search the cars. Although to be fair, she'd been in a state of shock. Still, she'd have most likely curled up in a fetal ball and died in the luggage closet.

Amber didn't know why it was so important for her to change his mind. Or why she wasn't more personally freaked out by the thought that time itself had shifted. That England—possibly the entire world— had been somehow ripped apart and put back together in a hodgepodge of mismatched timescapes, like a patchwork quilt.

A crazy quilt, she thought, *put together by inmates at the most fucked-up insane asylum that's ever existed.*

"If we keep up this pace," Blake said, "we should make Whitehall in good time."

"How will we know?"

"What's that?" He sounded distracted.

"How will we be able to tell if we're there? What if there aren't any buildings? What if it's like this?" Amber waved her free hand, taking in the seemingly endless sea of frost-tipped grass around them.

"It won't be." His tone was clipped. Final.

"How do you know that?" she insisted. "Look, we have to keep an open mind about this or—"

"Or *what?*"

Blake stopped so suddenly that she nearly ran into him. He turned, glaring down at her. She recoiled from the ferocity in his eyes. For a brief instant, the only thing there was bleak and utter madness.

Then the moment passed, and while he still looked angry, at least he looked sane.

"Look," he said, taking a deep breath. "There's no point talking about this. We can speculate all we want, but right now we'd do better saving our breath for the journey ahead." He mimicked Amber's gesture at the landscape around them.

"We don't know what's out here with us," he continued. "Possibly more of those creatures that nearly killed you. Or worse." He leaned in. "So I need to keep my attention on the possibility of predators. If you still insist on talking, we'll discuss it after we're safe at Whitehall."

With that he turned and resumed his determined stride through the grass.

Amber didn't see any choice but to follow, thoughts churning furiously in her head. With no one to share them with, she remained silent.

They stopped two hours later to rest and eat only slightly stale currant scones, taking shelter in a small hollow under the arched remnants of an old stone bridge. The kind that seemed to be scattered willy-nilly all over the UK and Europe, adding that touch of quaintness and history.

The ground under the five-foot expanse of moss-covered curved stone was still damp, water puddling in several places. Amber again thought of Gavin's fate and shuddered.

Blake glanced her way. "Are you cold?" he asked around a mouthful of scone.

She shook her head. "No. I just—" She stopped, feeling the prickle of tears yet again as she relived those horrible moments.

"What happened?"

Amber took a deep breath, doing her best to steady herself. Crying wouldn't help, after all, but maybe it *would* help to tell someone else what had happened. Maybe then she'd stop replaying it in her mind's eye.

"I was out on a picnic," she said, speaking quietly. "I guess you'd call it a date. We were on the river in a boat—a punt, I guess—when whatever happened, well, *happened*. Gavin, my date, he—" She broke off, trying to think of a way to describe what happened and make it palatable. The horror of that moment was still too fresh. "It was like back at the parking garage. The building itself and those cars. Part of him was just... gone."

She swallowed, then continued.

"Most of the punt was gone too, and the river..." She shook her head. "It was as if someone had pulled the plug and all the water in the river just ran out down the drain. One minute it was there, and the next—"

She took a sip of some sickly-sweet orange soda to steady herself.

Blake gestured toward her bare legs.

"What on earth were you doing on a boat in those clothes?"

Amber didn't know if he really cared or was just trying to distract her. Either way, she was grateful for the change of subject.

"Gavin and I were both attending a cosplay convention at the hotel," Amber replied.

"Cosplay. That's like a costume party then?"

"Sort of, I guess. People recreate costumes from their favorite TV show or movie or comic book."

Blake snorted. "Bloody waste of time."

Amber ignored his dismissive comment and continued with her story.

"The weather was so beautiful, it seemed silly to change. It was hot out. Not like this, and I didn't think I'd be walking any farther than from the dock back to the hotel." She heaved a sigh and took another sip of soda before asking, "What about you? Where were you when it happened?"

Even as the words left her mouth, Amber flashed back on 9/11. Every year on the anniversary of that horrible day, Facebook and other social media filled with stories of where people had been when the twin towers had fallen. She wondered if, years from now, whoever survived this event would do the same thing. Except if the electricity never came back, they'd be telling the stories while huddled around campfires. Not on Facebook or Twitter.

She shoved that thought back into the recesses of her brain. She didn't want to think about the possibility of a world without electricity. A world without the Internet. Maybe Blake was right, and when they got to Whitehall they'd find people in charge. People who knew what had happened, and how to fix it.

Meanwhile she waited for her companion to answer her question. He stared down at the muddy ground for a few beats, then looked at her.

"I was at home, making dinner," Blake said. "I'd made plans for that evening, but when I opened the front door and saw what lay outside my house, I knew my plans had changed."

"Do you always dress like that for dinner?"

He gave a small humorless laugh.

"Don't be daft. I changed soon as I realized things were different. The rules of peacetime don't apply anymore."

"You're in the military." It was not a question.

He gave a brief nod. "I was in 8 Commando, and then the SAS."

One of Amber's uncles on her dad's side had been an Army Ranger. She was familiar with just enough military history to realize Blake was a genuine badass, if he was telling the truth—and she had no reason to believe he was lying. Why would he?

He didn't seem inclined to elaborate, though, so Amber didn't pry any further. Besides, their voices seemed inordinately loud, bouncing off the underside of the bridge. They finished the rest of their meal in silence, each taking a turn dealing with the call of nature while the other kept watch. When it was her turn to play lookout, Amber stared nervously off across the grasslands. The constant wind made it impossible to tell if anything was moving out there, perhaps stalking them, so every ripple on its surface made her heart race double-time.

She wondered if she'd ever feel safe again.

Packing up, they started off once more and walked steadily for another hour, passing a few oddities along the way that stood out—not necessarily in and of themselves, but because they had no place in the grasslands.

A child's tricycle, lying on its side in a small rectangle of bisected concrete—a patch of sidewalk, perhaps.

A bed of rose bushes several yards long, abruptly ending where the grass took over, pink and red blooms withered and dropping in the frigid wind.

The front end of a double-decker bus lying on its side on a swath of cobblestones. The seats and walls were splashed with drying blood, but there were no signs of any survivors. No bodies. Blake stayed by Amber's side after that, slowing his pace so she could keep up with him.

Trees appeared in the distance, incongruous somehow. Suddenly the grasslands ended, replaced by ominous-looking swampland, as if one film set had given way to another. Patches of muddy ground connected pools of ominously dark, stagnant water. Large, ancient trees cut out most of the light. What little filtered through cast twisted shadows over the water.

The new terrain appeared to stretch in either direction

as far as they could see. As Blake and Amber stood at the edge of the bog, a bubble rose in the pool nearest them, bursting at the top. It smelled of rotting vegetation, the odor thick and foul.

"Do we have to go through here?" Amber asked in a whisper.

"No help for it," Blake replied. "We don't know how far it stretches on either side, or how far out of our way it would take us to go around. We don't want to be caught out in the open after dark."

She couldn't argue with that.

Still… the thought of venturing into something that looked like a creepy version of the bayou in Disneyland's *Pirates of the Caribbean* ride made the hair on the back of her neck stand up in skin-crawling apprehension. Something buzzed through the air in between the trees, its movement too quick for Amber to catch more than a brief glimpse. It was the size of a blue jay, but with nothing else birdlike about it.

"Stay on dry land, and keep close," Blake said.

"Like Velcro," Amber replied.

He gave her a blank look.

"Glue," she amended. "Like glue. Very sticky glue."

That earned her a very small but genuine smile.

"You'd do well to keep the crowbar in hand, I think." Without waiting for an answer, Blake liberated the tool from its backpack loop and handed it to her. She switched the staff to her left hand and hefted the length of iron in her right.

He drew his rifle and together they moved cautiously forward into the boggy landscape.

14

The air seemed to grow thicker and the temperature rose by at least ten degrees. Maybe the thick canopy of trees trapped heat and humidity. Whatever the reason, Amber felt as if they'd walked into a slice of an entirely different world. One she couldn't wait to leave.

There were new sounds, as well. The persistent buzzing of winged insects. A chirping noise which might be crickets. A low chorus of what sounded like very big frogs. Underneath it all were occasional splashing noises, as if things slipped in and out of the water. She looked around nervously, but saw nothing other than ripples.

Blake moved slowly and cautiously, choosing each step with care. Amber made sure to follow closely in his footsteps, gripped by an almost morbid fear of stepping off dry ground. As they moved deeper into the trees, brackish green water covered more and more of the terrain until they were hard put to find a path on which to walk. She grew uncomfortably warm in her coat, yet didn't dare stop to remove it. Sweat dripped down her face and neck, pooling in between her breasts. A little while ago she would have been grateful for the heat, but this felt wrong. Out of place.

How could the air go so quickly from the cold, dry climate of the grasslands to this sickly, almost tropical humidity, thick and smelling of disease? Amber shook her head, wondering if the miasma in the air was making her loopy, not to mention overly dramatic. The further they ventured, the less this reminded her of some cheery Disney ride, and more like the Dead Marshes in *Lord of the Rings*. She couldn't stand to look down, for fear of seeing what might float just beneath the oily surface of the water, barely visible in the undergrowth.

No sooner had that thought crossed her mind than something grabbed her foot. Amber looked down then, and what she saw made her choke back the scream that rose in her throat. The only sound that emerged was a strangled sob, enough to make Blake turn back.

Blood-streaked fingers with incongruously well-manicured nails clutched desperately at one of Amber's pink high-tops. The hand belonged to a pale arm emerging from the murky fen. A woman's face, skin leached of color, breached the surface near the water's edge. Blood dribbled out of her mouth, forming graceful swirls of pink in the water.

"Oh god," Amber breathed.

The woman's fingers scrabbled weakly at her foot, catching hold of the laces and holding on as if they were a lifeline.

"Oh my god, she's alive!"

Blake immediately hunkered down and reached into the water to grasp the woman under her arms. As he started hauling her onto the hummock, she gave a weak scream that still managed to convey agony. When he'd pulled her halfway out of the bog, Amber saw why.

Her right forearm was covered in blood to the elbow. Something big and toothy had bitten into the left side of her chest, and her left thigh was a mangled mess. She was clutching an ugly wound on her abdomen—it had been sliced open by a claw or a blade. Her eyelashes fluttered open, the remnants of heavily applied mascara smeared around and below her eyes, giving her an almost clownish appearance.

How is she still breathing? Amber thought, appalled at the extent of the injuries. It was terrifyingly reminiscent of the little girl back at the Romford Arms.

Blake gently eased the woman down so that her head rested on a patch of moss, then carefully lifted what was left of her legs out of the water. Amber knelt at her side, reaching out to take hold of the hand on the woman's uninjured arm.

"It's okay," she lied softly. "You're safe now."

The woman's eyes closed again, her breathing shallow and labored.

"We have to do something." Amber looked up at Blake. He was sitting back on his heels, just behind the woman's head.

He shook his head. "There's nothing we can do. The stomach wound alone is enough to kill her."

"We can't just leave her here," Amber insisted.

"Even if she weren't dying, she's too injured to travel," he said with brutal honesty. "And there are no ambulances out here." The woman moaned, although whether it was from the pain or because she understood Blake's words, there was no way to know.

"But we can't just leave her here like this," Amber argued. "What if—" She dropped her voice. "What if whatever did this comes back?"

"Then we don't want to be here."

Amber stared in disbelief.

"How can you be so callous? There has to be *something* we can do!"

Blake stared back, his expression unreadable. Finally, he nodded.

"Move away," he said. Amber started to do as he said, but stopped when the woman's eyes opened again.

"Please don't leave me…"

"We won't," Amber reassured her. "My friend is going to help you, okay?"

Blake cleared his throat. She looked at him and then struggled awkwardly to her feet, using her staff to prevent the weight of her backpack from sending her tumbling backward off the relative safety of the hummock.

Blake took her place at the woman's side, placing one hand on her shoulder, the other reaching for something in his belt.

"Everything will be fine," he said softly.

He shifted just enough for Amber to see the combat knife in his right hand. Before she could do more than gasp in horror, he sliced the blade across the woman's throat in one swift cut. What little blood was left in her body welled out of the gash. Her eyes stayed open, staring sightlessly at the canopy of trees above.

"There," he said. "Nothing else can hurt her."

Amber stood there, shock freezing her in place as she tried to parse what had just happened. A very small voice in her head told her that there had been no other option. That Blake had done the right thing. It was the lack of regret in his eyes that made the voice hard to hear.

"Let's go," he said, coming to his feet in one easy move. "And stay close. Whatever attacked her could still be lurking below."

Amber followed, sticking next to him despite the desire to run in the opposite direction.

* * *

"I think we're almost out of this forest."

After an hour or so of what felt like an endless slog through the fetid swamp, Blake pointed ahead to where it did indeed look like the trees—and hopefully the swamp—were coming to an end. It wasn't very light, though, and what brightness there was looked strange, as if diffused through a filter.

Closer to the tree line, a thick mist started drifting through the branches, settling lower and covering both water and dry land so that each step forward had to be tested before they could proceed. To Amber, the last hundred feet seemed to take longer than the rest of the journey. She became hyper aware of the sound of *things* splashing in the pools.

Were the noises growing louder?

She tried to shut the image of that poor woman from her mind's eye, and kept moving until suddenly they were out of the trees and into yet another landscape, one that appeared with the same abruptness as all of the others they had already passed.

The hummocks and pools gave way to hard-packed dirt, and the tendrils of mist turned into what seemed like a wall of fog that obscured everything around them. Visibility was only a few feet in any direction, and sounds became muffled.

Amber had heard of London's infamous "killer fogs," a combination of coal smoke and mist. There didn't seem to be any pollutants here, though. The dense fog was whitish gray, not yellow or black, and free of any acrid odor.

It could still be hiding things.

It wasn't as cold as it had been in the grasslands, although her hair now hung in damp tendrils around her face and her coat grew heavy with moisture. At least the ground beneath their feet was dry.

Blake paused to look at his compass. "Just a few miles away," he said. "Two or three at the most."

They'd gone a few hundred yards or so when a large object appeared in the mist in front of them. They walked up to it slowly. Amber half expected it to be breathing, but closer inspection revealed it to be some sort of primitive structure made of what looked like dried mud and straw, with a thatched roof.

Wattle and daub, she thought.

They continued around the hut until they came to an opening about shoulder height—at least if those shoulders belonged to Blake. He held a finger up to his lips and Amber nodded. Even if she hadn't completely understood his need for caution, she wasn't about to argue with him about anything right now.

He might decide to put me out of my misery.

Even as the thought popped up, Amber knew it wasn't entirely fair. What else was he supposed to have done? He was right. There *were* no ambulances just a phone call away. Which meant that if she got injured badly enough that she couldn't continue, he very well *might* decide she'd be better off dead.

Worse yet, maybe he'd be right.

Blake took a cautious step to peer through the window. A spearhead shot out of the opening, and he jerked away just in time to avoid being skewered through the throat. As whoever was inside started to pull the spear back, he seized the wooden shaft with both hands and braced one foot against the bottom of the hut.

Small hands emerged, clutching desperately at the other end of the weapon. Blake gave a strong jerk and slammed whoever was on the other side into the wall. There was a grunt from inside and the hands slipped off the shaft, causing Blake to stumble backward a little before he righted himself. He hauled the rest of the weapon out through the window.

Whoever was inside broke into sobs, punctuated by the wailing of what sounded like a little kid. Blake swiftly went around the corner, Amber following on his heels, until they came to a door-sized opening covered by a coarse cloth attached to the top of the primitive doorframe. There Blake used the tip of the spear to push the cloth away, and looked inside.

"A woman and two children," he said, letting the cloth drop back in place. The wailing grew louder, and she thought she could hear a baby crying, as well. She couldn't stand it and pushed past Blake before he could stop her.

Amber stopped short when the woman—no older than she was and at least a foot shorter—gave a cry of fright. Next to her were a little girl no older than maybe five, and a toddler barely able to stand, clutching his sister's leg. All three wore shifts of the same rough cloth that curtained the doorway. The woman's hair and the little girl's were pulled back in single braids.

A pile of straw with furs and blankets on it hugged the far wall, and a fire pit sat in the center of the hut, an iron pot suspended above it.

Amber opened her hands as the woman cringed away. The two children screamed in fright.

"It's okay," she said softly. "We won't hurt you. We're friends."

The woman cowered back even more at the sound of Amber's voice, pulling her two children behind her. Blake poked his head inside.

"Come on," he said, "we need to keep going."

"We can't just leave them here," Amber protested. "They're the first living people we've seen since…" She trailed off, not wanting to think about the woman in the swamp.

"We can't help them," Blake said, his tone uncompromising. "We can't even talk to them. She doesn't understand a word you're saying."

He was right.

Amber hated him.

"They'll just slow us down," he continued, the cold truth of his words steamrolling over her objections. "And that's even if we could get her to understand where we're going, and why. The best thing we can do is stay the course, find out what's happening. Then we can send someone back to help those in need."

If there's anyone but us left alive, Amber thought bitterly.

He laid the spear down on the ground right outside of the hut, pointing to the woman and then at the weapon. Then he gripped Amber by one arm and pulled her out, never taking his gaze off the woman until they were well away from the doorway. She pulled away from Blake's grasp. She didn't want him to touch her.

At least he left them a weapon, Amber told herself as they began walking again. Moments later the hut behind them was swallowed up by the fog.

The hard dirt beneath their feet abruptly gave way to cobblestones, wending their way in a downward curve. It was a road. Blake nodded in satisfaction.

"Civilization at last," he said, and he picked up his pace, renewed energy in his stride. Amber wasn't so sure, but she followed anyway.

Other shapes appeared out of the mist. Buildings flanked them on either side of the cobblestone road, but there was no consistency to their shape or, in some cases, to the materials used. Amber noticed a storefront on one side where the first few feet of the wall looked brand new, while the rest of the wall could've been several hundred years old. It looked as if someone had drawn a line between the two portions. The rooftops didn't match up.

A store on the other side looked as though the signage had been cobbled together by three different people, with totally different ideas as to what kind of store it was and what type of lettering should be used. In places, the cobblestones were replaced by asphalt and sidewalks. It was surreal to the point of nightmare.

Once or twice Amber thought she saw human shapes moving in the heavy fog, but she couldn't be sure. If there *were* other people lurking about, they obviously didn't want to be seen.

Blake appeared not to notice any of this. He seemed so positive that things would be okay once they reached Whitehall.

How could such certainty be wrong? Perhaps when they emerged from the mist, sanity would be restored.

Amber knew that was false logic, but she clung to it the way that Blake held onto his conviction that there was a government center waiting for them just ahead.

Cobblestones and asphalt gave way to grass again and the ground sloped gently upward, making their progress more difficult, at least for Amber. She'd been doing her best to ignore her throbbing feet, but now the muscles in her legs were screaming, as well. Nothing in her life had prepared her for this kind of grueling physical activity. If—no, *when*—she got back to San Diego, she would start walking every day. Go to the gym, take some sort of physical fitness classes.

They kept forging upward, the gentle rise giving way to a steeper slope. Still the mist swirled around them. When they reached the top, or at least where the ground appeared to level off, Blake signaled for her to stop.

"We've earned a break," he said in what was the closest to a jovial tone he'd used since she'd met him. The fog swirled around them as Amber took off her backpack and Blake plunked down the duffle bag. They each pulled out a bottle of water and a packet of chips.

Crisps, Amber reminded herself, although she supposed it didn't really matter anymore.

"We're nearly there," Blake said in satisfaction, taking a long pull of water. Amber didn't ask why he was so sure. It was enough that he was.

And oh, let him be right.

They drank the water and ate their chips. Amber did her best to stretch out her legs, trying the exercise he'd taught her the day before. Her hamstrings felt as if they'd been cut in half and then reattached. Short and painfully tight. She wanted to change the Band-Aids on her feet, but didn't think Blake would want to take the time. He seemed almost relaxed, but his eagerness to reach their destination was obvious.

Instead, Amber pulled out her iPhone and powered it on, waiting for the Apple logo to disappear and the main screen to show up. She punched in her password. The battery was at eighty-eight percent, but there still was no service. Even though she'd expected as much, her disappointment felt like a gut punch.

"What's that then?" he asked.

"It's my cell phone," she replied.

Blake didn't ask any more questions, which seemed weird. Then again, questions might bring answers that he wasn't ready to deal with. Like the date on the *Romford Bee*.

"Are you ready?" He stood, hoisting the duffle bag. Amber nodded, albeit reluctantly, and put her phone away. She could've used an hour or twenty, just sitting there resting her feet and legs. Not to mention her neck and shoulders, sore from the unaccustomed weight of her backpack. Instead she stood up, muscles groaning in protest, and swiveled her head in a gentle circle to release some of the tension.

A gust of wind blew across their vantage point, chilling the air. Amber was reaching down for her backpack when Blake gave a sudden inarticulate cry. He pointed ahead, in the direction they were going.

"Look! It's Tower Bridge!"

Amber's heart gave a leap in her chest. Maybe there was hope after all. She moved to Blake's side and looked where he was pointing. Sure enough, the familiar shape of one of the bridge's two towers poked out of the fog, which looked as though it might be dissipating somewhat. The wind blew again, sending the mist swirling, thinning it out down around the bridge.

As they watched, the fog parted below so they could see the entire tower at the far end of the bridge. Another violent gust made it possible to see beyond, where the River Thames had widened out into a tidal flat. The one tower and a small chunk of the pedestrian walkway was all that remained of the iconic Tower Bridge.

Other things rose out of the fog and the water—long spindly things that curved upward, ending in rough oval shapes. One of the oval shapes opened, emitting a long, low noise that echoed across the water. More eerie cries arose as a herd of brontosauruses slowly made their way past what was left of the Tower of London.

Blake dropped to his knees as if someone had sliced his legs out from under him.

"God, no," he breathed. "It can't be. It's… it's gone. It's all gone."

Amber put a hand on his shoulder, not sure if it was safe to do so but needing at least to offer him some comfort. He didn't shake it off—he just turned and looked up at her with haunted eyes.

"It's all over," he said hoarsely. "We'd be better off dead."

15

"We'd be better off dead."

Amber lay on her sleeping bag, huddled under her blankets, car coat under her head. She knew she needed to get some rest, but it just wasn't happening. The only time she remembered ever being outside without ambient light was years ago on a family camping trip up in the mountains. Even then they'd had a campfire, along with a full moon and a spectacular display of stars in the skies above.

Here there were no moon or stars to be seen—just a seemingly endless stretch of fog.

"We'd be better off dead."

The words haunted her, kept her awake. She continued to watch Blake, checking to see if he was actually asleep. Every strange noise, every creak, every howl, every other eerie sound from outside was less frightening than the possibility that the man sleeping next to her might wake up and decide to show her the same "mercy" he'd given the woman in the swamp.

After they'd seen the dinosaurs lumbering through the mist, down where the Thames used to flow, Amber thought Blake was going to charge down the hill in some sort of suicidal last stand. Instead he'd stayed on his knees and stared numbly at the reality that had replaced his hope. The shock had broken something inside of him, at least temporarily.

Unwelcome sounds—howls, yips, grunts, growls, and worse—had echoed in the fog that surrounded them, with no way to tell where they were coming from. He might have remained there until something ambled out of the mist and ate him, had Amber not pulled him away.

"We need to get to shelter," she'd said.

Even as she'd spoken, the sun had started to set, and visibility became that much worse. Blake had pulled himself together long enough for them to backtrack and take shelter in one of the few buildings—a men's clothing and tailor shop. It looked like it had survived the event relatively unscathed. The door had been unlocked, the only sign of disturbance being several impeccably dressed tailor's dummies lying on their sides on the plush hunter-green carpet, along with a few bolts of cloth and a pair of shears.

Amber had quietly pocketed the shears.

When she'd tried to talk to Blake and make plans for the next day, he'd acted as though he hadn't heard her, busying himself by throwing down a couple of long Edwardian-style coats as a makeshift bed. Now he lay silently in the corner, his face turned toward the wall.

Should I stay or should I go?

The Clash song played in Amber's head, its lyrics totally apropos. She wouldn't have survived up to this point had it not been for Blake, but now she was certain that he'd end her life as unhesitatingly as he'd saved it.

Yet the thought of setting out on her own again terrified her. She'd been lucky to make it to the Romford Arms unscathed. The last day and a half had taught her that anything could be lurking out there. For all she knew, packs of raptors roamed the grasslands, like in *Jurassic Park*. There might not be any place left that offered genuine safety, with or without Blake.

The bottom line?

She wanted to survive.

Which means I need to leave.

Waiting until the sun began to rise felt like common sense. But if she waited until daybreak, she'd never be able to make it past him. He'd demand to know where she was going, and he wouldn't just let her walk away.

At least, she didn't think he would.

I need to leave and I need to do it now.

Her backpack had food and water in it. She and Blake

had divided up the supplies. *"If we're separated,"* he had said, *"you'll still have the basics you'll need to survive."*

She wouldn't be able to get very far, however, regardless of when she left. Her feet still hurt, and even at her best she doubted she could match Blake's rapid pace. He'd catch up for certain. So she needed to figure out a way to disappear, and give herself a real head start. Yet how would she get far enough away in the dark without running into who knows what, with no chance to see it coming or protect herself?

How could she keep him from following her trail?

Unless…

She knew what she had to do.

Amber sat up, slowly and silently. Taking care to make as little noise as possible, she pulled out her flashlight. She covered the beam with her hand before she switched it on, then cautiously allowed no more than a sliver of light to leak out in Blake's direction, careful to not let any fall on his face. He didn't move. His breathing was deep, punctuated by surprisingly soft snores.

Switching off the flashlight she pulled on her coat, careful not to make a sound, then quickly folded up the blankets and secured them to her backpack. Gathering everything up, she rose to her feet and crept stealthily across the carpeted floor to the back of the store, away from the street. She moved as if she was blind, inches at a time, feeling cautiously for obstacles, not daring to risk the light again.

Slowly turning the knob, she pulled on the back door, and it gave a tiny protesting squeak. She froze.

"Amber?"

His voice sounded far away.

Should I answer?

She said nothing, waiting, barely daring to breathe, listening for any further sound.

Nothing. Not even a snore.

Amber crept into the hallway and with the utmost care, gently shut the door behind her. She risked using the flashlight beam to guide her to the end of the hall and down the stairs, and then out the door below, where she slipped into the fog-shrouded night.

An hour before dawn, just like clockwork, Blake opened his eyes. He'd always been quick to wake, even as a child. The habit had served him well in the military.

This morning, however, his eyelids were uncharacteristically heavy, the remnants of unpleasant dreams still lingering at the edges of his consciousness. He shook his head to clear it and turned his head to see if Amber was still asleep.

The girl was gone.

So was her gear.

"Amber?"

He sat straight up, and scanned the room.

She's gone.

No.

No, this was unacceptable.

It was suddenly clear. Blake had been floundering. Whitehall had been his final anchor, and once his troubled mind had accepted that it was well and truly gone—lost to whatever mad hellscape had claimed them—he'd nothing to which he could cling.

Except for Amber.

And now she too was gone.

The sobering realization pulled him from the mental wreckage in which he had been trapped, snapped him back into a semblance of his regimented self. It gave him a goal once again. He had to find her. Springing to his feet, he grabbed his duffle bag, and quickly inspected the front door. The latch was still locked, just as he had left it. He turned and left through the back door.

Once outside, he scanned left and right. The fog still lay thick over the landscape, but he could see there had been an alley here, now split lengthwise. Beyond the half-road, where there should have been buildings, cobblestones melted into asphalt. A few yards beyond, nothing stood but knee-high grass.

"Amber!" he called out. "Amber, can you hear me?"

No response came, apart from faint echoes off the building walls behind him. He fought a growing irritation, choking it down in order to keep his focus.

Making a circuit of the surroundings, he took an inventory of his options.

The remains of the shops formed a small urban island, surrounded on three sides by a border of grass. To the north, east, and south he found no signs of passage, no trace of footprints leading away. That only left the portion to their west, a stretch of asphalt that finally gave way to scattered patches of cobblestone, concrete, and the debris of other ages.

The girl had to be heading west by southwest, then, back into London. The most she could have had was a three-hour lead. If he made good time, and she went at her usual slower pace, he thought he could catch up to her in no more than two hours.

Blake returned to the shop to gather his supplies, packing them quickly into the duffle. Then he set off at a brisk pace toward the southwest.

The hunt was on.

Amber peered from the upper-story window of the adjoining inn, remaining carefully hidden behind the curtain. She watched Blake head deeper down into what was left of London.

When at last he disappeared from sight, she gave a sigh of relief. Then she sat back and made herself watch the clock on the wall. When it had ticked away a full twenty minutes, and not a moment before, she picked up her things and strode out again, heading off through the grassland in the opposite direction.

16

Trudging through ankle-high snow, Amber shivered as the frigid wind sent icy fingers under the coat to assault her bare legs. Her toes were numb under the socks and high-tops, and she wasn't sure she could unclench the hand holding the staff.

She didn't think she needed to worry about frostbite yet—surely it wasn't *that* cold—but if she didn't find her way out of this snowy landscape by nightfall, that could change. Using the staff to test the ground under the snow, Amber stepped up her pace, hoping for a glimpse of something other than skeletal trees set against white ground.

It had been hours since she had entered this new region. She'd wrapped one of the blankets around her head to keep body heat from escaping, with the other draped over the coat to help keep the wind at bay. It was arranged in a cross between a Roman stola and a shawl, held in place with a couple of large safety pins.

Where's a toga party when you really need one?

These random thoughts surprised her every time they popped up. Her dad would call them "graveyard humor." Amber wondered if it was a sign of impending insanity.

Then again, what was she *supposed* to think or feel under circumstances as incredible as these? Not even her oh-so-unflappable mother would have been able to keep it together if she'd seen brontosauruses ambling through the streets of La Jolla.

With a sinking heart, she realized that there actually *might* be dinosaurs wandering the canyons of the Southern California coast. If this phenomenon was worldwide, there was no telling what her family was experiencing.

Just let them still be alive.

Amber's right foot suddenly punched through a thin crust of ice that she'd somehow missed with the staff, submerging her shoe in a couple inches of icy water.

"Shit!"

She pulled her foot out, but not before the sides of the High Top got totally soaked. Instantly she felt frigid water seeping into the sock. She'd just have to suck it up, though, and keep moving until she reached someplace where she could rest in relative safety. Maybe even someplace with hot water so she could bathe. While her thick hair didn't require daily washing, this was pushing it. Her scalp itched, she smelled funky, and her underarms needed shaving.

God, what a stupid thing to even think about.

Still... she'd kill for a shower.

Starting up again, she used more care to test the ground ahead of each step, ignoring an inner voice that kept urging her to hurry up. She hadn't seen any scary wildlife since leaving Blake behind, but she'd heard ominous noises more than once, and something had left massive paw prints in the snow not far from where she'd first entered the bleak winter wasteland. Heart pounding in her chest, she'd made sure to walk away from the direction those prints were headed.

The icy crust started giving way to patches of slush. Water dripped off branches as more snow melted and the chill in the air went from frigid to merely butt-ass cold. Amber caught her breath as she saw a splash of green off in the distance. She walked just a little faster, resisting the urge to break into a run. After all, she might find herself back in the swamp again. Without Blake and his compass, she had no idea what direction she was traveling.

It soon became apparent that the green she saw wasn't a swamp, but rather a line of trees stretching out in either direction, their leafy branches interlocked like a chain of protestors with their arms linked. As she drew closer, Amber saw that there weren't any trees— or even grass—on the other side of the line. It was as if someone had plucked a row out of an orchard, so orderly and yet so out of place. A precise line in the middle of so much chaos.

But the precision was an illusion, she discovered. The line of trees lay in a long, narrow slash of terrain that trailed off shortly to her right. She couldn't see the other end, to the left. It continued as far as she could see.

She slowed her pace and approached the tree line, glancing nervously upward as something suddenly rustled in the leaves above. Amber gave a little yelp and a lone squirrel scurried from a low-hanging branch to one higher up, where it turned and chittered at her.

Amber didn't know whether to laugh or swear.

She passed underneath the tree and through the line, then stared in dismay at the landscape on the other side. There the ground looked as if it had been transplanted from a dead planet—perhaps one that had died in a nuclear holocaust. It made the swamp seem cozy and inviting by comparison. Nothing good could be here.

I could follow the tree line for a bit, she thought. *See where it takes me.* That seemed like a better idea. At least the trees gave her an illusion of cover, and she could always climb up into the branches if the necessity presented itself.

Amber took another look at the desolate scenery in front of her.

I should at least check this out.

She didn't know where the thought came from, but it hit with an immediacy and urgency that couldn't be ignored.

Amber stepped out onto the fallow land and continued forward. She moved slowly and quietly, stepping over scorch marks that crisscrossed the ground. The terrain was devoid of plant life, reduced to a gray and black speckled crust that crunched softly underfoot, puffs of dust rising with each step.

It looked like photos she'd seen of Hiroshima.

She repressed a shudder.

"I've got a bad feeling about this," she muttered. Her voice sounded too loud, and totally out of place. Nervously she glanced around.

Nothing.

Lots of nothing. A dead zone.

So why was she so scared?

This is stupid, she decided. *I'm out of here.*

She turned to walk back toward the trees, but that niggling itch returned, like a mute ghost in the poorly lit back corridors of her mind, trying wordlessly to persuade her to continue.

Keep going.

Don't be afraid.

She frowned.

"Well, crap."

Turning around again, she marched across the gloomy quasi-moonscape, one softly crunching footfall after another. But toward what?

Suddenly she felt a sudden urge to halt, right where she was—but there was nothing there. Just more of the same black-and-white limbo. It began to creep her out and she started forward again. Before she had gone more than a dozen steps, however, the ghost was back, silently urging her not to leave.

Not yet.

"This is getting ridiculous," she said to herself irritably. Nevertheless, she dutifully obeyed her gut and walked back a few paces. The rush of relief was downright palpable when she stopped at the same spot as before.

"Okay, what is *up* with this?" she called out loudly, to nobody. She looked around to see if there was anything she was missing, even scanning in the sky above, then gave the ground a few exploratory jabs with her staff.

Nothing.

Wait a minute!

The staff hit some resistance—there was something down here. She crouched and dug a little more, scratching at the crusty ground. There was definitely a hard surface, buried just below the powder and grit. She used her hands to clear away the gray crust and ash.

Her eyes widened.

"Holy shit," she breathed.

Amber had uncovered what seemed to be a square hatch of stone or concrete, about a yard square. A thin groove ran along the edges of the block, but there didn't seem to be any hinges or latches. She ran her palm across its cool, smooth surface, then looked around again, struck by a flutter of paranoia, suddenly certain she was being watched.

There was no one.

Turning back to the hatch, she stared at it. Willing it to give up its secrets.

"Open sesame?" she tried.

Nothing.

She felt around the edges for any sort of clasp or hidden button, racking her brains to think of all the ways James Bond or Scooby Doo might trigger a secret door. When nothing came to mind, the initial wonder of discovery began to be chipped away by frustration.

Shaking it off, she rocked back on her heels and tried to puzzle it out, drumming her fingers on the hard surface. She didn't know what was in there—hell, she didn't even know if there was *anything* on the other side of the concrete square. Even so, at that moment nothing else in the world seemed quite as important as finding out.

She didn't try to reason why. The "why" wasn't important.

Think. Think, think, think…

Her eyes glazed over. A not unpleasant drowsiness washed over her, along with a lazy lack of urgency. It was oddly comforting to be here, not doing anything but relaxing peacefully and contemplating the fine blankness of the hatch, letting her gaze sink deeper and deeper into its solidity, into its emptiness, into its void…

Time passed.

How much?

Who knew? Who cared?

Red Triangle Upright

The image of a red triangle appeared unprompted in her mind's eye. It sat upon the hatch, at least in her imagination.

Indigo Heptagram Anticlockwise

Amber imagined a dark violet star shape, serenely spinning in place next to the solid red triangle. She realized with surprise that she knew—in that curious way you just know things in dreams—that the star was a heptagram, and it had seven points.

Sinoper Nonagon Yaw

A third shape joined her imaginary lineup. This one looked like a stop sign on steroids—it had just one side too many, but somehow it worked. It was a rich rust color and it wasn't just spinning, it was doing a three-dimensional pirouette.

Yep, classic Sinoper Nonagon Yaw.

She visualized all three shapes at the same time, a mental feat that gave her a disproportionate feeling of satisfaction. She let the image hang there a little longer, until the hatch suddenly made a sharp *clack*—the noise so loud Amber jumped back with a shriek of surprise.

The three shapes scattered. She couldn't remember any of them now, not exactly. But that had ceased to matter. The hatch was *sinking*. When it had dropped about half a foot, the whole thing halted with another *clack* and slid away into a recess. Through the opening she saw a stone ramp that angled down into blackness.

What just happened?

Amber peered down the ramp. It was pretty dark down there.

"Anybody home?" she said. "Hello?"

No answer.

She was surprised to find herself already walking down the incline.

Jeez, I'm brave today. Then again, maybe this was just a dream, so what did she have to lose?

The ramp led down in a narrow corridor, barely illuminated by a series of tiny pale blue florescent lights. For a moment she just stared at them, stunned to see electricity again. The air felt surprisingly warm, and Amber pulled off her wrap of blankets, then her coat, as well. She left them on the floor and continued down the ramp.

Below was a small, low-ceilinged chamber, carved out of the same stone as the hatch and ramp. It was dimly lit and empty except for one thing—a black hexagonal pillar.

Or was it nonagonal?

Nonagonal? What the hell is nonagonal?

The pillar was about two feet wide in the middle and tapered to a tiny flat hexagon at either end. It seemed to be humming, though that made no sense, Amber realized, since it wasn't making any sound. It was suspended in midair, without any visible means of support.

On a whim she set her staff against the wall and took a few steps closer. As she did so, the object slowly began to spin. She moved closer still, even while a small part of her was thinking *moth to the flame.*

The spinning, humming, floating object began to generate a trace of incandescence from deep within. The glow began as faint gossamer veins of flickering lightning, and slowly spread throughout, gathering strength and brightness.

It's so beautiful.

Amber wanted nothing more than to reach out and touch it.

So she did.

17

Abruptly Amber awoke, surprised to find herself upright and walking in the afternoon sun, moving at a steady, unhurried pace. The sky was surprisingly clear, though here and there on the horizon there were piles of clouds, some of them dark and ominous. She stopped, disoriented, though not so much alarmed as startled.

Where am I?

She looked around. Though there was still a bite to the wind, it was warmer now. She stood in the middle of an open meadow, lots of coarse grass interspersed with pinkish-purple heather and yellow gorse. There was a standing grove of silver birch up on a rise a short distance away. The air smelled clean and fragrant. It looked... peaceful. No slavering wolves in sight. But...

How did I get here? Her eyes went wide. *Have I been sleepwalking? Holy crap, how long have I been sleepwalking?*

There was a fleeting memory of something she couldn't quite recall. She felt the tickle in her mind, though, as if she had just awakened from one of those vivid, amazing dreams, only to have it vanish like a handful of fleeing butterflies. She had a flash… of a smell of ashes, of dancing geometric shapes, and a trapdoor?

A cave?

Nope.

Gone.

Focusing, she shut her eyes tightly, but it was no use, she just couldn't bring it back. The last thing she remembered was trekking through the seemingly endless expanse of snow-covered land, shivering even under her coat and blankets.

Speaking of…

Where are they?

Her head jerked right, then left, scanning the ground. Nothing. She still had Gavin's Han Solo jacket over her Codex garb, her backpack in place, but no coat. No blankets. Surely she wouldn't have taken them off? Even where there wasn't snow or frost, the temperature still felt like an icebox. She looked back in the direction she thought she'd come from. No sign of anything lying discarded on the grass.

That's just weird.

A gust of wind whistled through the trees, rustling the grass and flowers. Amber lifted her face and let the chilly air caress her cheeks, bringing her back to reality. She should be panicked, she knew, at the loss of her only sources of warmth. Yet for the moment it didn't seem terribly important. She wasn't cold. In fact, checking in with herself... she felt fine. All her assorted aches and pains that had seemingly settled in for a long visit—like irritating relatives over the holidays—no longer bothered her very much.

Which actually bothered her a little.

She also felt oddly rested, though she sure as hell didn't remember sleeping since she left Blake, and very much doubted there was any place around that would have afforded her the opportunity. And yet, she felt strangely energized, as though she had gotten ahold of a big cup of coffee and was bouncing off the caffeine.

However she'd gotten to wherever she was now, she gave a silent thanks that she made it there safely. Sleepwalking in this nightmare world could prove fatal. She didn't believe in angels, but it sure felt like something—or someone—had to have been watching over her.

Or someone. That bothered her, that some unknown person might have been involved. The memory gap should have felt alarming... but rather than dwell upon something she couldn't do anything about, Amber decided to keep moving. The sun was low to the horizon, and the most important thing was to find some sort of shelter.

Picking up the pace, she constantly scanned the landscape in front of her. Then, as the shadows began to lengthen, she came to a stop again. At her feet was a sight that offered new hope.

A trail. An actual man-made trail with human footprints, several sets of them.

Staff in hand, Amber changed direction and set off up the well-trodden path, through the grass and up the slope.

18

Cam ran on into the night until at last his aching legs gave out and he collapsed onto the cold wet heather, panting and out of breath. He rolled onto his back and granted himself the luxury of dying if it was his time to do so.

Yet no pursuing enemies stood over him. He lay still and listened for any sounds of the battle. Off in the distance he could still hear the faint rumbling.

There he remained, catching his breath and letting his heart settle down. He felt exhausted and more lost than ever. At least the constellations shining above him in the night sky were still familiar.

Raising a hand to the silver torc around his neck, he ran his fingertips along the ridges of its intricate coils. Before this unexpected journey, the necklace had given him strength and pride. Now, it only reminded him that his homeland and people had vanished and he was hopelessly lost in some strange nightmare land.

Cam sighed, and finally let his muscles relax.

At least I'm safe again, for now.

No sooner did he entertain the thought than a silent shape dove past him through the air, landing on a nearby patch of gorse—an owl pouncing on a vole. It startled him. To see an owl on the wing was an ill omen. A warning to be wary of evil sorcery close at hand.

He sat up, fully alert.

Just a few heartbeats later, he heard a soft rustle. The silhouette of a figure appeared, stalking along the crest of the heath above him. Carefully, quietly, Cam slipped the sword from his belt. He held the sword low at his side, reversing his grip until the blade faced down, concealed by his forearm so it wouldn't make a telltale gleam in the moonlight before he had a chance to strike.

Amber trudged wearily along the ridge, her unexpected burst of energy pretty much fizzled out. She had to take care not to make a misstep and end up tumbling ass over teakettle into some ravine. She longed to stop and rest, find some shelter where she could stretch out and sleep even if only for a few hours, but she hadn't found any place that felt safe enough from the things that wanted to eat her.

So she kept going, forcing herself to keep putting one foot in front of the other.

And soon I'll be walking out the do-o-or…

She groaned inwardly.

Not that song again.

Amber shook her head in an attempt to clear it, but she was so very, very tired…

The figure on the ridge was searching for prey, and supremely confident, making no attempt at stealth. No doubt he was armed with one of the deadly handheld fire-weapons. Cam would only get one chance to kill him, if even that.

I need something to wake me up.

Amber stopped and shrugged off her backpack, digging into one of the side pockets where she found a roll of peppermint Life Savers that she'd bought before leaving San Diego. There were only two left, and the paper stuck to the candy as she tried to pry them apart. Frustrated, she gave a yank, only to have both Life Savers go flying onto the grass. The gleaming white candies vanished into the bushes below.

* * *

Like a panther, Cam kept low as he stalked silently, approaching at an angle toward his opponent's flank. He drew as close as he dared before changing the grip on his sword. A single, swift chop to the neck would be best.

Andraste, guide my hand, he prayed silently.

He charged, blade out and swinging.

"Shit!"

Possibly the last Life Savers in the world, and now they were gone.

Rather than wasting the time digging for a flashlight, Amber flicked the switch on her staff. The orb lit up with its eerie green glow, quickly proving to be useless for searching in the grass.

But the cheap Halloween LED light was strong enough to reveal the man, charging toward her, sword raised.

Amber tried to scream, but could only stand there, frozen with fear.

An unnatural ball of sorcerous emerald light burst suddenly into life. Stricken with shock, Cam froze, his attack halted in mid-strike.

This was no alien warrior or sinister druid. Instead, before him stood a beautiful young woman in dazzling splendor. Jewels glittered on the circlet in her honey-red hair, on the delicate necklace about her throat, woven into the rich fabrics of her scarlet and gold bodice. Her shift was of white linen, the skirt short like that of the Roman goddess, Diana of the Hunt.

Is she a goddess?

No malevolence lurked in those soft eyes. No wrath, no cruelty, no seduction—only wonder and surprise. Her innocence and beauty struck him hard as a thunderbolt. To have been so discourteous to a feminine being of such noble bearing shamed him.

He dropped to his knees and bowed his head.

"I beg your forgiveness," he said softly.

Amber stood shell-shocked. The attack was over before it began.

What the hell?

She stared at the barbarian warrior, now on his knees with his head down.

"*Drog yew genev,*" he said softly.

Amber's first instinct was to turn and run away, but the rational part of her knew she could never outrun him. Besides, if he'd wanted to, he could have easily killed her just now. In fact, he almost did.

What changed his mind?

He remained kneeling before her until she started to get embarrassed. Whatever happened next, she realized, she would have to make the first move. She screwed up her courage, then gingerly reached out and touched him on the shoulder.

"Hey."

He looked up, his eyes wide with... fear? She couldn't tell.

Holy crap, he can't be any older than me!

He had coal-black hair, and a fresh cut across one cheekbone. Everything about him seemed fierce, except for the look in his eyes. There were stories hiding in those eyes. He had been through a lot, just as much as she had. He had the eyes of a lost boy.

That was it.

He's lost. Just like me.

Amber knelt beside him and smiled to put him at ease.

"Hey, it's okay. You don't have to bow or anything." She doubted he could understand her words, but kept talking anyway, hoping her tone would get the message across. "I'm in the same boat as you. Lost and just trying to find my way home."

It seemed to be working. He listened intently and then, when she'd finished, he replied in his language again.

"*Gav dhymm, ny gonvedhav. Ple'th os ta trigys? A wodhes'ta kewsel Brydaineg?*"

Amber shrugged and smiled.

He tried again.

"Loquerisne linguam Romani? Latinam?"

To her surprise, Amber picked up on a couple of familiar words.

"Oh! Roman! Latin! You can speak Latin?"

"Evax! Sic, paululum linguae Latinae dico!" A happy burst of more Latin followed. Amber struggled to remember any of what she'd learned in college, and drew a total blank. She held up her hands.

"Wait, wait, I'm so sorry, but I can't speak Latin. No parley Roman, um, nolo habla Romano."

He frowned in confusion.

"Oh, wait," Amber said with sudden inspiration. *"Expecto Patronum! Expelliarmus! Riddikulus! Horcrux!"*

He held up his hands, laughing. *"Eho, eho, nullo intellego! Nullo intellego!"*

She began laughing as well. It felt amazingly good to be laughing again, as if some horrible crust of fear and sadness had covered her, and had cracked so that a little bit of happiness and relief came pouring out. The two of them sat there in the light of her scepter and let the simple joy of a stress-free moment roll over them, each one's laughter making the other laugh even harder.

Finally it subsided. He smiled at her.

"Riddikulus."

They burst into laughter all over again.

When she had to stop because her sides were aching,

Amber wiped the tears from her eyes and composed herself.

"Okay, let's try something else." She patted her chest. "My name is—I am Amber. Amber. Understand?"

He nodded.

"Am-ber."

Her eyes lit up.

"Yes! I'm Amber! That's me! Now you."

She poked him in his chest.

He seemed to understand. He patted his own chest.

"Ego sum Camtargarus Mab Cattus sum Trinovanti."

He saw her confusion and tried again.

"Cam. Ego sum... Cam."

She smiled shyly.

"Hi, Cam."

19

Cam seemed afraid to go back the direction he came, so Amber followed him along a different route than either of them had been following. She felt at ease with him in a way she hadn't with Blake. It was strange. Even with the language barrier, she felt she could trust him. He seemed genuine—and he *hadn't* killed her when he'd had the chance.

Am I being an idiot? she wondered. *Just trading one lunatic for another?* The more she thought about it, though, the less that seemed likely. For now, she figured she'd go with her instincts, and hope they didn't get her throat cut.

She used her flashlight to illuminate their way as they walked. Its steady blue-white light amazed him. He flinched when she pointed the ray of light near him, so she ran her hand through it to show him it was harmless.

After a moment Cam tentatively put his hand through the beam, laughing in relief when it didn't turn him into a toad, or carve him up like a lightsaber.

Eventually they came to an overhang on the ridge. Moss coated the rock on the underside, which formed a natural hollow that offered protection from the chill wind. Cam spread his cloak out on the bracken, and Amber pulled out her two blankets. The two lay close to each other, not quite touching, and Amber almost immediately fell asleep.

Cam lay awake, listening to the slow, rhythmic sound of the woman's... Amber's... breathing. He marveled at her. For a goddess she was curiously vulnerable and shy, and yet had amazing magical powers. Truth be told, he was no longer sure she was a goddess, though that didn't make her any less wondrous. Her hair the color of banked fire.

That shy smile...

Those green eyes.

He shook his head. She had to be of Sídhe blood, though thankfully she seemed free of the capricious malice the fair folk often possessed. Perhaps she was a druid princess from the Isle of Mona, or a lost nymph spirit.

She rolled over and curled up against him. Cam stiffened at first, then tried to relax as he realized she was still asleep, unconsciously seeking the warmth of his body like a child burrowing against its mother.

Surely the goddesses above would know he meant her no disrespect, and was not taking advantage of her. In his heart, he knew it too. He also knew he'd be a liar if he tried to pretend he didn't like the feeling of her curves against him, yet he did his best to squash his body's instinctual response.

Cam vowed to himself and all the gods that he would protect her, even as he drifted off into slumber.

No sooner had her eyes closed than Amber opened them again. She found herself in a beautiful Victorian library. Fine rosewood shelves lined with rare and precious leather-bound books ran from floor to ceiling, bracketed by Corinthian columns. Warm sunshine bathed the room through expansive skylights, while leaded-glass windows looked out on the grounds of an immaculate landscaped garden that stretched for miles.

Chamber music played softly.

Clad in an elegant Regency dress and sporting a parasol, she wandered past the shelves, admiring all the fabulous books. But she wasn't walking. Instead she was sitting, prim and proper, back once again in the punt, which—although split perfectly in half through the middle—still floated placidly down the library's plush carpet.

Gavin stood there, picnic basket in hand. Amber smiled, happy to see him.

"Might as well enjoy the moment, don't you think?" he said with that cheeky grin of his. The half-punt continued past, and he waved to her as she went by. Amber turned in her seat.

"Wait!"

"It's too late for it now," he said softly. "I'm done for."

She tried to get the boat to stop, but it continued merrily, merrily along as the library morphed into a hallway, still lined with books. Without paddle or pole, the punt glided past all the shelves, through a marble hall of busts and grandfather clocks, and right out into the garden.

The grounds had been landscaped with exquisite care into the shape of a giant jigsaw puzzle. The first pieces were normal-sized, each less than an inch wide, but the more she passed, the bigger they became. Soon, each individual piece was the size of a plate, and then the size of a pizza pan, big enough on which to hold a picnic. No matter how large they were, however, all the pieces together fit like a charm. Strangely enough, all of them seemed to come from completely different puzzles.

As the half-boat floated onward, the pieces grew larger and larger still—blanket-sized to swimming pool-sized to parking lot-sized. Her punt cruised along into a new puzzle piece—one she didn't much like—a dismal gray landscape crisscrossed with scorch marks and flecked with tiny fragments of black and white. Just a few yards in, her vessel abruptly ran aground on the delicate ashen crust. The sudden stop jolted her right out her seat and onto her feet. She found herself back in her Codex costume, Gavin's Han Solo jacket draped over her shoulders.

At her feet was a square stone hatch, fixed in the ground. It seemed familiar, and she passed one hand over it. A trio of bright colorful little symbols appeared, floating above its surface. The hatch slid open, revealing a ramp dimly lit by tiny blue firefly lights.

Déjà vu, Amber thought, descending the corridor into a dark inner chamber. There a spindle-shaped pillar awaited, hovering above the ground. It looked like an opaque obsidian carving. She could hear it hum, though it made no sound. As she approached, it almost seemed glad to see her, starting to slowly spin as an eerie, almost marine luminescence began to flicker to life in its depths.

So beautiful, Amber thought.

She wanted nothing more than to reach out and touch it.

So she did.

Her palms tingled as she brought her hands close to the slowly moving crystalline spindle. As they came to within an inch of its surface, the brightness streaming from the core of the object roared to life. What had been opaque became pure crystal, shining brighter than a lighthouse lantern.

Without warning the light engulfed her, trapping her in place. Her hair stood on end and arcs of violet-blue chain lightning crackled between the object and her fingertips. Her eyes rolled back in her head and her spine arched as the energy overload set off spasms throughout her body. She rose up on her toes, leg muscles straining from the surge, and then gravity abandoned her altogether.

The unrestrained energy pulses lifted her completely off the ground, suspending her helplessly in midair with arms outstretched like a crucified angel, while lightning played over her and crackled in chaotic waves.

Then, as suddenly as it began, it was over.

The outpouring of power drew back into the crystal spindle, and slowly her toes touched down on solid ground again. At that moment her whole body collapsed beneath her, and she slumped to the cold stone floor in a heap.

Wait, Amber thought, back in her fancy dress in the Victorian library. *That part wasn't a dream…*

She licked her thumb and flipped the parchment page of the oversized leather-bound folio. The next page was an old-fashioned woodcut, roughly carved and stylized like something out of a medieval manuscript.

The woodcut was of her, collapsed on the subterranean chamber floor. Abruptly it came to full-color life, and her eyes lit up as she watched herself rise from the floor and shake her head, collecting her staff again before returning up the ramp to the surface.

The Amber in the picture emerged from the hidden passage and strode off toward the horizon, leaving a trail of footprints in the ashen crust.

As Codex Amber departed, Victorian Amber turned the page.

CHAPTER XIII: ÆGYPT

This new page also had a woodcut illustration. It featured the Great Sphinx and a trio of pyramids beneath the moon and all the constellations of the Egyptian night sky. At the base of the colossal leonine statue, just front and center of its great limestone paws, stood a man wearing an inky black hooded robe. Given a big sickle and a skeletal head, he would make a perfect specter of Death.

As it was, she could just make out the hint of the man's face on the tiny figure. She proceeded to read the page's text.

Amber.
AmberAmberAmber.AmberAmberAmberAmber

**AmberAmberAmberAmberAmberAmber
AmberAmberAmber.Amber Amber.**

**Amber. Amber. Amber. Amber. Amber. Amber.
Amber. Amber. Amber. Amber. Amber. Amber.**

Amber. Amber. Amber.

Amber.

She frowned, then suppressed a laugh.

What is this?

The woodcut caught her attention again as it came to life, just like the other one. Clouds drifted past the moon. The man's black robe wafted gently. She read further. The words felt squirrely and ticklish on her eyeballs.

Eve ry th in gi s e ve ryt hi ng isev er yth in g ise ve ryt hin gisev ery thi ng is

The line of gibberish began to wiggle and dance.

Ever Yth in gise Very Thin gi Sever y Thing iSeve Rything iSeveryth Ingis

The words continued to mutate, slowly becoming more familiar, though still frustratingly cryptic.

Every thingise verythingiseverything iseverythingi-
severythingiseverythingis

B ro kenb roke nbro ken brokenbrok enbro kenbro
kenbr ok en bro kenbr oken

Bro Kenbro Kenb Rokenbr Oken Brokenbro Kenbro-
ken Brokenbroke Nbrok

Everythingisbrokeneverythingisbrokeneverythingis-
brokeneverythingisbrokenever

And then with one final twist, the jumble of mish-
mashed letters untangled.

Everything is broken.

She looked again at the picture. The scene had
zoomed in on the hooded figure beneath the Sphinx. She
resumed reading, and the text continued its stumbling
dance from gibberish toward clarity.

It' Shard It Shard It'shardi t'sh ard It'shar d it' shard
it's har dit'shar dit'sh ardit's ha rdit'shard itshardit'sh
ardit'shardit'shardit'shardit'shardit's

it's hard it's hard it's hard it's hard it's hard it's hard

To tal kthi swa ytota lkt his wayto tal kth iswa yto

She held her breath.

Total kthi Sway to ta lkth Is wa ytot Alk thi Swa ytotalkthiswaytotalkthiswaytotalkthiswaytotalkthiswayto

It's hard to talk this way.

Amber exhaled, and concentrated on making sense of the text.

**Idon thave mu chti meido n'tha vemu chti me
Ido N'tha Vemu Chti Me Id On'th Avem Ucht Ime
I Do N'thav Emu Ch Tim Eido N'th Avemuc Hti Me
Idon'thavemuchtimeidon'thavemuchtimeidon'thavem uchtimei**

**An dso mu cht os ay an dso muc htos ay
An Dsomu Chtos Ayan Dso Mu Chtos Ay
Andsomu Chtosay An Dsom Ucht Osay
Andsomuc htosayan dsomuchto sayand**

Idon'thavemuchtimeandsomuchtosay

I don't have much time and so much to say

Amber nodded to herself. *Okay, I think I'm getting the hang of this,* she thought, turning the page. Another archaic woodcut stared out at her—a close-up of the hooded face of the man below the Sphinx, his features still hidden in shadow.

Again there was dancing text.

i'lld ow ha ti canto hel py ou I'lld Owha Tican Tohel Pyou
I'lldowhati Cantoh Elpyou
I'lldowhaticantohelpyou

I'll do what I can to help you

bu tfir sty ouh ave tof ind meBu Tfi Rsty Ouh Avet of in Dme Bu Tfir styouh Avetof Indme

Butfirstyouhavetofindme

but first you have to find me

hel pmeam ber
Hel Pme Am Ber
Helpmeamber

Help me Amber

She gasped. The woodcut came to life right on cue, and the hooded man's eyes locked on hers. The rest of his face was still cloaked in shadow, but his eyes—

My god, his eyes!

The irises were a blue-violet so dark that the black holes of his pupils were lost in them. The most remarkable thing, however, wasn't their near-perfect blackness, but the hypnotic display playing out on their surface.

Infinitesimal pinpoints of white light streaked from the whites toward the center, and vanished there. Looking into his eyes was like watching a slow, steady cascade of stars falling down a well...

Help me Amber.

20

Amber woke up with a start, flashing on the image of a dark violet eye with a cascade of falling stars, so clear in her mind even as she shook the remaining cobwebs of sleep from her brain. She still lay on top of Cam's cloak, both blankets carefully tucked around her.

The space next to her was empty.

"Cam?"

Sitting up, she was careful not to smack her head on the rock. She stood and stepped away from the protective overhang, peering out into the misty morning. There was no sign of her new companion.

He wouldn't have left me, she told herself even as her heart rate sped up. *I mean, he left his cloak. He needs his cloak, right? He wouldn't just leave it behind.* Her breathing quickened and her heart pounded in her ears as panic started to settle in at the thought of being alone again.

Taking a deep breath, she forced herself to calm down.

He wouldn't leave me behind.

The panic attack backed off as quickly as it had begun. Amber took a few more deep breaths and then sat back down, digging into her backpack for a bottle of water. She found her hairbrush first, and decided this was as good a time as any to pull it out.

Brushing her hair felt deliciously indulgent. The bristles snagged painfully on numerous tangles, but she tackled each one slowly and methodically, pulling out twigs and leaves that had gotten caught in there, as well. The ritual soothed her. Finally her hair spread out over her shoulders in a smooth blanket. Quickly she braided it, then secured it with a scrunchie dug out of her backpack, heaving a small sigh of satisfaction.

The sound of a cough made her jump. She looked up to see Cam standing a few feet away, a dead rabbit slung over one shoulder, his arms filled with a bundle of firewood. He looked embarrassed, as if he'd seen her naked or something, and immediately turned away. Setting the wood and the rabbit down, he busied himself with building a fire.

What's got him so…?

Had she fallen out of her top?

Oh jeez.

She looked down at the dirty Han Solo jacket and her poor filthy Codex dress and corset underneath. Nope, everything was in place, tucked away where it should be—although the top did show a fair amount of mud-spattered cleavage.

Maybe that's it.

Cam woke with the dawn. He was hungry, wanted to go forage for breakfast, and knew that they would both need a solid meal to face whatever this new day might bring. He looked down at the young woman still deep in slumber next to him, face half buried under the blankets.

Should he wake her up?

No, he thought. *She needs her rest.*

Hesitating at the thought of leaving her alone, he decided that finding something for them to eat was worth the risk, as long as he didn't go too far. The outcropping did a good job of concealing their sleeping place. He knelt low and scanned the horizon for any potential trouble. There was no sign of any dragon like the one he had seen back in the strange forest, or of the herd of tri-horns that nearly stomped him to death. There was nothing visible larger than a red fox hunting field mice.

Taking care to stay within earshot, it took him no time at all to catch and dispatch a rabbit, and then forage some tender young hawthorn leaves and wild mushrooms. Last, he gathered the driest wood he could find to make a small fire to roast the rabbit, and then hurried back to the little hollow where they had passed the night. He moved with deliberate stealth, trying not to wake Amber if she was still sleeping.

When he reached the overhang she was awake, sitting cross-legged with the blanket spread out over her lap, slowly attending to her hair. She worked the brush from the scalp to the ends, her hair covering her shoulders in a mane of spun gold fire. He was transfixed. There was something so intimate about the moment that Cam felt as if he'd interrupted a private ritual. Waiting until she'd finished, he gave a deliberate cough to let her know he was there.

She jumped at the sound. Cam felt even more awkward for startling her, and immediately set about building the fire and skinning the rabbit. He felt a hand tap on his shoulder and turned to see her smiling at him.

"*Can I help?*" Amber gestured to the wood, then the rabbit, then to herself. Cam smiled back and shook his head, concentrating on drilling a sharpened branch into a chunk of deadwood. The overhang helped block the worst of the wind, but the gusts still made a challenge out of starting a fire.

The woman watched for a moment, then dug into her bag and pulled out a small box. She tapped on Cam's shoulder again, then scratched a small sliver of wood against the box. His eyes went wide as her magic produced a tiny flame.

A gust of wind blew it out immediately, so she pulled out a second sliver. This time Cam held up his hands around hers to protect the flame from the wind, trusting her to prevent him from being burned. Together, they brought the miraculous little flame down to the tinder, holding it steady until it caught.

He blew on the newborn fire, careful not to put it out, nurturing it into a small but respectable blaze. Then he looked at the little box and grinned at Amber, nodding his approval.

Oh my god, Amber thought, *I'm so glad he's not one of those guys with something to prove.* Her brother would have insisted on starting the fire from scratch, just to prove that nature wasn't the boss of him.

Cam finished skinning and dressing the rabbit, putting the sharpened stick through it and propping it up to cook above the fire. He offered her a handful of mushrooms wrapped in little green leaves, then mimed her eating them, and she gingerly took a bite. They weren't bad.

She rummaged through her backpack to see what else she could contribute to their meal. She pulled out her last bottled water, a can of orange soda, a small bag of chips, and a Cadbury Dairy Milk bar. Opening the chips, she ate one before offering him the bag, just to show they were edible. He nibbled cautiously at first, a look of surprise spreading across his features, then devoured as many of them as she offered. She popped the soda can tab, and Cam jumped.

Amber covered up a laugh by taking a sip.

"Oooh, boy. This is gonna give us both a sugar rush." She held the can out to Cam.

He took it somewhat warily, looking both impressed and suspicious. He sniffed the opening, then took a cautious sip. He wrinkled his nose, and seemed to think about it for a long moment. Then he took another obviously polite sip before handing it back to her.

Okay, maybe that was a bit too much for him. Amber set it down, figuring she'd save the water for after the meal. As she did he retrieved the rabbit from the fire, and she steeled herself.

Any squeamishness she had over eating a cute little bunny quickly faded once they started digging in. The meat was fresh and melted in her mouth. She had never felt like such an enthusiastic carnivore before. Afterward she pulled out the chocolate bar, and she doled out each square with great ceremony. Cautious at first, he was sold after the first bite, apparently liking it even more than he did the addictive potato chips.

When their grand feast was finally over, they wiped their hands clean on the dewy grass. Cam lay back, hands clasped behind his head while Amber, on a whim, pulled out her cell phone.

Her iPhone had a burgundy protective case on it, which meant it was relatively indestructible, even if dunked in water. So far it had survived a lot more than that. She hit the power button.

No bars and only thirty percent battery life left. She had a charger cord, but when would she ever find a place to plug it in again? She pulled up her photos anyway, knowing she should save what little juice remained, but unable to resist the comfort of seeing her family and friends, even if just through pictures.

Cam shifted position, moving closer to her to cast an inquiring look. Then he reached out and touched her cheek with one gentle finger, wiping a tear that had seeped out without Amber realizing she'd even been crying.

"Crap." She gave a shaky laugh and brushed a few more errant tears away before they could fall. Then Cam said something she couldn't understand, pointing to her phone. He stared with wide eyes at the pictures on the screen.

"My parents," she said. She tried to think of the word for "parents" in Latin. *All my Latin comes from Harry Potter*, she thought sheepishly, but then a few words came to her.

"My *alma mater* and *pater*. Is that right?"

He nodded, and pointed to them.

"*Matrem tuum et patrem.*"

She nodded back and scrolled through the photos.

"And my brother and sister. My um… fraternity and sorority. My best friend Amy." Lots of pictures of her and Amy in various costumes at Comic-Con. Cam was spellbound by every image.

"My cats. And—"

She stopped.

The last pictures she'd taken were from ImagiAnimeCon. The very last picture on the roll was a selfie of her and Gavin, the river and the punt behind them. They were smiling. Happy.

"Oh," Amber said in a very small voice. She swallowed hard, choking back a wave of grief she couldn't afford to indulge in right now. Not just for Gavin, but for life as she'd known it. Even if she could charge her phone somewhere, somehow, the world she had known was gone.

The Internet? Gone.

Electricity? Gone.

Everything?

Just gone.

Cam put a hand on her arm, his brown eyes warm and concerned. She swallowed again, swiping stray tears away from her eyes.

"I'm okay," she said with a feeble attempt at a smile. He looked down, lost in thought for a moment, then brightened.

"*Dicite mihi de te. Unde venistis?*"

Amber shrugged her shoulders, completely mystified by the question. He pointed all around them, and then pointed to her.

"*Ubi in mundo?*"

Amber felt terrible. She had no idea what he was trying to ask her. Frustrated, he furrowed his brow and then had another idea. He knelt down and smoothed out a spot of dry ground. Then he traced a circle in the dirt.

"*Hic est totius mundi.*" He looked up and gestured broadly around them, encompassing everything.

"Oh! The world." She nodded. "Yes, I understand. Okay, *mundi*, the world." She swept her arms out to indicate that she got it. Encouraged, he grinned and drew an irregular, roundish blob shape in the center. She was baffled yet again.

"*Hic Mare Mediterraneum.*"

"Ah, alright. That's the Mediterranean Sea." She made a wavy motion with her hand. He nodded, and drew a little squiggle in the center of that.

"*Roma.*" She nodded again. He indicated three broad regions surrounding the blob like slices of pie.

"*Hic Africa, hic Asia, hic Europa.*"

She smiled and nodded. It didn't look like any world map she'd ever seen or drawn, but she recognized nearly all the places he pointed out—*Libya* and *Aegyptus*, *Arabia* and *Anatolia*, *Germania* and *Gaul*, and to the far north of his circle, *Ultima Thule*. Well, she recognized *almost* all of them. She had no idea where or what *Ultima Thule* was supposed to be.

Last he drew two more little kidney shapes on the left-hand side of the circle's outer rim, which he identified as *Ériu* and *Pritan*.

No idea. Amber shook her head.

"*Hibernia et Britannia*?" He patted the ground. "*Hic sumus, Britannia.*"

"Britannia! Right. We're in Great Britain, yes!"

Cam grinned in satisfaction and continued. He pointed out *Londinium*, and drew a line to represent *Tamesas*, the Dark River, flowing out from it to the sea.

"London… the Thames… okay." Amber smiled, encouraging him.

He patted his chest. "*Trinovantus sum.*" He waved his hand over the area east of London and the Thames.

"*Haec est mea patria. Terra Trinovantes.*" He put a finger at a point by the sea.

"*Camulodunum. Mea patria.*" He patted his heart again.

"*Camulodunum…*" She repeated the strange word. She had no idea where *Camulodunum* was, but she understood what it meant to Cam. He was trying to get back there. She nodded.

"It's your home."

Cam nodded. "Home." Then he reached out and touched her chest with his finger. "*Unde es? Ubi est patria tuam?*"

"Where's my home? Um..." She looked at his map, unsure how to tell him her home lay far off the chart.

Amber pointed to their location, and dragged her finger westward, past Londinium, past the isles of Britannia and Ériu, and out into the rim of the World Ocean which ringed everything. She frowned, drawing a line from beyond the Pillars of Hercules to a point far, far off the map. She looked up at him, and waved her hand over the area.

"*Atlantic Ocean. America. California.*" She patted her heart. "*San Diego.*"

Cam's eyes went wide with surprise, and after a moment he nodded. Even though he could only make out part of what she had said, he understood completely— and it explained much.

Amber was from Atlantis.

21

Amber wasn't sure how much Cam had understood when she'd tried explaining her home to him, but he'd seemed satisfied. Having gone as far as they could with sign language and bastardized Latin, the two packed up and set off to try and find Cam's home, if it still existed.

It was as good an idea as Blake's notion of Whitehall, she thought. She didn't really have any better suggestions to offer, no desire to set off on her own again. Being with Cam made her feel less of a Hufflepuff and more of a Gryffindor, both safer and braver at the same time.

They continued together without incident for the rest of the day, only slowing down when the sun started to set. They didn't need to discuss the idea—both understood all too well the need to find some kind of shelter. Ahead lay a small stand of birch and oak and other native trees Amber didn't recognize.

Cam led her to one of the bigger oaks and let her sit and rest while he set to work cutting branches from the nearby birch trees. Once he had a thick armful of branches and saplings, he started to assemble a lean-to against an arm of the big oak. When he began to gather bracken and leafy branches, Amber joined in, too. Soon they had enough to fill out the walls and cushion the floor of their makeshift shelter.

Amber made a pillow of her backpack and lay down, feeling at ease with her companion. He removed his cloak and gently laid it over her, then sat Indian style, watching out of the lean-to for trouble. Stray gleams of moonlight illuminated his face, and after a time she reached over and touched him softly on his back. He turned, gave a weary smile, and lay down beside her. She pulled the cloak over the two of them.

In the near dark, he turned to her.

"*Nos dha*, Amber. *Bonam noctem.*"

"Good night, Cam."

He rolled over, away from her, and she curled up snug against the warmth of his back. In a matter of moments, both were sound asleep.

Back home in San Diego, she ran down her street as fast as she could. No matter how quickly she ran, she wasn't tired. She took longer and longer strides, and suddenly remembered that she knew how to turn off gravity. Her running leaps grew longer and longer, until she flew in the warm sunshine over all the houses and yards.

Soon she was sailing so high that her fear of heights kicked in, so when she saw a door in the sky, she banked over and opened it. The chamber inside was made of glass, giving a brilliant view of the bright sunlit clouds.

An invisible man waited for her. She couldn't see him, but she knew he was there all the same.

"Amber, you need to come find me," his voice whispered in her ear. She spun around in confusion.

"Where are you? I can't see you."

"You will. You need to come find me. Help me, Amber. Before it's too late."

"But where are you?"

"Here."

The world beneath them blurred past until the room in the sky hovered over the Great Pyramids. Far below there was a tiny figure standing between the paws of the Sphinx. He held up his hand, and suddenly she was staring into his eyes—those blue-violet pools with their endless cascade of tiny pinpoint stars falling down into darkness...

The stars pulled her down with them, and then the darkness transformed into bright light—great balls of dancing brilliance swirling all around her. It was so beautiful, so—

* * *

Harsh shouts and barking dogs tore her from her dream. Amber sat up in confusion, only to be blinded by bright lights shining directly in her face. She held up her hands to shield her eyes.

"Am-ber!"

The sound of Cam's voice shredded away the rest of the cobwebs.

"Cam?"

The roof of their shelter crumpled beneath repeated blows even as rough hands seized her, yanking her to her feet and nearly jerking her arms out of their sockets.

22

Bound with coarse ropes around their necks and with their wrists lashed together, the prisoners were marched through the darkness. Amber felt strangely detached from the situation, most likely in shock and total denial. Yet another part of her mind fought to stay calm and alert. She was pleased to see that Cam was keeping his cool, as well, despite the ugly bruise rising on the left side of his face.

She blamed herself for that bruise. When she demanded to know where they were going, the soldier holding her leash had started to backhand her. Cam had gone near crazy at that, almost ripping the rope tether from the hands of the soldier leading him. Three more soldiers immediately leapt in to restrain him. Even then, he'd only stopped fighting when Amber, fearing for his safety, called his name and shook her head.

Their captors were right out of a Rembrandt painting. Some had muskets, others had pikes, all had swords. They wore red coats, steel breastplates and helmets that made her think of riot cops or Spanish conquistadors, but this bunch spoke English—an old-timey Shakespearean kind of English. Not that they spoke very much.

Amber was enough of a geek to recognize that they weren't from Ye Olde Elizabethan Renaissance Faire times, but a century or so later. From what little they *did* say, she gleaned that they were troops from the English Civil War—the ones on Oliver Cromwell's side.

What were his guys called again? It was just on the edge of her thoughts. *Oh yeah, Roundheads.* She wished she knew more about them, but military history wasn't her strong suit, nor was this particular time period. She'd dug into the Victorian era because of the whole steampunk esthetic. Buff coats and breeches didn't do so much for her.

Nor could she recall if the Roundheads were Catholic or Protestant, but whichever it was, she knew they took their religion dead serious—although maybe not so much the "love thy neighbor" parts. They were superstitious, too. She filed away that fact for possible use later.

None of the soldiers would speak or make eye contact with her, and they carried her backpack on a pike as if it were radioactive. Even unlit, they didn't dare lay a hand on her dorky cosplay scepter. They transported it on a

219

jury-rigged stretcher as if it were the Ark of the Covenant.

Shortly after the sun rose they came to a stone road. The design seemed ancient, but the road looked brand new. They moved along the road and, before long, the stones turned into a modern two-lane blacktop, complete with dotted lines, highway signs, and the occasional scrap of litter cluttering the side of the road. Amber stared at a crumpled McDonald's bag and crushed soda can. The sight brought a rush of emotions for reasons she didn't dare try to figure out right then.

Something brushed her arm and she glanced up to see Cam at her side, sympathy and concern clear in those expressive brown eyes.

"None of that, you!"

The guard leading her tugged hard on the rope, causing her to stumble and nearly fall. Cam gave a low growl deep in his throat. Out of the corner of her eye, Amber saw his muscles bunch up, tensing.

"Cam, no!" she hissed. As much as she appreciated his anger on her behalf, it wouldn't help if he got himself killed trying to protect her. He subsided, but she could tell it cost him some effort to do so.

The highway and terrain around them continued to change as they marched on. Sometimes the road was no more than a narrow footpath. Other times it disappeared altogether, so they just stuck to the direction it had been going. After a while, however, it became a wide horse-trod dirt road, and stayed that way for the last hour of their journey.

Finally, they arrived at a rise topped by a great old oak. One thick branch lurched out to the side like a massive arm, a perfect anchor for all the ropes tied there.

It was a hanging tree.

The sight of the gallows tree in front of them gave Cam a cold, hard knot in his stomach. He didn't think he and Amber were going to be hanged. At least not right away—a squad of soldiers were currently readying another trio of prisoners for that fate.

Two were bearded warriors of Skandia, who silently regarded them with grim eyes the steely color of Arctic Sea ice. Cam gave the Northmen a short, quick nod of respect. He knew of the tribes beyond the Mór-Maru, the cold Sea of Death to the east. From the look of them, they hadn't been taken prisoner without making their foes pay a heavy price for it, in blood.

A pair of soldiers cursed while they strong-armed the third condemned man toward the tree. A wild-eyed shaggy-headed savage who struggled and howled unintelligibly like a trapped animal, he was barefoot, dirty, and near-naked, dressed only in stinking, ragged furs. Cam had no idea where he'd come from, but still felt pity for the wildling.

* * *

Amber stared at the prisoner's thick brow and janky overbite. With a shock, it hit her that he was some kind of Neanderthal, a real-life caveman. Her head swam at the realization.

The echoes of his primitive shrieks haunted Amber as she and Cam were led away down into the town—a Ren Faire-ready country village of quaint thatched cottages nestled at a crossroads. The intersection was dominated by a stone church. A handful of anxious villagers hurried here and there, but for the most part the town was populated by an army of Roundheads. Horsemen and knots of soldiers moved along the earthen streets, and the commons were covered with row after row of drab army tents.

She noticed four heavy rugged timber posts standing close by, and more gibbets lined the south side of the main drag. The bodies of Royalist officers dangled from them, swollen tongues protruding from slack lips. Beyond this gruesome display, a large stockade had been erected in the fields. Inside, scores of Cavalier prisoners under heavy guard awaited their unknown fate, exposed to the elements with no shelter, blankets, or fires to warm them.

The squad that held Cam and Amber waited at the crossroads while their corporal spoke to an officer. Amber looked from the line of hanging corpses to the glum captives huddled inside the stockade. The idea of joining them in there alarmed her—she could hear more than one rattling, phlegm-filled cough.

The corporal returned.

"Take them up top," he ordered. "Master Stearne shall wish to attend to them."

The soldiers started moving again and led them over to the church. They didn't enter the sanctuary, but went straight into the tall bell tower, marching Cam and Amber single file up the stone steps, which wound their way to a narrow landing. There two uneasy Roundhead soldiers stood guard in front of a heavy wooden door.

One of the guards gave the newcomers a sour look, licked his lips, and then fished out a heavy brass key from his pocket to unlock the thick door. Amber noticed that someone had recently taken the trouble to nail four horseshoes to the wood in the form of a clover shape—or maybe a cross. The door opened onto another series of steps leading to the very top.

"Against the walls!" the corporal called out. After a brief pause he stomped up the steps. The soldiers pushed Amber and Cam, and they started up after him.

Originally the church belfry, the topmost chamber now served as a jail cell. It was a smallish circular room, about ten feet in diameter, and—despite the corporal's orders—didn't have much to offer in the way of real walls. A single waist-high rim ringed the chamber, while four thick stone columns supported the bell tower's peaked steeple. Otherwise the room was open to the elements, and offered a view in all four directions. In one direction Amber could see smoke rising above the trees.

There were three other prisoners already there— four if she counted the body lying on the floor. At the sight of it, she gasped. It was covered by a bright yellow raincoat that acted as a shroud, with the word "POLICE" stenciled in big block letters on the back. The corporal regarded the prone figure with a dispassionate glance, then turned to the others.

"Two more to keep you company," he announced, and he jerked his head toward Cam and Amber. A soldier cut Amber free from her bonds, and then turned to Cam.

"Put him in irons," the corporal ordered. "He's apt to be more of a handful than the rest, I reckon."

His men complied, shackling Cam's wrists together with a pair of manacles. That done, they clambered down the steps, slamming the oak door shut behind them. The moment they were gone, Amber stepped over to Cam's side and gave him a reassuring hug before they both turned to face their three new cellmates, all of whom stared back with equal curiosity.

The first was a tall, lanky, distinguished-looking gentleman in a black frock coat, waistcoat and top hat. He was somewhere in his mid to late forties and reminded Amber of a fox in human form, down to his sharp features and russet-colored hair and sideburns.

She wasn't quite sure what to make of him. He reminded her of someone from an Arthur Conan Doyle story, but didn't seem heroic enough to be a Sherlock Holmes, nor sinister enough to be a Moriarty.

Next was a sharp-eyed, dark-haired British policewoman, attractive in a no-nonsense way. Maybe late twenties or early thirties. She wore a short-sleeve white shirt with a checkered kerchief, a black skirt and a black bowler hat with a checkered sash and badge.

Last was a young man in his twenties with tousled brown hair wearing a smirk and what had been a truly elegant outfit. Judging from the state of their clothes, all of them had been through a rough couple of days, and yet he still managed to look snappy in a charcoal-gray long coat with black velvet collar, worn over a waistcoat and tie, with tight drainpipe trousers. His outfit was Edwardian, but his attitude was pure rock and roll.

He lowered his shades to peer at them with a wry grin.

"Well, hello, hello, hello," he said in an affected posh accent. "Welcome to the witch house."

Seeing the others in their more or less modern dress clothes, Amber suddenly felt self-conscious in her costume and muddied high-tops. She rubbed her arms and cleared her throat.

"Hi. I'm Amber, Amber Richardson, and this is Cam," she said, gesturing. "He doesn't speak English."

Cam, meanwhile, stared at the others, wearing a frown as if trying to decide whether they were friends or enemies. Noticing that Amber seemed at ease with them, he relaxed a bit after a moment, but continued to glance suspiciously at the young Edwardian in particular.

The older man looked them over with an incredulous expression.

"Curiouser and curiouser! Well now, do we have an American girl joining us? A circus performer to boot, by the look of you."

He turned to Cam and raised an eyebrow.

"And a howling barbarian. Judging from his torc and plaid, I daresay your friend must needs be an ancient Celtic Briton. One of Queen Boadicea's chaps, perhaps. Wherever did you find him?"

The policewoman frowned at the older man and extended her hand.

"Please excuse the professor's lack of manners, Amber," she said. "I'm Police Constable Alex Brice. In here, though, I think just Alex is fine."

Amber shook the policewoman's hand, and Cam followed her lead, despite the manacles on his wrists. Not to be outdone, the professor regained his composure and doffed his hat to them, adding a slight bow.

"A thousand pardons. Professor Winston Harcourt, at your service."

The younger man just grinned, seeming to enjoy the

mutual displays of social awkwardness. He removed his sunglasses and bowed low with an overly ornate, swirling salute fit for Marie Antoinette.

"His imperial majesty Lord Simon William Albert Edward George Broad of East End, Cosh Boy, defender of the faith, protector of the commonwealth, and your most humble servant." He straightened up again and flashed another mocking grin. "But in here, I think just Simon is fine."

Cam started to return the bow, but Amber grabbed him before he'd completed the gesture. He looked at her, his expression confused. It darkened when Simon snickered.

Constable Brice—Alex—shook her head.

"You'll want to take his imperial majesty here with a pinch of salt, I'm afraid. We've only been in here since yesterday, and we're all pretty much ready to kill him." Simon's grin widened. She ignored it and looked at Amber and Cam with concern. "Are you two alright? Do you need any medical attention?"

"We're okay," Amber replied, grateful for the concern. "I mean, it's been a crazy couple of days, and we're pretty freaking far from okay, but we don't have any major injuries or anything. We're just pretty beat up." Her stomach growled. "And hungry."

"We're all hungry about now," Alex said with a wry smile. "They haven't been in any hurry to feed us, or even give us water. I don't suppose you have any information about what's happened, do you?"

Amber shook her head. "I was *really* hoping you guys might know what's going on. I mean, seriously, *what is going on?*"

Alex took a sharp breath before answering.

"Well, that's the thing, isn't it? It's hard to wrap our heads around it, but as far as we can tell—" She shook her head before continuing. "—it's utterly unprecedented. And for all we know, it's happened worldwide, as well."

Professor Harcourt cleared his throat.

"Indeed," he said, "and most understated. Were I not a man of science, suffice to say I might be tempted to suggest that Judgment Day has arrived, and all the souls from throughout the ages have been summoned to appear before the Almighty." He paused, then added, "Whether it involves a deity or not, there can be no doubt that some dreadful cataclysm has struck, every bit as powerful as the inescapable forces that long ago sank the continents Atlantis and Lemuria."

You've got to be kidding, Amber thought.

"Perhaps they've risen again, through some powerful method unknown to us," he continued. "For that matter, who can say that this isn't an attack upon our planet by the inhabitants of some other celestial body? Or more likely, the planets and stars have aligned in some cosmic configuration that has unintentionally concentrated its energies upon our hapless world. Whatever the proximate causation, this unparalleled and extraordinary calamity has thrown the very procession of time itself into disruption."

Simon leaned against the closest column and folded his arms.

"No disrespect to your worthy Atlantis or little-green-men-from-Mars theories, Doctor, but it seems more likely that some eggheady lot went mucking about with some daft new atom-splitting scheme, and things got out of hand. Now the entire planet's gone tits up, and we're left to pick up the pieces."

Harcourt turned on him with an affronted glare.

"See here, you impudent reprobate! There are members of the fairer sex present, and I won't stand idly by while you offend their gentle sensibilities. So curtail your vulgarity and spare us your boorish behavior and wretchedly ignorant pseudo-scientific nonsense before I am obliged to box your ears like the unruly schoolboy you are!"

Simon leaned in and went head to head with the professor.

"I wouldn't fancy your chances, mate," he growled. "I may not have my flick-knife, but I can still lay the likes of you right out."

Cam bristled, reacting to the hostile tones. Worried he might try to jump in, Amber put a hand on his arm and shook her head. Meanwhile Alex stepped over to intervene, sounding more like an exasperated school teacher than an angry cop.

"Look, that's enough from the two of you," she snapped. "You're both insufferable." She pointed a finger at Harcourt. "*You* with your bloody arrogance! And *you*—" She turned on Simon next. "You with your incessant wisecracks." She shook her head in exasperation. "For all your smart-arse load of bollocks, I know you're both just as scared as the rest of us."

Harcourt sniffed and tugged on his coat sleeves. Simon resumed slouching against his column like an offended alley cat, pretending nothing had just happened. Alex gave them both a warning glare, and then continued.

"But you're quite right, Professor," she said. "We've got a very serious situation here." She fell silent for a moment, cocked her head, and shot Simon a sideways glance. "Come to think of it, in the short time I've known you, that may be the closest you've come to saying something sensible."

He just gave a sullen shrug.

Amber took the opportunity to jump in.

"Look, I hope this isn't a silly question, but I really want to ask you all—" She stopped, shaking her head. "God, I'm not even sure how to ask it, but, well… what year *is* it now?"

The professor frowned.

"To be perfectly honest, that question posed much

less difficulty three days ago, before matters became quite so… shambolic."

Amber nodded sympathetically. "I totally understand, but can you at least tell what the date was for you before everything happened?"

"Certainly," he replied. "The morning of the twenty-first of November, 1889."

Amber turned to Simon.

"What about you?"

"The eve of Guy Fawkes Night, 1956," he replied with another of his cocky grins. "It was a good night."

"And you, Alex?"

"April the seventeenth, 1985," the police constable answered. "I'm guessing that's fairly close to your time, too?"

"Actually," Amber said, "I'm from 2016."

The others stared at her with a new appreciation. Simon whistled softly. Even the cool, pragmatic constable gave her a look of surprise before catching herself with a chuckle.

"The twenty-first century! I know that's only thirty years away, but it still sounds so futuristic when I say it out loud."

Amber gave a rueful smile. "It seems awfully far away from here right now. I feel like Dorothy trying to get home to Kansas."

"Would we were in Oz," Simon muttered.

"Where exactly are we?"

"Well," Alex said, "as far as I've been able to tell, we're in the county of Essex. To be exact, we're in the quaint little hamlet of Lexden, just down the road a bit from Colchester." She pointed out a column of smoke rising slowly above battered city walls, a mile or two away, "Which our charming hosts have been in the process of attacking."

"These soldiers are—they're called Roundheads, right?" Amber looked out over the wall at the army below. "Oliver Cromwell's men?"

"Full marks, American girl," Harcourt said with more than a little condescension. "However, Cromwell isn't in charge as yet. Currently he's still the second-in-command to Lord Fairfax—at least as far as they are concerned. But yes, they're the Parliamentarian army, and they've been laying siege to the Cavaliers inside there." He pointed toward Colchester. "Those are the Royalists who still support King Charles I."

Amber leaned further out to get a better look.

"Careful now, Red," Simon cautioned. "Don't stick your head out too far. If they catch you watching them, they throw nasty things at you. Like musket balls."

She pulled back, turned, and noticed that Cam had taken a seat with his back to the wall, Indian style, and commenced trying to slip out of his manacles, without success. Simon turned to watch his painful lack of progress with an annoying Cheshire Cat grin. Cam glared back at Simon, then pointedly ignored him.

"At present," the professor said with a self-important air, "—if one can still employ the term with any meaning—it seems we are looking at the siege of Colchester, which means this is the summer of the year 1648, and the Second English Civil War is on. Or at least it was until poor Father Time went completely senile and scattered the pages of the calendar to Hades and back. Now time is more a matter of geography than chronology, I'm afraid. Go a few miles down the road, and who can say what year it will be."

Pompous but accurate, Amber thought.

Alex nodded. "Right. From what we can tell, this super storm, or whatever it was, destroyed parts of Colchester's outer walls, but also took away a great deal of the Roundheads' army. A few more seem to have run into some sort of dinosaurs, so now the fight's a little more evenly matched than it was in the history books."

"Is that good news or bad news?" Amber asked.

"To be perfectly dispassionate," Harcourt mused, "the political consequences of the Puritan revolution would arguably lead one to declare it was not only morally justified, but ironically, laid the foundations for England's rise to greatness as the world's most glorious imperial power."

Alex rolled her eyes.

"Well, be that as it may," she said, "*I'm* going to root for the side that isn't keeping us in custody."

"A pox on both their houses," Simon chimed in.

"Why *do* they have us locked up?" Amber asked. "What do they have against us? We don't have anything to do with their stupid war."

"They think we're witches, of course." Alex raised an eyebrow. "They've decided that *we're* the ones responsible for this whole wonky time business."

23

A cold knot tightened in Amber's belly, and she slid down against the wall, wrapping her arms around her legs.

"But this isn't much of a jail, is it?" she said, trying to regain her equilibrium. "I mean, wouldn't they have us chained up in a dungeon somewhere, if that's what they thought?"

Alex gave a rueful smile. "I'm sure there's a perfectly horrible dungeon in the cellar of Colchester Castle. Fortunately for us, this belfry tower is the strongest confinement our little village here could offer. To begin with, it's one of the few places built with proper brick, and not thatch. Otherwise, we'd probably be out in the cow fields with the Royalist prisoners, catching whatever dreaded lurgy those poor bastards have."

"I guess we should just be glad nobody's going after us with hot pokers," Amber joked nervously. No one laughed. The others stared in silence. Cam looked up from his labors, sensing the sudden tension in the room.

"You don't really think they'll..." Amber's voice trailed away. "Do you? They wouldn't..."

"Why don't you ask him?" Simon jerked his thumb toward the body covered by Alex's raincoat.

"That's not very funny," Alex said crisply.

"I'd never joke about torture." Simon's voice suddenly went serious. "That's coming soon enough."

Amber paled.

"Shut it, Simon!" Alex hissed. "You're not helping."

The policewoman went over and knelt down to Amber's level, putting a hand on her knee and speaking gently.

"Hey," she said. "Listen to me carefully, Amber. I need you to be strong right now. We all need to be strong, and not give up. I'm not going to lie to you. We're in quite a serious situation, so let's stay sharp, yeah? I doubt we can reason our way out of this, so our first priority is finding another way out of here. Understand?"

Amber heaved a shuddering sigh, looked up and nodded.

Alex smiled. "Right. Good girl."

She offered her hand and helped Amber to her feet again. Cam gave up his painful attempts at slipping out of the shackles, which had only resulted in angry red scrapes on his wrists. He stretched the full length of the chain, as if testing it as a weapon. He looked over at Simon, and smiled.

"Well, gentlemen." Alex turned to the group. "Any thoughts on escape?"

The professor put on a thoughtful look and Simon chewed his knuckle. Amber risked another peek outside. It felt dangerously high, towering not just above the ground, but even the precariously steep church roof next door. The thought of scaling the tower was terrifying to her, but it seemed like their only hope.

"Do you think we could climb down the tower? It's awfully far to fall, but—"

Harcourt snorted in derision.

"That sort of acrobatics is all well and good for a flying trapeze artist like yourself, but I daresay the rest of us would be dashed to smithereens if we were to attempt such feckless folderol."

Alex nodded.

"I hate to say it," she responded, "but I think he's right. These slick walls would be near impossible to climb down. Though if we could manage to make a rope somehow, we might be able to pull it off. We'd have to wait until dark, though."

"Have we got enough clothes to make a rope that could hold our weight?" Simon asked. "Not that I much fancy making my way across the countryside in just my underpants. It might make for an interesting trip, though."

Amber pointed to the body under the wrap.

"What about his clothes?"

The others turned to look at the corpse, mulling over the idea. Harcourt appeared to be squeamish at the thought.

"What was his story?" Amber asked.

Alex shrugged.

"We didn't get much of a chance to hear it, I'm afraid. They caught him before any of us, and they'd already worked him over rather badly. He was in pretty rough shape."

"That, and he was barking mad to start with," Simon added.

Harcourt glared at him in disapproval.

"There is that," Alex agreed reluctantly. "He may have been schizophrenic. He certainly didn't make much sense…" She shot Simon a heated glance. "Let's see what you have to say when they're done with you."

"You'll get your chance, I'm sure."

"I'm sorry, Simon." Alex shook her head. "That was a terrible thing for me to say."

"Don't mention it," he replied with another of his shrugs. "It's a fair cop. Besides, I wasn't wandering the moors dressed up like Gandalf. No wonder the Roundheads nabbed the old blighter. If any of us look the part of a warlock, it's poor old Merlin there. Of *course* they roughed him up."

"For all we know, he *was* an enchanter," Alex said. "He never managed to tell us when his time was, or where he came from." She turned back to Amber and added, "That's why we called him Merlin. Not to his face, mind you."

"How did he die?" Amber asked.

"After they were done, they dragged the poor demented chap back up here and tossed him in with us," Harcourt said. "He fell asleep last night, and never woke from his slumber."

"Don't look at me to give him a eulogy," Simon said. "Barmy old codger gave me the creeps, what with all his muttering and those right peculiar eyes of his."

"Wait, what do you mean?" Amber's heart started racing. "What was wrong with his eyes?"

Simon raised an eyebrow. "Well, they were… it's a bit hard to explain, like."

"Was it the color?"

"Yeah, the color, and, well, they just had this odd gleam. Seemed sensitive about it. Didn't like making eye contact. Why?"

Abruptly Amber turned away and stepped over to the body, kneeling by its side. She reached out, then hesitated, her hand hovering uncertainly, before she gathered up her courage and slowly pulled the rain slicker down to uncover the dead man's face.

She gasped. It looked as if he had been tortured with

knives, branding irons, and perhaps a hammer. The left side of his forehead had suffered a horrible crushing wound, leaving a mess of coagulated blood and matted hair. For an instant Amber thought she would be sick, but she breathed through it and took another, closer look at him, focusing on details other than the horrific wounds.

He was wearing a sort of monk's robe made of a black fabric she didn't recognize. His skin had an almost bronze tint, and his features were such an odd mishmash of different ethnicities, it made it difficult to tell his race or nationality. But she recognized the face.

Her heart was beating so hard now she thought the others could hear it, too. She leaned in and gently touched him. Then she took a deep breath, and carefully opened the dead man's eyes.

They were exactly the same as they had been in her dream. A deep indigo color, with a slow, constant rain of myriad tiny pinpoints of light dropping away before her eyes, like stars tumbling down a well…

She knelt there, entranced by the vision. Finally, she turned to the others.

"He's not dead."

24

The other prisoners crowded around Merlin to see the miracle for themselves.

Alex crouched down next to Amber, looking at the prone man.

"Are you sure?"

Amber nodded. "I'm sure."

The constable went into action to check his vitals, feeling his wrist for a pulse. She placed first her fingertips, then her cheek against his face and chest to sense any trace of breathing. She shook her head.

"Still not getting any sign of respiration or a heartbeat." She examined his eyes carefully, then turned to Amber. "You're right, though. He must be in some form of a coma. His eyes are certainly responding to something, though I'll be damned if I know what it is." Alex looked down again, captivated by the play of brilliant tiny sparks across the surface. "I've never heard of anyone's eyes doing anything like *that*."

"How extraordinary," the professor marveled.

"He was cold as a cellar stone earlier." Alex placed her palm against the man's neck. "My god, he's so much warmer now—I don't know how that's possible, but there it is."

"He's a tough old bastard, our Merlin." Simon gave a reluctant nod in admiration. "Shall we take bets whether he pulls through?"

"Do shut up, Simon," Alex snapped.

"What?" he responded. "I salute the old bugger. Besides, just half a tick ago we all thought he was dead as mutton. Simple common fact." Alex opened her mouth to rebuke him, but Simon held up a finger and jerked his head toward the stairs.

"Sounds like company's coming. Better leave him be."

No sooner had the words left his mouth than they heard the sound of a key in the lock downstairs. Everyone cleared away from Merlin's body as the door below opened.

"Against the wall!" a guard ordered from below.

Amber expected a Roundhead soldier to march up the stairs. Instead, a young woman in shawl and bonnet appeared, hauling up two wooden buckets. She had a scarf wrapped around the lower half of her face, like a bandit, as if to avoid inhaling any contagious witchery.

"Oh no, it's that madwoman again," Harcourt muttered.

"Sweet Lord Jaysis preserve this goodly Christian woman from all harm and vexations of Satan!" she cried loudly. "Get ye back, underlings of evil, and eyes down, all of ye. I'll not suffer any to look upon me with the evil eye. Ye cannot ensorcel me with thy black arts!"

"Just be quick about it, woman," the jailer said from below. The peculiar woman hefted the buckets before the prisoners. One was empty, the other sloshed with water. She continued her high-volume rant, addressing the two newcomers.

"Hear now, ye workers of iniquity! My name is Nell Prudence, and I have two buckets. One is water for ye to drink—and be thankful of it, undeserving wretches. The other is empty, for ye to do thy filthy business, God save us." Nell carefully handed the water bucket to Amber. The other she abruptly thrust at Harcourt, who caught it in his gut with a pained and surprised grunt.

"Go on with ye now, get to it, just like before. They'll turn their backs."

She spun the hapless professor around and pushed him toward the other end of the chamber. He sputtered, trying to protest, but Simon came straight over and snatched the bucket away from him.

"Oh for fuck's sake, give us. I've been dying for a slash!"

He turned his back and proceeded to do just that. Amber and the others did their best to ignore the sounds as he began to fill the bucket.

Nell turned and regarded the rest of them with her hands on her hips, before finally settling her gaze on Amber. Then, with cool deliberation, the strange woman walked right up to the girl, uncomfortably close, and turned her head toward the stairs. She spoke loudly again.

"Nay, there's no gruel for the likes of ye! Think you to sup whilst honest Christians suffer?"

She turned back to Amber and winked. Then Nell put a hand on her own belly, and pulled out a small round loaf of coarse brown bread from under her shirt. She put a finger to her mouth and quickly handed it over.

"Take this now," she whispered.

Stunned, Amber just stared.

"Go on now," the woman insisted. "Just don't let them catch you with it."

Snapping out of her daze, Amber quickly knelt to stash the bread under the raincoat that covered Merlin. Nell leaned closer to the prisoners. "Listen. Don't do anything rash yet. They want to get information before they're finished with you, but I don't think they'll have a chance until tonight, and I'll do everything I can to get you out of here before then."

"Who *are* you?" Alex asked.

Nell shook her head.

"No time to explain now. Look, this is what—"

"Make haste with you, girl!" the jailer yelled up from the door. "What's the delay already?"

"Fie on you, sluggard!" she hollered back, her Olde English accent firmly back in place. "Surely ye don't want witch shite stinking up the holy church belfry now, do you? God be thanked they haven't pissed it up already!"

The jailer growled some unintelligible reply.

"Bad enough all the good folk be in the church praying, instead of tending to their chores," she continued. "Don't care if it *is* Doomsday, there's still work to be done!" Turning back to Alex and Amber, she pulled down the scarf from her face. Nell was even younger than she acted, maybe in her mid-twenties, with sea-green eyes and a determined, pretty face.

"The Royalist counterattacks are keeping them occupied," she said quietly, "so that's good news. If we're lucky, they'll be too busy to bring you before their witch hunter. His name is Stearne. He's trouble." She shot a glance at Merlin's still body. "I'm sorry about your friend."

Amber grabbed her arm.

"Thank you! But quick, how are you going to get us out?"

The young woman smiled.

"Why, with my witchcraft, of course!"

At that, she hurried back down the stairs and out of their sight. They heard the door slam and the lock click.

The prisoners stared at each other for a moment.

"Well," Alex said, "that's the first bit of good fortune we've had since we were tossed in here."

Professor Harcourt looked dubious. "How do we know we can trust her?"

"Do these fellows look like they train double agents?" Alex shot back.

Amber nodded. "She brought us food and water, and she's definitely not from around here, right?"

"You worry too much, old man." Simon made a lazy yet dismissive gesture with one hand.

"Don't start again, Simon." Alex gave him a quelling glare. He grinned back at her. Amber went back over to Merlin, and Cam joined her at the unconscious man's side.

"Maybe we could clean some of his wounds, now that we have some water," she said.

"Shame to waste good drinking water," Simon quipped.

The Celt leaned over the prone man and inspected his injuries. He scowled. Their captors had abused the older man shamefully—cuts, burns, and bruises all attested to that. When Cam lay his head against the man's chest, it took a long time for him to detect the faint heartbeat.

Next he examined the ugly wound on the side of the man's forehead. It was staved in as if he'd been struck with a war club—his skull looked to be cracked, though it was hard to tell under the sticky black-clotted mass of blood and hair.

Rising, he went to the bucket of water, conscious that Amber was eyeing him hopefully. He looked around for a piece of cloth, then turned his attention to his cloak. Before he could rip off a strip, though, the older woman stopped him and offered him the checkered cloth from around her neck.

He took it, and put a hand to his heart in thanks. Then he dipped it in the water, took it over to the stricken man, and set to work carefully cleaning the head wound, moving slowly and deliberately so as not to let his manacles get in the way of his ministrations.

Amber eased back down on the floor to rest her aching feet. Alex sat down next to her.

"I have to hand it to him," Alex noted, nodding toward Cam. "He's taking all this remarkably well, considering he's probably older than Jesus. Wouldn't you love to hear how *he* got here?"

"Mmmm, I reckon I can guess." Simon cocked his head to one side and put a finger to his head in a parody of deep thought. "He woke up one morning, crawled out of his cave and said, 'Blimey! Where's me precious rocks and bearskins? Did those Neanderthal types the next hill over nick 'em all?' And he's been meandering about looking for them ever since.

"No, strike that," he said, motioning toward Amber. "Ever since he laid eyes on her, he's been chasing after our Yankee bird here." He gave her an appreciative glance. "Not that I blame him, of course."

Amber flushed with embarrassment.

Harcourt crossed his arms and remained silent.

"Honestly, why do I bother?" Alex sighed and rubbed her brow.

Simon grinned. "Aw, don't be like that, Constable. Go on, tell us how *your* apocalypse started out."

Wary of playing his game, she tossed him a sidelong glance. Simon raised his eyebrows, trying to look innocent.

"Right," she said, giving in. "Well, why not? Not much to say, actually. I was driving through Dedham Vale on my way back into town. First there's a weird sound, maybe a siren, then there's a massive blast ahead of me—in all honesty, I thought the Russians had dropped the bomb on us—and before you can say 'Wham UK!' there's no road, and my patrol car's collided with a stand of poplars that wasn't there a moment before.

The front end is complete scrap, so I started walking through a howling wilderness. After a day or more our local historical society here scoops me up on one of their bloody patrols."

"That's not too far off from my story," Simon offered. "Our part of town got it so bad during the Blitz, I could scarcely tell anything was the matter when it all went tits up. Except then the rest of the world up and disappeared. Spent the next couple of days looking for something to eat and running from the odd dinosaur until I wound up too close to these parts. The welcoming committee nicked me, too."

"What about you, Professor?" Amber asked. She had a feeling she'd just invited one of Harcourt's long, rambling monologues, but even that was preferable to his current sullen silence. Besides, she welcomed anything that could take her mind off what might happen to them if Nell didn't make good her promise.

Harcourt brightened under Amber's encouraging smile.

"Mine is truly a tale worthy of Jules Verne," he began most grandly. "I had just commenced upon the first leg of my Continental lecture tour through the most distinguished cities and universities of Europe. I had secured passage on a first-class vessel leaving Folkestone Harbour. Nothing but the best, of course, as I'd been invited by the crème de la crème of society and academia…"

25

The clerk at the ticket window shook his head again.

"Sir, I don't wish to be rude, but to be perfectly frank, it makes no difference if you're the queen's own ambassador, and this the first leg of your diplomatic mission to the emperor of China," he said firmly. "If you want to cross the Channel, you'll buy a ticket for the ferry like the rest of the good folks here, or you can buy a ticket for the next train back to Southampton and charter a ship more to your liking. Begging your pardon, but unless you wish to walk or swim, those are your two choices. Now, which of those may I sell you this morning?"

Professor Winston Harcourt sputtered.

"But this is outrageous, man!" he exclaimed. "Are you telling me there is *no* first-class accommodation available whatsoever?"

The customers behind him in the queue responded before the clerk could.

"Did you not hear him the first seven times?"

"Come on, mate. It's bloody freezing out here!"

"Get on with it!"

Startled by the outbreak of mob unrest, the professor quickly purchased a ferry ticket, picked up his traveling case, and took his leave of the Harbour Station. The stone face of King Neptune, aloof on the wall above the ticket window, watched him depart while the irritated customers still waiting heaved a collective sigh of relief.

Exiting the building, Harcourt spotted a carefully printed white sign.

FOLKESTONE—BOULOGNE-SUR-MER

He made his way down the pier to where the ferry boat was waiting. The last few people were coming down the gangplank. Only after they'd disembarked would the waiting crowd be allowed to board. Professor Harcourt glumly handed over his ticket and joined the rabble, his visions of a comfortable and tastefully decorated private cabin rapidly evaporating.

They looked to be in for a rough crossing, he observed.

Ominous gray storm clouds roiled over the Channel and the wind was already brisk, blowing stray spatters of rain. His options for shelter were few. An uninviting cabin beneath the deck, close and musty-smelling, filled up quickly with most of the female passengers. Many brave souls dared the sky to do its worst, spreading out in chaise lounges or simply turning up their collars and thrusting hands into pockets to ride it out on deck.

There were luggage racks available, but the professor had no wish to let his case out of sight, so he kept it at his side as he claimed a spot on deck along the railing. His fellow sojourners were predominantly male, a mix of French and British, with a young and eager American couple at the railing, as well.

At last all the passengers were aboard. Lines were cast off, the horn sounded once, then again, and the steamship's twin screws pulled them away from the pier, and then propelled them on their way. Before long, the sea churned gray-green, and the wind blew bitterly cold. Harcourt clung to the bar with one hand and to his hat with the other, hoping to keep his footing on the rolling deck and to avoid seasickness. He kept his case clutched tightly between his feet.

Seagulls wheeled above the boat, taunting him with their rusty squawking. The gusts of rain blew in more frequently and the chill increased. The professor had no real experience in marine matters, and his fortitude wasn't usually tested so severely. In abject misery, he peered down at the case by his feet. His stomach wrestled with temptation… and lost.

Slowly and carefully, he bent down and opened the traveling case. Inside rested scores of small bottles containing his "Special Galvanic Nerve Elixir (*At last, Lightning in a Bottle!*)." The label on each bottle claimed it harnessed the new miracle-working power of pure electricity in liquid form as "a most surpassingly efficacious tonic for all manner of physical and cerebral ailments, complaints, and maladies, both common and exotic."

Breaking into his stock went against his own rules, but circumstances were dire. He desperately plucked one out and his cold, wet fingers struggled with the stopper. The boat pitched suddenly and the tiny bottle flew from his hand out into the churning waves below.

"Pissing damnation!" he swore explosively, nearly losing his top hat in the process. Recalling there were ladies present, he quickly added, "I mean, *dash* my wig!"

Bracing himself again, he pulled out a second bottle, and after long minutes of more tortured fumbling, successfully pried off the stopper, raising the glittering vial in a toast.

"To the victor, the spoils," he said, and lifted the bottle to his lips. Before he could drink, however, a loud keening sound arose, causing him to think the captain again was engaging the ship's horn. As it rose to an almost painful level, drowning out the sound of the wind, the storm clouds all around the vessel abruptly burst into a prolonged and thunderous incandescence.

Astonished, Harcourt and the other passengers stared at the spectacle. The second bottle slipped through his fingers and plunked into the sea. He scarcely noticed this time. More passengers crowded up on deck to see the spectacle. Even the sailors came out to witness the atmospheric phenomenon.

"What is it?" one of them asked, shielding his brow with his hand.

"Sheet lightning of some rare type, I should think," the professor replied. "Quite remarkable."

Through the fog and rain, the light grew ever brighter, suffusing the storm clouds with a marvelous radiance. Then, quite without fanfare, nature's aerial display abruptly ceased. The people on deck oohed and awed. Some even applauded.

"No extra charge for the fireworks show, ladies and gentlemen!" the captain joked from the wheelhouse. The sky brightened, the storm clouds rolling away as if the ferry had chased them off. The chilly air warmed a few degrees and the roiling ocean calmed down enough to offer some relief to Harcourt's stomach. Off to starboard, the retreating fogbank uncovered another ship approaching from the south.

The vessel was a towering sight to behold. A majestic

triple-masted ship at full sail. As it drew closer, Harcourt and his fellow passengers were delighted to see that it was a magnificent recreation of a classic pirate galleon, complete with sailors in full costume crowding the decks and the rigging. It even flew the Jolly Roger.

The passengers waved and smiled as the galleon pulled alongside the ferry. An excited cheer of surprise went up when the vessel opened its hatches and a battery of cannon emerged.

"Look, it's Long John Silver!" one gentleman said. He laughed, pointing to the agitated pirate captain, who stood on the forecastle, waving his cutlass at them and bellowing inarticulately. Suddenly, one of the cannons opened fire with a booming report, sending a shot whistling over their heads. The crowd gasped, and then broke into wild applause.

"That was cutting it a bit fine, wasn't it?" Harcourt remarked to the sailor beside him, but the seaman was distracted, looking back to the bridge.

The pirates raised a bright red flag, provoking another round of applause from the passengers. Inside the wheelhouse, the ferry captain didn't appear to be entertained. He came out, a megaphone in hand.

"What the devil are they playing at?" he said with a scowl. "That could have taken someone's head clean off!"

A second cannon roared, and the captain's head vanished in a spray of red. His decapitated body collapsed to the deck. Someone screamed. Then all the guns began firing. The ferry shuddered and rocked as a fusillade of cannonballs struck amidships. Chaos broke out on deck, screams and shouts filling in the gaps between cannon fire. The passengers panicked, diving for cover or running pell-mell across the tilting deck. Some even leapt overboard, only to be left swiftly behind in the icy water. An alarm bell rang frantically.

The professor hugged his traveling case to his chest and ran around to the other side of the wheelhouse for cover. The boat's mate dashed for the bridge and took the wheel, wrenching it hard to port.

"Full steam ahead!" he yelled.

The ferry lurched away from the angle of attack and began to speed off, but it wasn't out of the line of fire yet. Blasts of chain shot—iron balls joined by links of heavy chain—screamed high over the deck of the ferry. They ripped both of the ferry's auxiliary masts in two, splintering and toppling them. Other hits slammed into the funnel. The smokestack rung like a bell and crumpled at the points where the balls impacted, but its steel held.

The pirate captain bellowed more orders and the next thundering volley peppered the air with lethal shrapnel. The salvo hit the ferry like bursts from giant shotguns. It scoured the wall of the bridge, shattered the windows, and tore apart those unlucky enough to still linger on the wrong side of the deck.

From the sheltered side of the bridge, Harcourt watched in horror as the windows exploded out above his head in a spray of shards and splinters. Nearby passengers dove for cover. When the rain of debris ended, Harcourt raised his head and risked a peek inside the wheelhouse. The first mate still manned his station, his mangled corpse clinging to the ship's wheel.

The battered ferry boat continued to limp along its new heading, even as it was hit by another barrage. The cannonballs beat against the aft hull like a drum, the boat bucking like a kicking horse under the onslaught.

When the awful sound of hammering stopped, Harcourt lifted his head to quickly take stock. Twisted corpses were strewn all over the slick red deck. The ferry had carried four hundred and fifty passengers. Of those who had been up top, less than a dozen remained, all huddling for cover with him.

They stayed low on the deck, not daring an attempt to move to the relative safety of the cabin below. The young American couple lay beside him. The three of them exchanged desperate looks. Then, with sickening anticipation, they watched helplessly as the busy pirates prepared to fire yet again.

When the next barrage came, the American woman screamed. This time, however, the bombardment merely sent huge spouts of water into the air as the cannonballs landed in the sea short of the ferry. The steamship had managed to pull itself just out of range, but the galleon turned to pursue. The stragglers left outside raised themselves up off the deck, cautiously optimistic that they had a chance now.

"Can they catch us?" the American man asked.

One of the surviving seamen rubbed his jaw, and shook his head.

"I shouldn't think so, sir," he replied in a broad Cockney accent. "But I don't rightly like the sound of our screws. I think those cannons may have knocked them about a bit." He went aft and leaned over the rail to take a closer look for damage. A small crowd of the survivors gathered to watch. He whistled appreciatively and another crewman joined him.

"'Ow's she look, then?"

"Well, the hull's taken its licks and it ain't very pretty, but no real damage, I reckon. We best take a look amidships to be sure there's no breach there, either."

"What are we to do now?" Harcourt asked, cradling his traveling case in his arms like a newborn. "Return to the harbor?"

"Aye, and as fast as we can, for as long as the boat holds together."

"What is your name, sailor?"

"Hixson, sir."

"Well, Mr. Hixson," Harcourt said, slipping on an air of authority to conceal his own fear, "you appear to have been promoted to captain of this vessel."

The sailor started to respond, but then blinked, gulped, and nodded without a further word.

The remaining sailors and several of the male survivors helped clear the wheelhouse of debris and arranged the bodies of the dead in tight rows along the rail. Harcourt preferred to accompany Hixson while he took a quick inventory. The ferry's hull had been pummeled mercilessly, but remained seaworthy. Most of the instrumentation on the bridge, however—including the ship's compass—lay in ruins.

"Bloody 'ell," Hixon swore. "We'll 'ave to navigate by sight as best we can."

The ferry forged ahead through alternating sunlight and banks of fog, each hand keeping an eye on the galleon tracking them, hungry to close the gap again.

Harcourt made a station for himself in what remained of the wheelhouse, along with a few of the crew and the American couple. The young man hunched in the corner next to him, arms wrapped around his legs. The woman curled up in her black-and-white checkered Scotch ulster long coat and cap, and had closed her eyes, using her leather gripsack as a pillow.

Harcourt turned to the man.

"Dreadful breach of protocol, I fear, but there's no one to properly introduce us." He extended his hand. "Professor Winston Harcourt, at your service."

The other gave a weary smile and shook hands.

"Likewise. I'm Tracey Greaves. My indisposed companion is Elizabeth Cochrane." The woman glanced up, managing a weak smile and a wave, and lay her head back down again.

"American?" the professor asked, rather unnecessarily.

"Yes, from New York. I'm the London correspondent for *The World*. Miss Cochrane is my colleague. You'll have to excuse her. She's barely slept since Wednesday."

"I daresay you'll have quite a story to report when we get back. Perhaps I should give you my card, in case you care to interview me for my account of the incident."

Greaves had no chance to answer.

"Look there!"

As the sailor on watch pointed, a surreal sight appeared dead ahead. The cliffs of Dover, a massive wall of dazzling white chalk miles long, jutted straight out of the gray-green sea.

"Cor! We've overshot Folkestone!" Hixson exclaimed, turning the wheel hard to starboard. Harcourt and the American joined him at the helm.

"What does that mean?" Harcourt asked.

"We can't turn around and make it to the 'arbor without putting ourselves back under their guns, sir. They'd blast our topside to pieces. If we want to keep out of range of their guns, we 'ave to keep feeding the coal and push the engines for as long as we can up the coast, just until we come to the nearest port or run into help."

Hixson swallowed, and wiped his brow.

"It's not so bad as it sounds, though," he added. "We're in a busy shipping lane, so we can't be far from the closest Navy or Coastguard ship. We'll send up a flare just as soon as we spot one. Those bastards won't last two minutes against a proper vessel."

The others nodded. It was a good plan. And yet…

Greaves bit his lip, looked up.

"Have you *seen* any other ships?"

The sailors exchanged uneasy glances, but said nothing.

26

"...so once I'd realized that we had overshot the harbor, and advised the mate, I did my best to dispel the fear of my fellow passengers and help keep the crew focused on our survival." Harcourt paused, coughed, and cast a longing glance at the water bucket over by Cam, then loudly cleared his throat.

"If I could perhaps trouble you for some water, dear boy? I find I'm still quite stiff from my exertions on my journey here."

Cam didn't respond and Harcourt frowned.

"Remember, he doesn't speak English," Amber reminded him gently. "He does speak a little Latin, if that helps."

"Indeed? Well now, why didn't you say so? Naturally I have more than a passing knowledge of Latin!" He turned to Cam, using the voice of a kindergarten teacher speaking slightly too loudly to a particularly slow student. *"Quo vadis, homo adolescens? A priori, bibendum aqua pura ex post facto, etcetera."*

Cam looked up and stared at him, baffled.

Harcourt looked around uncomfortably and cleared his throat.

"It appears the savage lacks a firm grasp on the language, so I shall fetch it myself. Unless…" He paused, looking hopefully at the others. None of them moved, so Harcourt lurched to his feet and went over to the bucket. He grimaced in distaste, pulled out a handkerchief and wiped the wooden rim before taking a gulp of water. Despite his best efforts, some dribbled down his chin and onto his shirt.

"Really," he muttered, "you'd think they would have included a ladle."

Simon gave a mocking laugh. "Because they take such care seeing to our comforts and well-being."

Alex nodded. "We're lucky to have it at all. I suspect our girl Nell had more than a little to do with it."

"I suppose you're right," Harcourt said reluctantly, then he brightened. "Didn't I see a loaf of bread change hands?"

"Now that you're up, you might as well bring it over here," Simon said with an insolent smirk. "There's a good chap."

"I'll get it." Amber wanted to make sure Cam got a share of the bread, and didn't quite trust Harcourt to divide it evenly. She scrambled to her feet, uncomfortably aware that Simon was checking out her legs as she tried to keep her skirt from flying up.

Smiling at Cam, she knelt down, pulled the loaf of bread out from under Alex's raincoat, and tore off a portion for him. His fingers brushed against hers as he accepted it. Then she handed out fair shares of the bread to the others, keeping a slightly smaller piece for herself. Some habits were hard to shake, like those developed by years of living with entitled siblings.

As they ate their meager fare, Harcourt continued his story. "Where was I? Oh, yes, so we sailed past the white cliffs of Dover…"

From Dover to Ramsgate and around the point to Margate, the ferry continued to crawl up the coastline as if in a dream. The survivors kept their eyes peeled, but it was always the same story. The coast was devoid of any sign of civilization, and the waters seemed deserted. Not a ship, not a tug, not a fishing boat, not so much as a dinghy—only their implacable pursuer.

"None of this makes any bloody sense," Hixson murmured for the hundredth time since he'd taken the wheel. "This can't be the right coastline. Where are the lighthouses? Where are the docks? Where are the bloody *people*?"

"Where are we now?" Harcourt asked, instantly regretting the question. The sailor shook his head.

"Damned if I can say, sir. We *should* be coming up soon to the Thames Estuary, but there's no landmarks I can recognize, and we've no instruments to guide us any better." He pointed at the coastline and added, "It should be right there." In response, the professor picked up their late captain's spyglass. He scanned back and forth.

The mouth of the Thames?

Impossible.

It was a wilderness on every side. They might as well have been steaming toward the mouth of the Amazon, for all he could tell. He snapped the telescope closed and turned to the steersman.

"See here, I'm certainly no mariner, but I *do* know, most categorically, that by no means can this possibly be the mouth of the Thames!"

"It *has* to be!"

"Look for yourself, man!" Harcourt held out the spyglass. "Do *you* see any royal shipyards? Do you see Southend-on-Sea? Do you see *anything*?"

The sailor shook his head in frustration.

"I don't understand 'ow it can be… but… you must be right, I think, sir. Right then. We'll keep heading north until we find the Thames, or anything of help." A thoughtful look crossed his face.

"Or until the props fail, or we run out of steam."

DANA FREDSTI | DAVID FITZGERALD

As they continued, waves of fog came and went, hampering their navigation even further. Behind them, still just out of cannon distance, the pirate galleon kept pace with its prey. Each time the mists cleared, they could see the ship still dogging their trail.

Leaning out over the bow, one sailor kept sweeping the horizon with the spyglass, looking for any sign of the Thames Estuary. Back at the wheel, Hixson, Harcourt, and the others waited anxiously for news. Finally, the lookout turned and gave them the thumbs up. Hixson and the others broke out in smiles of relief.

"It's a miracle our coal 'eld out," the man sighed, "let alone our poor screws and rudder." Turning, the ferry steamed toward the middle of the wide estuary, the shore on either side barely visible in the mist, like a watercolor of a landscape. Hixson exhaled happily. "We'll be 'aving lunch by a roaring fire before you…"

His eyes grew wide and his voice trailed off.

He stared at the land that lay dead ahead.

"Oh Christ… It's the Isle of Mersea."

"It can't be." Professor Harcourt shook his head. "Mersea is miles to the north—"

"Don't you see?" Hixson cut in. "That *was* the Thames we passed, you bloody fool!"

"Impossible!"

"*All of this 'as been bloody impossible!*" Hixson shouted. "*All of it!*" He spun the wheel hard about. The ferry groaned as it banked into a sharp turn to starboard.

"*'ang on! We've got to get out of here!*"

But that was no longer an option. This was the moment the pirates had been waiting for. The ferry was hemmed in, and the galleon closed the trap, turning hard to starboard and bringing all of its guns to bear. The pirates opened fire with another thundering barrage.

Cannonballs rained down on them. One bounced off the ceiling above their heads, eliciting a shriek of terror from Harcourt. Another smashed into the deck a few feet from the wheel, cratering it with a spectacular crash of flying timbers and splinters. Still more hammered away at the hull.

As the dust settled the survivors lifted their heads, only to see that the pirates were lowering their longboat into the water, packed with a boarding party armed to the teeth with swords, pistols, and muskets.

"Bugger me," Hixson muttered.

"Do we have any weapons on board?" Greaves asked.

The helmsman shook his head. "We're a ferry boat. We've a signal pistol. The stoker's got a shovel. I have a pocket knife."

"How many flares do you have for that pistol?" Miss Cochrane asked.

Before Hixson could answer, another booming crack came from the pirate galleon, followed by the terrible sound of breaking timbers and men screaming. The masts of the galleon shuddered and then fell in opposite directions, taking the rippling sails with them. Seamen tumbled from the rigging.

No more than a second later, the galleon was torn abruptly in two, both halves sinking fast. The pirates in the longboat were struck dumb, staring uncomprehendingly as the remains of their ship—along with their crewmates—sank below the waves in a froth of bubbles.

Aboard the ferry, the survivors stared at their terrible miracle in disbelief.

"Good lord," the professor gasped. "What could do that? Some kind of a submarine warcraft?"

Unspoken notions of Jules Verne and the *Nautilus* ran through his head, but there was no time to dwell on such thoughts. While they looked on, a colossal shape suddenly erupted out of the water, moving at tremendous speed.

It looked like a massive shark, but was the size of a whale. It seized the end of the longboat in its jaws and tilted the entire craft up out of the water. Then it crunched down once, twice, three times. In just three horrific bites it had completely consumed wooden boat and screaming pirates alike.

No one spoke. It was Miss Cochrane who first collected herself enough to point at the deck.

"Look," she said softly. The men then saw what she

did—the rivulets of blood flowing from the bodies stacked against the rails, slowly dripping off the deck and down into the water.

Harcourt looked at the steersman in horror.

"Surely the creature can't tear *this* vessel in half," he whispered, as much to himself as the first mate.

"I don't think so," Hixson replied slowly. "The ferry is made of steel, not wood like those poxy bastards' ship. But… we've taken so much damage from the cannons…" He paused. "If belowdecks has taken anywhere near the same beating as the bulwarks—" He shook his head. "It might not hold."

"Can we outrun it?" Miss Cochrane asked as swirls of red rose to the surface of the water. "Head up into the river?"

Hixson considered this. "If we go in too far, we'll run aground."

"Yes," she replied urgently, "but if we run aground, the water will be too shallow for that thing to follow. Sharks can't swim in the mud, after all."

"A shark?" the professor sputtered. "The size of that monstrosity? It's a physical impossibility."

"Well, whatever it is," she shot back, "it looks like it's finishing up with those cutthroats."

Hixson turned and took the wheel again. "All ahead full!" he bellowed. "Quickly now. Our lives depend on it!"

The battered ferry lurched forward, picking up steam

as they made their desperate run up the river. Harcourt, Greaves, and Miss Cochrane stayed at the railing, watching for signs that the monster was following.

"It's coming," Miss Cochrane said. Her voice was surprisingly calm. Harcourt and Greaves followed her gaze. As they watched, the water stirred, then parted as something large headed their way.

"Faster!" Harcourt yelled. "Can't you go any faster, man?"

Hixson didn't answer, all of his attention focused on navigating the fog-shrouded river ahead of them.

"There!" Greaves pointed off to the right. "There's land over there! It has to be too shallow for that thing to—"

With a thundering crunch, the deck pitched violently, sending Harcourt and the Americans reeling. The professor nearly flipped over the railing to the water below. More screams came from the cabin below deck.

The ferry lurched forward again, driven by the collision, gaining a few more yards toward land. The engine sputtered, but still held. Hixson stayed at his post, holding onto the wheel with a death grip, grim determination on his face.

The gigantic monster rammed the ferry a second time, tossing everyone to the deck again. The creaking sound of buckling, crumpling metal struck terror into the professor's heart.

"We're taking on water," a crewman hollered. As if to

prove his words, the ferry lurched, listing sickeningly to one side.

"We can still make it," Greaves shouted as the land drew closer.

Hixson gave an inarticulate yell as he tried to steer the vessel to the riverbank, not a hundred yards away. Then the entire ship lurched up with massive force, as if Neptune himself had punched through the heart of the vessel. The center buckled, not quite breaking the boat in half, but causing both bow and stern to bend apart as the whole ferry rose out of the water, then crashed back down.

Water sloshed over the rails with enough force to wash several men overboard, the decks tilting downward at precariously steep angles. The ferry listed further to one side, sending the cabin underwater.

Miss Cochrane grabbed her companion by the arm. "Tracey, we have to swim for it." She turned to Harcourt. "It's our only chance." She grabbed one of the life preservers that dangled from the railings. It was chewed up by shrapnel, but still intact.

Harcourt stared at her as if she were mad. *Go into the water with that monstrosity?* He'd rather—

The thing hit the ferry yet again. Hixson lost his grip on the wheel and tumbled into the river, vanishing into the black water.

"The boat's done for," Miss Cochrane snapped. "That

thing's going to keep hitting until it sinks and then it'll start going after whoever's left. Our only chance is to get to shore before that happens."

Greaves nodded, although clearly terrified.

She pointed to another life preserver. "Grab that and—"

The thing struck again and this time the ferry tipped onto its side, sending Harcourt and the two Americans tumbling into the river.

Harcourt's scream of terror cut off as frigid salt water filled his open mouth and went up his nostrils. He kept hold of his traveling case, clutching it in one hand so unconsciously that he didn't notice when the weight started dragging him further into the depths. He flailed his other arm to reach the surface. Something clutched the back of his jacket, hauling his head up above the water.

Screams immediately assailed his ears.

"Here! Grab this!"

He thrashed, sputtering and choking as Miss Cochrane, clinging to the life preserver, guided him to the other side. There was no sign of her companion.

Harcourt grabbed onto the preserver, looping one arm through, trying to lift his case up to rest on top. Its weight immediately sent the preserver dipping into the water.

"Let go of it," Miss Cochrane said urgently. "It'll swamp us."

He shook his head, teeth chattering with cold.

"Don't be a fool! We can make it in if we share this, but it won't—"

Whatever she was going to say was lost as a wave washed over them both and the huge shape of the monstrous creature passed underneath. In his terror, Harcourt let go of the case, kicking out with both feet as he yanked on the life preserver and made for land.

It wasn't until he was crawling up onto the muddy ground that he realized he'd left Miss Cochrane behind to fend for herself. He scanned the river for other survivors, but there was no sign of anyone, only the wreckage of the ferry, sinking into the depths.

Then he spotted a bit of flotsam, bobbing against the riverbank like a little boat. He ran over in disbelief and beheld a minor miracle.

His hat, only slightly the worse for its soaking.

27

"And so, after I did all I could to help the rest, I dove off the sinking ship and swam to shore. Only the legacy of my college athletics saved my life."

Harcourt paused and sighed heavily before finishing, "Alas, no one else was up to the challenge. To quote the mariner Ishmael, 'And I only am escaped alone to tell thee.' So I set out up the river in search of help. You're all too aware of the kind of help I encountered."

Cam paid no attention to Harcourt's story. Even if he hadn't been preoccupied with tending the stricken Merlin, and even if he could have understood the other man's words, he would still have probably ignored him. The man's type was familiar. There'd been more than one braggart in his village. The Trinovantes had a saying:

Empty cauldrons make the most noise.

He did, however, keep track of the group, and he noticed the way the younger man kept looking at Amber. Cam trusted this shifty-eyed fellow even less than the blowhard.

He gently daubed at the sticky blood that had pooled on Merlin's forehead. It was tricky with his wrists in manacles. Keeping the cumbersome chain out the way was a challenge. He took care to hold it in one hand while he ministered with the other, trying hard not to let the cold metal links bump up against the stricken figure. It made for slow work, but there was nothing else he could do, so he kept at it.

As Cam cleared away the clotted mess surrounding the wound, the slightest trace of something silvery began to emerge. Peering closely, he could make out a cluster of tiny shapes, like a honeycomb crafted from lines of the very finest wire, thin as strands of hair. The precise little shapes seemed to follow the lines of the wound, and before his eyes, they seemed to grow, slowly sending out more lines, to form additional honeycomb shapes.

"*Nev Kawgh,*" the Celt murmured, and he pulled away in surprise.

It wasn't just happening on the forehead. All of Merlin's cuts and burns were growing the same tiny metal shapes. Some druid's art was at work here, stitching the man's wounds together with marvelous bands of silver.

"Amber," he called, wanting to share this miracle with her. She looked up and started to walk over.

"*Against the wall!*" the jailer shouted from outside.

Amber let out an involuntary squeak of alarm as the door slammed open. She turned as their guard came up the stairs, sword out, with two other men following behind. Cam tensed but the woman, Alex, put a warning hand on his arm.

They all stared at the newcomers. One man was tall and swarthy, sporting long curls of black hair, a trim mustache, and a small pointed beard. He wore gleaming blue-black armor over a rich red velvet doublet and breeches, an ornately engraved breastplate and shoulder guards fit for a warrior, with a white lace collar over a metal neck guard.

Beside him stood an older man, a brooding figure in an inky black wool cape whose flat eyes chilled Cam's blood. His gaze gave the impression of a praying mantis tracking a smaller insect.

"*This is His Grace the Lord-General Fairfax,*" the jailer growled, "*and Master Stearne. Mind that you lot show some respect, ye dirty bastards.*" Cam didn't understand the words, but he understood the tone perfectly well.

The general—Lord Fairfax he was called—came forward. He had a slight limp, yet his tread was heavy and imposing. He took his time, going from prisoner to prisoner, inspecting each of them carefully as if silently weighing their worth.

Finally his attention fell upon Cam.

"*Where are you from?*" he asked.

Cam only returned his gaze defiantly.

"He doesn't speak any English," Amber tried to explain.

"What *does* he speak?" the man snapped. "Is he some manner of Scot? And address me properly when you answer, girl." His voice was sleek as steel and hard as iron, a voice accustomed to instant obedience.

"I… I'm sorry. I'm sorry, your—your…"

"*Your Grace,*" the jailer said icily.

"Your Grace," she said. "I'm sorry, I don't know what language he speaks, sir. Your Grace, sir."

He frowned at her, as if she had just posed a riddle for him to solve.

"*You* are not English."

She gulped, and balled her fists tight to keep them from trembling.

"Mean you ever to tell me where you hail from?"

Amber's mind raced and her mouth quivered as she fought to follow the question, let alone provide a suitable answer that wouldn't get her killed.

"I… I'm American, Your Grace," she finally blurted out.

Lord Fairfax cocked his head almost imperceptibly, and then burst out with a loud laugh that made her

DANA FREDSTI | DAVID FITZGERALD

jump. His laughter provoked the jailer to risk joining in. Only the caped man in the tall pilgrim hat—Master Stearne—kept his stone face. The lord-general let his laughter run its course, and then his expression became impassive again.

Amber felt as though she was in some sort of bizarre play where she didn't know the script.

"Sergeant, go stand behind this line of prisoners."

Their jailer obeyed.

"All of you heed my words most carefully," Lord Fairfax continued. "For as long as I decide, none of you shall speak. None of you shall move or signal to your neighbor in the least. On pain of death. For all of you, this very moment." He let that sink in for a moment before turning to the jailer. "Sergeant, is your sword at the ready?"

"Aye, my lord."

"Sergeant, mark our savage warrior. I shall proceed to count to three. Reveal no sign of your intention, but at the very stroke of three, unless our wild friend bids you stop, you shall at once swiftly cut the throat of this American girl without fail. Do you understand?"

"Completely, my lord-general."

Amber thought she was going to faint.

Oh god. Oh god. Oh god.

Lord Fairfax cleared his throat. Stearne, the witch hunter, watched the drama as intently as a cat tracking a mouse.

"One."

Cam remained in stony silence. None of the other prisoners dared breathe.

"Two."

Amber's thoughts raged. *He can't say anything! He doesn't understand anything you've said! Oh god, I'm going to die.* She closed her eyes tight. Her heart beat so hard it hurt her chest. She could feel the sergeant's breath on the back of her neck, hear his inhalation as he steadied himself for what was coming.

Oh god.

"Stand down, Sergeant."

"Aye, my lord."

Amber exhaled suddenly, with an audible sob. Fairfax paid it no mind.

"I've seen what I need."

The relief of the prisoners was palpable—except for Cam, who remained defiant. He was entirely unaware how close Amber had just come to death. The relief, however, was short-lived. The lord-general had another order.

"Sergeant," he snapped, "before we go, face the wildling to the wall and compel him to kneel."

The jailer grasped Cam's irons and yanked him into place with some kicks and shoves. He pressed Cam's face into the bricks of the wall, and then lifted his sword overhead, awaiting his commander's order. Amber wanted to scream, to beg for Cam's life, but she didn't dare make a sound or even move.

Fairfax turned away from the proceedings and looked to the witch hunter.

"Master Stearne? What say you?"

The Puritan leaned in and whispered to the general. Fairfax listened, then gave a curt nod.

"I suspected as much."

He turned back to the prisoners.

"No need for that, Sergeant. Leave him." Before Amber could begin to process her relief, however, Fairfax added, "Bring the girl with us. She has an appointment with Master Stearne."

If their jailer was disappointed at not being allowed to execute Cam, he didn't show it. He merely let his prisoner go, sheathed his cutlass, and took Amber by one arm. Cam lifted his face away from the rough brick wall and pulled himself up from the kneeling position. He had kept his temper in check throughout the ordeal, but now he saw their captors taking Amber away.

He roared the only word he knew in her language.

"Amber!"

Then he charged the sergeant. The startled soldier released Amber's arm and drew his sword, fast as a serpent's strike. But the Celt flung up his manacles and caught the falling blade in the chain, barely inches away from his forehead.

"No!"

With a shout Amber wheeled and threw herself between them, grabbing the jailer's sword arm with one hand and pressing against Cam with the other. She looked up at the sergeant, eyes wide and stinging with tears.

"Please," she begged. "You don't have to do this. I'll go, and he won't give you any more trouble. He just wanted to protect me. Please."

The soldier gritted his teeth, ready to press the attack, but his resolve softened in the face of Amber's unexpected plea. He turned to Fairfax, confused. The lord-general raised a conciliatory hand.

"It's alright, Sergeant. Our colonial girl must be the genuine article—that valiant gesture was worthy of the Indian princess Pocahontas. She just saved her young bravo's life by it. Let us hope he does not cast her gift aside lightly."

Amber caught her breath, still shaking, and nodded to Fairfax.

"Thank you, Your Grace."

Amber released her grip on the jailer's arm and he stepped back a pace, lowering his sword but not sheathing it yet. She helped Cam to his feet, holding his uneasy face with both hands.

"It's okay, Cam," she said, with a lousy attempt at a reassuring smile. "I'll be okay, I promise." She pointed to the man lying on the floor. "Him. Merlin. Take care of Merlin, understand? *Expecto patronum* Merlin."

Cam looked at the unconscious man, then back at Amber, and nodded.

"Ego sum… Ego sum patronus."

She smiled for real this time, and softly kissed him on his cheek. Then, before she could change her mind, she turned and went with the men out the door.

Downstairs, the sergeant passed her off to two more soldiers. Now that she was out of the bell tower, Amber could hear the desperate, quavering hymns being sung by sobbing parishioners in the adjoining church. Villagers hurrying on their way into its sanctuary shot her venomous sidelong looks, but didn't dare speak to her.

Probably afraid I'll give them the evil eye, she thought, wishing she had that kind of power so she could get out of this mess.

As the soldiers marched her down the lane, hands resolutely locked on her arms, Amber risked one last backward glance up at her fellow prisoners. Cam and the others watched her go in silence. Alex gave her a little wave for good luck.

Amber turned in numb dread as they passed soldiers who were busy heaping bushels of dry kindling atop stacks of firewood. These surrounded the rugged wooden posts that lined the main drag, and they were

already erecting two more. Now there would be six—
enough for all of them.

Cam watched as the soldiers came out of the bell tower
with Amber in their grip. Just for a moment, she turned
her head to give them one last look before the captors
marched her away, passing the line of tall wooden stakes
being loaded with bundles of kindling and firewood. He
knew what those were for.

He watched the men take Amber down the lane and off
onto a side road leading into the countryside to the north.
He waited until she was well out of sight before finally
turning away. The female prisoner laid a comforting
hand on his shoulder, sympathy clear in her warm
brown eyes. He gave a small nod of acknowledgment
and then, true to his word, went over to the unconscious
man Amber had called Merlin, resuming his place by the
man's head.

The other three found places to sit as well, trying to
stay out of the cold and damp as best they could.

28

Just past the cluster of cottages, shops, and the one inn at the center of town, a side road headed off north toward the river. Amber kept an eye out as her escort turned up the road, using the sun to mark their direction, trying to memorize the landmarks of the surrounding area.

They passed orchards and hedgerows enclosing fields of sheep or black cattle, a pair of mills at the river, and crossed a little stone bridge. From there the road rose up into low hills. The sounds of cannon and musket fire coming from the east grew clearer the further they walked uphill.

A fine manor house appeared ahead, looking out from the crest of the hill, half a mile or so up. However, her entourage stopped at a more modest, solitary structure. Its once white-washed walls were covered with moss, the exterior unkempt. Fairfax and Stearne entered first, closely followed by Amber and the soldiers. The Puritan filled two pewter tankards from a cask, while Fairfax took station at a long dining table.

Amber's armed escort quickly hustled her through the front room into a smaller room beyond, where they locked her inside without a word.

Her new prison at least had windows, but they were small and barred, making for a gloomy interior. It had been cleared of all furnishings except for a few empty shelves, a long iron-bound chest against one wall, and a stout wooden worktable. Its surface showed marks from years of busy service. That had to be the home of a local craftsman, she surmised.

Or someone who beats up their furniture on a regular basis.

She wasted no time kneeling down at the door and peeking through the keyhole. An ominous dark lump loomed beside the doorknob. She frowned, then realized it was just the back of one of the soldiers standing guard.

At the dining table, Fairfax was busy spreading out a map and placing several small wooden figurines on top of it, as if he was setting up a game of chess or Risk. Holding her breath, Amber eavesdropped as Fairfax pointed to various pieces while explaining their battle plans to Stearne.

"Our palisade—Fort Essex, here on the Great Broom Heath—covers us against the sorties from the town, but the fort is under fire most oppressive from two of

Lord Goring's regiments posted outside the head gate, here... and here. The worst of it comes from the battery of cannons in St. Mary's churchyard at the walls... here. The rebels have had the audacity to make it their fort."

"They shall surely be damned," Stearne murmured.

"They have a one-eyed gunner in position in the church tower," Fairfax added, "and the villain's marksmanship is devilishly keen. He's sent a great number of ours to their eternal reward, so accordingly we must bring up more artillery to pound upon that profaned tower until it and the accursed gunner are both fallen down to Hades.

"Our first line of foot was three regiments, about seventeen hundred men in all," he continued. "A good part of them fought their way through the head gate— only to be driven back into High Street and cut to pieces. We attempted to storm the south gate again three times after that, and each time were beaten back in great havoc, with their cannons raining fire upon us all the while. So we retreated, having lost several worthy officers, along with near a thousand men, and the wounded besides."

He looked up from the map and pressed a hand against his brow.

"The Royalists still have a good body of horses, and give us no rest. They scour the fields every day, falling on any of our men they find straggling from their posts. Thus we are not able to carry the town by storm. I have sent to London and Suffolk for more forces. While we wait, I've posted soldiery on the roads and on patrol to prevent aid or escape."

Fairfax paused, and Amber could see that the strain hung heavily on him. The lord-general took a drink from his tankard, moved to the mantel, and leaned on it, staring into the fire.

"Notwithstanding, ever since that night of the infernal lightning storm, our five thousand has been slashed in twain, or worse," he said. "Meanwhile Lord Goring and Lord Capel continue to fortify the town and shore up the gaps in their walls. There's no sign of any of the Parliament ships from Harwich. No new communications arrive from outside, and none of my outgoing messengers have returned. It would seem we are utterly alone.

"Both we and the rebels seem to be inhabitants of the same 'island' now, one scarcely four miles long and three miles wide, and dropped into pandemonium. So who are truly the besieged? Is it they? Or we?"

He drained his tankard. "I cannot fathom what dread fate has befallen us, or detect any rhyme or reason in it. O'er half my men and horses melted into thin air, damn it! And with them, all the land for leagues around us has faded away, transformed into fallow earth—or worse." He turned and faced his companion. "You're the theologian, Stearne. Can you explain it? Can you direct me to the scripture that speaks of such a thing?"

Stearne, who had remained very still, now spoke carefully.

"We know that we do but serve God's will here, my lord," he said. "Of that, there can be no doubt. The Revelation of St. John does speak of the angel who, once the seventh seal hath been opened, would take a golden censer filled with fire of the heavenly altar, and cast it into the earth, and with this would come voices, and thunderings, and lightnings, and an earthquake." He drew close to the lord-general, looking as though he wanted to put a comforting hand upon Fairfax's shoulder, but didn't quite dare.

"Surely what we all witnessed on that terrible night is its very fulfillment," he continued, "and now we await the seven angels which have the seven trumpets prepared to sound their call, that Christ himself may return in glory with all his heavenly host." The Puritan fished a stack of papers from his pocket.

"These broadsheets report news of other signs," Stearne said. "A pool in Lancashire has turned to blood, while elsewhere children have been born with horns, or with two heads. The strange beasts we have seen and the queer outlanders we have captured all bespeak to the truth." His voice rose as his excitement increased.

"Our battle with these Royalists here in Colchester, as with Lieutenant-General Cromwell's battle in Pembroke, are but the outward manifestation of a far larger but invisible struggle between the mystery of iniquity and the divine host—"

Fairfax turned on the man.

"Spare me, Stearne," he growled. Abruptly he pounded a fist against the tabletop. "I would have *real* intelligence, not sermons and rumormongering! We have a battle to fight, an army to feed, and no sign of aid from any quarter. How long do you think we can hold out?"

Stearne blanched, taken aback.

"My lord, I—"

"Hold your tongue and listen well. I care nothing for your apocalypses and the witch-madness you stir up among the troops and the town. The men we fight here are but Englishmen like ourselves, not some satanic horde. When this damnable conflict is over, the king will return to his throne, the abuses of his reign curtailed, and we shall all drink to his health together, Roundhead and Royalist alike, God willing. No matter what doomsday the likes of you and Commander Cromwell preach."

Go, Lord Fairfax, Amber thought.

Stearne kept silent, lips pressed together in a thin line as if to hold the words trapped inside.

"Do you know why I have you here, Stearne?"

The Puritan hesitated. "My lord, the witches here—"

"I care not three damns who you suppose is a witch," Fairfax cut in. "What I care about is knowing what these strange prisoners know."

Stearne licked his lips, and tried a different tack.

"Aye, my lord. If they prove to be spies for the rebels, then—"

"Spies?" Fairfax gave a snort of derision. "Those poor, terrified wretches? I have no idea where they are from, or their business here. I wager a hundred sovereigns the savage is the only one who has ere even picked up a blade, and he is here for the girl, a love-stricken whelp.

"But spies?" Fairfax shook his head. "I know spies, Stearne. I employ many. A spy blends in, says little but sees much. He is a bold and cunning rascal, a consummate actor, a man who can insinuate himself into a table of off-duty guardsmen or a military headquarters."

Fairfax paused, cocking his head to one side.

"Someone like you, Stearne. I daresay you would make a most excellent spy."

Master Stearne said nothing to this, but Amber could see his hand held tightly at his side, twisted into a quaking fist.

"*Think*, man!" Fairfax urged. "What manner of infiltrator dresses in outlandish garb, his speech passing strange, as he wanders the countryside without course like a stray lamb? I know not why they are here. In truth, I doubt they know themselves, but they came from *somewhere*, and I would have you discover where that is. How they came to be here, and all things they know concerning our circumstance. Think you that you are up to such a task?"

Stearne gave a curt bow of his head.

"I shall not fail you, my lord."

"Good as the best." Lord Fairfax pulled his gloves from his belt and drew them on. "See to it." He strode over to the outer door with a stiff, heavy gait, but paused at the threshold. "Tell me… how many witches have you killed, Stearne?"

"When I served as witch-pricker under Matthew Hopkins—the witchfinder general, God rest his soul— we brought some three hundred of the malefactors to justice, my lord."

"Indeed." Fairfax's tone was dry. "And is it true your mentor was himself finally subjected to his own tests, and so condemned to death as a warlock?"

"Oh no, my lord." Stearne shook his head. "That is naught but a scurrilous lie."

Amber couldn't see Fairfax's expression, only that he silently nodded and walked out the cottage. Stearne turned toward her door, the look in his eyes grim. He'd been schooled by Fairfax in front of common soldiers, and he was ready to take out his anger on someone else.

On her.

29

Amber scrambled to pull herself away from the keyhole and get across the room. She quickly took a seat at the far end of the worktable, just as Stearne swung the door open wide. She did her best to look innocent.

The witch hunter stood there regarding her for a long, uncomfortable moment. Without removing his gaze from Amber, he spoke to the soldiers.

"Leave us. Stand guard in front of the cottage, and see that I am undisturbed."

They saluted and took their leave. The witchfinder closed the door and walked over to the long ironbound chest that lay against the wall. Amber realized with a sickening shock that it was large enough to serve as a coffin.

"I trust you overheard our little exchange, did you not?"

Amber said nothing, her mind racing between possible

options. None seemed promising. Stearne reached down and unlocked the oblong chest, then pulled something out from inside. He let the lid close again.

"You'll quickly find that truth is the only acceptable response. Speaking falsely is no better than refusing to speak at all. So I ask you again. Did you hear us?"

She hung her head and nodded. He rose and walked behind her, deliberately concealing the object he carried.

"You will answer all my questions truly and clearly, aloud and without delay. Anything less justifies punishment. Do you understand?"

She nodded, and quickly added, "Yes."

He smiled. It didn't suit his face.

"See? Excellent. Now we can proceed."

Amber risked a sidelong glance. The witch hunter stood at the far wall and, for the first time, she noticed an iron hook mounted there. He continued to hide whatever was in his hand under cover of his heavy dark cloak. With the other hand he gestured to her.

"Come over to stand beside me, girl."

A pit opened up in her stomach. She began to shake helplessly and all the strength in her limbs melted away like spent candle wax. When she tried to protest, the words leaked from her mouth in pitiful fragments, the same words over and over again.

"Please don't… please… you don't have to… please, please, don't…"

"You will come stand at the wall beside me now." His voice dropped to a low growl, his eyes flinty.

Slowly she rose, making a soft involuntary keening noise in her throat as she forced herself to walk toward him like a disjointed marionette. When she was near enough, he shot out his hand like a mantis and seized her wrist, causing her to shriek in fear. He smiled and produced an iron bar from behind his back. It had a manacle at either end, and in the middle, a ring suitable for hanging.

With a practiced hand, Stearne shackled first one wrist, then the other—despite Amber's struggles to resist. Then he pulled her arms high and hung up the bar on the iron hook. The constraint was a little too high for her, forcing Amber to stand on the balls of her feet to prevent the bar from pulling painfully on her wrists. The position hiked her already short skirt up even further.

Stearne left her dangling there and nonchalantly strolled back to again open the lid of the strongbox. He pulled out a bound leather parcel, untied its cord, and rolled it out on the table, making sure Amber had a clear view. It contained a variety of pouches holding small knives and metal instruments. She flashed on thoughts of the Spanish Inquisition, of Salem, of Edgar Allan Poe stories.

He smiled again. "Lord Fairfax is a courageous man and a good soldier, but he knows little of the spiritual battle.

That is my expertise. Where he has doubts and misgivings, I have unshakable certainty and perfect knowledge."

Stearne pulled out a small brass brazier, and filled it with a measure of charcoal taken from a sooty hide bag.

"The lord-general would learn from whence you came, but I know well where you are from, and who it is that hath sent you."

Next he pulled out a twist of cotton from a little tinderbox and busied himself with flint and steel until he produced enough sparks to fan them into a flame and light the brazier. She watched the procedure in horrified fascination, unable to turn away. A terrified whimper escaped her, but he ignored it.

"The End is drawing nigh fast," he said almost casually. "What then shall we discuss?"

Amber's fear was so great she could barely think, let alone make her mouth work to form words in coherent sentences. In an isolated part of her mind, she knew her only chance was to say the right thing—but what could she possibly say that Stearne would understand, or even believe? Could she reason with him? She doubted it. Though he was a religious man, there was no appealing to his mercy or kindness—one look at him told her he didn't have any.

His faith was the kind that fostered darker qualities.

"Please believe me," she said finally, with as much sincerity as she could muster. "I'm not your enemy. I'm not a witch either. I'm just... I'm just a normal person, and I would never hurt anyone. I'm lost and I just want to get back home."

He looked at her with an unreadable expression, then turned back to the coffer. Pulling out a heavy sack, he unceremoniously dumped the contents on the table. An odd assortment of items spilled out, including a policeman's billy club, a leather handbag, a flashlight, a gold watch on a chain, handcuffs, a switchblade... and her backpack.

Lastly he reached down, and lifted up a long bundle wrapped in sheepskin. He unwrapped it, revealing her ridiculous Codex scepter.

With all the artifacts spread out in front of him like a vendor displaying his wares at a market, Stearne took a seat at the table and steepled his fingers. His poker face was unreadable. Was the look in his eyes meant to further intimidate her, or dangle some glimmer of hope? He let her stew a while, letting the ache grow in her arms and feet as the heat built in the softly smoking brazier.

Finally he spoke.

"The Lord hath delivered thee into my hands, thou and all thy works of heathen idolatry," he said. "Come then, and let us discuss these tools of magic." He rose and let his hand wander above the table before settling on the scepter.

"This, for instance. Am I to believe this is but the

workaday staff of a normal girl from, where did you say? Somewhere in the Americas?"

"San Diego, California," she replied automatically.

Why did I say that?

For once, Stearne actually laughed out loud.

"The island of *California*?" he sneered. "At the farthest end of the world? Did Sir Francis Drake maroon your grandfather there, and did he take an Indian maiden to wife? Has it taken all these many years for your ancestors to trek across the continent and sail back to England, my red-haired, red-skinned mulatto?"

He roared at his own wit, and Amber's heart sank.

Now he thinks I'm either crazy or lying.

"I didn't mean it," she said, with a weak attempt to smile. Stearne's short-lived amusement evaporated as quickly as it had sprung up. He fished an iron poker out from its pouch in the leather parcel, holding it up for her to see before he stirred it into the hot coals.

"That small jest has earned you one taste of hot iron." He lifted the scepter. "Now, shall we try again? Tell me what powers it possesses, and how one employs it, with what words or gestures. Tell me everything, and tell me *now*."

Amber stared at him in shocked disbelief. Here was a grown man who seriously believed that her cheap plastic costume prop could have sorcerous powers. How ridiculous, how insane, that he was willing to torture and kill her, just to get them.

Unless…

She steeled herself, took a deep breath and let out a loud laugh. The unexpected sound rattled him. She glared at him with her best mad gaze, speaking as deeply as she could manage.

"Foolish man! You dare lay your bare hand upon the scepter of, of *Feliciaday* without saying the magic words?" She struggled to keep her voice from cracking. "Now its curse is on *you*!"

For the first time, she had wiped the certainty off his grim face, she realized with a hint of triumph. He dropped the scepter to the ground as if it was on fire, real fear in his eyes.

And then anger.

She had overplayed her hand.

"You Jezebel!" he hissed. "Deceitful harpy. Would you put my immortal soul in peril?" He seized the red-hot poker from the brazier, sending a shower of sparks into the air, and plunged it at her face. She screamed and tried to turn her head away, but he seized her roughly by the neck and held the sizzling iron an inch from her eye. The heat from it threatened to singe her cheek and eyebrow.

"Tell me," he spat. "If you do not this very instant reveal how I might break this curse, and give me the power over this scepter, I promise you I shall plunge this iron as deep into your eye as my strength allows."

Amber screwed her eyes shut, and hoped desperately

that she still might have a shot. When she spoke, her voice remained defiant.

"Kill me and you'll never know," she said. "You'll be damned to hell, forever and ever." The words sounded desperate and childish to her, a stupid and hollow threat, but it was all she had.

She tensed herself for the agony that would come, the sound of her own heart hammering in her head.

Stearne released her throat.

She risked opening her eyes.

He slowly pulled back the poker, just a few inches. The heat receded, and she faced him again. Stearne's eyes were uncertain, uneasy. He carefully slipped the poker back into the hot coals. Then he turned to study her again, his new expression causing Amber almost as much dread as the poker. He eyed her body, her short skirt, her exposed legs. His fingertips rubbed against each other in an odd gesture, as if he was gearing up to touch her, but didn't yet dare.

"You assume a most pleasing form." He leaned in close, so close she could smell the ale on his breath. "But think not it will dissuade me. I know well that is naught but your disguise. It will peel away to reveal your true nature, soon enough. But first…"

She remained silent, although inwardly she was horrified.

"The scriptures say, when we go forth to war against

our enemies, and the Lord God hath delivered them into our hands, if we see among the captives a beautiful woman, and hath a desire for her, and wouldst have her, then thou shalt go in unto her, and humble her, and take thy delight in her." He stroked her face with one finger. "So you are rightfully my handmaiden."

She shuddered, cringing as he brought his arms over her head and lifted her off the wall. He kept a grip on her manacles as he pulled her close.

"You *shall* tell me, one way or the other. My methods can be harsh or gentle, that choice is yours. But either way, you shall now undress and lie on the table."

Behind them, the door suddenly opened.

"I ordered no interruptions!" Stearne barked furiously.

But it wasn't his guards.

Nell stood in the doorway, a basket on one arm and a pistol in her other hand, pointed straight at him. He shot her a look of outrage combined with pure hate.

"What is this, *woman*?"

"Why, nothing, Master Witch Hunter," Nell replied. "Or should I say Witch Pricker? I've just been out and about, blending in, you know. Saying little but seeing much. Insinuating myself at the tables of off-duty guardsmen and the military headquarters, much like a consummate actress, if I say so myself. Rather bold and cunning of me, wouldn't you say?"

Stunned, the Puritan could only stare at her.

"You? A... *spy*?"

Nell smiled at him.

"Oh, it wasn't very hard to peek in on your meeting with his lordship. Or to persuade your guard outside to let me come in and pay you a little visit. But I'm no spy, Master Pricker. No, I'm a *witch*—" She hissed the word dramatically. "—and so is she, even more powerful than I am. Now, you can let her out of those wrist irons harshly... or gently... the choice is yours. Either way, do it *now*."

She raised the pistol in line with Stearne's face. He nodded, dumbstruck, and with shaking hands freed Amber from the manacles. She fell back against the wall in relief, rubbing her aching wrists together.

"Nell, I can't tell you how happy I am to see you."

"Honestly? It's my pleasure." Nell grinned at her, then turned back to Stearne, the pistol unwavering in her grip. "All right now, Quaker Oats, make yourself useful for once and put all these things back in the bag. You can leave your torture tools. Go on, get to it!"

Stearne started in surprise, then hurried to obey. While he quickly filled the bag, Nell glanced over to check on Amber.

"Are you alright there?" she asked. "Don't worry, this brute won't lay another finger on you now—"

Stearne suddenly lashed out, swinging the bag like a weapon. It struck Nell squarely, knocking her to the ground and sending the pistol flying out of her hands. He followed with a vicious overhead swing that narrowly missed her skull, raising his arms for a second strike that wouldn't miss its target.

"Stearne!" Amber called out from behind him. He froze, and couldn't resist glancing back at her. "I give you the power of the scepter!" She held it in both hands, its orb glowing an unearthly green. She held it aloft just long enough for the terrified witch hunter to get a good look before she swung it with all her might, bashing it into his head. The green sphere shattered, and Stearne crumpled to the floor, unconscious.

"Totally worth it." Amber smiled and tossed the broken remnants of her cosplay prop on top of his prone body. Nell sat up, rubbing her shoulder.

"I owe you for that."

Amber gave her a hand up.

"And I owe you for getting me out of those manacles—but I *do* have questions for you."

Nell grinned at her.

"No doubt you do," she said wryly. "But first, let's go free the others."

30

On the north road from Lexden, one of the local millers stepped off to the side to let a horse-drawn wagon amble past toward town. He raised a hand to the two Roundhead soldiers driving it. They were hunched over, eyes to the ground, but they returned his greeting.

Amber turned to Nell.

"Do you think he spotted us?"

Nell adjusted her helmet and risked a quick glance behind them.

"No, I think we're fine. Just remember, keep your head down, and if anybody stops us, let me do the talking. Be ready to hightail it just in case."

Their stolen uniforms were ill fitting, but sitting up as they were in the wagon, the bagginess was less noticeable. They had left Stearne's two sentries tied and gagged—just like the unconscious Stearne himself—inside the cottage.

Nell had persuaded them to disrobe the same way she'd gotten them to leave their post—at gunpoint.

After she and Amber had donned their disguises, they'd located the wagon out back and helped themselves to it. They loaded it up with the rest of the things Stearne had hoarded, and as much food and provisions as they could find.

"Oh, by the way—" Amber extended her hand. "I'm Amber." Nell shook it, easily handling the reins while doing so.

"Glad to make your acquaintance. I should tell you something, though." She looked at Amber with a gleam in her eye and a wry little smile. "You see, my name's not really Nell—it's Elizabeth Cochrane. But everybody calls me Nellie Bly." She raised an expectant eyebrow. "It's my pen name. I'm a reporter." She scanned Amber's face for a reaction. When none was forthcoming, she shook her head and laughed.

"Oh, I'm so glad my editor isn't here," she said, shaking her head. "I'd never hear the end of it. Here I thought I was so famous."

"Oh no, no, no, please don't mind me," Amber said, mortified. "I just don't watch any of the news shows on television. I get all my news online, but I'm sure I must've seen you. Um, what network are you on?"

Nellie pursed her lips and puzzled over Amber's response.

"I'll tell you what," she finally said. "We can talk to our heart's content after we rescue the others. Right now what we need is a plan. Let's see. First we need to do a head count of the guards."

Amber nodded. "There were two at the top of the stairs, keeping watch on the door to the belfry."

"Right, and they've turned the downstairs into a guardroom, too. There are always three or four soldiers hanging around down there." She frowned. "I'm not feeling overly optimistic. These old-timey pistols are pretty dodgy. I know we could buffalo a pair of sentries, but dealing with any more than that, and we'd be getting too high for our nut trying to keep them all at gunpoint. What we need is a good Colt revolver."

"Or an Uzi," Amber mused. Nellie opened her mouth to speak, but Amber had another thought. "Also, it's broad daylight. How are we going to smuggle them out past all these soldiers and townies?"

"Maybe we can pull around behind the churchyard and sneak everyone into the wagon there. Either way, we have to get those guards out first."

"What we need is a distraction."

Nellie nodded thoughtfully.

"A distraction, and quickly!" They were running out of time. The outskirts of town were already in sight. In another minute they'd be at the church.

"Oh!" Nellie brightened. "What if we start yelling

that the Royalists are counterattacking?"

"Maybe… except that we'd blow our cover."

"Blow our cover? Whatever does that mean?"

"Um, it means they'd see through our disguise."

"Ah. Yes, of course. Silly of me."

Amber frowned. "I've seen so many movies and TV shows, you'd think I could remember a good distraction from at least one of them. What would Mal Reynolds do?"

"I'm afraid I don't know what you're talking about, my girl."

Before Amber could reply, a raucous screech pierced the air from above, spooking the horses and making both women jump. The terrible sound was answered by more of the same. They twisted around in their seats, looking up as a flock of winged shapes flew overhead.

More than a dozen of them appeared, great flying monsters, each the size of a hang glider. Their crested heads were as long as a man's torso, their mouths like giant tongs bristling with teeth. And they were flying straight for the town.

"Pterosaurs," Amber breathed in awe and disbelief.

Nellie stared at them in horror.

"What on earth *are* they?"

Amber turned back, grabbed the reins and gave them a sharp snap, urging the horses into a gallop.

"They're our distraction. Let's go!"

* * *

As they charged into town, chaos had just started to erupt. The massive pterosaurs were strafing the rooftops and the roads. They snapped up the unlucky chickens and sheep that didn't get out of the way in time, then swooped away again. Screaming women grabbed their children and ran for shelter. Roundhead soldiers scrambled for cover and fired their muskets and pistols as the monsters circled overhead. No one took any notice of the horse-drawn cart careening past.

True to plan, they sped toward the bell tower and turned into the churchyard itself, driving the cart between narrow rows of gravestones before pulling to a halt under a large tree in the shadow of the church and belfry. The imposing stone structures helped soothe the anxious horses, which neighed and stamped nervously with each screech from overhead.

Amber and Nellie leapt off the cart and ran for the door, where a stream of panicked soldiers poured out. The three or four men they had expected to find inside were closer to eight or nine. When those ran out, the young women ran in, only to collide with the two sentries. Amber was bowled over and hit the ground.

"Out of the way, you fools!" the jailer roared.

Nellie ran up and body-slammed the burly man, but only bounced off him to the ground. The two sentries swore but barely broke stride, hurrying to catch up with the others. Amber leaned over to her fallen companion.

"Are you okay? Why did you *do* that?"

Nellie rose up on her elbows and gave her a wide smile. She held up the jailer's ring of keys and jingled them. Amber grinned back. Then the two dashed up the stairs and pounded on the heavy oak door.

"Guys? It's us!" Amber called.

Someone shouted something back, she couldn't make out quite what over all the noise. Nellie wasted no time unlocking the door, and the two ran up the steps to the belfry.

"Look out!" someone yelled.

A huge crocodile mouth full of knife-like teeth snapped at Nellie's head, clamping down on her helmet. She screamed and it pulled back, taking her body nearly all the way out of the tower. Amber grabbed her tight around the waist, but only managed to get dragged up the steps with her. The pterosaur beat its wings furiously, trying to make off with its prey.

Cam let out a Celtic battle cry and leapt at the massive creature. He raised his arms and swung his chains down like a war flail on the thing's long head. The iron links cracked hard against its skull, and the beast's jaws flew open with a rattling, ear-piercing shriek, dropping Nellie back inside. He swung again, and this time the monster launched itself backward, and with an aerial twist it fled into the sky.

Another one, however, swooped in from a different angle to take its place, followed by still another flying over to get its share of the food. The pterosaurs seemed oddly fixated on the nooks and crannies of the tower, with all its delicious, wiggling creatures huddled inside the exposed belfry. One fished around for Merlin's dormant body, but Alex grabbed up the bright yellow police rain slicker that covered him and lashed away at the prehistoric horror, yelling in an attempt to drive it off.

A third beast took Simon by surprise, clamping down on his arm. He cried out in shock as the toothy monster wildly flapped its wings and tugged, lifting him clear off the floor and into the air. Harcourt tried to pull him back, but a swipe of the thing's head sent the professor flying across the space and crashing against the wall.

Cam turned to see Simon in danger of being carried off. He didn't like the man, but couldn't just let him become bird meat. Letting out another battle cry to muster his courage, he made a running leap over the ledge, catching a precarious handhold on two teeth of the creature's lower jaw just as it took to the air. The pterosaur thrashed its head violently, shaking the men like a dog with a rat.

Simon managed to twist himself free, and hit the floor of the belfry.

Buffeted by the wings and flung about, Cam abruptly lost his grip on the teeth and slipped off, but the snapping jaws bit down on his chains. The links tangled in the thicket of long teeth, leaving him dangling in midair at the verge of the bell tower wall and a death drop. As the giant winged creature tried to fly away with him, Amber and a newcomer, another young woman, struggled to grab for his legs. Cam fought to hook a leg around one of the support pillars to avoid being plucked out of the tower altogether.

At last Amber caught one of Cam's legs, and the newcomer grasped hold of the other. Both pulled with all their might, while he twisted and jerked at his chains. They struggled to keep their footing, feeling the pterosaur trying to pull away with all three of them. Then, with a wet crunching snap and a spray of blood, the tug of war flew apart. The pterosaur shrieked and fell backward out of sight, and the trio collapsed to the floor.

Cam sat up and shook his head, still stunned. He looked down at his manacles and saw what had happened. A pair of teeth eight inches long, their roots bloody and wet, had been caught in links of the chain and torn out.

He turned to find Alex fending off the remaining monster. It seemed unreal to watch the courageous woman keeping the ferocious bird-thing at bay, with nothing but a twirling yellow cloak. Time seemed to slow to a crawl as he stared in wonder.

With a sudden influx of noise and motion, the world rushed in again and he snapped to his senses. Alex yelled desperately. He snatched up one of the two teeth in his fist and rushed to her side. The beast was still distracted by her—it didn't see his attack until it was too late. He stabbed his makeshift weapon deep into its eye. The thing let out a scream and its head collapsed on the ledge.

Then its whole body tumbled away, limp as a rag.

Alex exhaled in relief and turned to Cam.

"Nicely done, sir," she said with a smile of admiration. He returned the smile, understanding her meaning if not her words.

"*Salutatio*," he replied.

"Nell, are you okay?" Amber asked.

The newcomer nodded breathlessly and undid the chinstrap on her helmet, slipping it off gingerly. The faceguard had been torn clean away, and a line of pockmarks in the metal showed where the helmet had saved her head from being crushed.

Harcourt picked himself off the floor and retrieved his hat, while Simon sat up and leaned against the wall, holding his injured arm and eyeing the remains of his tattered left sleeve.

"Is it serious?" Harcourt asked him.

"The arm's been better, but me poor sweet vintage coat got the worst of it," Simon said unhappily.

"Here, let me take a look at—"

"There's no time for that now!" Alex cut in. "We've got to get out as fast as we can, and right now."

No one argued.

Amber hurried over to Merlin's side. "Quick, help me get him up." Cam saw what she was attempting and came over to lend a hand.

"What? You want to drag him along?" Simon scowled. "Come on, he's as good as dead already."

Alex frowned. "I hate to admit it, but he's right, Amber. He's unconscious and probably dying. He'll just slow us down."

Nellie and the Professor stood uncomfortably silent.

Amber looked up at them.

"Listen, I know what you're saying, but please, you've got to believe me. He's important. It'll take too long to explain, just trust me, there's more to him than we realize."

"Whatever are you talking about?" Harcourt demanded.

"You wouldn't understand—"

"Amber!" Alex said. "We don't have time for this! Come on!"

Nellie looked to Alex, then to Amber.

"We can do it," she said. "Go on, there's a wagon just outside. We'll be right behind you." She joined in helping Amber and Cam lift the unconscious man. Alex frowned, but gave a quick nod.

"Right." She turned to the others. "Come on then!"

They hurried down the steps.

Amber mouthed a silent *thank you* to Nellie, then she and Cam pulled Merlin's unresisting body up to his feet. Each slung one of Merlin's limp arms around their shoulders to carry him out, with Nellie trying to steady him from the front. After just a few wobbly steps, however, his legs and arms suddenly stiffened.

Nellie stared at his face in disbelief.

"Wait! He's awake!"

She was right. The man had lifted his head, and for the first time, Amber noticed the latticework of tiny silvery hexagons stitching the lines of his wounds. His dark indigo eyes were still doing the same eerie falling-stars trick. She looked into them hopefully.

"It's me, Amber. Do you remember? You contacted me."

He frowned, peering at her without a hint of recognition. When he spoke, his deep voice crackled.

"The… Event. How much time?"

Amber looked to Nellie, but she was equally puzzled.

Merlin looked around at the belfry, at his rescuers. He turned to Cam, staring at him. Uncertain, the young Celt stared back and then spoke softly.

"Mat an traoù ganeoc'h ar bí, a dhrewdyh uasail?"

The man's eyes fluttered for a moment, and then opened again.

"An Darvoud… Assa a-gensow? Kedhla pandr'a hwer?"

The two women were shocked to hear him respond fluently in Cam's native tongue. The Celt shook his head and gave a longer answer in the same language as Amber and Nellie listened to their exchange in wonder. Then the man turned back to them and, without missing a beat, switched back to English.

"Where are we now?"

"We're escaping from the Roundheads," Amber answered. The man mulled this over for a moment.

"Yes… yes… that could work…"

"So, let's go down these stairs, okay?" Amber suggested gently.

He looked at her as if she was the one touched in the head. "Yes, of course!" he cried out suddenly. "Let's go down these stairs!" He immediately headed down the spiral stairs at a brisk clip. The three rushed to catch up with him. At the bottom he fairly threw open the door, but then stood there, frozen.

Alex, the professor, and Simon were there. So was a ring of some twenty or thirty Roundhead soldiers holding their firearms at the ready.

So, too, was Master Stearne.

31

The witch hunter looked on with malevolent approval, arms crossed, as the seven were made to kneel so the soldiers could bind their arms at the wrists with thick coarse rope. The villagers, re-emerging after the pterosaur attack, gathered to see the show.

"So thought you to terrorize us with winged gargoyles?" Stearne thundered for the benefit of his audience, striding up and down in front of the prisoners. "Bear away our children to the depths of Hell? Thought you that your hellish minions would aid in your escape? Your master Satan has failed you! The Father of Lies has betrayed you." His gestures were sweeping, his oration theatrical.

"We should have tied him up better," Nellie muttered under her breath.

"We *should* have killed him," Amber growled back.

Stearne turned his eye on her and slowly strode up. He knelt until they were eye to eye.

"Thought you to make a fool of me?" His soft, silky voice made her skin crawl. "See now who is the fool, brazen harlot. Look upon your fate." He pointed, and she followed the gesture to the line of stakes. Several soldiers poured oil on the kindling, while others stood by with lit torches.

Amber had heard the phrase "burned at the stake" dozens of times without giving it any thought. Now she knew *exactly* what it meant. The growing realization horrified her, and made it hard to breathe.

She turned her head to escape Stearne's triumphant gaze and saw Nellie glaring daggers at the Puritan. Alex and Harcourt stared ahead in numb despair—even Simon was silent. Cam was the only one still fighting, gripped firmly in a headlock by a pair of soldiers who struggled to keep him under control.

Merlin, on the other hand, gazed into the distance and mumbled to himself, seemingly oblivious to the drama around him.

Tears stung Amber's eyes. Had she doomed these people by insisting on rescuing a madman? There had to be more to him than what they were seeing, she *knew* it—and yet at that moment, none of it mattered. They had failed, and they were going to die. Horribly.

"These are dark times." Stearne rose and stretched

out his arms, addressing the crowd again. "These are the end times, when dreadful omens appear across the land and all the works of man, yea, even the very foundations of the earth, have been shaken by the hand of the Almighty. Soon shall come the end of days, and with it a new Jerusalem for those who remain faithful to His holy word."

"And what sayeth His holy scripture?" He turned to the prisoners and pointed an accusing finger at them. *"Thou shalt not suffer a witch to live!"*

A roar went up from the crowd.

"What about Lord Fairfax?" Amber yelled, struggling to be heard over the ruckus. "He's the one in charge. You know he wouldn't want this. You soldiers! He didn't order this!"

"You know she's right!" Nellie shouted. "Lord Fairfax knows we're innocent! He'll court-martial all of you if you go along with this madman!" Their words rattled the soldiers visibly. Some shot sidelong looks at each other.

"Keep silent, you lying Jezebels," Stearne spat. "We ought to obey God, rather than men! As for me and my house, we shall serve the Lord."

"You can't just kill people without a trial," Amber protested. "That's murder!"

The witch hunter ignored her. "Take them to the stakes," he shouted. "We have endured their presence too long already. The time has come to obey the Lord's command, and put an end to it!"

The crowd erupted in another righteous bellow of anger and fear. The soldiers dragged the condemned to their feet and marched them over to the stakes, hauling them atop the crunchy, rickety stacks of oil-drenched tinder.

Amber stood in shocked silence as their erstwhile jailer wrapped her in links of chain, a grin on her ugly face. She watched the twisted, hateful faces of the villagers who cheered him on, and the soldiers standing carefully off to the side with torches, awaiting their part. She looked anywhere but at Stearne—she didn't want to see his triumphant expression.

It took four soldiers and an armored fist to the head to secure Cam to his stake. Even then, he strained against the chains.

Camulos, grant me strength. Andraste, Queen of Ravens, give not our flesh to your birds yet. She who has not fallen, let me not fall here without vengeance. Break these chains to let me battle them now, or consign my howling spirit, merciless and terrible, to haunt them forever.

He turned to look at Amber, a mixture of fury and helplessness in his expression. He would give his life to save her from this fate.

* * *

Certain that she was about to die, Amber tried to think of her family, and everyone she'd loved in her life. Instead she found herself distracted by the sight of Merlin, and by the thought she'd never even know his real name. He continued to mutter to himself, and looked like a real-life martyred saint now, gazing up to heaven in an unending stream of rapturous prayer.

Except he wasn't gazing skyward.

Instead he stared fixedly out to the west, down the long main road. Amber followed his gaze and saw a group of horsemen, swiftly approaching. They looked important, yet they were coming the wrong way for it to be Lord Fairfax.

"Look! It's Cromwell!" a soldier cried out.

As a wave of recognition spread through the crowd, cheers of joy broke out from villagers and soldiers alike. Only Stearne didn't seem to share their enthusiasm.

"Make way!" one of the newcomers cried. "Make way for the lieutenant-general!" And the crowd quickly obliged, creating a path that allowed Cromwell's horse to pull close to the stakes and kindling. Amber couldn't help but stare at him as he rode up.

He looked so... so *ordinary*. So unexceptional. Not like someone who'd changed the course of history. Cromwell raised a hand to calm the crowd's excitement, and addressed them.

"Divine Providence has brought us to you," he called

out, "with reinforcements and good tidings!" A cheer went up. "The Welsh have been defeated at Pembroke!"

Another cheer erupted.

"The Scots have been defeated at Preston, and the rest of the Parliamentary army and horses march behind us, coming to put a swift end to this rebellion." At this last bombshell, the crowd went wild. Even the most hardened soldiers gestured enthusiastically. Then Cromwell's face darkened as he took in the scene before him.

"But what is this Papist spectacle?" He looked around accusingly. "Who gave the order to permit some damnable Spanish *auto-da-fé*?"

"Sir, my lord lieutenant-general—" Stearne looked shell-shocked. He removed his hat and attempted a nervous bow.

"Are *you* the varlet responsible?" Cromwell's voice was hard as iron. The witch hunter seemed to virtually melt under the commander's gaze.

"Begging your pardon, my lord. I am, but you see—"

"Arrest this man at once!"

After just a moment of confused hesitation, a pair of soldiers seized Stearne. He sputtered and tried to protest, but the lieutenant-general shut him down.

"Get him out of my sight! He will stand trial for this outrage." Then he gestured toward the prisoners. "Free these people at once, and fetch yonder wagon. These blameless folk are innocent, and possess much critical information needed by Parliament. They shall come with us back to London. Step to it, post haste!"

Stearne squirmed and begged for mercy, but the Roundheads dragged him off with the same enthusiasm as they had shown his victims. Still more soldiers hurried to unchain Amber and the others, helping them down from the tangled piles of firewood. Some were gentler than others.

Professor Harcourt practically swooned when he was released, forcing two soldiers to support him.

When they released Cam from his chains he leapt to the ground and hurried to Amber's side, looking uncertain at what had just transpired. The moment she saw him, she grabbed him and hugged him hard.

The stolen wagon, still loaded with their things, was quickly brought around—complete with a volunteer driver. The soldiers, so recently ready to burn them alive, became the very models of courtesy while helping Amber into the wagon, each eager to have Cromwell take notice.

Cam snarled, shaking off the helping hands, then hopped up in the wagon on his own and sat down beside Amber. Alex and Nellie got in, followed by Simon.

"Get your poxy hands off me, you wankers," he growled at the soldiers when they tried to help him up.

Amber turned her attention again to Merlin. Though seeming to have recovered from his horrific wounds, the man seemed unaware of the soldiers. He'd stopped mumbling, and walked like a zombie, his unblinking stare fixed on some infinitely distant point as Amber and Cam pulled him up to join them. He sat down, Indian style, across from Amber, though he kept his head turned to the front.

"You've all done well," he whispered, so softly that even Amber had to strain to hear him.

"What's that?" she asked him.

"You've all done well," Cromwell called out in a loud voice.

"Now we must needs make haste for London," Merlin breathed.

"Now we must needs make haste for London," the lieutenant-general announced to the crowd. Amber looked from Merlin to the soldier, thoroughly confused.

Last up to board the wagon was Harcourt. He had one foot on the running board when he suddenly broke away from his helpers and practically staggered over to where Cromwell and his entourage waited on horseback.

"My dear Lord Cromwell," Harcourt said, teary-eyed. "Please allow me to extend my deepest thanks at your fortuitous and most gentlemanly rescue of my companions and myself. We are forever in your debt, and indeed, perhaps I speak for all of England when I say—" He reached up to grasp Cromwell's hand, closing his eyes as if in prayer. "—thank you."

A gasp went out from the crowd.

A woman screamed.

The former prisoners—except for Merlin—all turned to see what was the matter.

"Holy shit," Amber said.

Harcourt moved close to Cromwell's mount, then *through* it.

"What sorcery is this?" an angry voice cried out. Others picked up the cry.

"You fool! Get in the wagon!" Merlin yelled, getting to his feet.

"You fool! Get in the wagon!" Cromwell implored the crowd.

Unnerved by the commotion, Harcourt opened his eyes. Finding himself in the *middle* of man and horse, he panicked and lashed out with both hands as if to clear a path through the horse's hindquarters. One flailing arm connected with something solid. Instantly Cromwell and his riders vanished, replaced by a glossy obsidian sphere about twice the size of a billiard ball, hanging perfectly still in the air.

Terror swept through the onlookers.

Without warning, and with surprising strength and vigor, Merlin shoved the gawking driver to the ground and took up the reins.

"Hang on!" he yelled. "We're out of here! *Giddy-up!* Yah! Yah!" The horses lurched forward, jolting the wagon's passengers.

"Hang on! We're out of here! *Giddy-up!* Yah! Yah!" echoed the little black floating sphere.

The professor's panic turned to terror as he saw the wagon leaving without him. He let out an involuntary squawk of alarm.

"Wait!" he cried. "Wait for me!" Merlin, however, showed no signs of stopping. Harcourt ran and leapt as the wagon went clattering past. Simon and Alex caught him, hauling him up as they would a flopping trout onto a boat.

"A gentleman… never… runs…" Harcourt wheezed.

Simon sat up and cupped his hands at the angry mob. "Bollocks to Cromwell! Fuck right off!" he hollered with malicious glee, finishing with a two-finger salute.

Merlin whipped the reins like a madman, sending the horses into full gallop.

He turned his head back for a moment.

"Groucho! Cromwell program off and return!" he called out. A few moments later a whistling sound rose on the wind, and the glossy black sphere came humming through the air after the wagon, quickly overtaking it. It settled into a holding pattern about a foot above Merlin's shoulder, matching their speed.

"Harpo and Chico," Merlin called out again. "Activate and run program two!"

About a hundred yards behind them, a forty-foot tall tyrannosaurus abruptly blipped into existence and let out an ear-splitting roar. Harcourt gave a high-pitched scream and Merlin cackled. His passengers watched the show in wonderment as they continued to speed down the road, past fields and farms.

Simon called up to the front.

"Oy! We've got company coming!"

Amber spun and watched as two-dozen riders or more thundered up the road in hot pursuit. Merlin whirled, eyes blazing.

"So quickly? Damn it!" he swore. He rubbed his chin. "Seems the primitives aren't as dumb as they look. Time for more sophisticated tactics."

The wagon gave a sudden lurch as the road abruptly ran out, turning into wild heathlands.

"Damn it! We're out of the shard. Somebody take the reins!"

"I'll do it!" Nellie replied. She hopped up and took over. Merlin turned around and directed his full attention to their pursuers. The black sphere moved closer to him. The horses continued to strain, but the wagon moved noticeably slower now on the uneven terrain.

"We'll never outrun them like this!" Nellie shouted over her shoulder.

"No… not like this…" Merlin agreed. He sat down Indian style again and settled into a guru-like stance.

With a look of intense focus, he began to calmly rattle off a string of commands.

"Harpo, Chico, kill program two and return.

"Groucho, climb two point five meters and give me a good wide bird's eye. Come down seventy-five centimeters… Hold it, that's enough.

"Now give me a full three-sixty degrees, full cone image. That's it. Record for five seconds and return…"

Amber watched him with a newfound sense of awe as he continued to direct his magical floating sphere. It dropped back down and took to hovering above his shoulder, quickly joined by two more flying in from far behind them.

They must be drones, Amber thought.

Merlin turned to Nellie. "As soon as we drop behind this next rise, stop the wagon." She looked back in fear at the riders pursuing them, just a few hundred yards behind and gaining. She turned to Merlin.

"We can't stop here!" she yelled back. "Look at them!"

"You madman! We daren't stop now!" Harcourt echoed with a wail.

"Just do it!"

Nellie shook her head, but the moment they crested the next low hill, she pulled up on the reins.

"Whatever you've got planned," she said, "do it fast!"

Merlin gave a sharp nod.

"Groucho, run a trailing cloak on these parameters."

The floating orb took station above the wagon, projecting a wall of light behind them.

"What's it doing?" Amber asked.

"Groucho here is projecting an image at the back of the wagon. It's not perfect, but for our purposes it's the next best thing to invisibility."

"But they're charging up now!" Alex cried. "They'll charge right into us!" It was true. They could hear—and feel—the thundering hooves of the approaching horses.

"Not if we can throw them off our trail," Merlin said with a determined glint in his eye. "Now everyone be quiet. Harpo, Chico, link to Groucho, upload feed for replay on continuous loop. Name your files decoy one and decoy two respectively, and put them on deck. Activate scatter pattern and leapfrog modes on my mark, and… now!"

The two other drones sped away from them again at a sharp right angle, heading across the heath. The sound of hoofbeats reached a crescendo and the Roundheads suddenly appeared over the rise directly behind them.

Amber gasped.

"Don't make a sound!" Merlin hissed.

The riders reined in their horses, coming to a dead stop just a few yards away. Amber grabbed Cam's arm and put a finger to her lips, while the professor stuffed a hand in his own mouth to keep from making any noise.

A moment later, an exact duplicate of the wagon,

complete with passengers, came to life two hundred yards to their right and raced noisily across the countryside.

"There!" One of the riders pointed, and the whole company turned as one. They spurred their steeds, some passing within a few feet of the real wagon as they thundered off in pursuit of its phantom twin.

32

This is totally surreal, Amber thought, watching the hologram speeding away in the distance, complete with sound, leading the Roundheads on a wild goose chase. Merlin took up the reins again. Once the horsemen were out of earshot they set off, veering in the opposite direction from their pursuers.

"Where do we go now?" Alex asked from the back of the wagon.

"We head south, Constable Brice," Merlin called back.

"Why south?"

"My vessel is that way," he answered. "We'll be safe once we get aboard her."

Harcourt stiffened. *"Safe on a ship?"* he shrieked. "God's teeth, man, that's madness! My ship was blasted by pirates, and then torn to pieces by a behemoth! Out of four hundred and fifty souls, I was the sole survivor, and only by the skin of my teeth!"

Nellie turned around and glared at him. "Harcourt, you are an insufferably obtuse man. Sole survivor, my foot!"

The professor stared at her for a long moment before the realization hit.

"Good heavens!" he said. "You're the American woman from the ferry. Miss Corcoran! You are truly a master of disguise."

"*Cochrane*, you idiot," Nellie spat back. "Yes, it's me, and no thanks to you. We might've made it to shore together, if it hadn't been for that precious case of yours. As it was, I narrowly escaped being gobbled up by that gargantuan shark, and wound up clear on the other side of the estuary." She took a deep breath to compose herself.

"It's just as well," she continued. "I was able to make it as far as Colchester without attracting attention, and you don't exactly have a knack for getting around inconspicuously, or blending in once you arrive."

Harcourt could only sputter in response. Simon grinned broadly, seeming to take great pleasure from this exchange, and even Amber had to suppress her smile. She felt just a little bit sorry for the professor, though. His role of hero had been blown completely out of the water.

"There's no need for you to worry, Professor Harcourt," Merlin said with a casual wave of one hand. One of the spheres still hovered nearby. "You'll find my vessel one hundred percent shark-proof, no matter how large the shark."

"Just a minute," Amber said. "How did you know the professor's name, or Alex's?" She hesitated for a moment, and then added, "For that matter, who the hell *are* you?" He turned slowly and gave her an indecipherable look, made all the more imposing by his dark violet eyes. She blushed.

"I mean, we all should thank you," she said, "but we don't even *know* you."

"Ah, but I know who you are, Amber from the twenty-first Century," he said matter-of-factly. "All of you. Even though I had been, to all extents and purposes, in a deep coma, my brain restored a low level of cognitive operation. I heard everything that happened back in the bell tower— or rather, my auditory system recorded it. I just wasn't able to access it until after I regained consciousness."

Simon stared ahead, suddenly very quiet. Amber suspected he might be recalling all the things he had been saying while he thought Merlin was dead.

"Well, that… explains *that*, I suppose," she said uncertainly, "but—"

"Well, my name is Dr. Jonathan Meta," he said, cutting her off. "Though you all can keep calling me Merlin if you like. I have to admit, I rather like it."

"Are you a medical doctor then?" Alex asked.

"No, an astrophysicist," he said. "The director of

the Advanced Transpatial Physics Lab's Omnia Astra Project."

"Astrophysicist?" Amber said, suddenly excited. "Like Neil deGrasse Tyson?" She loved astronomy. Then she became serious again. "So do you have any idea what's going on? I mean, what's causing all this, this... insanity?"

"You mean the Event?" Dr. Meta—Merlin—pulled the wagon to a halt and turned back. The thoughtful look in his strange violet eyes was made even more surreal by the cascade of infinitesimal stars playing across their surface. "Well, yes. I know what it is." He paused, then added, "And if I'm right, we can put the world back the way it was. It will be just as if it never happened."

33

The others looked at Merlin in shocked silence while the enormity of his words sank in. Then they began peppering him with questions, words overlapping to form an incomprehensible wall of sound. Only Cam was silent, distracted by something behind them.

"Wait, wait, wait!" Merlin raised a hand. "I'll explain everything as soon as I can, but for now the first order of business is to get to safety, yes?"

Before anyone could answer, Cam urgently pulled on Amber's arm. She turned, then gasped.

"We've got a problem," she said.

Merlin frowned. "Now what?"

Cam pointed. The wheels had left a deep, unmistakable trail behind them. Simon raised an eyebrow.

"So how are your gadgets at erasing wagon wheel tracks?"

"Damn it. I should have thought of that." Merlin shook his head grimly. "It may not be long before our pursuers will retrace their path and pick up our trail. There's nothing for it. We'll have to lose the wagon." He scanned the horizon. Slightly off their current course to the southeast, a forest of linden and hornbeam trees beckoned, erupting suddenly out of the surrounding heath. "We'll head for those woods up ahead. We can lose them in there. Quickly now!"

Gathering up what little they had, they disembarked from the wagon, then Merlin turned it around to the west and slapped the horses, sending them galloping away.

"Step carefully," Alex cautioned them. "If we're lucky, they won't catch sight of our footprints, and will just keep following the wagon."

"Until they catch it up and realize they've been had," Simon muttered.

Alex shot him a look. "Aren't you the optimist?"

"Hopefully, they'll be chasing the rovers a little longer before they even notice the problem, and then they'll have to backtrack to where they first lost us," Merlin said. "We really need to be out of sight before then, though."

The thought spurred them all forward.

After half an hour or so of swift hiking, the group reached the safety of the forest, dark and shadowy in the late day.

Still Merlin urged them on, and another thirty minutes later, they found a small clearing, and he indicated that they could rest for a bit. After hours of being on the run, Amber's exhaustion caught up with her, and she dragged with every step she took. The others didn't seem to be doing much better.

They collapsed on the ground or rested against tree trunks. Cam stretched out full length on his back, looking up at little auburn squirrels that chattered away at their intrusion. Overhead, thrushes and larks went from tree to tree in search of a meal. The shadows were long.

"How far away is your ship?" Nellie asked Merlin.

"Once we get out of this forest, I'd guess another hour or two."

"It'll be nightfall before that," Alex said, looking up through the trees. "I don't fancy our chances, stumbling around here in the dark."

"Do you think we'll be safe here?" Harcourt looked around in apprehension.

"That depends on how long it takes for Cromwell's boys to realize they've been sent on a wild ghost chase," Simon mused, "and how quickly they can track us back here, right?"

Merlin nodded.

"What about your drones?" Amber pointed to the sleek onyx orb silently hovering just above the scientist's shoulder. "Any word from them?"

"Good question. The rovers are running what I call a leapfrog program. As soon as one gets out of sight of the Roundheads—manages to duck beneath a rise, or veers around a stand of trees—the other will speed further along and start re-projecting our audio-visual.

"That way, the pursuers never come close enough to get a good look. Of course, the soldiers might just give up, and decide to go back to town before it gets dark," he said. "Or they might run into another shard. Either way, it's a good idea to check on how they're doing." He raised his voice slightly. "Groucho, show us the views from Chico and Harpo, please."

The helpful drone projected two images in midair, inciting a gasp from Cam, Harcourt, and Nellie. One hologram showed heathlands speeding past, while the other revealed only a black void. Merlin frowned.

"That's not good. Reverse to last transmission from rover three, rear view." Both screens recalibrated and showed the horsemen behind them in hot pursuit. One rider moved close enough to hazard a pistol shot, and with a boom of smoke and a crackling electronic squeal, the right-hand screen abruptly went black.

"Damn lucky shot!" Alex swore.

The illusion must have been shattered along with the drone. The remaining screen showed the Roundheads halting in surprise, and it was clear the jig was up. The cavalrymen milled about in confusion for a few moments, then one of them took command. He gestured, they did an about-face, and sped their horses back the way they had come.

"So much for that trick," Simon said sardonically.

"We were lucky it held up as long as it did," Merlin replied. He rubbed his chin thoughtfully. "That was almost twenty minutes ago. Now it all depends on how well the Roundheads can track us." He looked off into the distance. "Harpo, cancel scatter program and return."

"I simply must know how your flying automatons are able to hear your commands over such great distances," the Professor gushed.

"It's a matter of electromagnetic radiation being sent out through a cranial implant," Merlin replied absently. "Normally, I wouldn't even have to bother speaking aloud to them, but I think the Spanish Inquisition brigade back there damaged my neural links. I'll have to check them later, all this talking to the robots is such a boring chore."

Harcourt started to ask another question, and Merlin held up a hand to forestall him. "I'll explain further when we're safely aboard my ship."

"What do we do now?" Nellie asked. "Keep going? Hunker down here for the night, and leave at first light?"

"That's not a bad idea," Simon agreed. "At least it's not as bloody cold here as it was in Roundheadville."

Amber nodded. She'd noticed the slight rise in

temperature as well, although she'd attributed it to the extra layer of clothes she'd stolen from Stearne's guard. The leather buff coat was almost *too* warm now.

"Let's face it. We've had a hell of a day already." Alex looked at the others. "If we try to keep pushing ourselves, in the state we're in, I doubt we'll get very far. At the very least we need some food and water, if not a few hours of sleep."

No one disagreed.

"Still, though, we can't let the Roundheads take us by surprise again," Harcourt cautioned.

Amber had an idea.

"Merlin, can your drones go track them?"

"Well, in theory, yes," he replied, "but they don't fly very high, and that kind of thing isn't really their strong suit. I would need to be guiding them manually. Although—" He paused to think. "What I *could* do is post them in fixed locations at the perimeter of the forest, to alert us if anyone begins to enter the trees."

"That seems like a good plan." Alex nodded. "In the meantime, let's see what we can do about our basic needs. Amber, do you think you and Cam might come up with a little firewood?"

"Sure!" Amber replied. She nudged Cam, pantomimed collecting sticks, and the two set off.

"It will need to be a *very* small fire if we don't want to attract attention," Harcourt warned.

"Of course," Alex replied. "Professor, would you mind splitting up the food into equal parts for everyone?" At first Harcourt looked as if he would object, but then he changed his mind.

"Why, certainly. At your service."

"Nellie, maybe you could assist the professor?" She turned so Harcourt couldn't see her face, and mouthed *watch him.*

Nellie smiled.

"My pleasure."

Harcourt frowned ever so slightly.

Alex turned to Merlin. "Say, Doctor, can you spare Groucho long enough to help us locate a creek or an artesian spring, anything with some water?"

Merlin nodded. "Finding a basic chemical signature like that will be simple enough for its sensors. Groucho, are you picking up any fresh water nearby?" The orb whirred for a moment, and then projected a red arrow pointing off to the east, deeper into the forest, along with data floating alongside the pointer.

Freshwater source
Approximately 400 meters

"Ta very much," Alex replied with a smile. She went

over to their meager pile of supplies and picked out a bucket, a water skin and few other small items which she quietly placed in an empty flour bag. She sauntered over to where Simon sat resting against a tree, and gave him a soft kick, almost affectionately.

"Hey, you lazy sod. I don't suppose there's enough gallantry in you to accompany a lady on a trip to fetch a pail of water, is there?"

He opened a suspicious eye. She stood over him, dangling the water skin by its cord just above him. He frowned, but grabbed it and stood up.

"About time you asked me out for a drink," he said with a grin.

Harcourt watched the two of them with thinly veiled disapproval.

"I say, would it be better if I accompany the two of you?"

Alex waved him back.

"Thank you for the concern, Professor, but it's quite alright." She gave Simon a smile. "We'll be right back!"

34

As Alex and Simon tramped through the ground cover, the fragrant forest air seemed to swallow the sounds around them, though odd snatches of birdsong echoed now and then.

"Aren't we there yet?" Simon looked around as they walked, unimpressed with the scenery. "How far did that gadget say it was again?"

"Four hundred meters," Alex replied. "That's around two furlongs for you, Grandpa."

Simon shot her a look. "I bloody well know what a meter is."

"Well, then let's cut the whingeing and carry on, shall we? Not too much further."

Simon opened his mouth to mount a suitable retort, but froze before he got a word out. Alex looked at him in alarm.

"What is it?" she whispered.

He took a moment before answering.

"We're not alone," he said softly.

As calmly as possible, they looked around. Anyone wanting to spy on them had plenty of cover, trees, and thick undergrowth. Then a crack sounded close by, then another. A red fox burst from the bushes, staring at them with a wild glare before bolting off.

They let themselves breathe again, exchanging sheepish looks.

"I think we're going to be okay," Alex quipped. "Let's keep going." Simon shook his head, but followed her without any further protest. He liked to watch her make her way through the woods. Policewomen's skirts had been much longer in his time. He approved of the change. And was it his imagination, or was Constable Brice putting just a little more sway into her normal no-nonsense stride?

"Jesus!"

Without warning, Alex halted in her tracks, causing Simon to nearly bang into her. He cursed—and looked up to see what was the matter.

A massive skull, far larger than any human cranium, had been impaled on a tall wooden stake, blocking their path at eye level. It was a cave bear, he guessed, painted with thick lines of red ochre. Leather strips hung in ribbons around the pole.

"Prehistoric?" Simon whispered.

"Undoubtedly." Alex traced a finger along the ridges of the bone. It came away red. "And freshly painted. I wonder who did this."

Simon shook his head.

"That I don't know, but I think they live up there." He pointed up through the trees at an outcropping of mossy rock. Deerskin hides were stretched out over a framework of lashed tree limbs to form a canopy over a cave entrance.

"Let's be very, very quiet now," Alex said in a calm, measured voice.

"And get the hell away from here."

She shook her head. "We can't just leave."

Simon stared at her in disbelief.

"Are you stark staring *mad*?"

"We have to make sure there's no one in there," Alex insisted, her tone still calm and low.

"And what if there is? What then?"

Alex shushed him as his voice started to rise.

"*Then* we get the hell out of here, yeah?"

Simon looked dubious.

"Look, we're going to be sleeping nearby," she insisted. "We don't want anyone sneaking up on us, do we?" She raised an eyebrow.

Simon frowned, but nodded. Alex set down her gear, stepped around the totem and started creeping up toward the mouth of the cave. Simon stayed where he was, looking left and right for any signs of hostile natives.

Alex made it up to the opening and cautiously peered inside, her heart pounding in her chest despite her brave words. Darkness and quiet and a truly rank smell—that of meat long gone bad. She waited long enough for her eyes to adjust to the gloom, ascertained the cave was empty of humans or animals, then straightened up. The tightness in her chest eased.

"It's okay," she called down. "No one's home."

She made her way downhill and rejoined Simon.

"Nothing to worry about," she assured him. "By the looks of things—and the *smell*—no one's been around for a while."

"That's good news for a change," Simon muttered. They grabbed their gear and continued on.

As they ventured further, the forest changed in subtle ways from prehistoric to primeval. The low undergrowth of fern and bracken grew denser, joined by horsetails and clusters of firmoss. Oaks and birches vanished altogether, replaced by towering tree ferns and what looked like stands of some giant form of asparagus.

"That's something then," Simon remarked.

Alex nodded without comment.

After another hundred yards or so, they came to a small lake. At first glance it appeared idyllic, a wonderful spot for a picnic. Closer inspection showed lobe-finned fish the size of alligators stomping around the mud chasing jumbo dragonflies and other oversized insects. As Alex and Simon approached, the budding amphibians quickly turned and scurried back into the water.

The little lake swarmed with life, predominantly trilobites and primitive fish—some funny looking, and some scary looking.

"What do you reckon?" Simon asked her.

"It looks safe enough from here, but be careful, there could be something big and nasty lurking beneath the surface."

"Isn't there always?"

Alex gave him a look.

"I'm dead serious, you know," she said. "Just watch yourself. Or don't. Suit yourself."

Simon set to work filling the water skins and bucket while Alex went down a little further away from him. She knelt by the water's edge and washed her hands, then rinsed out her neckerchief and used her reflection in the water to clean up a little.

After a few minutes Simon paused in his work and turned to her with raised eyebrows.

"You're a big help."

Alex shrugged. She stood and straightened her skirt and stockings. In the process, she looked up to catch him ogling her.

"Do you *mind*?"

"What?"

"I've seen the way you look at me, Simon. And at Amber. And Nellie."

"What of it?" he said with mock indignation. "You can't blame a bloke, can you? You lot trouncing about the countryside in your sassy little skirts and low-cut tops and all."

"Have you always been such a right cocky little shit?"

He shrugged. "Now, why shouldn't I be?"

She finished fussing with her stockings, and stood up straight. Crossing her arms, she gave him a long appraising look.

"You know, Simon, the funny thing is, if you were even just the *slightest* bit better-mannered, some girls might even say you weren't a half-bad looking fellow."

He shot her a look. "Constable Brice, are you fraternizing with the enemy?"

"I have to confess, I had an ulterior motive for setting out on this little expedition." She gave him a half smile. He grinned in response.

"Don't you have police regulations forbidding that sort of thing?" he responded. "Chatting up bad boys? Or... could it be... that you're a bad girl?"

She refused to answer him. Instead, she stretched down, pretending to straighten out her stockings one last time, but in reality showing off her legs to good advantage. She tilted her head and gave him the barest hint of a smile.

"Do shut up and come over here, will you?"

Simon didn't have to be told twice. He grinned and strode over to her with a jaunty little walk, hands in his pockets.

"What did you have in mind?" he asked.

"Something like this."

She put her hands on his shoulders, and slowly ran them down his arms. He looked down at her chest.

"You have a pair of absolutely smashing breasts."

"Do you want to touch them?"

"Thought you'd never ask."

"Go on, then."

He smiled as she took him by the wrists and lifted his hands. But then she seized his left hand in a wristlock, reached behind her back with her right, and expertly cuffed his right wrist.

"Hey now, easy!"

"Come with me, if you please," she said crisply, pulling him over to the closest of the tall asparagus-looking trees and handcuffing him to it.

35

"Sweet Jesus, you *are* a right kinky bird, Constable!" Simon said, and he laughed. Alex turned and faced him, all business.

"Not at all, actually."

His laugh died away as he saw the resolve in her eyes.

"What are you doing?" he asked flatly, as if he already suspected the answer.

"Does the name Pippa McDermott ring any bells?"

He frowned.

"What about Veronica Cordingly?"

"Are these meant to be old girlfriends of mine? Never heard of 'em." His eyes flashed with their usual defiance, but his voice betrayed a growing unease.

"Oh, you will. Or would have, I suppose—but you've already started, haven't you?"

"Already started *what*?" he answered, a little too

quickly and a little too sharply. Alex continued.

"I suppose you don't recall Chloe Wenham either."

He closed his mouth tight and said nothing, his face as impassive as a chunk of concrete—but not before she'd caught the telltale look of surprise in his eyes.

"Oh, you *do* remember her, I see." A look of triumph flickered across her features. "Yes, I expect you'd remember one of your first. You stalked her for months beforehand, didn't you?" She peered at him intently.

"I don't know what you're talking a—" His protest was cut off when she pulled out the short length of cord from her bag and gagged him with it. He boiled with muffled outrage and pulled at the handcuffs, his eyes furious, but she ignored him.

"I don't want to hear any more of your blather, Simon. I just want you to listen to me, understand what I'm doing, and why." She cocked her head to one side and studied him. "I didn't recognize you at first, you see. Not surprising, really. The first time I ever saw your picture, you were an old bastard. But when you rattled off your whole name for us this morning, that rang a bell—and I finally placed where I know you."

He stopped his thrashing.

"You're Simon William Broad," she continued. "You were busy in the late fifties and early sixties, all throughout East London and Essex. The papers called you the 'Simon Says' killer—daft name, that. You killed almost a dozen young women—just like Amber, Nellie and me. Did you ever use this knife for the job?"

She pulled out his flick-knife, and held it up to his face before releasing its blade with a touch of the button. Simon's brows rose at the sight, and he shook his head, trying to plead with her through the gag.

"I'm an officer of the law, Simon," she said, staring into his eyes. "I'm not a vigilante, and I'm not a murderer like you. Maybe I'm wrong about the timing and you haven't even killed anyone yet, but here's the problem. There's no jurisprudence anymore. There's nothing in place to rein in people who go wrong, and I can't just let you go. It's not fair, but neither is being a serial killer." She heaved a small sigh, then continued. "Sorry, Simon, but that's why I have to kill you. Maybe it's just to clear my own conscience, but I needed you to know why first."

He furiously rattled the tree trunk, trying frantically to uproot it or pull it down, but it wasn't going anywhere. Alex coolly watched his struggles, until at last he gave up and stood there, trying to breathe, staring at her with an unreadable expression.

"Simon, I can make it quick and easy for you, but only if you cooperate with me." Her voice was unnervingly calm. "I know it's not much, but I'd bet that's a damn sight better deal than you offered any of your victims. Now why don't you get down on your knees for me."

He swallowed hard, still staring at her. Then, without a sound, he sunk down onto the damp ground and lowered his head.

It was Alex's turn to hesitate. She took a deep breath. Part of her had been steeling herself for this since they'd escaped from the witch hunter and his soldiers, but now that it came right down to it, she fought to steady her nerves.

She wasn't a killer. The man in front of her *was.* Not just a cold-blooded murderer, but one who enjoyed torturing his victims—doing so for days before putting them out of their torment. That brute fact was the only thing that gave her the strength to carry her plan through to the end. She tightened her grip on the blade and rapidly considered her options. A good, steady penetration just above the left collarbone, she decided.

Then Simon raised his head again, a new look of terror in his eyes. Looking over her shoulder he pulled away as much as he could, his eyes wide with fear, screams muffled by the rope. Alex furrowed her brow.

"Don't be pathetic, Simon. It won't work."

She caught just a flash of movement in her peripheral vision and wheeled around to see the thing swiftly emerging from the water—a giant aquatic scorpion, as big as a couch. Its massive armored claw arms bristled with spines like racks of elk antlers. Its huge head boasted a horrible maw, with an inner pair of clawed mouthparts as long as her forearms. It clamored and chittered hungrily for her, a sickening sound.

"Shit!"

The thing grabbed for Alex and she threw herself sideways to avoid its sweeping grasp. Her desperate dive sent her crashing painfully to the ground and she landed hard on her shoulder, rolling over with a sharp groan of pain. The switchblade went pinwheeling out of her hand and disappeared from sight. In an instant the scorpion scuttled up and was on her, hissing and chittering. She looked up and screamed as the massive spiny side limbs grasped her.

Trapped face-up and on her back, she began kicking and scrambling, fighting to back away as fast as she could. Stuck on her elbows she couldn't outrun it, and its short outer arms quickly pulled her in. Lashing out frantically with her legs, she could only barely keep clear of the ravenous maw.

One inner claw clamped down on her ankle, drawing blood and another scream from her. With a desperate kick, then another, she stomped away at the thing's twitching mouthparts until it released her. With her legs pulled free, she twisted around to her knees and half-crawled, half-fought, trying to break through the grasp of its side arms.

A stabbing pain in her back made her scream again.

The scorpion had stuck her with the spike of its tail.

* * *

Simon's panic at seeing the gigantic monster emerge from the water hadn't gone away, but at least it was focused on chasing down Alex, thus ignoring him. He grabbed the trunk of the prehistoric tree and pulled at it as hard as he could, using his whole body to try and either uproot it or pull it down.

No use. The tree wasn't budging.

Alex struggled to break free, but the monster's spiky front arms still had her ensnared. She twisted and squirmed to avoid its stinger, though the primitive scorpion lashed at her repeatedly. If the thing was venomous she'd be dead soon anyway, but she kept fighting. Finally, with a lucky twist, she squeezed out of its grasp, though not without taking another sting on the arm.

The gag was making it hard for Simon to breathe. He leaned against the trunk, trying to take in more air through his flaring nostrils. Alex screamed again, startling him back into action. He reached up with his handcuffed wrists and pulled himself up the trunk. He dug in with his feet and reached up again, lifting himself a little higher.

And then a little higher.

And then a little higher.

Alex came up on her feet and reached for her truncheon, but it had come out of its sheath at some point during the struggle. She grabbed the nearest weapon she could see—a long, jagged branch of something like bamboo. With a grunt, she broke it off and had just enough time to turn and raise it before the thing was on her again. She brought it down with all her strength, stabbing between the scorpion's huge compound eyes.

Her makeshift spear shattered on the carapace. She swore loudly and leapt forward, rolling over the scorpion's body and past its flailing, stinging tail.

Coming out of her roll she scrambled to her feet again. The hulking creature began twisting its body to circle back on her. With the water behind her, she backed away as much as she could, scanning left and right for the fallen switchblade. It was nowhere in sight. She cut to the left, to the trunk of the nearest asparagus-tree.

The scorpion charged her again, scuttling to cut off her escape. Alex backed up further, trying to keep trunks between her and the giant hissing, chittering creature, but she quickly realized she was only trapping herself in the dense foliage. The scorpion seemed to realize it, too. Its arms tore away at the greenery, and it was becoming harder for her to back away from the frenzied attack.

Then there was no more give behind her at all.

The vegetation was too dense for her to move any further. The scorpion's front arms clamped down on one of the stalks she was trying to squeeze past, snapping it in two. She kept her grip on the cut piece, and jabbed her new weapon deep into the scorpion's clattering crab mouth.

Lunging, the creature only succeeded in impaling itself further, and let out a hideous shrieking sound as its own momentum drove the stake deep into its primitive brain. The segmented legs flailed and stamped, its arms and tail extended out and up at bizarre angles, and then the thing simply came to a stop.

Alex slumped in relief and lay there a minute, crushed up against the stand of tree trunks. She tried to breathe, her heart racing a mile a minute. Her shoulder blade hurt like hell. She cupped her elbow for a closer look at the sting on her upper arm. The bleeding—and the pain—were considerable, but she had seen worse. Her real fear was poison, but with every breath she felt more confident that this primeval scorpion hadn't yet evolved the venom that its smaller descendants would possess in a few hundred million years.

You'll be fine, she assured herself. *Now get up.*

She managed to extricate herself from her cage of tree trunks and insect limbs. As she painfully pulled herself up and over the dead creature's armored carcass, a new thought suddenly occurred.

Where's Simon?

Her answer came instantly when he dropped down on top of her. The shock of the impact hit her like a truck. She screamed and tumbled off the scorpion's back, falling to the ground, her back and upper arm on fire. Simon tumbled, too, but he swiftly rolled with it and came up from behind while Alex tried to stagger to her feet. Without hesitation, he flung his handcuffed arms around her throat, and pulled tight.

She clutched at the chain links and fought to stand. Simon drove his knee into the small of her back, increasing the pressure on her windpipe, bending her spine and pulling her off balance. She strained to stay upright, then suddenly slammed the point of her elbow sharply into his ribs. He gasped and buckled. Taking advantage of his weakness, she lifted both her knees up into the air and brought them down again, flipping him over her head.

He thudded flat on the ground, winded. She gasped for air until he started to sit up. She snap-kicked him in the head, sending him sprawling. He yelped in pain and tried to get to his feet. She ran forward and followed up with a high kick to his face that knocked him into the fern.

As she rushed to finish him, a sudden spasm of pain jolted through her body, emanating from her back and arm. Her heart beat far too fast, and a wave of dizziness washed over her. She stumbled and extended her other arm to catch herself. Both her vision and her balance grew shaky and wobbly.

Shit. Guess the bloody thing was poisonous after all…

The world started spinning, then all she could make out was Simon rising up again. Coming toward her. With his flick-knife in hand.

Simon wiped his knife on Alex's blouse before standing, retracting the blade into the handle, and pocketing it. He smiled down at her corpse.

"You really do have lovely breasts, Constable." He briefly considered unbuttoning her blouse to take a look at them, but quickly discarded the notion. No time to play. He needed to get back to the rest of his group.

Besides, he'd never found his toys particularly interesting once they'd lost the ability to beg.

He hoped to have more quality time with Amber.

36

When they'd gathered enough wood to start building a fire, Amber went back to the clearing with their first armful. In the meantime, Cam continued looking, all the while keeping an eye out for danger and for food. Both habits were second nature to him. Their meager stock wouldn't last long but fortunately, foraging was something he did very well.

He felt very protective of his new companions.

Spying a cluster of mushroom caps growing amid the roots of a large hornbeam, he knelt to inspect them. They weren't any kind he recognized, so he reluctantly left them where they were. He'd seen how quickly the wrong kind of mushroom could kill a man. Cam considered offering them to Simon. The thought made him smile. If the man ate them with no ill effects, no harm done.

And if they proved fatal?

Well, at least he would've done something useful for the group.

Cam left that happy notion behind, along with the mushrooms. He wouldn't do it, of course. True, he didn't like or trust Simon, but the man hadn't done anything to warrant such treatment. Besides, poison was the weapon of cowards and Romans. If he ever killed Simon, it would be face to face.

A crackling of branches caught his attention. Instinctively, he slipped behind a tree until he could see who—or what—was making the noise. A figure stepped into view. Cam peered cautiously through his screen of leafy branches. His eyes narrowed.

Simon.

Cam had no great wish to greet the annoying man at the best of times, so he decided to remain out of sight. Simon strolled casually with a little smile on his face, that of a man without a care in the world. Cam looked behind him for the woman, Alex, frowning when he didn't see or hear her. What possible reason could she have for staying behind?

As Simon drew closer, Cam noticed worrisome signs. The man sported a bloody gash on the side of his forehead. His clothing was torn and encrusted with mud, along with other, darker stains that spoke of something more sinister. Yet he didn't wear the look of a person who had run into trouble. If anything, he looked *pleased* with himself.

Cam also noted that he didn't have any water. Hadn't they left with a bucket? Was Alex following behind, carrying it? He shook his head, watching Simon saunter by. Why had he saddled her with all the work? Why had he left her unescorted in the woods? He had no doubts about Alex's courage or strength, but what kind of man would ramble off and leave a woman behind to fend for herself?

His dislike continued to grow.

Cam waited a few minutes to give Simon time to go past him and out of sight again, staying concealed while he kept an eye on the woods to see if Alex would appear. When she didn't, he quickly headed back to the clearing.

Back in the clearing, Amber stacked the bundle of firewood she'd gathered. Sweat dripped between her breasts and trickled down her back, and her shift was damp under the corset.

Oh, for a hot shower, she thought.

She shed the buff coat, but left the breeches and boots on for the time being, along with the Han Solo jacket. The soldier's boots fit her well and were surprisingly comfortable, the leather supple and well worn.

Guess people really were *smaller, back in the day.*

"That's a nice look," Nellie said, grinning at Amber's new outfit. She'd changed out of her stolen uniform, too, so that she was in her original garb—a dark blue two-piece traveling dress made of broadcloth and camel-hair trim. Over that, she wore a Scotch ulster overcoat and a jaunty matching ghillie cap, both of black-and-white plaid.

"So glad to be back in my real clothes!" she sighed.

"Where did *those* come from?" Amber asked in amazement, admiring all the vintage wear.

"This was the bundle I brought when I came to rescue you. I couldn't bear the thought of being stuck in those horrid peasant clothes a minute longer!"

"You know, that cap makes you look like Sherlock Holmes."

Nellie laughed. "What? Cheeky girl! I'll have you know, this is the height of fashion. At least it was a few days ago. Does no one wear hats in the future?"

Amber gave her a tired smile, and sat down to wait for Cam to return. She felt a little guilty that he was still foraging without her help, but mostly grateful for the chance to catch her breath and rest for a bit.

Still, she couldn't help but worry about their pursuers. The risks increased with every moment they stayed in one place. She wasn't sure how far away they'd have to travel to shake off the fanatical Roundheads, but she doubted they'd gone far enough yet.

The day's events played over again in her mind's eye. Nearly tortured. Nearly raped. Nearly burned at the stake. Any one of those "nearlys" could have turned out so much worse, but that didn't help her relax. She wasn't sure she'd ever relax again.

She felt better knowing Cam was keeping an eye on things, and that Merlin had his drones flying on patrol. She wished that Alex and Simon would get back with the water though, if only to stop Professor Harcourt griping about it.

"Why do you suppose they're not back yet?" Harcourt asked again. He turned to Merlin. "Didn't you say it wasn't far at all?" He phrased it almost as an accusation.

Merlin and Nellie ignored him. This left only Amber. She wasn't hard-hearted enough to blow him off. She *wished* she was, but she wasn't.

"It may not be that far," she said, "but they had to make their way through trees and who knows what. And a bucket full of water is heavy, so it's going to take them longer to walk back." She smiled at him, face hurting from the insincerity. She would have gladly thrown him back to the megalodon to shut him up. "I'm sure everything is fine."

At that moment Simon burst out of the trees, limping heavily, blood running down from a gash on his forehead.

"Jesus! I couldn't do anything..."

He took a few more stumbling steps, then dropped to his knees.

Amber jumped to her feet and ran forward, Nellie close on her heels. Merlin—sitting Indian style as he concentrated on directing the rovers—looked up in surprise. Professor Harcourt followed a few steps behind, as if making sure it was safe before getting too close.

The first to reach Simon, Amber steadied him as he started to slump forward. She struggled to hold him up, but managed to stop him from doing a faceplant in the grass.

"Simon! What happened?"

"We—" He stopped, his breath coming in short, shallow gasps. He had a full water skin slung around his shoulder and she quickly uncorked it, lifting the spout to his lips so he could take a drink. He nodded his thanks, taking another draft before continuing.

"We found the water," he said. "We'd filled the skins and the bucket. Alex... she wanted to rinse off a bit, you know? Clean herself. Said she felt mucky. She was leaning down there at the water's edge, splashing water in her face, so she didn't see it when it came out of the water."

"Oh my god!" Amber covered her mouth.

"When *what* came out of the water?" Nellie hunkered down next to her.

"Ah fuck, I dunno." Simon shook his head as if to clear it. "It was some sort of giant scorpion thing. The one that grabbed Alex was as big as the wagon. Bigger, maybe. Another one—a smaller one—attacked me before I could do anything. I had my knife, stabbed it in its eyes..." He trailed off, swallowed, then looked up, his eyes filled with pain and regret.

"By the time I got away, it was too late. The fucker had stung her, ripped into her. She wasn't moving."

Nellie looked at him in disbelief. "Do you mean to tell me that you *left* her there?"

"Well, I—"

"You *left* her there, without checking to see if she was still *alive*?"

Simon shook his head in denial, tears streaking through the mud and blood on his face. "You weren't there," he insisted. "Jesus, I barely got away myself. Do you think I would've left her if there had been anything I could've done to help?"

Nellie shot Harcourt a quick condemning glare.

"Not everyone does what they can."

Harcourt flushed a fiery, shamed red and stayed unaccustomedly silent.

"Merlin," Nellie called out urgently. "We need to go see if there's anything we can do for Alex."

A sudden movement caught Amber's attention and she looked up, startled. Cam stood at the edge of the clearing, at the same spot where Simon had emerged. He watched them in intense silence, his face unreadable as stone. The fury burning behind his eyes terrified her.

"Cam, what—" she began.

* * *

The Celt suddenly stormed forward, grabbed Amber by the arm and hauled her to her feet. She yelped in shock. Simon tried to hold on to her and Cam shoved him back, hard. He hit the ground with a wince and a whimper of pain, then glared up, furious.

"What the hell, mate?"

"Cam, what the hell is *wrong* with you? Can't you see he's hurt?" Amber pulled away from him and turned back to Simon.

Cam gave a frustrated growl and ran over to Merlin. The doctor sat with eyes closed, deep in concentration. Cam hated to risk disturbing the wizard if he was in the middle of spellcasting, but he had to warn them.

"*Mo thiarna asarlaí...*" Cam began.

My lord sorcerer...

Merlin shook his head and held up a hand to silence him.

"We have contact from the rovers!" he called out to the others. He put a hand to his ear, even though Cam couldn't see anything there. "A Roundhead horseman has dismounted and is entering the forest to our north and advancing. May just be a scout, or he might be the first of many."

"How much time do we have?" Harcourt gasped.

"No time. They're coming our way. We need to pull things together now and leave."

Cam threw a brief, almost pleading look at Amber,

then took off at a dead run back into the forest.

"Cam!" Amber turned to Nellie. "I think he's going to look for Alex. He shouldn't go off alone." She started after him, but Simon grabbed her by the arm.

"You can't go off by yourself," he said. "It's too dangerous."

"Let go of me!" Amber shook his hand off her arm and ran after Cam.

Simon turned to the rest of them. "You lot take care of whatever's coming. I'll take care of Amber."

"Just get them and hurry back!" Merlin said. "We can't stay here for much longer."

Simon nodded and vanished back into the trees.

Harcourt shook his head. "That one never struck me as a heroic type."

"Something has our boy Cam riled up," Nellie said worriedly.

"I'll talk to him as soon as I can," Merlin said. "Right now we need to get out of here. Load up!"

Cam sprinted through the ancient forest, charging between the trees with reckless speed. He hated to leave Amber, hated that he couldn't explain his outburst, but there was no time to waste. He was frightened, but his fear was for the woman, Alex, not for himself.

He feared it was already too late for her.

Daylight was almost gone, though a full moon had risen, adding some illumination as it filtered through the trees. Following the route Simon had taken, he ran straight until the foliage changed, and he could detect the scent of water ahead. He burst out between two fern trees, coming to a skidding halt to avoid stumbling into the middle of a nightmare.

He was too late.

Giant clawed beetle-things, half a dozen or more— some the size of badgers and others larger than wolves— scuttled about at the water's edge, fighting over the mutilated remains of a human body. Cam recognized Alex by the clothing and a brief glimpse of her face, frozen in an expression of dazed horror.

No one should die this way, he thought. *A warrior with as much courage and heart as this woman should leave this world with honor and the keening of her loved ones to send her on her way.*

One of the smaller things sat on top of what was left of her chest, chewing at one shoulder with its disgusting mandibles. Then another clawed horror—at least three times the size of the one that was feeding—smacked it away with furious chittering sounds. The little creature tumbled into the claws of a yet another larger relative, only to be snatched up and swiftly devoured while it squirmed and wriggled to escape. The biggest monster proceeded to drag Alex's corpse into the water. As it did so, her head lolled back drunkenly, giving Cam a good look as the red line in her neck opened like a second mouth.

As Cam stared in horror, her body slid into the water, vanishing along with the monster. The smaller creatures regrouped and scurried toward him with purpose. He backed away from the creeping, scuttling nightmares, his mind reeling with horrible realizations. Any doubts were now gone.

If Simon had truly witnessed her death in the clutches of these chittering abominations, he could never have looked as carefree as he had in the forest. The show he'd put on for the others was clearly false.

Simon was lying.

Alex's throat had been cut, not torn by the coarsely serrated claws of these beasts, but with a sharp metal blade wielded expertly.

Simon was a murderer.

And he had just left Amber and the others in Simon's company.

Cam turned to race back to the clearing, praying to all the gods he worshipped that he would not be too late this time.

37

Amber did her best to follow Cam's trail, but hadn't gone very far into the prehistoric forest before a hand came up from behind to grab her arm and stop her.

"Hold up a bit," Simon said. "You can't go haring off into the forest all on your own like Little Red Riding Hood."

"There are wolves all over the place now, not just these woods," Amber shot back. "Cam shouldn't have to face them alone." She tried shaking him off again, but he was ready for it this time, and held on tightly.

"Look," he said reasonably, "I'm not saying don't go after him. I'm just saying don't go after him alone. I'll go with you. It'll—" His voice cracked and he swallowed hard. "It'll give me a chance to make up for losing Alex, you know?"

Amber stopped trying to pull her arm away, thinking of the little girl who'd been dragged off by those wolf creatures in the Romford Arms Hotel. How there'd been nothing she could have done to stop it, and yet how gutted it made her feel, like she'd somehow failed.

"It wasn't your fault, you know," she said. "You know that, right?"

He gave the barest hint of a smile.

"It's true… really. I've been there," she added. "It's not easy. Now let's go find Cam, please? It's going to be dark soon."

"Yeah, let's do that." Simon let go of Amber, instead offering her his arm by way of support over the uneven terrain. She shook her head.

"I'm good," she said, and they set off again.

As they went deeper, it became harder to discern Cam's route. The shadows were deep, and Amber kept the flashlight pointed at the ground, scanning for signs of where he had passed.

Simon tried to hurry her along, but she shrugged off his efforts and slowed her pace, focusing on following Cam's tracks. A faint white form gleaming just ahead made her look up for a moment, thinking it might be him.

A huge skeletal face streaked with red appeared in the beam.

She screamed and dropped the light.

Simon gave a low chuckle and scooped it up.

"It's just an old cave bear skull," he said, the obvious

amusement in his voice making Amber feel like an idiot. He straightened and shone the beam back on the skull to give her a better look. "See? Look closer."

"No thanks," she said with a shaky laugh. "I've already seen as much of it as I want to." Shaking her head, she tried to convince her pounding heart to slow things down to a normal rate, angry at herself for being startled in the first place.

Simon grinned.

"Here, I'll get rid of it."

He pulled the skull off the pole and tossed it away into the bushes. Then he pulled the wooden stake out and tossed it out of sight, as well.

"Is that better?"

That undercurrent of mirth was starting to disturb Amber more and more. How could he find anything funny, after witnessing Alex's horrific death? Then again, people dealt with trauma in different ways. Maybe it was Simon's only coping mechanism.

Who was she to judge?

Still, he was creeping her out. She'd be glad when they reached Cam.

"Thanks," she said, reaching for the flashlight, only to flinch as he shone the beam directly in her eyes, momentarily blinding her. She lifted a hand.

"Simon, what the—"

Before she could finish her sentence, Simon grabbed

her wrist, pulled and spun her around. One arm latched around her body while his other hand clamped painfully tight across her mouth. She tried to scream but the sound was muffled beneath his fingers. He yanked her off balance and then half dragged, half carried her up the incline, toward a destination she couldn't see.

She did her best to struggle, but he was stronger than he looked—all lean, wiry muscle combined with a frightening willingness to hurt her.

"Let's just make this easy, my girl," he said softly. "You can try and fight me, but then I'll have to smash you over the head with this torch. That'll give you one hell of a headache, and trust me when I tell you you're going to be in enough pain as it is."

His words made Amber's blood run cold, but she wasn't about to stop fighting him. She tried to bite the hand that covered her mouth, dug her heels into the ground, clutched at anything she could to slow him down, to stop his progress up the hill. She grabbed at trees, the rough bark scraping her fingers, yet couldn't get enough purchase on anything to hold on for more than a few seconds before he pried her away.

Suddenly they were on level ground again, at what looked like a cave entrance. Amber caught a whiff of funky, musky leather as Simon pulled her past a canopy of animal hide. The smell of the leather was nothing compared to the stench inside the cave itself.

The fridge had died one hot summer day while Amber and her family had been away on vacation. They'd come home to a freezer full of spoiled meat. She'd thrown up when she first smelled it, and it had taken several days and lots of bleach and air fresheners to get rid of the lingering odor. Amber recognized that same rancid smell now and had to fight the urge to vomit, swallowing the bile that rose in her throat.

"That's nasty now, isn't it?" Simon sounded positively cheerful as he muscled her inside the nearly pitch-black cave. He forced Amber toward the ground, kicking her legs out from under her when she tried to resist. The impact drove the air from her lungs, and something small but hard—a rock, maybe—dug painfully into her lower back. It ground in even further when Simon straddled her, pinning her arms down with his knees.

Before she could take a breath and scream, Simon grabbed her chin and shoved a wadded cloth into her mouth, quickly tying it off with another strip of fabric. He lifted a knee enough to seize one of her wrists and wrap some coarse rope around it, repeating the process on the other side. He then secured both wrists together and sat back, his weight resting on Amber's thighs as she lay there in stunned disbelief.

"Now then," Simon said, the sheer happiness in his voice turning Amber's blood to ice. "I'm so glad Stearne didn't hurt you." He leaned in close to her ear. "I never did care for leftovers."

Cam sped through the trees as fast as the dim twilight would allow. When he reached the clearing, Nellie, the blowhard, and Merlin were packing up camp. Amber and Simon, however, were nowhere in sight and Cam's heart sank. He went straight for the magician, the only person who could understand his tongue.

"Noble druid, I must ask you—where is Amber?"

Merlin answered him in the same language.

"She went after you, and with her went Simon, to keep her safe."

Cam grabbed his arm. "You must listen to me. That filthy traitor Simon, he killed the woman Alex."

Merlin looked up sharply. "How know you this?"

"I saw him return without her. He did not see me, but I saw him. He walked with a light heart, smiling and pleased with himself—until he knew others were watching him. Only then did he cry, but the tears were false."

"Simon told us Alex was killed by some monstrous creature."

"He lied," Cam said fiercely. "I went to the lake where they sought water. Aye, monsters lurked there, that much was true, but her throat had been sliced open with a killer's blade, not ripped by claws or teeth. He killed her and left her corpse behind for those creatures to feast upon."

Even by the light of the moon, brighter in the clearing, Cam could see Merlin's face drain of color. He quickly barked out something to Nellie and the blowhard in their language. Nellie gasped, pressing a hand to her mouth while the man looked outraged.

Merlin clapped a hand on Cam's shoulder.

"Come. We need to find them swiftly. Our enemies are already coming for us."

38

"So what shall we do first?"

Simon was little more than a moving shadow in the near-perfect blackness of the cave. He sounded almost relaxed—except for an undercurrent of dark glee in his voice, which spoke of enjoying things best done behind locked doors and thick walls. How had she missed hearing it before? Amber was almost glad she couldn't see his face.

"No suggestions?" he said. "Not to worry."

Amber heard a *snick* sound.

"We'll have plenty of time to play."

She felt the warmth of his fingers on her neck and then the chill of steel as he pressed something sharp right under her throat.

His switchblade.

She froze, hardly daring to breathe for fear that the steel might cut into her flesh.

"The others are going to look for you at the lake. If there's anything left of that rozzer bitch's body, maybe they'll figure those giant scorpions got a hold of you, too. With any luck they've already made a meal out of your prehistoric Romeo."

Amber gave a muffled cry. Simon chuckled.

"Aww, now don't worry too much. He's strong, that one. He might take a few out before they eat him alive. Now then…" He shifted his weight forward, changing his position to one that was uncomfortably intimate. "That's better, isn't it?" He pressed his groin into hers. "Yeah, that's nice… We're going to have fun, you and I."

His breath was warm and sour against her face, and the knife bit into her throat. Amber fought the impulse to kick, to try and throw him off. Instead she lay perfectly still as Simon proceeded to feel her up while describing what he planned on doing to her in horrifically graphic detail.

"It's nice to have some quality time to get to know one another," he said. "If we've learned anything today, it's that life is short, brutish, and utterly un-fucking-predictable. You have to grab hold of it and take what pleasure you can, while you can. *Carpe diem*, indeed, and *carpe noctem*, too.

"When that pilgrim prat was going to burn us alive this morning, I realized something. I was so jealous, so *envious* of him. Right then he was everything I ever aspired to. I really should have become a preacher… or a god." He gave a small chuckle. "Never appreciated just how bloody much power they have when folk are shitting themselves. Now see, if you apply yourself, take the time to learn how to manipulate fear and hate—well then, my lamb, you've got the power of life and death right in your bloody hands."

He paused and shifted so he was pressed even closer.

"Killing Alex wasn't much fun. I had to rush things, and she was already pretty much done in by the poison. No real time to play. Anyhow, she was a bit too uncompromising for my tastes. I like my women… softer, y'know? My last houseguest, she was right up my alley.

"Real pretty bird," he said, sounding wistful. "Big blue eyes, lots of brown hair. Slender and soft. We were just about to have some real fun when things went tits up and she vanished. Now *that* was a missed opportunity. She cried, y'know—so much she had trouble breathing." He heaved a sigh. "I liked that. Liked the fear in those big blue eyes."

He brought his lips down right next to her ear and whispered, "You're gonna cry for me, Red. Until I decide it's time for you to stop." Amber gave an involuntary whimper and Simon put a deceptively gentle hand on her face, wiping a finger under one of her eyes.

"Oh, that's nice. You've already started."

He pulled back slightly, easing the pressure, and a bright light shone in Amber's face, momentarily blinding her. She turned her head to one side, shutting her eyes to escape the beam.

"Sorry about that, love." He tilted the flashlight a little to one side, taking the beam out of her face. "Better?"

Amber opened her eyes and saw Simon's face eerily illuminated above her, the flashlight held in between their bodies. She didn't stop to think.

Snatching the flashlight with her bound hands, she swung upward, pretending she was bumping the ball in volleyball and his chin was the point of impact. The metal connected with a loud *crack*, snapping Simon's head back. At the same time, she bucked her hips and rolled to one side, throwing him off her.

She didn't give him time to recover.

Clutching the flashlight, Amber scrambled awkwardly to her feet, tore through the deerskin, and stumbled out of the cave. The animal skin came tumbling down, wrapping in a tangle around her.

Back in the cave Simon gave an inarticulate yell of rage even as she stumbled down the hill in the night. Random branches slapped her face and arms as she plunged forward. Her toe caught on something hard and she pitched forward, losing hold of the flashlight. It flew out of her hands and for a few terrifying, helpless seconds she was sure she was going to tumble face first all the way down the incline. She jerked backward, falling painfully hard on her knees instead, then fought through the pain to get to her feet and kept running, thankful she hadn't broken an ankle or her neck.

The ground leveled out and Amber stumbled through the trees, struggling to take in a full breath through her congested nostrils. Reaching up with her bound hands, she ripped the outer gag off, spat the rest out onto the ground, and sucked in sweet, life-giving air.

Which way?

Her sense of direction had completely failed. She could hear Simon cursing above her as he threw scraps of the canopy aside, and knew there was no time to find her bearings. She picked a direction and ran.

Twilight had given way to night. The moon shone above, but the thick canopy of trees only allowed a faint gleam of dappled light through—barely enough to prevent her from running face first into a tree. She heard her pursuer crashing down the hill and kept moving, hoping to find the safety of their temporary camp—or anywhere—before Simon managed to find *her* again.

She glimpsed more moonlight through the trees ahead and stepped up her pace, biting on the rope that bound her wrists, pulling with her teeth as she ran, trying to loosen the knots he'd tied. She got one free, but the second one wouldn't budge, no matter how she tugged at it. Finally, she gave it up and just concentrated on reaching the gap in the trees.

Almost there.

In a final burst of speed, she dashed into the moonlit clearing—and nearly barreled straight into a lake. She slid to a stop a foot or two away from the water's edge, trying to catch her breath as quietly as possible. This had to be the source of water Merlin's rover had detected.

The clearing permitted more moonlight here, making it easy to see how much life teemed beneath the lake's surface. The water seethed with activity... as did the shoreline. Something vaguely amphibian skittered up onto the bank, followed by a monster right out of an atomic-era sci-fi movie, a horrible chittering noise emanating from its mandibles.

Holy shit.

Amber froze in her tracks.

It looked like a scorpion on steroids, as big as a Shetland pony. Its barbed tail whipped over its head and stabbed the fleeing amphibian. The lizard-thing shuddered and collapsed in the sand, limbs twitching feebly as the scorpion descended upon it and fed.

Amber's paralysis broke and she started backing slowly into the trees, one careful step at a time before finally turning to run and—

Simon stood at the tree line, flashlight in one hand pointing up under his face so she could see his grin, like a summer camp counselor about to tell ghost stories around the fire. She backpedaled a few paces, then went after the rope around her wrists again. The scorpion chittered, nearly done with its meal.

Simon shook his head. "Y'know, at first I was pretty cheesed off at this chase you've led me on, but now that we're here, I realize it's... well, this is a splendid opportunity. We'll just leave some of your clothes here. Nothing important—your dress, underwear. Nothing you'll need again. That way if the rest of them *do* search for you, they'll think you died here. They'll go on their merry way, and you and I will have plenty of time to play together. Unless..."

He paused, cocked his head to one side, toward the scorpion.

"Unless you'd rather get it over with and let that thing have you for its next meal while I watch." He considered the idea. "That could be almost as much fun—especially if you scream."

"Fuck off," Amber spat—the first time she'd ever said those words to another person.

He shrugged. "Your choice, love."

Amber cast a frantic gaze at the scorpion, and then back at Simon. Could she make a break for it further down the shoreline, darting into the woods? She almost had the second knot undone...

He pointed the flashlight in her direction, yet the

monster didn't acknowledge her presence.

"I don't think it actually sees or hears the way we do," Simon said conversationally. "Not sure *how* it hunts, but I've seen it in action. Felt it, too, actually. Once it knows you're there, it's fast. I think maybe it hunts by vibration. Let's find out."

He stomped his foot hard on the ground. The scorpion chittered again, clicking its mouthparts as it turned.

"Yeah, I think that's it."

Simon stomped again. Amber gasped as the monster scurried toward him—and toward her, since she was standing between them. "Of course, now that it's spotted you, it's not likely to forget that you're here." Amber frantically worked at the rope with her teeth. The last of the stubborn knot gave way just as Simon offered one last emphatic stomp on the ground before ducking behind a tree.

The monster charged. She screamed and threw herself to one side as the scorpion lumbered past. It quickly redirected its attention, drawn to the vibration when she hit the ground. Amber rolled onto her back and scrambled away, scuttling backward like a crab on her hands and feet as the thing lunged for her. She screamed again, holding up her arms and hands in a vain attempt to shield herself as the gore-drenched mandibles dipped toward her.

A sharp cracking sound echoed over the lake.

Then another.

The creature buckled as if the weight of its body suddenly became too much for its legs. Amber rolled out of the way as it collapsed where she had just been sprawled on her back.

"Amber!"

A familiar voice shouted her name, over to the left where the shoreline curved in the opposite direction. Amber's jaw dropped.

It couldn't be...

"Amber! Stay there! I'm coming."

Rough hands seized her from behind, one entwining in her hair to yank her head back, the other painfully wrenching her arm behind her.

"Guess you'll be coming with me after all," Simon whispered. As he did, she watched creatures swarm over the dead scorpion in a chittering feeding frenzy. Then the pain caused her vision to blur.

Another shot cracked from the left. Simon flinched and swore, letting go of her wrist as he clutched at his left shoulder. Amber wrenched her hair out of his grasp, feeling some of it tear away at the scalp. She faced Simon, fiercely happy to see blood spurting out from between his fingers.

He snarled and lashed out with his left hand, catching her across the face hard enough to rattle her teeth and send her stumbling back toward the feasting creatures.

One of them hissed and scuttled toward her. She dove out of its path, landing heavily on one side, nearer to the tree line. Simon followed her, his frock coat swinging about his legs.

"I'll kill him and then cut you apart, piece by tiny piece," he said between clenched teeth. She scrabbled in the sand for a piece of wood or a rock—anything to use as a weapon to protect herself. Simon let go of his wounded shoulder, blood dripping blackly from his hand as he reached down to grab her. He seized her, fingers digging into her upper arms, just as her fingers closed over what felt like a ridged wooden club—Alex's truncheon.

Tightening her grip, she lashed out with the billy club, smashing Simon across the bridge of his nose. He howled in pain and fury, and she immediately followed up with a direct blow to his wounded shoulder, and then smashed him on the collarbone. Then she kneed him in his groin as hard as she could. He groaned, reeling like a drunken man as he stumbled over his own feet and fell backward—

Straight into the path of the scorpions.

Simon screamed as one of them caught him up in its claws and sunk its mandibles into his bloody shoulder. Another, smaller one immediately skittered over his torso, settling there before going to work on his stomach. His scream rose higher, changing in pitch from pain to agony. The agony became unspeakable when the rest of the creatures closed in.

Amber staggered back away from the horror show, seeking shelter in the trees before her legs gave out on her. She sank to her knees, folding over until her head rested on her hands.

She heard shouts, but stayed in that position until Blake reached her, joined quickly by Cam, Nellie, Merlin, and Harcourt.

Only then did she let herself cry.

39

Amber and Blake sat a few feet away from the small, crackling fire, silently sharing a cup of coffee. Amber had heated water in a little tin cup from Blake's duffle and added one of her packets of instant. She even had a bit of sugar and powdered creamer tucked away in her backpack. She'd offered some to Cam, but he'd taken one sip and handed the cup back to her, his expression making it clear what he thought of coffee.

He seemed equally unenthusiastic about Blake.

The urgency to flee had eased once they realized that Blake was the person Groucho had detected. They'd relocated nevertheless, and when Amber told them about the cave, it seemed the ideal alternative. She hadn't been so sure, but had allowed herself to be overruled. Merlin used the drones to locate it. When they arrived, Nellie located a hunk of maggot-ridden meat in the corner, and tossed it into the forest.

As soon as she did they heard rustling coming from more than one direction. Putrid or not, the meat wouldn't last long.

Once they'd settled in, they dug into the food they'd brought from the wagon, along with some of what Amber and Blake had left in their respective backpack and duffle. There was bread, cheese, dried meat, and some harsh red wine—which caused Harcourt to nearly cry with happiness—as well as the nearly full water skin Simon had brought back.

The various snacks Amber and Blake contributed were met with suspicion from Harcourt and curiosity from Nellie. Cam managed an air of nonchalance that Amber found sweetly funny, considering his reaction to the same things two days earlier.

The cave had a natural chimney in the roof, so they managed to build a fire that couldn't be seen from below, and the burning wood helped to eliminate some of the rancid stench still lingering in the air. Cam and Merlin sat next to the fire, deep in conversation, while Harcourt lay on his back, snoring deeply and rhythmically after consuming several cups of wine. Nellie leaned back against Blake's duffle bag, eyes half-lidded but still awake. Cam caught Amber looking at him, and the two exchanged a quick private glance, each silently checking to make sure the other was okay.

Amber never thought she'd willingly go back to the cave where Simon had taken her, but the group needed a place to hunker down for the night and, well, if Psycho Simon had thought it a good hiding place, it probably was.

As the fire cast light onto the walls, they made an amazing discovery. The prehistoric inhabitants had painted on the walls, the kind of thing she'd only seen in photographs, like the ones from the Lascaux caverns in France. Stick figures with bows hunted huge-antlered elk, hefty wild ox, and shaggy rhinoceros. Alongside all these were less-identifiable symbols, abstract shapes and squiggles. The artists had also produced rust and white powders to leave vibrant handprints. It gave Amber chills to be able to touch them—the same kind of feeling she got when she touched the walls of medieval castles or standing stones from centuries ago.

All of a sudden she wondered how "old" Cam was, and if his people had done artwork like this. Maybe later she'd ask Merlin to translate for her.

She felt oddly normal—if such a state even existed anymore. Almost eerily calm after yet another near-death experience. She'd trusted Simon. Despite his annoyances, he'd been one of them, and yet he'd wanted to not just kill her, but to take his sweet time doing so. Shouldn't she be a quivering heap of nerves about now, all tears and hysterics? Instead she'd eaten her share of the food with a hearty appetite, and had a sense of well-being that seemed out of place.

Maybe it was the coffee.

That, and the fact that Simon was dead.

Unequivocally dead.

Amber looked at Blake. He wore a buff coat and breeches that he'd taken off some unfortunate Roundhead cavalryman who'd run across him while on patrol. Amber almost felt sorry for the fellow. She doubted he'd stood a chance.

"How did you find me?" she finally asked, breaking the silence between them.

He shrugged. "Once I realized I was looking in the wrong direction, it was easy enough to track you. I lost a good day heading down into London though. Clever of you to hide right next door." He drank some more coffee, the look on his face the most contented Amber had seen there since meeting him.

"When I saw what those Roundhead bastards were up to, I figured they'd taken you prisoner, so I kept out of sight, trying to figure out how to get into their little enclave without being seen. Easy enough to go undercover and blend in. Stole this—" He indicated the buff coat. "—and a nice horse from a rider on patrol."

Nellie, who'd been quietly listening to the two of them, nodded her agreement.

"I saw them drag the lot of you out to the stakes,"

he continued. "Wasn't sure how I was going to get you out of that, but then your friend there…" He nodded at Merlin and shook his head in amazement. "How the *hell* did he conjure up a fake soldier, let alone the dinosaur?"

"I'm still not exactly sure," Amber admitted. "It has something to do with his drones."

"I won't even pretend to understand what that means," Blake said with rare self-deprecation. "At any rate, I followed the other soldiers, far enough behind that when they went galloping away, it was obvious that your wagon tracks were heading in the opposite direction." He smiled. "Knocked me for a loop when I finally caught up with the real wagon, and realized you lot had bailed out somewhere earlier. Once I backtracked far enough, I had a gut feeling I'd find you in these woods. It's what I would've done. Stumbling on you at the lake, though…"

He shook his head.

"That was pure luck."

Amber nodded, not entirely sure what to say. She felt like an asshole for running away from him in the first place.

"I'm sorry," she finally said. "I didn't mean to put you through all that trouble."

"Oh, I don't blame you for leaving." Blake laughed, a harsh sound with no amusement in it. "I lost my head. Became a liability, no good to you or myself. No, you did the right thing, the smart thing, leaving me before I got you killed."

Amber stared at him. "Blake, I didn't leave you because I was afraid you'd get me killed," she finally said. "I left because I was afraid you were going to kill me."

He stared back in confusion. "You thought I was…" He trailed off and shook his head.

"You said—and I quote you—that we'd be better off dead," she replied. "And that woman in the swamp…" She swallowed hard. "I get it—that it was a mercy killing. That she wasn't going to make it. But how could I know you wouldn't decide I would be better off dead, too?"

Blake said nothing. He stared off into some unseen distance for a while before he turned to look at her again.

"I'm sorry," he finally said. "In hindsight, it seems perfectly clear why you thought what you thought. I just didn't cop on to it at the time. Ah, hell." He set the cup down and rested his head on his hands. "God, I'm a bloody idiot."

"No you're not," Amber said. "Come on, you've saved me from giant wolves, prehistoric scorpions, and a serial killer. I'd be dead three times over if not for you."

"She has a point there, soldier boy," Nellie chimed in.

Blake took a deep breath, then another. He lifted his head, looked around for the cup of coffee he'd set down. Amber handed it to him. He drank the rest in one swallow and nodded.

"Fair enough."

Amber glanced over at Cam. The Celt was listening

intently to whatever Merlin was saying—and looking totally shell-shocked. Curiosity aroused, Amber got to her feet and went over to join them.

"Hey, is he okay?" She nodded at Cam. "What did you tell him?"

Merlin looked up and smiled at her.

"I was telling Cam what I'm about to tell all of you."

"Which is?" Nellie scootched over to sit next to Merlin.

"Ah, that I am a powerful wizard, and that through terrible magics, the mystical balance of the world has fallen into ruin."

Amber and Nellie exchanged glances.

Nellie snickered.

"Really?" Amber's tone was doubtful.

Merlin gave an unexpected grin. "Sadly there's no word for 'astrophysicist' in Cam's culture, but maybe I can explain it a little better to the rest of you."

"How did you learn his language?" Amber asked.

"I didn't. It's just a linguo-implant I have that includes early Brythonic Celtic in its programming."

Amber's eyes lit up.

"Is there any way you can do that for me?" she asked. "So that I can talk to him, too?"

"Of course. Remind me when we're aboard the ship."

Cam said something to Merlin, pointing at Amber. Merlin nodded, then grinned.

"He just asked the same thing."

Amber beamed. Being able to talk to Cam, *communicate* with him in the same language, was more than she could have hoped for.

"Could someone wake the professor?" Merlin looked over to the sleeping Harcourt. "It will be easier to tell all of you this at the same time." Nellie obligingly leaned back and smacked the snoring man on one shoulder.

"Rise and shine, Professor!"

Harcourt's snore ended in a startled snort as he sat up, shaking his head in confusion. Taking pity on him, Amber patted the ground next to her.

"Merlin's going to tell us what happened, Professor," she said. "Here, sit by me. You'll want to hear this, I'm sure."

Harcourt harrumphed in reply, but moved over as she'd suggested. Blake stayed where he was, but listened intently.

"Where do I begin?" Merlin said, the light of the fire casting exaggerated shadows across his face. "As I said, I am an astrophysicist. In particular, my focus of study is underlying cosmological structure theory. I am—or was, more accurately—leading a project engaged in cracking the secret of traveling faster than the speed of light through space."

Amber hung on his every word. This was seriously the stuff that nerdgasms were made of.

"I apologize if some of you already know this," Merlin continued, "but the universe is so incomprehensibly large that interstellar journeys would occupy hundreds of thousands, even millions of years. It would take more than a century to reach even the nearest star systems to ours. Our project was trying to find a way to travel the universe faster by warping space-time—the fabric of the universe, if you will."

"Why on earth would anyone wish to travel through *outer space*?" Harcourt snorted with a dismissive *harrumph*. Merlin ignored him and continued.

"Unfortunately, four days ago, there was a terrible accident. The containment field ruptured somehow—I... I still don't know how or why—and an unexpected event occurred. This Event was... is... well, the Event is a schizochronolinear catastrophe."

"A schizophrenic what?" Blake scowled.

"What does that mean, a, uh, schizo... chrono... linear catastrophe?" Amber asked, wrestling with the word. Merlin paused, and creases appeared on his brow. His indigo eyes looked almost black, but the tiny strands of silver honeycomb on his forehead glittered in the firelight.

"Let me see if I can explain it." He stood and stretched out his hand, pointing from one end of the painted cave wall to the other. "Imagine time seen as a continuum—an infinite line containing everything that was and everything that will be...

"Time perhaps as a tangible object," he suggested.

"One that can be touched, like a mural on a wall that stretches infinitely in both directions. Portraying everything that has happened, is happening, and will happen." He began striding along the length of the wall. "In one direction is the future unfolding." He reversed his course. "In the other direction the past, much of it forgotten, back to the beginning of time itself."

He stopped and faced them.

"Finally, imagine time as a stained-glass window. The story of everything laid out in a glittering mosaic of trillions upon trillions of moments, from the big bang to the fiery death of the universe." The intensity of his gaze held everyone in captive silence, waiting for him to speak again.

"Then the window shatters," he continued finally, "everywhere... and every when." He paused, took a deep breath.

"*That* is what has happened."

He sat back down.

"Oh," Nellie said flatly.

Amber struggled with the overwhelming concept, straining to take it all in. Harcourt glared at the floor, as if personally offended by the universe. Blake rubbed his eyes and shook his head, like a man trying to wake up. Cam put a hand on Amber's arm, checking to make sure the druid's words hadn't alarmed her too badly. He put his hands together and flapped them like a bird's wings.

"*Tempus... fugit,*" he said, and quickly brought his hands crashing down to the ground like a fallen eagle, wiggling his fingers to mime a scattering collapse.

"*Tempus...* fuck it," she agreed. She turned to Merlin. "Doctor, this accident—when did you say it happened?"

"Four days ago. February 2nd, 2219. Currently, all of us are living in the twenty-third century. Today is technically February 6th, 2219—only 'today' is made up of pieces from a million yesterdays."

"So, all these different places," she said, "this prehistoric cave, the Cromwellian village, what's left of Romford and London, those are all..." She trailed off, unable to find the words to finish her sentence.

"They are all shards of space-time," Merlin said, "from our shattered timeline."

"So that means... now, the whole world is like a big jigsaw puzzle, but made up of pieces from different times?"

"Yes! That's an excellent analogy." Merlin looked relieved.

"But then..." Amber was almost afraid to ask her next question. "Where are all the other pieces?"

The scientist hesitated before answering.

"I simply don't know."

No one spoke for the rest of the night.

40

Amber jumped when Blake placed a hand on her shoulder.

"What's wrong?" she demanded.

"Nothing. Everything's alright," he said, "but it's time for us to move out. Your friend Merlin is waiting outside with the young savage."

Even half asleep, Amber couldn't miss the lack of warm and fuzzy on the words "your friend, Merlin." She sat up on her elbows and looked at Blake.

"He's a good guy," she said quietly. "I think."

"That he might be, but he's also stark raving mad." Blake shook his head. "All of that nonsense he was spouting last night. Don't tell me you actually *believed* him."

Amber raised an eyebrow. "Do you have a better explanation?" she asked. "You didn't want to believe me when I told you that time had changed. You believe me now, don't you?"

Blake didn't reply.

"Then why can't you believe Merlin?" Amber heaved a frustrated sigh. "Blake, you need to get with the program, or you're going to be the one losing his mind. There are brontosauruses in the Thames, dire wolves in Romford, pterosaurs in Colchester, and who knows what else out there. You saw what came out of the lake last night. You *know* I'm right. You wouldn't have come after me if you didn't."

"No... you're quite right." Blake ran a hand through his hair. "It's just... it's madness, what that man said. Utter madness."

"It's also the only vaguely plausible explanation anyone's offered so far, the only one that makes any sense."

Blake was silent for a moment before finally nodding. Amber wasn't totally satisfied, but it would have to do for now.

Outside the cave the indigo sky was just starting to soften to blue. Blake and Amber quickly woke up Nellie and Harcourt, and they gathered their things. In a matter of minutes, they were all on their feet and making their groggy way out of the cave to join Merlin and Cam.

The rovers dutifully identified their path with discreet flashlight beams, and Merlin led the way. They hiked south, giving the primordial lake a wide berth, and eventually emerged from the forest just as the sun was edging above the horizon. Stray skeins of geese streamed across the morning sky. The wide countryside beyond was heartbreakingly beautiful and inviting, like something out of a painting.

"It's gorgeous, isn't it?" Nellie said in a low whisper.

Amber nodded in agreement, although now she was morbidly aware of how little cover it offered them, and how completely visible they would be to anyone or anything that might be stalking them. She looked back.

Blake brought up the rear, constantly sweeping the horizon for any potential threats. Cam stayed close to Amber and Nellie. Merlin strode ahead at a healthy pace, eager to reach their destination. Harcourt seemed oblivious to any danger as he stamped along unhappily, clutching his coat with one hand and holding onto his hat with the other to keep the wind from plucking it off his head.

Fortunately for all of them, so far nothing fiercer than field mice and wild rabbits seemed to be lurking in their vicinity. They hiked onward, time passing swiftly. For the most part, no one spoke. Everyone seemed lost in his or her own thoughts, or maybe just shell-shocked.

"How far do we still have to go?" Nellie whispered after a while, but Amber could only shrug.

"Let me talk to Merlin." She increased her pace and sidled up to him.

"So why did you park your car so far away?" she asked. He smiled, getting the joke.

"You don't know the half of it," he replied. "There wasn't a lot of choice, really. I rushed to Britain looking for some of my colleagues at the Greenwich Royal Observatory—only to discover that I couldn't locate my friends, the observatory, or London. There was scarcely any trace of civilization anywhere. So I decided to head back to my lab, but it would be a long trip and I knew I wasn't going to make it very far. The generators needed to recharge, so I needed to find a place to stow the ship somewhere safe and out of sight."

"That makes sense." Amber considered his words. "But why did you leave the ship at all, if you got a good look at how messed up everything was outside?"

"Ha!" He snorted. "I've been asking myself the same question a thousand times since. I was a fool to go out on a reconnaissance, let alone go out without any sort of weapon. In my defense, though..." He paused, heaving a sigh. "Well... it's been quite a while since I had the opportunity to go for a walk freely in the open countryside. Unfortunately, I didn't get very far before a patrol of Cromwellians came upon me.

"Their hostility was quite a shock," he continued. "I didn't expect to run into any other people, but just in case, I wore a simple black robe. That way, I could pass myself as a druid to the pagans, and a monk to the Christians." He shook his head, smiling at his own naivete. "So much for that plan. I underestimated just how seriously the Christians took their theological divisions—and how viciously."

Amber nodded. The thought of Stearne was still fresh enough to bring up a sharp twinge of anxiety. *How much further to safety?*

"And then, of course, there was this hard-to-explain matter," he said, pointing to his starry eyes with a wry smile. She gave him a nervous little sidelong glance, then turned her head away again, embarrassed.

"You know, I hope you don't think this is rude, but I keep meaning to ask you about your eyes—only I never think of it at a convenient time. Um… you're not an alien, are you? Does everybody in the future have eyes like yours?"

"Oh no, I'm pretty sure I'm the only one," he replied. "I probably should explain to everyone a little later, once we're all safely aboard." She was relieved he wasn't offended, and pleased to finally address the elephant in the room.

"Do you know how much longer we have to be out here?" she asked.

"It's not too much farther now," he replied. "No more than—"

Abruptly the two remaining rovers began beeping and swirling around his head and shoulders, projecting holographic data.

Multiple contacts
Presumed hostile
1500 meters and closing

Merlin stopped in his tracks.

"Show me." The drones dropped down to eye level and jointly projected a viewscreen. It showed the company of Roundhead horsemen, and the face of their leader was all-too-clearly visible.

"Stearne," Amber breathed.

"What's going on?" Blake caught up to them, his expression tight with concern. Amber pointed at the viewscreen. He nodded grimly and turned to the others.

"We have company, and we've been spotted!" Blake shouted. "Run!"

They broke into a sprint across the open country, Cam falling into step beside Amber and Nellie. He soon fell back next to Harcourt as the man was outpaced by the rest of the group. He slung an arm around the Victorian to make him move faster.

"Make for that rise ahead," Merlin called out. "My ship is just beyond it."

"You heard the man," Blake hollered. "Move it!"

The sound of hooves became audible from behind. Amber risked a quick glance over her shoulder and saw the horsemen thundering toward them. The sight spurred her on, despite a growing stitch in her side.

The ragtag group crested the low rise without daring to stop, but just as suddenly found they no longer had any choice in the matter.

No more than a dozen yards away, a new shard spread out before them. Judging by the scent of saltwater, this one contained nothing but a chunk of ocean, but if so, it was now a stranded inland sea. It stretched for miles.

There was no sign of a ship anywhere.

Amber's heart sank. *Now what?*

Blake stared for a moment, then turned on Merlin. He grasped the man by his shoulders, nearly lifting him off his feet.

"Where the hell is the ship you promised, you bloody bastard!" he roared in Merlin's face. "You dragged us all this way to an oversized lagoon for nothing? You're a madman." He turned to the others. "We've been following a madman!"

"Wait! You don't understand—" Merlin began.

Whipping back around, Blake seized him around the throat with white-knuckled hands and squeezed.

"Stop it, Blake!" Amber cried. "You're going to get us all killed!" She threw herself between the two men, pulling at Blake's arms until he let go of Merlin's throat. She could see the effort it took for him to choke down his rage as he fought to control himself

"We've got to get out of here, now, or we're all dead," he said through gritted teeth.

Coughing, Merlin rubbed his throat and held up a hand.

"Listen—the ship is here," he said, his voice a hoarse croak. "I don't understand the delay, but I promise, it's here."

Harcourt burst in, his voice laced with panic. "Good god, man, there's no time! Have your flying spheres create something for us to hide behind. They're nearly upon us!"

But it was too late.

The Roundheads were already there.

41

Twenty armed riders lined the crest of the rise above them, Stearne in the forefront. Amber's throat tightened with fear.

"No one move," Merlin murmured under his breath. "Everyone stand perfectly still. *Cam, ní gwaya ar bí*. Harpo, stand by to run mirror maze program on my mark. Groucho, stand by to run shock and awe program on my mark." The Roundhead horsemen gathered in a rudimentary formation on the ridge, unmoving and silent.

"What's going on? What are they waiting for?" Nellie hissed.

"They're trying to intimidate us," Blake said tersely.

"We need them to come closer," Merlin whispered. "No one move. If we stay here, it will force them to come to us." For long moments that seemed to stretch on forever, no one moved.

"Come on," Merlin urged them softly. "Come down a little closer…"

Nothing.

"What now?" Blake whispered.

Abruptly Stearne gave a slight wave, and the company urged their horses down in a line, staying in tight formation.

"Yes!" Merlin breathed in. "Harpo to my left, Groucho to the right." The rovers rose two meters, taking position on either side of him.

"*Now*," Stearne yelled. The soldiers drew their pistols and opened fire with a thunderous salvo. Harpo burst into a splintering cloud of metal fragments. Groucho instantly moved right, but only got a few meters before it also took a hit, plummeting to the ground. The witch hunter snapped his fingers and his horsemen holstered their spent pistols. Each drew a second or slipped a musket from the saddle scabbards. A moment later they stirred their horses forward again, down the incline to swiftly encircle their exhausted quarry, guns trained on them. The six were entirely hemmed in, their backs to the water.

"I need more time," Merlin murmured quickly. He gestured strangely, with slow, deliberate motions. "We've got to stall them."

Stearne rode up close, and smiled.

"Your flying familiars seem to have run afoul of Providence, wizard. Still, such a most beauteous sea spread out before us. A fine day for a swim, is it not?" he said with mock civility. "Pray, let us not keep you. Though in truth, you scarcely seem dressed for such sport. Perhaps you may yet partake of more running for us instead? What say you?"

His soldiers chuckled.

Amber fought to come up with an answer. Something—anything—to buy Merlin a little more time. She could see Cam's muscles tensing, and knew Blake was thinking along the same lines. She had to do something, but she had no idea what.

"My dear fellow, there's no need for any of this," Harcourt said loudly, taking a step forward with arms wide open. "Can't we come to some sort of mutually advantageous agreement?"

"Bargaining now?" Stearne's eyes narrowed. "What manner of double-dealing are you playing at?"

"No chicanery, I assure you," Harcourt said with a small laugh. "Surely a man of your ability can discern that even in our present sorry state, we are folk of distinction and means." He glanced at Cam. "Some of us, at least."

"Go on." The Puritan's voice betrayed curiosity.

Harcourt did. "Surely, given your position, you might make use of us, rather than… squandering our unique talents and resources, all because of an unfortunate misunderstanding."

"How so?" The witch hunter sat up straighter in his saddle.

The professor glanced at Merlin, and then continued.

"Myself, I possess degrees in a multitude of scientific fields," Harcourt said, "and that advanced learning could be applied to a wide variety of projects and consultations. For example, I possess the formula needed to create a special galvanic nerve elixir—which can be used to address all manner of physical and cerebral ailments, complaints and maladies, both common and exotic."

Stearne glared darkly at him.

"Your stratagem comes clear," he hissed. "You will not tempt me with your worldly so-called knowledge, or your alchemical trifles." He turned to address the rest of his prisoners. "Thought you to distract me with your bevy of tricks and dodges? The lot of you have led us on a merry chase, and that ends here."

Amber shuddered and the witch hunter noticed, giving her a look that hinted at vile things to come. She clenched her hands into fists as heat flushed her cheeks.

"Here your revels cease," he proclaimed. "Each of you will pay dearly for your wicked mischief—" He looked straight at Amber as he continued. "—for a very long time before we suffer you to die. There is no escape from divine justice."

"Justice?" Nellie let out a mocking laugh. "What do

you know about justice? Do you tell your men what you do to the women behind closed doors? Is that divine? Is that justice? Are any of their wives or daughters safe from you?"

The witchfinder didn't deign to reply, but his stare promised a world of pain.

Emboldened by Nellie's words, Amber stepped forward, refusing to look at Stearne and instead turning her attention on his soldiers, looking up at the barrels of their pistols.

"Why do you hate us so much?" she asked. "We're not your enemy. We're not witches, or spies, or whatever else you think we are. We're just people, just like you, and all we want is to get home safely." The soldiers gave no response. She took a deep breath, trying to keep her voice from shaking.

"Don't you see? There are monsters out here. They'd be more than happy to turn every one of you into a meal." Pointing an accusing finger at Stearne, she continued. "Hate and fear are the easiest things in the world to sell. Don't buy it. Don't be his slaves. Don't be idiots. Stop wasting your time and concentrate on your real enemy." Amber glared at the witchfinder. "And stop listening to assholes like him."

She couldn't read their expressions as they continued to watch her in stony silence—like gargoyles, their faces brutish, ugly, and hard. For what felt like a never-ending moment, she stood there, vulnerable and trembling, trying hard not to let them see what she felt inside—a spiky iron hedge of black fear closing in on a single fragile hope.

"Girl, you've a right rare gift for speech-making." Stearne's lieutenant, a stocky, grizzled man with the scarred face of a bulldog, lowered his pistol and spoke in a deep, gravelly voice. His face remained unreadable, but his flat gray eyes fixed on hers.

The other riders looked at him.

He leaned forward in his saddle.

"I for one want to hear what else you have to say—" There was a fire in his eyes now as he raised his voice. "—when we truss you back up on the stake in Lexden Common and roast you like a Papist's plump Christmas goose, you poxy hell-bound bitch!" The other Roundheads threw their heads back into long hyena howls of raucous laughter, dark and ugly. The sound shriveled Amber's soul.

At a nod from the witchfinder, the soldiers began to dismount. Most kept their guns trained on the prisoners, while others pulled manacles from their saddlebags. Stearne urged his horse forward and leaned down, cuffing Amber savagely across the face, hard enough to knock her to the ground. She lay there, stunned and heartsick as one of the soldiers tramped up to her, bindings in hand.

The Puritan stared down at Amber with gloating satisfaction.

"Thought yourself so clever, wench? Now you wi—"

As the Roundhead reached down for Amber's arm, Cam charged forward, delivering a high kick square to the soldier's face. A stream of blood gushed from the man's nose and mouth, his helmet flying off as his body snapped backward. Stearne's horse reared up in a panic. The closest soldier turned at the commotion—as Cam snatched up the chain meant for Amber and swung it up into the man's surprised face.

Rattled by the suddenness of the Celt's attack, the Roundheads twisted to bring their guns to bear on him and opened fire. Most of the barrage went wild, though several rounds struck Cam's second victim from behind, killing him on the spot. Amber rolled out of the way as Stearne struggled to rein in his rearing and kicking steed. Smoke and the smell of gunpowder filled the air.

Seeing his chance, Blake lunged forward and cold-cocked the nearest Roundhead as the man turned to shoot Cam. He grabbed the soldier's musket and shot the next closest one point-blank in the throat, then swung around to smash the musket butt-first into the face of a third soldier coming up from his flank.

He turned back for just a moment to face his astonished companions, who stood in shock, watching the chaos.

"*Run!*" Blake yelled.

"*Ov Camtargarus Mab Cattus na Trinovanti!*" Cam roared at his shaken foes as he charged again, swinging the chains into a mass of them. They scrambled over one another to get out of the arc of his red-stained makeshift flail. Not all succeeded. Behind them, the rest of the company's horses stamped and snorted anxiously.

One Roundhead dropped his spent pistol, quickly drew his cavalry sword, and thrust it at Cam's eyes. The Celt ducked out of the line of attack and came up again, whipping the chain around the soldier's sword and forearm. With a wrench of his arm, he yanked the man past him to the ground—but lost the chain as it snagged on his stricken foe.

Blake flipped the musket in the air to change up his grip, turning it from a crude spear to a club. He swung it in a wide swathe, trying to draw in as many of the soldiers as he could keep engaged, but there were too many to keep them all at bay.

Still, he'd faced worse odds in North Africa…

* * *

Nellie scanned desperately through the smoke and chaos, seeking to spot Amber.

"He said run!" Harcourt shouted, already backing away, though there was still nowhere to run except into the water.

"No!" Merlin yelled back over the din of the fight. "Stay together!" He was still gesturing oddly.

There! Nellie finally spotted Amber, still on the ground, terrified, scrambling to avoid being trampled by Stearne's rearing horse.

"Amber!" she shouted.

Despite Blake and Cam's efforts to keep them all busy, the other side had more than enough soldiers to completely surround the two fighting men—with still more soldiers free to come after the rest of them, as well.

Empty-handed, Cam rushed his closest foe, grappling with him before the man could connect with a swing of his sword. He flung the assailant to the ground, rolling and struggling fiercely for control of the blade, while the other Roundheads tried to get in on the fight.

Blake raised his musket in both hands just in time to block an overhead blow, then struck out at his opponent, clocking him with both ends of the firearm. A split-second later he twisted to sidestep another attacker before slamming the musket down on the soldier's head, sending him to the ground, too.

More closed in to fill the gap.

Four Roundheads came around the edge of the melee and spotted Nellie, Merlin, and Harcourt. The nearest two came straight after Nellie, one with arms outstretched, the other with shackles in hand, both laughing as if playing some schoolyard game.

She bolted to evade them, but they chased her down quickly. One seized her around the waist, the other grabbed at her arms, cackling with glee as she tried to hit him and claw his face. Together the filthy pair tackled her to the ground, pinning her down to get the manacles on her.

Another rushed up to Harcourt, sword out. The professor shrieked and put up his hands, but before he could even say a word in surrender, the soldier struck him down with no more concern than if he'd been swatting a fly.

The last of the four soldiers came for Merlin. The scientist raised his hands slowly and carefully in response.

"Easy now," he said gently. "I'll go quietly." The soldier's cheeks were pockmarked with smallpox scars, his eyes narrow and suspicious. He held up a chain.

"No tricks," the man grunted.

* * *

Prone on the slippery ground, Cam gripped the soldier's sword arm, straining to keep the small-sword from plunging down on him. His other hand grasped the soldier's neck, while his foe clenched Cam's throat, just below his silver torc—a contest of strangulation. Only a hand's span lay between their faces. His opponent's was red and sweaty, the cords in his neck stretched to the breaking point beneath Cam's fingers.

Then Cam heard the piping of the fairies growing louder, and at last he saw them dancing before his eyes, tiny blue stars, old familiar friends. His opponent's grasp on his neck suddenly loosened, and Cam released his own death grip in order to wrench the soldier's wrist inward, driving the blade into the man's neck. Blood drenched him and the soldier slid off, limp as a dead fish.

He shot up, gasping for breath. Instantly the other troopers were on him. One struck him with the butt of his musket to the face, knocking him back to the cold ground. Another launched a vicious jab to his guts. As did another. And another, until Cam could no longer feel anything at all.

With an unexpected low swing, Blake caught one Roundhead just below the knee, dropping him like a felled tree. The commando kept moving, weaving and dodging, but the soldiers kept him ringed in, and he knew the fight was going on too long. His speed was starting to lag. He beat back two sword thrusts, ducked a swinging weapon, and jabbed his musket stock into the opening of another soldier's helmet.

He wheeled about, just as Stearne's grizzled lieutenant got into the fray. The burly man had another flintlock pistol ready, out and aimed at Blake's heart. On sheer reflex alone Blake gave a backhanded swing of the musket as he ducked to the right. It connected just as the Roundhead fired, knocking the weapon aside. Blake reeled, ears ringing from the pistol's booming report.

Behind him, another soldier fell with a scream.

A musket swing caught him in his blind spot. Rolling with the blow, he came up again and parried a sword cut, but a second one sliced open a red line along his arm. He swung the musket wildly, but took another hard blow on his shoulder. The impact knocked the musket out of his hands, and then a third solid hit to his side knocked him to the ground.

A heavy foot caught him in the pit of his stomach, causing Blake to curl up reflexively. The same foot rolled him on his back before planting itself on his chest. Blake opened his eyes to see the lieutenant standing above him with a triumphant sneer. Another soldier with manacles bent down toward him, but the big man pushed him back.

"No shackles for this one," he growled, pulling out yet another flintlock pistol from his brace, and aiming it down at Blake's head.

Merlin kept his arm movements slow and deliberate, his voice meek and reasonable. The soldier cuffed one wrist, then the other, locking both tight. Then he looked up, catching sight of Merlin's face up close. His eyes widened and he stood transfixed, staring into the violet blackness of Merlin's eyes and the tiny stars cascading down their depths.

"You—you have the evil eye..." he stammered, backing away in horror.

"No, no," the scientist said gently. "No, there's a reasonable explanation."

The pockmarked soldier raised an accusing finger at him.

"*You do!* You're a warlock and you're casting a spell on me!"

"No, let's calm down." He raised his hands. "There's no such thing as a warl—"

"*You're the Devil! Christ Jesus save me!*"

The soldier took another step back, pulled out his flintlock, and shot Merlin dead in the chest.

* * *

Smoke, confusion, the sound of gunfire, and the screams of panicked horses and dying men filled the air. Crawling on her belly to avoid the stamping hooves, Amber wormed her way past the clusters of vicious fighting. Everything in sight was moving with dreamlike sluggishness—the horses running rampant, the flash and thunder from musket and pistol barrels, the soldiers swarming around her friends like ants.

What was happening? *Was* she dreaming?

Pulling herself to her feet, she looked about in a daze. *Oh god.*

No matter where she looked, her eyes were met with horror. Cam's body lay unmoving on the ground while Roundhead soldiers beat him with muskets. The grizzled lieutenant who looked forward to her death on the stake was kicking Blake to the ground. Nellie was cursing and fighting while a laughing pair of soldiers straddled her body and shackled her wrists.

Harcourt's body lay in a crumpled heap in the heath.

And then as she watched, an enraged soldier drew his firearm and shot Merlin. A burst of red spray stained the air. Chained arms thrown high, the scientist's body flew backward and hit the ground. There it remained, motionless.

She snapped out of her stupor. Eyes wide, she screamed Merlin's name. The soldier wheeled at the sound and fled, as though he were the victim and not the murderer. Amber scrambled to her feet and ran over to the fallen man.

"Dr. Meta? Merlin?" she said softly, her voice quavering. "Can you hear me?" He was unmoving, shackled arms over his head. She knelt down and listened for breathing. There was none. She touched his chest, running her finger over a wet patch on his black robe, right in the center.

With trembling fingers, she smoothed out the material, revealing first a torn, scorched ring, and below that, a ragged red hole, big enough to slip her fingers in. She pulled her hand back in shock.

Merlin was dead.

There was no word for the howling emptiness that ripped through her. She knelt there, as numb as if the entire world had been murdered.

In a very real sense, it had.

She looked up again, her eyes wet. The fighting was over. Stearne had regained mastery over his spooked horse, and he was once again issuing orders. His lieutenant stood with one foot on Blake's body, yelling something back up to his master.

Stearne turned and pointed to her. His gaze reflected more than mere triumph—it managed to blend hunger, wounded pride, vengeance, and lust. Through her haze, she could just make out what he was saying, his voice ringing with righteous fury.

"Enough," he cried out. "Take the witches and gag their lying mouths. See that they are shackled and hitch them to your saddlebows to march them home. If they resist, let the horses drag them all the way back to the stakes. If the warlocks are too wounded to stand, cut their throats."

Off to Amber's left, soldiers dragged Nellie to her stumbling feet, her escorts hauling her away despite her struggles. Knots of soldiers leaned over the unmoving bodies of Cam and Blake, while others trudged toward her and Merlin.

They were coming for her.

She turned her head away—she couldn't bear the thought of meeting their eyes. With one final shuddering inhalation, she placed a soft kiss on the dead man's forehead and rested her head on his chest. She waited for the soldiers to drag her away.

A strange sensation tickled her ear.

It was an almost electronic hum—and it was coming from his chest. Sitting up, Amber gripped either side of the tear in his robe and pulled, ripping the fabric open.

Holy shit.

The hole in his skin was overlaid by an intricate mesh of tiny silver hexagons, replicating and spreading out to completely cover the wound.

His eyes opened.

Amber shot straight up to her feet, startling the pair of

soldiers coming up to fetch her. Then Merlin sat up. The Roundheads fell back in shock.

"Shouldn't you two be running away now?" he suggested.

They staggered, turned tail and ran.

42

The rest of the company turned to see the pair of hardened troopers wailing in fear as they fled from the young woman standing calmly... next to the man they had just seen shot dead.

Stearne and his burly lieutenant caught sight of the panic spreading across the troops, and they spurred their horses forward to see what was causing the uproar. The witchfinder pulled back hard on the reins when he saw Amber and Merlin standing there, a wave of speechless horror spreading across his face before he straightened in the saddle, visibly fighting to compose himself.

Beside him, his lieutenant's ugly bulldog mouth gaped open.

"Pay no heed!" Stearne called out to his remaining men. "It is naught but a last trick of the warlock! His infernal powers of illusion cannot avail!" Pulling out his pistol, Stearne took aim at Merlin's chest, but his spooked animal danced nervously from side to side, preventing him from taking a clean shot.

"You have no idea what we are, or what we can do." Merlin took a step forward, his expression cold and distant. "But you're about to find out." Behind him, the waters suddenly began to churn. A low, thrumming vibration began, silent but palpable, causing Stearne's already anxious horse to rear and whinny in fright.

Then, with a roar of rushing air and water, a massive shape rose up and hovered in the air, rivulets cascading off every angle of its sleek surface. It was a flying vessel, double-decked and a hundred feet long—big enough to be a jumbo jet, elegant enough to be a luxury yacht. It floated above the waters, perfectly still and serene. The name emblazoned on the side of the vessel was *Vanuatu*.

Blake sat up, shaking off the now stunned ring of soldiers who had been trying to gag and shackle him. He rose to his feet and caught sight of the ship, then froze in wonder. Nellie pulled free, snatching the keys from her captors and shoving the pair away from her for good measure. Harcourt sat up, rubbing his head where he'd been struck down by the flat of the Roundhead's broadsword. He gawked at the ship along with the others.

From the vessel's flanks, twin fields of brilliant prismatic energy fanned out on either side into wings, made up of beams of light arranged in a feather-like configuration. At the fore, another sheet of raw energy beams formed a spearheadshape extending out from the nose. The energy fields shone with a multi-colored brilliance like the gleam reflected off a diamond. Taken as a whole, it made the vessel look like an abstract statue of a bird in flight, created from glossy metal and planes of shimmering, iridescent crystal.

The Roundheads knew this was no mere trick of light and sound. They could feel the wind and the spray of the water on their skin. As they stared in awe, the gigantic craft turned its bow toward them, pivoting effortlessly in the air. A long cannon-like device emerged, projecting from an aperture in the ship's nose. It trained itself directly on Stearne, while a booming electronic voice came from within.

"SURRENDER AND DISPERSE OR WE WILL OPEN FIRE."

For the span of a few heartbeats the soldiers could only stare, wide-eyed and open-mouthed. Stearne and his lieutenant were just as transfixed as the rest of them. Then at last, the lieutenant lost his nerve completely.

"Bugger this!" he swore, clambering onto his horse, whipping it around, and galloping off over the ride. A moment later, like a startled murder of crows taking to wing, the rest of the company scattered in panic, leaving the witchfinder to his fate.

Wearing a look of utter shock as he watched the last of his soldiers abandon him, the Puritan dropped his pistol and dismounted, standing stock still.

Merlin called out a quick order. "Get the lights on those horsemen and give me voice amp." The ship flashed spotlights on the fleeing horsemen, bright enough to pierce the day.

"Halt!" his amplified voice demanded. "Halt or die!" The cavalry obeyed instantly, wheeling their horses around as Stearne dropped to his knees.

"Have mercy," he begged. "I implore you to spare me, unworthy wretch that I am."

"Quiet, you," Merlin growled. He addressed the riders again. "Take this bastard back with you to your Lord Fairfax. And tell Fairfax to cease the fighting in Colchester. You all have bigger problems than... than... whatever the hell you're fighting over. There are a lot more things in the world that want you dead." He paused, then looked down at Stearne and added, "When you get there, you *will* confess your crimes. We'll know. We'll be watching. Tell Fairfax."

Stearne peered up, his face a mask of confusion.

"Go on, get out of here, you despicable worm," Nellie told the miserable Puritan. "Go back and tell them what you've done... or else... *grrkkkk.*" She drew her finger across her throat.

Nodding, Stearne grasped the reins of his skittish steed, mounted, and rode back to join the others in a swift retreat.

Blake stormed up to Merlin.

"Damn it!" he snarled. "Why the hell didn't you just blast him? He's just going to keep killing people."

The scientist just looked at him thoughtfully.

"You may be right. But I couldn't just blast him."

"After all he did?" Blake shook his head in disgust. "Tell me why the hell not."

"Primarily, because this is a research vessel, not a warship," Merlin said. "That's not a laser cannon—it's a telescope."

"Bloody hell…" Blake swore softly.

"Merlin!"

Turning at the sound of Amber's voice, the scientist saw her kneeling next to Cam. The Celt lay unmoving on the ground, battered and bloodied. Merlin knelt beside her and examined him briefly, before turning to the others.

"He's dying," Merlin said.

43

A gangplank extended seamlessly from the ship to the shore. At the top, a large door opened and out floated what looked like a smooth, slightly oversized surfboard. Sailing through the air down the gangplank, it came to a graceful, feather-light landing on the ground right alongside Cam, then flattened out at the edge in order to slip itself entirely under his body.

Having scooped up the patient, the board twisted like taffy, extending a quartet of slender, flat restraining arms up out of the sides to secure Cam safely as the stretcher lifted him away again. Holographic indicator panels popped up in the air above his body, giving readings and flashing red over areas of trauma.

As far as Amber could tell, Cam's entire body was trauma.

The stretcher's aerial glide up the gangplank was

smooth and rapid. Merlin hurried after it onto the ship, followed closely by Amber and the other survivors. The outer door opened onto a long central hall.

"*This is the ship,*" a calm, disembodied voice announced. "*Cabin One has been converted to a med unit and is standing by.*" The stretcher vanished through an open door.

"Thank you, ship," Merlin answered. He moved quickly to the door, hotly pursued by Amber, pausing to allow a sheet of blue light to project down from ceiling to floor. Turning to the others, he pointed further down the hall. "Wait for me in the common room!" Then he went through the sheet of light.

Like hell, Amber thought, following Merlin into the blue light without a moment's hesitation. It gave a gentle hum as she went through it to emerge into a completely featureless, windowless white rectangular cube. In the center hovered the stretcher, which unfolded into a full-blown medical gurney. Cam's ghost appeared suddenly, floating above his body—a translucent blue-green hologram showing his internal organs. A series of small holographic panels sprang up all around the body to provide medical readouts.

Merlin pored over the diagnostic monitors. Amber flattened herself against one wall, as close to him as she dared. A multitude of tentacles extruded out of the walls and ceiling. They set to work swiftly undressing Cam, gently cleaning away the blood and grime, and prepping his body for surgery.

He looked even worse with all the blood and dirt gone—so bad that Amber could hardly bear to look at him. His face and body were covered in dark blossoms of deep red and blue-black contusions, so swollen that he was unrecognizable. She kept her eyes raised to the holographic display above, but that was frightening in a different way. False-color images showed the extent of his massive internal injuries. They were all over his body, internal bleeding spreading and branching throughout in vibrant hues.

Red flashing indicators continued to spring to life. She turned to Merlin, as he watched the med unit work, his face grim. He clearly understood exactly what the diagnostic indicators were telling them.

"Dr. Meta… Merlin? Will he…?" Amber couldn't finish.

Merlin met her eyes, but he didn't speak. She could read the truth there, all the same. He turned away for a moment. Then, after a moment of deliberation, he turned back to the displays and interfaced with one of them.

"Don't worry, Amber." Merlin gave her a weary smile. "Cam's going to be alright." A second holographic ghost appeared in the room, hovering next to the scientist.

Amber needed a second glance to realize that this readout was for Merlin himself. His internal organs were adorned with a golden latticework, radiating from the middle of his chest. He looked free of any trauma, despite having taken a musket ball in that very place.

A large lump emerged from the wall, forming into a rectangular shape. The scientist leaned against it as it tilted up into a second floating gurney that came to rest alongside Cam's. Merlin lay unmoving while a trio of tentacles spiraled down to his chest.

"*Ready for transfusion*," the ship's voice said. Merlin nodded and closed his eyes.

"Proceed."

As Amber watched, the golden latticework in Merlin's hologram began to dissolve.

A little less than an hour later, Merlin's eyes fluttered open again. Amber leaned over him anxiously.

"Merlin, can you hear me? Are you okay?"

He looked up at her with a soft smile and a little nod.

"Is... Cam...?" he asked. Amber broke into a relieved smile, and nodded.

"See for yourself."

Cam lay sleeping peacefully on the surgical table, a drape covering his lower body. The swelling had gone down, and he looked like himself again. There were lines and clusters of tiny silver hexagons where cuts and bruises had dominated before. Above him, his holographic display showed none of the alarmingly red areas—all the bright patches were gone, replaced by constellations of golden hexagons.

"You saved his life," Amber said softly, "but I couldn't tell if you were sacrificing yourself to do it."

"I'll be fine," Merlin said. "It was a calculated risk. The medical nanites in my system had done all the hard work necessary to repair me, so I was happy to loan them to Cam. I'll take them back in a few days, after they've finished on him. In the meantime, I've made up the difference in my own body with some good old-fashioned stem-cell tissue." Amber shook her head, too tired to even begin to parse what he'd just said.

"I'll just take your word for that." She leaned over and kissed his cheek. "Thank you."

"It's the least I could do."

"Everyone will want to know what's happened," Amber said. "Can they come in?"

Merlin held up a hand. "In a few minutes," he said. "I want to talk to you first." He slowly sat up and faced her. "I know what you all did for me while I was unconscious. Alex risked her life to save me from those pterodactyls—"

"I think those were pterosaurs."

"You know what I mean," Merlin said. "I need to thank Nellie, too, but I especially need to thank you and Cam. The others were going to leave me behind. You two saved my life. In doing so, you may have saved the world, as well."

"You're welcome." She hugged her arms tightly. "I'm glad I could help, but honestly, you reached out to me first. How did you know who I was?"

"What do you mean?"

"You know, all the messages you sent me in my dreams. That's how I recognized you. You showed me your face."

"I'm sorry, but I have no idea what you're talking about."

"You have to know," she insisted. Amber found herself getting upset. "That shard of blasted earth— the one that looked like it had been nuked. Where the hatch was hidden? You put the key in my head. It had an underground bunker with that giant flying crystal thing?" He looked at her blankly. "With the lightning? It came to life and lifted me off the ground? And all those dreams with your face looking at me. Asking me for my help to save you."

He continued to stare.

"None of this rings a bell?" she said, her voice rising. "Seriously?" She wanted to hit him in frustration. Merlin frowned, and put out a hand to calm her.

"Hold on now," he said. "There's never been that sort of nuclear conflict, so unless it came from Hiroshima or Nagasaki, there couldn't be a shard like the one you described. More to the point, there's no such thing as telepathy."

Amber shot him a look. "Says the man who controls flying spaceballs with his mind."

"That's different," he countered. "That's pure technology. People can't go into other people's dreams."

Amber frowned. "Then something seriously weird is going on." Almost as soon as the words were out, she stopped herself, giving a small, self-deprecating laugh. "God, talk about understatement. But I *know* it was you—and you knew who I was, too. I really did open that hatch. I know it sounds crazy, but all those things really happened."

Merlin rested his chin on his hand.

"I believe you," he said. "I just don't know what to tell you. There must be a rational explanation, however, even if we can't arrive at it yet."

Amber nodded, taking a deep breath and expelling it.

"So where exactly are we headed?" she asked, trying to put her frustration behind her.

"We're heading back to the main site of the Omnia Astra Project," Merlin replied.

"How far is that?"

"It's at the South Pole."

"Holy shit."

"I know it's a long way," Merlin said, "but it's our only chance to reverse the Event before it's too late."

"What do you mean?" Amber replied. "I thought you said you could fix it. That everything would be the way it used to be."

"No, what I said is that another Event is going to occur, further shattering the timeline," he replied. "And then another will strike, and another, and another, their frequency increasing as time becomes more unstable. The fracturing will never stop, not even when the shards that remain are microscopic."

"So everything will just… disintegrate?" she said.

"Precisely," he replied. "Down to the subatomic level."

Amber stared at him in horror. "How can you be so sure about all of this?" she asked, unwilling to accept this worst-case scenario.

Merlin gave a deep shuddering sigh.

"Because," he confessed, "as I said before, I know what caused it."

"So what *was* that?"

He looked at her, the stars in his eyes glittering.

"I caused it."

EPILOGUE

Amber lay exhausted on her bunk, staring out the ship's window at the passing clouds. For the first time in days she was clean and had a real bed on which to sleep. Hot water and soft pillows had never felt so good. Best of all, Cam would be okay.

She desperately *wanted* sleep, but her mind kept replaying a never-ending loop of the day's events, including Merlin's doomsday revelations. Finally, her eyes shut of their own accord and all her anxiety simply drifted away into a deep, deep sleep...

She was dreaming almost instantly.

Merlin was there again.

Help me, Amber...

ACKNOWLEDGEMENTS

First and foremost, huge thanks to Steve Saffel, our Dark Editorial Overlord. Steve, your skill and understanding of what your authors are trying to create always results in a better book.

So much appreciation to Jill Marsal, amazing agent. Jill, your enthusiasm for this series has been a gift.

As always, thank you to the crew at Titan Books! Our eagled-eyed copy editor Steve Gove made some excellent catches, and we couldn't be happier with the end result. Thanks to Hannah Scudamore—one of these Comic-Cons, we WILL have that drink! To Nick Landau and Vivian Cheung, Paul Gill, Julia Lloyd, Katharine Carroll, Lydia Gittins, Jenny Boyce, and anyone we may have missed.

Many thanks also to Adele Wearing, Barbara Butler of the Colchester Young Archaeologists' Club, and Jenni Gray for their help with research. And so much appreciation to fellow authors Patrick Freivald, Jonathan Maberry, Mark Wilson, Craig DiLouie, and Maria Alexander!

ABOUT THE AUTHORS

Dana Fredsti is an ex B-movie actress with a background in theatrical combat (a skill she utilized in *Army of Darkness* as a sword-fighting Deadite and fight captain). Through seven-plus years of volunteering at EFBC/FCC, Dana's been kissed by tigers, and had her thumb sucked by an ocelot with nursing issues. She's addicted to bad movies and any book or film, good or bad, which includes zombies. She's the author of *The Spawn of Lilith*, the *Ashley Parker* series, touted as *Buffy* meets *The Walking Dead*, the zombie noir novella, *A Man's Gotta Eat What a Man's Gotta Eat*, and the cozy noir mystery *Murder for Hire: The Peruvian Pigeon*. With David Fitzgerald she is the co-author of *Time Shards*, a new trilogy of time-travel adventures, and she has stories in the *V-Wars: Shockwaves* and *Joe Ledger: Unstoppable* anthologies.

David Fitzgerald is a historical researcher, an international public speaker, and an award-winning author of both genre fiction and historical nonfiction, such as The Complete Heretic's Guide to Western Religion series and *Nailed*. He is also a founding member of San Francisco Writers Coffeehouse. He lives with his wife, actress/writer Dana Fredsti, and their small menagerie of cats and dogs, and is often accused of being the Ferris Bueller of San Francisco. His latest fiction is the *Time Shards* series.

THE SPAWN OF LILITH
DANA FREDSTI

Out of the spotlight, in the darker corners of the studio backlots, Hollywood hides a remarkable secret. Actor or actress, set designer, electrician, best boy, or grip— in la-la land, it pays not to be human. Vampires, succubae, trolls, elementals, goblins—studios hire anyone and anything that can take direction, be discreet, and not eat the extras. (The less you know about your agent, the better.) Though only human, stuntwoman and struggling actress Lee Striga is a member of the legendary Katz Stunt Crew. They're the best in the biz, in part because they can fly, and boast superhuman strength. When Lee lands a job on the movie *Pale Dreamer*, however, not everyone is following the script. It's up to her to figure out who or what is killing the cast and crew. Especially when Lee goes from stuntwoman to lead role... and the next target.

For more fantastic fiction, author events, exclusive
excerpts, competitions, limited editions and more

VISIT OUR WEBSITE
titanbooks.com

LIKE US ON FACEBOOK
facebook.com/titanbooks

FOLLOW US ON TWITTER
@TitanBooks

EMAIL US
readerfeedback@titanemail.com